DANGEROUS MASQUERADE

"I don't even know your name," Caleb murmured huskily.

Kate stirred restlessly in his arms, then hesitated. "Cathy," she breathed. Her hands pulled his shirt loose from his trousers, her fingers quickly freeing the studs, and slid beneath the fabric, moving with slow sensuality through the light hair on his chest. "Call me Cathy, Captain."

He gasped as her fingers dipped lower, following the dwindling trail of hair downward across his flat stomach. "I'm not a captain tonight, lovely Cathy," he insisted. "Just a man named Caleb."

She swayed against him. "Love me then, Caleb," she urged. "Teach me."

Other *Leisure Books* by Elizabeth Daniels:

BIRD OF PARADISE

ELIZABETH DANIELS

PARADISE IN HIS ARMS

To my brothers:
Jim, Rick, and John—
each a dashing hero in his own way.

A Centurion Book®

Published by special arrangement with Dorchester
Publishing Co., Inc.

Printed in the United States of America.

Prologue

San Fransisco Bay
December 1851

The young woman's forceful grip on the arms of the chair made her knuckles white and her lovely face was frozen as she fought the pain. Her pregnant body was as still as that of a marble statue as she tensed. Her face had gone from a healthy pink to a ghastly white in the space of a breath.

Only she wasn't breathing, Captain Caleb Innes realized.

"Lacy?"

The contraction passed, and Lacy Phalen Paradise let out her breath in a long drawn-out sigh. "Oh, dear," she said softly. "I'm afraid it wasn't very bright of me to come out here today."

Elizabeth Daniels

They sat on the quarterdeck of the *Puritan Paramour*, one of the tall-masted clippers that made up the fleet of Lacy's father's Puritan Shipping Line. The golden-haired woman and the young captain. Two old friends catching up on old times. Or they had been until the present intruded again. And quite dramatically, Caleb thought.

Lacy was as lovely as his memory had painted her. But she was no longer the girl he had grown up with, the girl he had once loved. She was now the wife of Benjamin Paradise, a gambler. She was the mother of a darling toddler, Benjamin Phalen Paradise, fondly called Phael to distinguish him from his father.

Little Phael now balanced unsteadily on his toes, his chubby hands between Caleb's. Fat, bowed little legs peeped from beneath his baby dress. Unaware that anything had occurred, the little boy grinned widely, pleased to be standing, and uttered a shrill cry of excitement. He bounced, lost his grip on the captain's hands, and sat back on the deck with a plop.

Caleb scooped the child up and studied Lacy's face to see that she was all right.

His dark uniform jacket hung open letting the wind whip at his snowy-white shirt as if it were a sail. The breeze lifted his blue-black hair over his brow, playfully tossing it in wild disorder.

Lacy took another deep breath. "I'll be fine, Caleb," she said as she looked at his worried face.

He wasn't convinced. "It's the baby, isn't it?"

Finding their attention diverted away from him, little Phael set up a howl.

Lacy reached for him. "Hush, sweetheart. Mama's here." Her eyes met Caleb's. "Yes, the pains started this morning," she admitted reluctantly. "I didn't want anyone to know. Besides, I was in labor almost two days with Phael." She paused a moment as she straightened Phael's clothing. When she spoke again, Lacy's voice was full of longing. "I did so want to come out."

Innes ran a hand through his hair. "Damn!"

Lacy stroked her son's curling dark hair, so like his father's. "Really, Caleb, I'll be fine."

He searched her face for signs—signs that told him what? He could read the message of his filling sails, could steer by the stars. But what did he know of the trials of birth? How could he care for Lacy? She appeared to be at ease once more, and Phael stirred in her arms, sucking his thumb.

Another grimace twisted her face. This time Lacy's hand went to her swollen stomach. "Goodness," she breathed at last. "That was a strong one. And so soon."

Innes was on his feet. His voice rang with a command as he hailed members of his crew. The men scrambled to the foot of the ladder leading to the quarterdeck. Caleb retrieved the squirming baby from Lacy. She let the little boy go without a word, her face almost white now.

Caleb thrust the baby into the arms of a seaman. "Keep him out of trouble and entertained."

"Aye, Cap'n," the man grunted, and made a funny face at the toddler, who squealed happily.

9

Caleb sent other men into San Francisco to the Paradise Palace Saloon to find Ben Paradise. He had only met Lacy's husband the day before and had liked the man. Now Caleb only prayed that his men would find Paradise and make it back to the ship in time. Lacy may have been in labor two days with Phael, but the strain around her lips told him that the new baby had no intention of waiting that long to make an appearance.

Lacy didn't argue when Caleb lifted her in his arms and carried her down to his stateroom. That in itself was ominous to the young skipper.

Caleb lay his light burden on the bunk just as another convulsion gripped the pale young woman. Lacy bit down on her lip to still a moan, and her nails dug into Caleb's arm as she clutched him.

"Phael," she said weakly.

Caleb smoothed back the near-white blond curls at her brow. Outside, a happy gurgle of baby laughter sounded. "He's well taken care of," Caleb assured her, pleased that the seaman was taking his new assignment as nursemaid to heart and apparently doing an excellent job of it. "I've sent for Ben, so just hold on, little puritan."

Lacy tried to smile. "I don't think this one wants to wait."

He patted her hand. Had anyone aboard ever delivered a baby? Even if they had, was he ready to allow them to assist Lacy? he wondered. Lacy. Sweet Lord! Lacy!

He ruffled his hair even more as he ran both hands through it, and his heart beat so fast he could hardly breathe. He felt like he was running before a storm, knowing that the squall would catch him, leaving him helpless as it savaged the ship and spit his crew into a hungry sea.

The next hour was pure hell for Caleb as he sat beside the straining young woman. He did as she instructed, readying both Lacy and the room. Her voice was shrill in urgency at times, soft and strained at others.

"Caleb."

The cry was so quiet he barely heard her.

"Caleb," she said. "It's time."

The steam from the pots of water on the braiser made the air heavy, almost suffocating, in the tiny cabin. Why hadn't he noticed it before? he wondered.

"Ben will be here soon, Lacy. Hold on." He squeezed her hand as if in supplication. His throat was dry merely at the thought of what lay ahead. "Please wait for Ben," he pleaded.

She smiled weakly. "It will be all right, Caleb. I'll do most of the work."

Her attempted at humor did nothing to ease his tension. He swallowed loudly as his courage quickly waned. "Lacy." His voice was tortured. "I can't do it."

Her hand touched his in compassion. "I'm afraid you must, Caleb," she murmured.

Lord, he felt so unprepared, so helpless, yet there was no one else. He had to be in command of himself, if not the situation, and he couldn't fail Lacy.

As if girding for battle, Caleb arranged his meager supplies near the bed.

Lacy bore down. Her fingers were like claws and as white as the sheet, as she gripped the sides of the bunk tightly.

Innes wiped the beads of sweat from her brow with a cool cloth, then swiped at his own dripping face with the sleeve of his shirt. It was the tension in Lacy's lightly covered body that told him the moment had arrived. Embarrassed and tense, Caleb moved the now damp sheets. "My God," he hissed between clenched teeth. "It's coming, Lacy. Easy. Just a little more."

A carroty fuzz, then a perfect little head slid cleanly into the world, followed by tiny narrow shoulders and slim, dainty legs. Caleb didn't hear Lacy's heartfelt sigh of relief. Gingerly, he held the tiny bundle between his hands. The child's skin was an angry red and slick with fluid. So fragile. So beautiful. So perfect.

Caleb placed the baby on Lacy's abdomen, draped a clean sheet over mother and child, and dropped back in his chair. There were still things to be done but not just yet. First he wanted to watch with wonder the miracle he had helped bring into the world. "She's perfect, little puritan," he told Lacy in an awed voice.

He stared at the tiny creature who tested her thin little limbs, pushing at the covering as she reclined on her mother. The miniature wizened face screwed up and her mouth opened to emit a lusty cry. One tiny fist waved out of the covering.

Lacy smiled drowsily at her daughter. She stroked the soft fluff of fine bright-red hair. "Katherine," she murmured. "My little Kate."

12

Caleb couldn't bring himself to look away from the baby. She would always be a part of him. A very special part. "The name is as pretty as she is," he whispered.

In answer, Katherine tested her lungs once more.

Chapter One

September 1873

Kate Paradise surveyed herself critically in the long mirror. She made a handsome boy, she thought. The long trousers, plain vest, and short sack coat effectively hid her figure. The stiff white collar and shirt front disguised the smooth, delicate curve of her throat and after three weeks of masquerading as a male, she'd finally learned to tie a decent cravat.

Kate rubbed the toe of her boot against the back of her leg to shine its dark surface quickly. Then she cocked the cloth cap that held her reddish-blond hair from view.

"Well, Davy, how do I look?" she demanded of the eleven-year-old boy who lay on his stomach across her bed.

David Paradise frowned, and his freckled nose wrinkled up in distaste. "You're gonna get caught, Katie. Whatta ya gonna do when Pop finds out?"

Kate continued to admire her reflection. "You're just jealous of my long pants."

David leaned over, his mop of straw hair appearing at her side in the mirror. His incredibly long-lashed blue eyes were wide. "I am not," he protested, although he had cast longing looks at her trousers. His own knickerbockers were childish, and he hated the fact that his mother was adamant about his wardrobe. She still treated him like he was a baby when he considered himself almost a man.

"I don't know," he mused. "I'd sure know you were a girl."

Kate pulled the jacket down and checked her reflection from a different angle. "This disguise is only to get me to the door without arousing suspicion."

"I know that," David defended. "But Pop is sure to spot you."

"He hasn't recognized me yet," she said, and readjusted the angle of her cap.

David's eyes widened in disbelief. "You mean Pop's seen you at Madam Lily's?" he demanded, incredulous.

"He does own a share of the parlor house." Kate had used that fact to talk Lily Walsh into helping her with the masquerade. "Don't worry, Davy," she soothed her younger brother. She sat on the end of the bed and ran a slim hand over his hair, tousling it in affection. "He doesn't know I'm the mysterious songbird."

David snorted. "Yeah, sure he doesn't. Pop ain't dumb, Katie. He'll find out."

Her back stiffened. "Are you planning to tell him?"

David scrambled to sit up. "Not hardly! I ain't fond of a hickory stick. If he or Mama found out I'd been helpin' ya sneak off to learn to be a . . ."

Her green eyes narrowed. "Don't say it, Davy."

The boy hurriedly moved out of her reach. Sisters could be as severe in their punishments as parents. With three older sisters and one younger, he'd learned to read the danger signs. At least his older brother, Phael, wasn't such a stickler, and Jack, the baby, wasn't a problem yet.

"I wasn't gonna say it. There *are* fancy names for it," he insisted.

"Like fair cyprian, soiled dove, or bird of paradise?" Kate curled her lip in disdain. "I'm not learning to be a prostitute. It's not like I'm going to one of the cowyards," she said of the shabby houses where a hundred or more girls entertained customers. They were barely a step above the tiny cribs where the women who worked the streets took men.

"Madam Lily's is a respectable parlor house," Kate defended. "It is demure, high-class . . ."

"Expensive," David completed. As the thunder clouds darkened her face, he hastened off the bed. "At least that's what Phael says," he qualified. He wished Phael would take him to Madam Lily's. Phael practically lived at the Paradise Palace, his father's saloon on Washington Street, and at Madam Lily's. "Does Phael know you're doin' this?" he demanded.

16

Kate laughed shortly and got up off the bed. She swaggered over to the dresser and took out a gun and holster. "Phael doesn't see beyond the tip of his cigar."

Her older brother was one of the more popular customers at Madam Lily's, with his handsome dark looks which were a younger version of their father's. At nearly twenty-three, Phael showed no interest in assuming his responsibilities at the Puritan Line office. He preferred the free life of a man of leisure to the regimented hours at the shipping warehouse. Kate knew that he was a sad disappointment to their mother, whose entire life centered around the Puritan Line.

Kate's fingers slid over the cool steel and soft leather in her hand. When she buckled the gun belt on, fastening the dangling holster to her thigh with the rawhide thongs, her disguise was complete. There were probably a few other young women of her class who would dare to dress as a boy and slip out, possibly to meet a lover or to have an adventure. But how many relished the feel of a Colt revolver in their hand as she did?

The six-shooter slid easily into the leather. Kate settled it lightly, testing the feel of the metal, the smoothness of the grip. It didn't do to travel the rough Barbary Coast of San Francisco without a little protection. The gun had been specially designed for her, a gift from her father, who had insisted each of his children learn to defend themselves.

"It's time to go, Davy. Will Quah Cue be ready?" she asked softly.

David punched the pillows beneath the coverlet into a better resemblance of a sleeping form. He pulled his own cap firmly in place over his fair hair. "Yeah. You're lucky he's been helpin' ya, Katie. I sure wouldn't want ya creepin' through Chinatown or the Coast alone. The crimpers 'ud be sure to get ya."

Kate's eyes softened with affection. "I'm lucky to have a brother with such resourceful friends."

David grinned. That smile was sure to break many hearts in the future, Kate thought, fleetingly feeling a pang of guilt for involving him in her escapade. In the past she had been able to dissuade David from stealing out when she left. But tonight was different. He knew that within a few hours her plan would be played and had insisted that she needed his escort at least to the edge of Chinatown. He wasn't her protector, David had taken pains to explain, but her lookout. Tonight of all nights, Kate couldn't take the chance of being caught on the streets alone.

She was twenty-one and much sought after by the young men in society. Yet she had rejected a number of suits for her hand, which caused her mother concern. Kate knew that Lacy Paradise was determined her daughters would make good marriages. It was the goal of every mother in the top six thousand social-register families in San Francisco to capture a European title for their daughters and Kate's mother was not totally immune to that ambition for her own offspring.

Kate was aware that her parents could buy whomever they wished. Their fortune was built on a combination of her mother's Puritan Shipping Line and her father's uncanny luck with Comstock mining shares and railroad stocks. They were one of California's many successful "shovelry" families, classified as such because they had arrived after the discovery of gold. The "chivalry" represented the few families who had settled in the area before the find at Sutter's Mill. The two separate elite factions fought among themselves for hierarchy.

It was no secret within Kate's family that Lacy Paradise longed to snub the matriarchs who decried her own interest in business. But, Kate thought with a smile, that didn't stop her from taking an interest in her four daughters' futures. She often told them that she hoped they would find men whom they could love as much as she loved their father, Benjamin Paradise.

Kate knew she puzzled her family. While other young women were more inclined to fantasize about their spousal candidates, Kate had scorned those who aspired to her fortune. By being indifferent to them, she had gained a reputation as an ice princess. The derogatory title worried her parents more than it did Kate. They knew she was a warm and loving child, perhaps a bit spirited, but that was hardly a fault.

However, in her sister Amelia's eyes, Kate knew she was a failure. At sixteen, Amy had her life planned, down to the social status of her unknown spouse. But nineteen-year-old Winona, who was the mirror image of their mother, from her incredibly pale blond hair to her deep green eyes and determinedly squared chin, wasn't interested in anything but the turn of a card. Only a card game brought a warm glow to Wyn's exotic eyes.

If Kate had been interested in collecting a court of admirers, she knew she would resent the fact that she had not inherited their mother's beauty. In her opinion, her coloring and features were unremarkable, and her hair had never settled into either a lush red or a sunshine-bright blond. Mixed together, the two colors formed a shimmering strawberry-blond.

Her eyes didn't echo the cool greens of the forest as her mother's, Phael's, and Wyn's did. Kate's eyes were green, but there was also a touch of her father's ice-blue. The combination was reminiscent of a sheltered lagoon. A rather murky lagoon, Kate thought.

Her features as well differed slightly from the rest of the family. Where Wyn, and to some extent, Amy, were often compared to their stunning mother, Kate took after her paternal grandmother. Except for the paler coloring of Kate's hair, she could have been mistaken for the demure young woman whose portrait had been rendered in 1815. It fit inside the cover of an antique pocketwatch, the only treasure that Kate's father, Ben, had of his parents.

Nine-year-old Lisa might be considered demure. But Kate would have been appalled if the word was used to describe herself. No, obstinate was the more frequently applied term, and Kate felt it fit her very well.

While her parents fretted about her lack of interest in young men, Kate mapped out her own future. She knew what she wanted out of life. It wasn't the comfortable house or the well-connected man of whom her society-hungry sister Amy dreamed. Kate wanted to see the world, to have a hand in her destiny. Learning the way the Puritan Shipping Line made contacts, bought goods and distributed them under her mother's tutelage had only been a starting point from which Kate's ambition had grown. She intended to be involved on a firsthand basis with the line and part of her plan to accomplish that involved a man.

A very special man.

Kate had always known and loved the man with whom she wanted to spend her life. Unlike the San Francisco beaux, Captain Caleb Innes couldn't he bought with her fortune. She'd often heard the story of how he'd once held the chance to win control of the Puritan Line in the palm of his hand and had refused it. He had grown up with her beautiful mother, had shipped on a Puritan vessel as a boy. Everyone had expected him to marry Lacy Phalen, but Caleb had declined the honor.

He had always been special to Kate. She had never found any other man she felt was worthy of her love. She meant to have him, no matter what obstacles were in her path. It didn't matter that he was so much older. That wasn't the problem. The hurdle was Caleb's seeming indifference to her as a woman. Kate was sure she could overcome that, if given the chance. And to gain her happy ending, Katherine Paradise was determined she would have the gentleman's full attention tonight, even if it meant tricking him.

21

Elizabeth Daniels

One last look in the mirror satisfied Kate that she could pass for a boy in the dark. She slid her revolver more securely in the holster. Perhaps a very dangerous boy.

She snuffed the lamp and motioned David to the window. They were through it quickly, scrambling quietly over and down the convenient toeholds of the cornice and frame of the first-floor window, to drop lightly to the ground in the side yard.

Kate gripped David's shoulder, holding him back in the shadows. Out on the street three men came down the front steps and turned, heading down the slope toward the gaudy lights of the Coast.

Kate waited until her father, brother, and their guest reached the corner of Stockton before she relaxed. Together she and David crept from the shadows. Rather than follow the men, they hurried along the crest of Nob Hill before turning down the steep incline of California Street.

Hoping David would think her shortness of breath was from the dash, rather than the narrow escape from detection by their father, Kate stopped just out of the glow of the street lamp. "You don't have to escort me to Chinatown, Davy. I can get to the rendezvous with Quah Cue," she insisted.

Her lagoon eyes sparkled with a brilliance that rivaled the lights in town, and a wild exuberance of part joy, part fear bubbled within her. Every breath she took was exhilarating.

Kate looked down into her younger brother's anxious face. "What can happen to me on Nob Hill?" she demanded with a bright smile.

22

David, however, was determined not to let his sister gyp him of his part in her adventure. He didn't understand her reasons for sneaking out. Kate was old enough to do as she pleased. He knew he wouldn't be sneaking behind their parents' backs when he reached her august age. It didn't make any sense to him when Kate tried to explain that things were different if you were a girl. If their father taught the girls how to ride and shoot, just as he had David and Phael, what was the difference? In fact, David remembered, Kate was a better shot than Phael. It was an impressive feat to best their older brother.

"I'm goin', Katie. Ya can't stop me," he insisted fiercely. "Cue told me what happened last week."

"It was nothing," she insisted. There had been two drunks who had decided to try the mettle of the boy she appeared to be. One had grabbed her shoulders and spun her around while the other snatched her gun—or tried to. Kate had landed a well-aimed kick that had felled the one man while Quah Cue had downed the other with an impressive open-handed blow. The whole confrontation had taken perhaps two minutes and she had walked off without a scratch.

Besides, Kate thought, what could an eleven-year-old boy do that she couldn't do for herself?

"You're going to tell me I'm still just a girl and girls need a man to protect them," she said.

David knew his sister too well to be foolish enough to tell her that, even though he believed it. Girls did need to be protected, especially if they were headed into the heart of the Barbary Coast. It was the reason he had arranged with his

23

friend, Quah Cue, to accompany Kate through Chinatown and to Madam Lily's. "Why should you have all the adventure?" David demanded, his voice pettish. " 'Sides, I'm only goin' as far as the spot where we're meetin' Cue."

He looked so ferocious and adorable, and Kate ruffled his hair once more. "All right, my dragon. Let's go."

Kate moved down the narrow alley that was barely wide enough for two men to walk abreast. Her fingers gripped the handle of her revolver, ready to draw at the slightest indication of trouble. In the shadows at her side, Quah Cue was poised for flight. He would see his friend David's sister safe to the door of the parlor house, then melt into the night before someone spotted him.

Kate could see the faint glow of light as Luther Sparks peered from the small window of the back door. The shutter was snapped closed and latched before he eased the massive door partially open. Sparks nodded shortly as Kate left the shadows and Quah Cue, and sidled carefully to the back of Lily's house. Luther held his rifle at his side, the muzzle pointed casually at the floor as he completely opened the heavy door. He glanced up and down the alley, then motioned for Kate to enter the house swiftly.

A quick glance over her shoulder assured Kate that her young Chinese escort had already disappeared. She would never admit it to David, but she was glad her brother had spent much of his young life roaming the streets of San Francisco. From the waterfront to the rabbit warren of

Chinatown, David had collected friends with his easy smile and dare-devil ways. Quah Cue was a budding member of the Sam Up tong, one of the Five Companies that ruled Chinatown. She never questioned David on his acquisition of friends. The boy had an insatiable thirst for knowledge and had always gone seeking his own answers. Quah Cue had been one of those answers, although Kate had never known the question.

"Madam's waitin' fer ya," Sparks growled at Kate as he barred the door.

Accustomed to his gruffness, Kate nodded. She stretched her fingers, easing the tension of gripping her gun tightly. Although she and Quah Cue had not been challenged, she never relaxed her vigilance once she left the Nob Hill house. David had slipped through the shadows as if he were one with them. But Kate lived on her nerves from the time she left the mansion until she reached the temporary sanctuary of Lily's establishment.

Kate slumped back against the table, not quite ready to face her co-conspirator upstairs. "How's the house tonight?" she asked Sparks.

Satisfied that the door he guarded was secured against intruders once more, Sparks settled back in his chair. He was a mountain of a man, and executed his job as a bouncer for Lily Walsh quite well. Sometimes, he even got the pleasure of tossing an unruly customer out on his keister.

"Bull Run Allen's out there tonight. Ya take care," Sparks rumbled.

Kate paused and pushed her hat back. "Ned

Allen? He's a little out of his class here, isn't he, Sparks?"

"Might be he's alookin'ta steal some o' the gals."

Kate considered his suggestion a moment, then shook her head. "I doubt if any of the girls would choose to work for Allen whether at Hell's Kitchen or one of his other establishments."

Sparks frowned, his heavy brows drawing together over his low forehead. "It wouldn't be the gals who did the choosin'," he said. "Allen don't call himself king of the Barbary Coast fer nothin'. Nobody says no ta that man."

Allen's turning up at Lily's posed a problem. Kate mentally reviewed the shipping schedule she had studied at the Puritan Line office. Captain Innes's ship, having just arrived in port, was due to sail back to China soon and he would not return for a number of months. It would be wise not to appear as the songbird tonight but it seemed cowardly to abandon her plans just because of Bull Run Allen. He was a dangerous man, but as long as he didn't know who she was, maybe she would be safe.

Ned Allen was a nasty character. His nickname, Bull Run, was a result of his claim to have participated in both battles of Bull Run a decade earlier during the War between the States. He owned a number of dives along the Coast and usually traveled in the company of hired thugs. When he visited a business establishment, it always resulted in trouble. There was no such thing as a social visit from Allen. If he was at Lily's, he wanted something.

Kate jerked her thumb toward the front rooms. "Lily know he's here?"

"Yeah. An' frettin'," he grunted.

Kate considered her options quietly. She had plotted and planned her campaign for so long. Prudence dictated she could wait awhile longer. But something inside her rebelled at the thought. No, her plan had to reach fruition tonight. Dangerous or not, Ned Allen's appearance could not be allowed to disrupt all her plans. In her disguise, even her father and brother had failed to recognize her. Why should Ned Allen? He didn't travel in the same social world as Miss Katherine Paradise. There would be no chance of a public scandal to shame her family.

"Best get a move on," Sparks said.

"Aye, I will." She flashed him a quick smile. "Thanks for telling me Allen's here. I'll give him a wide berth."

Sparks watched her disappear up the back stairs, taking them, boylike, two at a time. She didn't think he knew she was Miss Kate Paradise. He couldn't figure out why a nice girl like her would come to a bawdy house. Lily Walsh's was a high-class place, but girls from Nob Hill didn't belong here. It wasn't as if she had a living to make like the rest of the "seamstresses" who worked in Lily's upstairs rooms.

Sparks had seen them come and go. Pretty young things who lost their looks and their will to live. Some took to drink. Some smoked opium to forget. Sooner or later, they moved down in the ranks of their sisterhood. Younger, prettier women came along and pushed the older ones out of the parlor houses into the cowyards, into the cribs. Or they'd end up in a low-class dance hall, a place like Allen's Hell's Kitchen.

Elizabeth Daniels

There weren't many women who made it out of the Coast on the coat tails of some new millionaire. Not like back in '49 or during the early Comstock days. Then it was easy to marry a rich customer.

In a way Sparks felt sorry for Ben Paradise. The man had a beautiful wife, a house on Nob Hill. He was respected by other businessmen. But he had a passel of the most hell-raising kids you ever hoped to see. Seven of them, Sparks had heard. The youngest was barely a year old while the eldest, Phael Paradise, spent his time losing at cards or exercising his John Thomas in one of Lily's upstairs rooms.

Sparks settled his rifle across his chest and stared at the door. It wasn't any of his business. He just hoped Miss Kate wouldn't get herself in trouble. He kind of liked her. She had spunk. Sparks appreciated that in a woman as much as he did a flashing pair of eyes or a nicely turned ankle. And, Sparks admitted to himself, Miss Kate Paradise had those attributes as well.

Upstairs, Kate continued her masquerade, swaggering down the hall, as if she were a male customer intent on visiting one of the seamstresses. The carpet was thick and patterned with entwining vines bestrewn with blooming morning glories in shades of blue against green, a common theme at Lily's. Her decor was opulent but not in the ruby shades preferred by most of the bordellos on the Coast. Dark-stained panelling stretched halfway up the wall. Wallpaper continued up to the high ceiling, its embossed geometric design gold against a rich sea-green background. The shapes were continued in the intricately carved molding.

Kate had seen it all before and knew each room was done in a soft shade of blue. It had become Lily's trademark. Of all the rooms, Lily's suite was the richest. There the wallpaper was of watered silk in a shade to match Lily's eyes. The same fabric draped the tall windows and covered the bed. The furniture was upholstered in a light cerulean brocade. Rugs from the Far East in deep shades of blue covered the highly buffed redwood floor. It was the perfect setting for the madam who was the pearl of the Barbary Coast.

Kate strode quickly to a door at the far end of the hall.

Lily answered her knock swiftly, as if she had been standing at the door waiting for Kate's signal.

The blonde clutched the sleeve of Kate's jacket and pulled her inside. "Where have you been? I was worried half out of my mind!" Lily exploded.

Kate shrugged and sauntered across the room to help herself to the decanter of wine on the table. "Allen's just got you jumpy, Lily," she said, and sipped at her goblet.

The bouquet of the wine was heady. The glassware was as fine as that on the Paradise table on Nob Hill. Kate wondered if Lily had gotten it from Italy, via a Puritan ship.

The pale blue silk of her skirts spread out around her as Lily Walsh dropped wearily into a chair and warily surveyed her protégé. The lines

Elizabeth Daniels

at the corners of Lily's slightly elongated eyes had
deepened in the last few years but she was still a
lovely and attractive woman. When she studied
her reflection in the glass, she often wondered if
the lines and the trace of gray in her wheat-blond
hair were the result of too close an association
with Ben Paradise's children. What Phael's amo-
rous bent had begun, Katie's wheedling had
surely completed. She might not look her age,
but when either of Ben's eldest children came
into her room, Lily began to feel old.

"Well, you sure as hell are cool, kid," she
said. "Don't you know Allen's a tough customer? Don't you know what he could do to your
reputation if he finds out who you are?"

"Why should he?"

Lily stared at the girl.

"Papa and Phael haven't recognized me. Allen
doesn't even know me. No one but you knows
my real identity, Lily."

"But . . ."

Kate was calm and her look almost challeng-
ing. "You weren't planning on giving me away,
were you?"

Lily chewed nervously on her bottom lip. It
was tempting, especially with Ned Allen appearing suddenly. She'd thought her house was
safe from his filthy touch. She'd been wrong.
But she could still keep Katie safe. All she had
to do was confess her part in this insane plan
to the kid's father.

"Hell," Lily groaned, knowing she could not
back out now. Katie was grasping at something
Lily herself had never had, the love of a special
man. The only man she'd ever had particularly

strong feelings for had married Katie's mother.

Lily capitulated. "Your pa is gonna kill me if he finds out what you've been up to. Give me a drink, kid. I'm gonna need it tonight."

Kate obliged. As she handed the crystal to the older woman, she smiled faintly. "Cheer up, Lily. Tonight's my last night."

Lily looked up over the rim of her glass. "You sure?" She almost feared the answer.

"Absolutely." Kate swirled the wine in her glass, watching it catch the lamp light as it moved. "Captain Innes came to dinner tonight and left with Papa and Phael. My guess is that they'll go first to the Paradise Palace, then come here."

Lily sighed. The girl certainly had her father's cool head and her mother's determination. To Lily Walsh, it was a dangerous combination.

Lily gulped at her wine. Who would have thought all those years ago in Missouri, when she had been one of the girls at the Paradise Saloon, that one day she would meet up with Ben and Lacy again? Or that Ben would finance her house? Things had been much easier in the backwater town of Paradise. Much easier.

"Then I guess I can't talk you out of singing tonight," Lily said.

"Hardly, Lil." Kate tilted her head to the side, musing. "I've wanted Caleb Innes all my life," she said softly. "I've waited for him to notice I have grown up and to take the initiative, but he hasn't."

Lily wished there was more wine in her glass. A lot more. "Hell, I can't blame the man, kid. He's old enough to be your father. He bounced you

31

on his knee. You'll always be little Katie to him."

Kate finished her drink and stripped the cloth hat from her head. A fall of copper-and-gold waves cascaded down her back to her waist. "That's why he can't know who I am tonight."

"I told ya before, Katie. The man's not goin' to like what you're doin' to him." She paused, hoping that the girl would consider all aspects before she acted. "He might even hate ya."

They had been over all this before, and though Kate felt giddy, and nervous now that the moment was at hand, she wasn't going to abandon her scheme. She unstrapped her holster and laid the gun aside carefully. Her dark tie, vest, and coat followed her cap before she stepped behind the screen in Lily's room to complete her transition from boy to young woman.

"I know he loves me, Lily. Not just as the little girl he brought presents to after every voyage. But as a woman. He is attracted to me. I can tell by the way his eyes follow me."

Lily stared at the delicate design painted on the screen. Rosebuds, violets, lily of the valley, spring flowers entwined lovingly on it. What could she possibly say that hadn't already been said? Kate was being stubborn, refusing to listen to logic. She was blind to any but the result she foresaw. Lily feared what would happen to the girl when things didn't turn out the way she wished.

"Sure, kid," Lily said. "Of course the captain watches you. Who wouldn't? But what if he's just marvelin' at what a beauty you've grown into? You don't look like either yer ma or yer pa, not like that rakehell Phael or your sister, Wyn, do. But you got something special." Lily looked longingly at the decanter. No more wine, she decided. Between Bull Run Allen's arrival and Katie's antics, she'd need to keep her wits about her.

"I resemble Papa's mother," Kate said, her voice muffled as she pulled the deep yellow taffeta dress over her head.

Lily got to her feet and began folding Kate's discarded clothing. Anything to keep busy and not worry. As if she could stop doing that! "Not in personality, kid. That lady was a Southern gentlewoman. She's probably turnin' in her grave watchin' you."

Kate stepped from behind the screen wearing a wide grin. "Maybe I take after my grandfathers then. From the stories I've heard, neither of them was staid nor proper." She turned her back, holding the gown in place. "Hook me, Lily?"

The older woman obliged, enviously noting the narrowness of Kate's waist. "I wish you wouldn't go down tonight, Katie. I got a bad feelin' about this. It ain't gonna turn out like you want, kid. I know it."

Kate settled the low neckline of her gown. She drew her skirt up to check her silk stockings and yellow-frilled garters. "You're worrying over Allen too much, Lil. Everything will be fine."

Lily handed the girl a pair of high-heeled slippers dyed the exact shade of her taffeta dress. "I hope yer right, kid." She sighed. "God knows, I hope yer right."

Chapter Two

Leaving Kate to finish dressing. Lily joined her customers in the main parlor below.

The nine girls who worked for her were already entertaining the gentlemen with light witty conversation, gentle smiles, and promises of delights yet to be tasted in the luxurious apartments upstairs. Each room had been decorated in soft shades of blue. The color enhanced Lily's blond beauty but the gentler tones also helped maintain the fiction that the girls were "seamstresses," boarders of the house rather than women of loose virtue. Lily traded on fantasy.

Perhaps that was why she had given into Kate Paradise's wild plan, Lily thought as she greeted her guests. The kid's pa had always had a little corner of her heart. She still remembered nights she and Ben had shared before Lacy Phalen had come to the small Missouri town. She was a soft touch for the Paradise brats, that was the truth of the matter. Why else would she let that rapscallion Phael ride roughshod over her? More than one of the girls had fallen for his handsome face just as she had for his father's.

Lily straightened her back, preparing for battle. For battle it would be to defend her business against a lowlife like Ned Bull Run Allen. Scum didn't come any dirtier, she thought, and the bastard wouldn't have come into her place unless he wanted something.

Allen thought he could take advantage of her because she didn't have a flash man to look out for her interests. Ned had been sniffing around more the last six months but Lily had resisted going to her silent partner for help. With Kate preparing to attract Captain Innes's attention with her masquerade at the parlor house, dragging Ben Paradise into her problems was the last thing Lily wanted. Ben had financed the house but he'd never been involved in the day-to-day business conducted beneath the sheets. He'd just been helping a friend get established.

Still, Lily knew all she had to do was mention that she was in a spot, and Ben would be there. But it was something she knew she would never ask of him.

Lily paused in the archway, glancing toward the large man near the door. Even in formal attire, Zack Lawson was a formidable hulk. Fleetingly, she worried that Zack and Luther Sparks would not be a sufficient show of force if there was trouble. But they would have to do. They were all she had.

Lawson's silent nod of assurance did little to relieve Lily's tension. It was up to her to bait the bull, to find out why Allen was guzzling Blue Ruin in her parlor.

Ned Allen's eyes flickered over her as Lily Walsh hesitated in the doorway. She had managed to keep her figure unlike many of the grossly fat madams he employed. He liked the way Lily looked, always dressed in blue, and the way she moved like a cat, each movement smooth and sultry.

He'd dressed particularly fine himself, sporting all his trademarks—frock coat and cream-colored breeches, and glittering diamond shirt studs. The dazzling display had lured many women into his employ.

Allen rubbed at his red bulbous nose, thinking he hadn't come to see Lily, though. It was the damned mysterious songbird. From all accounts, she was a regular canary and unapproachable. She had appeared from nowhere and did not perform every night. The men who had listened to her claimed that she was a cool customer. She seduced with her voice, then left, leaving the other whores to console the randy buckos.

Lily joined Allen at the bar. Her smile was strained, tight, but her actions looked relaxed. Allen wasn't deceived. Lily had been in the business long enough to become a very talented actress.

She leaned back against the brass rail that ran the length of the counter and ran her fingers along the polished oak surface until they met his blunt-shaped hands. Her touch was a caress as she smiled lazily into his eyes. "Been a long time, Ned," she purred. "What's the matter, business slow down your way?"

Allen grinned. His eyes were cold and watchful. "You know better 'n that, angel. I'm always interested in expanding my interests, though."

"So I heard. Jest that our . . . interests don't seem the same," Lily said softly. "I like a little class, you know, Bull?" Her fingers continued to trace paths along the back of his hand. "Can't quite see my girls in short coats and black stockings with their asses hangin' out like your waiter girls at the Kitchen."

His lips stretched in a sneer. "Don't knock it, Lil. It's a fetchin' sight and the gals ain't complainin'. Got more business than they can handle."

"I'm a might more selective," Lily insisted.

"Humph. We ain't in the two-bit business, angel. You like the color of the buckos' money as much as I do. Might be I could help ya, Lil."

She withdrew her hand, turning with a rustle of blue silk. Allen approved of the view of her breasts straining against the form-fitting bodice. "I already got a partner," she said shortly. "We been over this long ago, Bull. Ain't no change in the arrangement."

It was Allen's turn to caress her hand as it lay passively on the polished surface of the bar. He thought she would withdraw her hand, but when she let him continue touching her, he knew Lily was afraid to rile him. "I'm not talkin' about takin' over, Lil. I thought there might be another way of doin' business together."

Lily's eyes widened, then narrowed to catlike slits. "I ain't interested in protection neither, Bull, if that's what ya got on your mind."

"You wound me, Lily. Still, there are some pretty desperate characters on the Coast. My name could spare ya a lot of trouble."

She pulled her hand from his.

He pressed a warning hand on her wrist. "I wouldn't refuse out of hand, Lil." He smiled mirthlessly. "Think on it. I can wait a day or two for your answer."

A tremor of fear ran through her stiffly held form, and Allen noted it with pleasure.

"That all you came for?" Lily demanded. "To threaten me?"

Allen's oily smile flickered. "A proposition, Lil. I wouldn't push yer luck." His gaze moved past her to the staircase. "Ah, the mysterious songbird," he murmured. "Perhaps for her sake, you'll reconsider, Lily."

Lily's frightened glance went to where a masked vision in yellow taffeta stood part way down the stairs, her hand stretched gracefully toward the bannister. Katie. Damn, the girl had an uncanny sense of timing.

Lily didn't like the way Allen surveyed Katie, as if she were property to be wrangled over. Lily had always considered her girls assets but never property. She had to admit the mystery of Katie's appearances and the beauty of her voice had increased business. At the moment it didn't matter that the girl was Ben Paradise's daughter. What burned within Lily was the knowledge that Ned Allen wanted her business. For that,

The deep golden-yellow of her gown enhanced Kate's skin. Even with the mask sheltering them, it turned her lagoon eyes into shimmering jewels.

Lily watched Kate's approach, her byplay with the customers who hovered around her. Perhaps the kid was right. Kate seemed to have a sixth sense where men were concerned. They flocked to her despite her coolness to their advances. They courted her as the lady she was. With the songbird, none of the men indulged in the heavy-handed groping they gave the other girls. Maybe, just maybe, Kate would win Captain Caleb Innes to a marriage bed and it had better be marriage the good captain had in mind in the morning. Lily frowned. She would not let Katie relinquish her virtue so willingly if she hadn't already known the type of man Innes was.

She would be sad to lose the captain as one of her customers. At forty-five, he was still an incredibly attractive man and Lily knew he was a virile and accomplished lover. She had never let Kate know that she had entertained Innes personally in the past. The kid would have scratched her eyes out.

Unconsciously, Lily smoothed the skirt of her gown. She was still a good-looking woman, even if she had settled into middle age, a comfortable time of life when a woman was still very vital. Lacy Paradise, Kate's mother, was barely two years younger than Lily and she had presented her husband with a third son a year ago.

For a moment Lily hoped that Captain Innes would bypass her parlor house that evening.

Then she caught the expression in Allen's eyes as he watched the songbird move toward the piano at the far end of the room. His look stripped the girl naked. His eyes lingered over her breasts before dropping to the silhouette of her legs beneath the clinging skirt. And Kate had noticed that intimate perusal, Lily realized as a warm blush rose from the low neckline of the girl's gown to color her shoulders and throat.

"Damn, Lily," Allen murmured in admiration. "You've got yourself an innocent!"

A breath of damp air followed the three men inside the entryway of Madam Lily's. Zack Lawson's broad shoulders temporarily blocked the light before he pulled the door open. "Evenin', gents," he greeted the newcomers. "Yer in luck tonight. The songbird's here."

"Our lucky night, indeed," Captain Caleb Innes mused. He stood aside while Ben Paradise passed a small deadly derringer from his vest pocket to the large man. It was a rule Paradise had urged Lily to enforce. No firearms or knives in the parlor house. Caleb was sure there were still a few concealed weapons but, in the years he'd been patronizing Lily's, Lawson's and Sparks' intimidating presences had usually been enough to discourage trouble.

Paradise handed his hat to Lawson. Although he had recently celebrated his fifty-second birthday, Ben was little changed from the man Caleb knew had led a wagon train into the tent-and-shack city of San Francisco twenty-four years ago. His handsome face was enhanced by deep smile lines about his ice-blue eyes and warm mouth. He had kept active, adding little weight to his tall, lean form.

A younger version of his father, Benjamin Phalen Paradise handed over his own small derringer to Lawson. Phael paused in front of the hall mirror to check the perfection of his evening clothes. He smoothed his dark brown hair back. "Pop won't admit Lily's newest addition has a voice to rival his favorite, Lotta Crabtree," Phael said.

Innes relinquished his hat to Zack. "I'll reserve my opinion," he said, and grinned at the preening younger man. "I'm an admirer of Lotta myself."

"Lily's find is a pretty little thing," Ben conceded. "I've only heard her sing once." He paused, his expression thoughtful. "But there's something naggingly familiar about her."

"Not to me," Phael insisted. "I hear she's an ice maiden, though. Lots of fellas have tried for a night with her and had their hopes dashed."

His father smiled wryly. "Yourself among them, I take it?"

"Not a chance. The ladies come to me, not the other way around."

Innes laughed. "A modest young pup, aren't you, Phael? Perhaps I should try my luck."

Innes's ship, the *Puritan Paramour*, put into the bay every three to four months. Once his voyages had run from Boston to San Francisco to China and back, voyages of six months or more. But since the completion of the transcontinental railroad four years earlier, trains did the work of shipping goods to the eastern coast much faster. So Innes had chosen to make San

Francisco his main port of call while continuing in the China trade.

Unlike many men their age, Paradise and Innes were little changed from the lean and trim men they'd been at Phael's age. Caleb had recognized the light in many women's eyes when they fell on his Puritan Line uniform. It fit like a glove, showing his broad shoulders and narrow hips to advantage. His blue-black hair was still thick and untouched with the frost of time. His brown eyes were enhanced by the smile lines that radiated from their outer corners, and the scar that slashed near his left eye. Despite his forty-five years, it wasn't only older women who appreciated his appearance. Still, few woman would consider an older man when beckoned by a young, energetic lover and that was probably true of the enigmatic songbird too. Caleb had never seen her but from what he'd heard, she wasn't only lovely, she was mysterious, hiding her features behind a white satin mask. If that were true, there probably wasn't a man in the room who hadn't entertained fantasies of being the one to discover what she looked like beneath it. With Phael's looks and youthful charm, he probably had an edge in being the first man to see the songbird's features.

Phael was cocky, as usual. "Wanna bet on it?" he suggested.

Caleb's sun-bronzed face creased in amusement. "You against me for the lady's favors?"

"Sure. Although I'd hate to take your money, Caleb. It's a sure thing . . . in my favor."

Paradise and the captain exchanged a quick glance. "I'm in on that bet," Ben said. "Let's see the color of your money, Phael."

The younger man reached inside his suit jacket. "A hundred says I come out the winner," he declared.

"Zack'll hold the bets. But two hundred says Cal walks off with the songbird." At his son's expression, Ben laughed. "Maturity counts, Phael."

Innes slapped down a like amount of money. "Maturity, hell. Experience will see me an easy winner."

As Phael handed over the rest of his bet. Zack Lawson folded away the money carefully. "That may be, gents," he allowed. "But what happens if neither of you win? The songbird ain't showed no signs of meltin'."

"Then, my friend," Ben declared with a firm pat on the giant's arm, "you have just made yourself an easy couple hundred bucks."

The big man's face creased in pleasure, then sobered. "Bull Run Allen's here. Thought you might want a warnin'."

Allen's name was familiar to all of them, as was his reputation. Ben's brow clouded as he nodded solemnly. "Thanks."

Bull Run had insinuated himself into a good number of Barbary Coast establishments. It had only been a matter of time before his greedy eyes had turned to Lily's profitable house. Caleb was a little surprised that Allen hadn't made an attempt earlier. Or if the man had, that word of it hadn't reached Ben Paradise. If he knew his friend, Allen would never have even attempted extortion a second time. Either Allen had never bothered Lily before, or she had managed to keep Paradise in the dark.

Ben's expression was wary. "Think he's here to cause trouble or just to be sociable?"

"Allen always spells trouble." Phael muttered.

"How's Lily taking it?" Innes asked.

Zack shrugged. "She's been keepin' him company at the bar but she ain't too happy about it. 'Specially with him ogling the songbird.'"

Phael squared his shoulders beneath the dark rich fabric of his jacket. "Well, he's not hedging me out of this bet," he declared, and strutted toward the parlor.

Amused at the younger man's attitude. Ben and Caleb followed at a slower pace.

Innes jerked his head in Phael's direction. His eyes crinkled in a smile. "Were you that cocky?" he demanded of his companion.

Paradise looked at his son's broad back, noting how the tailor-made jacket accented Phael's trim build and height. "God, I hope not," he muttered.

The rustle of petticoats near the archway drew Kate's attention to her brother's arrival. She sighed in relief. If Phael was here, it meant that Caleb was as well. She was a little surprised at the expression on Phael's face and the practiced way his eyes traveled over her. Would he recognize her? It was her one fear that Phael or her father would unmask her before she had a chance to seduce Caleb Innes.

Phael's practiced leer assured her that her identity was safe. It seemed that he had decided to join the crowd of men vying for her favors. Knowing her brother, Kate was sure a hefty bet was riding on his success. It pleased her that giving him the cold shoulder would put a dent in Phael's ego. Unfortunately, it would be only a temporary one. Phael's male pride was encased in armor twice as thick as that worn by a medieval knight.

Kate's weeks at Lily's had taught her that Phael worked very hard to promote his reputation as a ladies' man, and it had only been a matter of time until he noticed her.

As Kate watched, her brother excused himself from the lovely cyprians who had rushed to greet him and made a beeline for Lily, drawing her from the bar and Ned Allen.

Kate finished her song and nodded gently as the gentlemen applauded. She murmured the title of the next selection to her accompanist, and looked up to find that the archway framed more late arrivals.

Lily's girls were greeting her father and Captain Innes. Pleased at the men's arrival, Kate smiled warmly at them.

Ned Allen noted the new brilliance in the songbird's smile, and glanced back at the entrance with interest.

Ben Paradise. Now why, Allen wondered, was the songbird interested in him? The man was a well-known figure around the Coast but he was also unusually faithful to his wife. Lacy Paradise was an extremely beautiful woman, but Allen found devotion to one woman, no matter how lovely or experienced, unnatural.

Allen had never seen the other man, although from his reception it looked as if he was a

frequent customer at Lily's. He was a man of
the sea. Not only his uniform but the way he
stood, his legs braced as if on a tilting deck,
gave away his profession. No, Allen decided
after searching his memory, he didn't know
the man. It wouldn't do to dismiss him as
insignificant, though. In his business, Allen
had found it best to be suspicious of everyone. Merely the fact that the stranger wore the
uniform of Lacy Paradise's Puritan Line made
him interesting.

Lily watched Phael as he absentmindedly patted Dora Acton's hand. She was his usual favorite
among the girls at the parlor house and he was a
refreshing breath of air compared to her worries
about Ned Allen's interest in her house. When
Phael drew her aside, she avoided answering his
questions about the songbird. She could almost
imagine his horror if he ever discovered that the
songbird was his sister, Kate. Phael, for all his
man-of-the-world airs, was very protective of his
sisters.

While Phael puzzled over her uncooperative-
ness and, Lily supposed, plotted how to corner
the songbird, Lily joined Caleb Innes on the
opposite side of the room.

"Looking for special company tonight?" she
purred, perching on the arm of his chair.

Sensing dismissal in Lily's tone, the petite
ash-blonde at his side left to join a group of
men near the window.

Caleb smiled up into Lily's pretty face. Years
of squinting against sun, wind, and waves had
created creases at the corners of his eyes. But

they still hadn't disguised the scar that slashed just shy of his left eye, the souvenir of a battle he'd nearly lost to King Neptune. He had told Lily that over fifteen years ago, a particularly vicious storm had toppled the foremast, taking men with it into a welcoming sea. Innes had lost four good men that day, and if the splintered yard had struck him a second earlier, he would have lost his eye. All that remained was the memory and the fading scar. A scar that intrigued beautiful women. Women like Lily.

"Jealous, my pet?" he asked her. "I thought you'd tired of me. My last two visits have found you unavailable, if I remember correctly."

Lily sighed. Unfortunately, Kate had confided in her six months ago and, in all fairness to the girl, Lily had withdrawn from entertaining the captain personally. In fact, she had been at pains to insure that a different girl accommodated him on each successive visit. "You didn't complain, Captain, if I recall rightly," she said.

A warm gleam lit his soft brown eyes. "Does that disappoint you, Lily?"

Strangely enough it did. Damn Katie and her plots, she thought. She almost pitied the captain. Something told her that he would not react the way Kate expected him to, that all Kate was doing was hurting herself and him.

Lily considered backing out of her part of the plan. She glanced to the corner where Kate's sweet, husky voice sang of love, then to the bar where Ned Allen still stood sipping his drink. There was no way for her to back down now. At least in going through with the deception she would be getting Katie out of the parlor house and thus out of Allen's sight.

She turned back to Caleb, a gentle smile curving her lips. "I'm not disappointed," she said. "It's my business to make sure you aren't disappointed. A little variety to your visits guarantees that you'll return. You see, I'm a businesswoman first, Captain."

"And a woman second?" Innes chuckled. "I beg leave to differ, Lily. But I never argue with a woman if I can help it. What delight are you about to bestow upon me this evening?"

Lily considered him carefully, as if trying to make up her mind. "Do you fancy Zoe?"

"The little blonde you chased away? She did remind me a little of Lacy," he admitted.

Lily stared at the trim figure of Zoe, her pale blond curls dancing as she laughed up into the admiring face of a wealthy, potbellied man across the room. It was easy to forget that Lacy Paradise belonged to Caleb's past as much as she herself belonged to Ben's past. "Still chasing that ghost, Caleb?" she asked softly.

He laughed, a deep, warm chuckle that destroyed any illusions that he pined for Ben Paradise's lovely wife. "I never was the right man for Lacy," he said. "Or perhaps she wasn't the right woman for me." He ran a hand up Lily's arm in a tender caress.

Sensing Kate's furious gaze upon her, Lily refused to be drawn in by his smooth statement. "Perhaps you'll find her tonight," Lily said, and paused slightly as if considering her next words. "I need to ask a favor, Caleb."

His brows rose in surprise. "Anything within my power, Lily," he assured her.

Nervous now, Lily fidgeted. She straightened the already-perfect set of his tie and brushed invisible lint from the dark wool of his uniform jacket. The color nearly matched the blue-black luster of his thick hair.

"I've a new girl, an untouched girl . . . Hell, listen, this isn't easy. The kid is determined but I wouldn't give her to just any man. She needs someone who's patient and considerate."

He was pleased, touched at her confidence in him. Despite the bet he'd made with Phael, Caleb doubted his ability to seduce the beautiful young singer, although there was something very alluring and haunting about a woman who chose to wear a mask. In port, he'd often sought the exotic in both nature and amusements. He was drawn to the primitive cultures that had thrived on the islands of the Pacific. He'd led the life of a voluptuary, enjoying strange foods, strange customs. But there was always something that drew him back to San Francisco. It was as if he was searching for something without ever knowing what it was.

Seeing the curvacious, masked singer tonight had brought the elusive quest to his mind once more. There was something about her that drew him. Was it the mask? The sound of her husky voice? The way the yellow fabric of her gown clung suggestively to her delightful form?

Did it matter? She would have no interest in him. Not when younger men like Phael vied for her attention. What woman wouldn't prefer a young man? Experience didn't count for much when he was sure Phael had gleaned a fair amount of talent since his first visit to Lily's establishment.

"Why, Lily, I'd be honored," Caleb said softly. "Who is she?"

Lily didn't have to tell him in words. Her eyes had already traveled to the girl in the golden-yellow gown near the piano, the enticing young woman in the silk mask.

Caleb stared a moment in disbelief, then began laughing.

Lily stared at him aghast. She offered him the most sought-after woman in the room and he laughed. Laughed! *My God, Katie*, she thought, *I believe the man's unhinged!*

The captain's chuckle dwindled to an amused sigh. "Dear Lily," he murmured, "you've just managed to clean young Phael of a tidy sum."

Confused, her eyes narrowed in suspicion.

"The lad bet he could bed the songbird first."

Lily drew herself up haughtily. "He would have lost the bet in any case since the girl is his . . ." The madam stumbled to complete her statement, realizing that she had almost told Caleb who the songbird actually was. " . . . is not his type," she concluded.

Curious at her sudden stammer, Innes eyed Lily carefully. "I would have thought Phael the embodiment of every young woman's dreams," he said.

"Not for this girl's dreams," Lily muttered darkly then softened. "Don't worry about that one, Captain," she said with a nod in Phael's direction. "He'll find consolation."

Chapter Three

Ned Allen leaned back against the bar, his elbows hooked on the brass rail. He knew there were many eyes watching him. The men were curious to know what his business was with Lily Walsh and the women avoided catching his eye. Whatever their reasons, they all watched him with fear—except for Ben Paradise and his uniformed friend, the one suspicious, the other curious. That irritated Allen. He liked it best when people feared him.

Tonight he'd come to toy with Lily, though. He had no doubt that she hated him. Something in her face told him she was terrified and that terror had something to do with her mysterious young entertainer.

Lily's pretty face had tightened whenever his gaze fell on the singer. If there was one thing that he had learned that evening, it was that

Lily cared more about the girl at the piano than she did about her parlor house. Allen wanted to know why.

There was certainly much more to this songstress than he'd been led to believe. That she was beautiful he had known. He hadn't been surprised at her throaty, seductive voice, either. It was her self-possession and obvious innocence that drew him. The two qualities seemed at odds, a contradiction, and Allen didn't like mysteries unless he created them himself.

The songbird's eyes were bright, glowing with an excitement that had nothing to do with the adulation showered upon her. A fever burned within that trim, feminine package. A fever that could consume a man once it was released.

Did he yearn to take her innocence, Allen wondered, or just profit by it? Many men would willingly squander a fortune for the privilege of breaking this beauty.

He studied the mass of black hair, the way it framed her face in perfect ringlets before brushing her bare shoulders. Her skin was pale with a sheen like a rare pearl, almost too perfect to be real. The color of her eyes was hidden in shadow behind the theatrical mask. If he could see them, would they seem as artificial as the rest of her costume? He'd wait and see.

There was nothing fake about her figure, though. The songbird was slim yet her bosom rose in a tantalizing slope above the low neckline of her gown. The snug fit of her bodice displayed a narrow waist without a hint of a corset to create the affect. No, the songbird had no need of constricting undergarments. The way the front

54

of her skirt clung to the contours of her legs when she moved, Allen doubted that she wore much under the gown. The songbird was set on seduction.

The idea amused him. Perhaps Lily had trained her, but he knew a virgin when he saw one. There was a certain look in the eyes, a combination of fear and desire that battled for dominance. It hadn't mattered to him in the past which emotion had won out. He had taken in many virgins in the past and made a tidy sum of selling them to men who relished the destruction of virtue.

The songbird eased away from her admirers, her performance at an end. Allen had caught the signal that had passed between the girl and Lily and the songbird's cheeks had brightened momentarily. With embarrassment, with excitement, with fear? He watched her actions. She had class. Her movements were smooth, natural, unrehearsed. She stared straight ahead, her thoughts apparently far from her recent performance and the parlor house.

The twitch of her hustle was alluring. Her rich yellow skirts swayed gently as she moved away from the piano, away from the men who sought to detain her. Her eyes were bright, her smile fixed.

Allen set his empty tumbler on the bar and motioned for a refill.

As she passed the bar, Kate was startled by the forceful touch on her arm that halted her progress. Although she could have broken away easily enough, the look on the man's face dared her to try.

"Nice show, angel," he said. "You could do better than this place, though."

Kate looked into the leering face of Ned Allen. Her own eyes narrowed as she jerked her arm from his grasp. "This suits me fine," she flared, her voice a low hiss.

Allen chuckled. "A temper. I like that, kiddo." He brushed a hand against her cheek. "I'd get rid of the wig, though."

Across the room, Lily started from her seat but a hand on her shoulder prevented her from rushing to her protégé's side. She glanced back at Ben as he forced her back in her chair. "The kid's out of her league," she pleaded.

"Stay out of it, Lily," he said. The intensity of his blue eyes didn't reassure her that he would, though. She'd seen that look before, back in Missouri when he'd fought for Lacy Phalen. Did he know the songbird was his daughter?

Lily turned to Caleb, imploring him with her eyes to intervene.

With easy grace, Caleb got to his feet. "Maybe I should try my hand at winning this bet," he said.

Lily's hand on his arm pleaded. "Be careful. He's a slimy lizard, Caleb."

Paradise's raised brow questioned Innes's ability to handle Allen alone. "He's probably armed."

The captain nodded in total agreement with his friend. Allen wasn't the kind of man to feel confident without a concealed weapon, "Contrary to this establishment's rules." Caleb said softly, "so am I."

*   *   *

Allen's touch was familiar, as if he owned her, Kate thought. She flinched. The action amused him.

"No need to be afraid of me, angel," he said smoothly. "I jest wanna talk a little business."

Her eyes were emerald blocks of ice. He admired the transformation and the color that tinted her throat. Her chin was regal as it tilted in defiance.

"I have no business to discuss with you, Mr. Allen," she said.

He smiled, sure of himself and of her fear of him. "Ah, now you have the advantage, kiddo. You know who I am but I don't know who you are. You sure ain't some floozy from the Coast."

She didn't flinch this time and he admired her bravado.

"Good night, Mr. Allen."

Her voice was icy. A society matron couldn't have carried it off better, he thought.

"The pleasure's all been yours," she declared.

"You got a smart mouth, angel. Maybe a might too smart. Could get ya in trouble."

Kate's shoulders straightened, her squared chin lifted infinitesimally. "I'm not afraid of you, if that's what you're hoping."

Allen's eyes narrowed momentarily. Then he laughed. "You're good, angel. But not that good. We'll meet again, you can be sure of it."

Kate clenched her fists. Her palms were sweating and, beneath the mask, her cheeks burned. It was an effort to keep her voice level. "A threat, Mr. Allen? Surely that is beneath a man of your stature."

Allen put a finger under her chin. "Not a threat, angel. A promise. A solid promise."

Caleb was conscious of a fleeting sense of familiarity as he approached the pair. Was it the pert, half-hidden profile of the girl or the harsh features of the man that jogged a memory in his mind? But it was gone in a moment, leaving him none the wiser.

"I hope I'm not intruding," Caleb said, stepping up to the bar. Two furious sets of eyes turned to him, one fiery, one cold. The girl's eyes cooled immediately, and she smiled warmly at him.

"Not at all, sir . . . ah, Captain," she purred, her eyes flickering to the rank insignia on his uniform. "Mr. Allen and I have finished our discussion. Have we not, sir?"

Allen's eyes flickered over the man quickly, recognizing him as Ben Paradise's companion. "For the moment," he agreed slowly. "We will meet again," he warned.

"I think not."

Kate's voice was cool, and Allen had the impression that she had dismissed him as insignificant. She would learn no one ignored Ned Allen.

"If you will excuse me, gentlemen?" she said. At Innes's nod, she made her exit, leaving him with a brilliant smile.

Allen stared after her, then picked up his glass. "Seems you've made a conquest, Captain," he mused. "Cut the rest out pretty neatly."

Caleb watched the sensuous sway of the girl's skirts as she paused in the doorway to look back.

"Oh, do you think so?" he answered, his voice relaying mild surprise. "My lucky day then."

Allen frowned at the man's disinterested smile. He acted as if he were unaware of the songbird's reputation, of the nightly contests to gain her attention. Yet there was something that didn't ring true in the sailor's manner. Although seemingly at his ease, the man was tensing as if for a fight. Allen leaned back against the bar, his glass in hand. "Then again, you could know more about the songbird than you let on," he suggested.

Innes laughed shortly. "I've just put into port after three months at sea. She's just as much a mystery to me as she is to every man here."

"If you say so," Allen replied carefully. "What 'er ya drinkin'?"

Kate found escape from the parlor was not easy to accomplish. She was accosted by two eager young admirers the moment she entered the hall. They were placated with smiles and excuses, but the next man was not as easily discouraged.

She had reached the first landing when she was startled by his sudden appearance. The tall man had lain in wait for her in the shadows. Before she realized his intention, he had seized her hand and kissed it lingeringly.

"Have pity on me, oh, golden one," Phael pleaded. "Grant me but one smile that I might cherish it as belonging to me alone."

Kate snatched her hand away and laughed at the disconcerted look on Phael's handsome face. "A smile?" she purred, the phoney accent more pronounced so that he would not recognize her voice. "I doubt that a mere smile is your goal, sir. Confess. You wish to lure more than that from me."

He looked relieved, but then she knew poetry of thought was not her brother's strong point. "The truth, fairest one?"

Kate turned away, afraid that Phael would know her in such close quarters. "Your reputation proceeds you, Mr. Paradise," she murmured as if sad. "I'm afraid I do not wish to be counted as one of your many conquests."

Phael moved so that he was facing her once more. He favored her with his special smile. Kate knew it was special for she'd seen him practice it in the dressing mirror in his room. "You might possibly be my last conquest," he suggested. "The one woman to hold me."

Kate kept her eyes downcast. "I wouldn't dare tempt the fates, dear sir. Now if you will excuse me, I do have an appointment."

Phael stopped her, his hand familiarly at her waist. "You would turn me down so coldly when I cherish only tender thoughts for you?"

Kate moved away from his touch. "There are certain facts that make what you suggest impossible."

Gallantly, Phael gestured as if sweeping such insignificant things as facts out of his way. "They need not concern the path of true love," he insisted.

Highly entertained to see her brother hot on the trail of conquest. Kate hid her grin behind her hand. "I fear I would still remain quite without interest, for you see," she said with a sorrowful, melodramatic sigh, "my heart belongs to another."

"Another?" Phael stepped back in surprise.

"Yes," she affirmed. "An older, more experienced man."

Suddenly suspicious, Phael's green eyes narrowed. "And who is this lucky fella?" he demanded.

Kate ran lightly up the next couple of steps, then paused to look back down at him. "I doubt if you know him," she said mischievously. "He doesn't reside in the city."

"Who?" Phael insisted doggedly.

Her gaze went past him to the anteroom below. Her smile warmed as she looked at the man in the archway, his broad shoulders propped against the molding.

Caleb raised the glass in his hand in salute to the younger man.

"I won't say the best man won," the captain said, his lips twitching with amusement. "But I certainly did beat you out, Phael."

Above him on the steps, the songbird giggled. "Are you coming, Captain?"

Caleb was surprised at the nervousness that pitched her voice higher. "In a moment, my dear."

Kate nodded happily and continued up the stairs, her steps unhurried, although her heart was beating quickly.

Both men admired the sway of her skirts and the brief glimpse of her slim ankle their location below her allowed.

A frown creased Phael's face as he watched the girl. There was something odd about her.

61

He felt he'd watched her before, had heard her giggle.

As she disappeared from view, Phael shrugged. "No hard feelings, Caleb. Hope you can handle her."

Innes laughed. "But you hope I can't."

"I haven't given up, if that's what you mean." Phael grinned. "Buy you a drink?"

The captain looked at the near-empty tumbler in his hand, then up the stairs. "I think I could use it," he agreed, and followed the young man back into the parlor.

When Caleb opened the door, the songbird was staring out at the dark night. The myriad of lights on the Coast made it impossible to see the stars, even if the fog had lifted and she had cared to count them or to wish on them. What would the songbird wish for? Caleb wondered.

She was nervous. He could tell from her stiff stance. Softly, he closed the door. For a moment longer, the songbird stood silhouetted against the night, the golden hue of her gown blending with the soft, dimmed light of a single gas wall jet. The mask was on the dresser, discarded for his visit, yet the mystery persisted. She remained in the shadows, lovely yet unknown. Caleb doubted that he would be able to see her clearly even if she stood next to him.

At the quiet click of the latch she turned, a smile of welcome on her lovely face. Without speaking, she moved across the room and her arms slid around his neck as she offered her lips to him.

Enchanted by the simple innocence of her

movements, Caleb kissed her gently, tasting the lush fullness of her mouth. It parted welcomingly and he kissed her more fully, crushing her body to his.

She sighed and pressed closer, as if she savored the moment.

Caleb found his pulse racing as she responded. It was a heady feeling, one that he had not experienced in many years. His hand found its way to her hair, intent upon loosening it, to feel it fall in lush midnight waves down her back.

At his touch, she pulled away, suddenly coy. Her eyes were dark and mysterious. He couldn't tell their color in the dim light. Were they brown, green, blue? He couldn't remember from when he had gazed into them briefly at the bar. His attention had been on Allen, not the songbird.

"Please, can we continue without the light, Captain?" she asked, her voice a softly accented, husky whisper.

Dazed, he agreed. He wanted to see her as he made love to her but would respect her wishes at the moment. Lily had told him she was a virgin. He grinned wryly. His first virgin, actually. A sailor's life was not filled with many untested maids. She was naturally shy, even if she had chosen a profession that would soon destroy such innocence.

The songbird breathed easier as he extinguished the single lamp near the door. She slipped away from him briefly to return with her hair loose, falling in thick waves free to her waist.

Caleb found her easily in the dark room. Once more he claimed her lips, and her arms went around him in wild abandon. She pressed close to him, all illusions of shyness forgotten. In the dark, she was secure and eager.

His lips moved, exploring the gentle curves of her face, the sweeping length of her throat as she arched back, a sigh of pleasure on her lips. He buried his hands in her soft, sweet-smelling hair.

"Would you like to undress me?" she asked softly against his lips.

He chuckled, his voice low. "Actually, I'd like to get rid of my jacket and tie."

"I'm sorry," she said. "I should have thought of that myself."

She sounded sweetly contrite, and he liked the exotic hint of her accent. He knew it wasn't French, but neither could he identify it. It was hard to connect the whispery voice with her passionate responses.

Caleb smiled as she loosened his tie, then slid her hands beneath his coat. Her touch gently caressed his ribs, continuing over his chest, as she eased the jacket from his shoulders. But, long before it hit the floor, his mouth claimed hers. What the girl lacked in experience, she certainly made up for in the mechanics of lovemaking. Or perhaps it was her eagerness. An untested girl's touch should not excite him as hers did. Her hands appeared to worship him as they stroked along the muscles of his back, across the short hairs at his nape before burrowing in his thick hair once more.

His hands found the tiny covered buttons of her gown, and she sighed as the dress gaped, revealing her thinly covered breasts. Caleb's lips dropped to taste the hollow of her throat and she shivered.

"I don't even know your name," he murmured huskily.

The songbird stirred restlessly in his arms, then hesitated. "Cathy," she breathed. Her hands pulled his shirt loose from his trousers, her fingers quickly freeing the studs, and slid beneath the fabric, moving with slow sensuality through the light hair on his chest. "Call me Cathy, Captain."

He gasped as her fingers dipped lower, following the dwindling trail of hair downward across his flat stomach. "I'm not a captain tonight, lovely Cathy," he insisted. "Just a man named Caleb."

She swayed against him. "Love me then, Caleb," the songbird urged. "Teach me."

He heard a rustle of taffeta as the golden dress slid to the floor. He followed her hands to the crinolette ties, helping her now unsteady fingers with the knots. Quickly, she stepped from the light cage and was back in his arms.

Caleb's hands ran down her back, past her waist to trace the full natural curve of her hip. "I wish you'd let me see you, Cathy."

He felt the movement of her hair as she denied him. "Please, Caleb. Not yet." Her hands touched his, drawing them over the cool silk of her drawers and camisole, up to her breasts. "See me with your touch," she urged throatily. "With your lips." Her mouth was searing in its eagerness.

Caleb tumbled her onto the bed, his head bent to savor the taste of her warm flesh. He freed her breasts, exploring the delicate contours with his tongue.

The songbird gasped with unexpected pleasure as he teased the eager upthrust nipple. With her hands in his hair, she held him close.

Without lifting his head from its task, Caleb stripped off his shirt, tossing it carelessly to the floor. Immediately, she ran a hand along the sinewy ridges of muscle, marveling at the feel of his leashed power.

He found her calf and stroked it easily, then his hand moved up the silk stocking to the frilled garter.

The songbird gasped as his mouth left her breast. She felt his weight shift on the bed as he took off his trousers, then his hands returned to her waist to push her silk underdrawers down over her hips.

Now that the moment was at hand, Kate was anxious. Would she please him? Had she remembered all of Lily's instructions, all she had learned in the months that she had stolen away to talk to the girls of Madam Lily's? Would Caleb admit his love for her or would she incur his hatred for giving herself to him in this anonymous way? Was she bartering her virtue for a brief glimpse of happiness?

Caleb's lips traced molten paths across her naked skin. His tongue charted the unsailed, smooth surface of her stomach and moved ever downward.

Kate groaned his name. No matter what the outcome at dawn, she knew she would never relinquish Caleb Innes. He had belonged to her at her birth. Tonight she would belong to him.

Her stretching fingers found the tautness ·of his naked buttocks and the urgency of her touch drove Caleb mad. Never had he wanted a woman as he wanted this girl.

"Cathy," he breathed brokenly. "I don't mean to hurt you."

She was beyond understanding. She arched eagerly toward him, her lips seeking his. "I love you, Caleb," she whispered. "I love you."

His heart contracted at the tender words, words he was saddened to hear because they were words he couldn't repeat to her. He pushed the sorrow the phrase evoked from his mind. He was a man of the sea, a man who called no port home. A man whose mistress was a tall-masted ship, not a woman in a port town.

The urgency of his own body overpowered all thought and gently, he moved her legs and lifted her hips. Her arms circled his shoulders, and pulled his head down to meet her demanding lips. He kissed her, his tongue plunging within the sweet recess of her mouth as he duplicated the movement, thrusting into her, possessing her totally.

Kate's cry of pain died in a moan of pleasure. She was his now and Caleb was undeniably hers.

The parlor was empty but for one remaining quest. He sat nursing his drink, his legs stretched out before him, his expression one of pain.

He should have returned home to Lacy, Ben told himself. Instead, he continued to sit, patiently waiting for the couples to pair off for the night.

He was fairly sure of the answer Lily would give him. Not that he wished for confirmation. It would make him feel old and a failure.

Perhaps he wasn't in his prime. But three grown children didn't mean he was a graybeard, either. He was barely fifty-two. His hair was still thick and dark. Only occasionally did he resort to the reading glasses old Doc Nichols insisted he needed.

Upstairs Phael was consoling Dora for his inattention earlier. Ben had always been inordinately proud of Phael's prowess with the ladies. Was it because his eldest son resembled him so strongly? The boy had Lacy's eyes, of course, but otherwise it was like looking in a mirror that stripped the years away.

Pride in a son and a sense of failure over a daughter.

Did he really need Lily's confirmation to know the girl Caleb Innes had joined upstairs was Katie?

Paradise moved to the back bar and poured a double shot from the front row of decanters. The good stuff, he mused, but barely tasted the fiery liquid as it burned his throat.

Perhaps he should have stormed up the stairs when he had made the connection between the mysterious songbird and his daughter. Instead, he had sat drinking, trying to convince himself that he was wrong.

What could he say to Katie? She was twenty-one years old. He had made Lacy his mistress when she'd been barely twenty and Phael had been born barely six months after he had married her.

It was the anguish he knew Innes would feel in the morning that kept him at his post. It was obvious that Katie had preserved her disguise, that Caleb didn't realize who he was bedding.

Paradise took another long pull on his drink, seeking answers in his glass. Had he failed Kate as a father? She had always been a loner. Phael had been his favorite, tagging along in his footsteps eager to learn anything, everything he thought to impart. Kate's interest had always revolved around the *Puritan Paramour* and Caleb Innes.

A schoolgirl infatuation, he'd thought. But Katie had grown up and why hadn't he noticed?

Tired now that the house was settled for the night, Lily stood in the archway. Ben noticed that she didn't look surprised to see him still there. He grimaced. Wasn't he the man who always went home to his wife? And tonight he hadn't even sent Lacy a message saying he'd be late.

"So ya know," Lily said softly.

Ben took a healthy swallow. He didn't even feel the burn of the whiskey any longer but the pain was still as strong as it had been earlier. "Yeah, I know."

He had aged suddenly, Lily realized. The vital man who had been ready to battle Bull Run Allen earlier was gone.

"I'm sorry, Ben," she murmured.

He put a second glass on the bar and filled it for her. He actually smiled. It was a shadow of his former grin, but it still charmed her. "It's not your fault, Lily. I didn't recognize her myself. Neither did Phael." He stared into his drink a moment. "She's headstrong."

Fury at Katie for inflicting pain on her father raged impotently in Lily's breast. What could she do? Pull the girl out of bed? It would just destroy Caleb's illusions sooner. Let him enjoy the hours that remained of the night. At dawn he would face the truth.

"What gave her away?" Lily asked.

Paradise swirled the whiskey in his glass. "Nothing in particular. Phael in a way. Everything. Nothing."

Lily pressed for details.

"The set of her chin when she was cornered by Allen. The way she treated Phael." He laughed shortly, the sound full of pain. "He waylaid her earlier. Over a bet. A fool's bet." Ben took another swig of his drink. "Tell Zack to keep the money. I don't think anyone will feel like claiming it."

Lily watched him, waiting patiently.

"Phael said the songbird had no compassion. That she was condescending, humoring him, treating him like an errant schoolboy. Or her brother."

"And you aren't mad?"

"Oh, no, darlin'," he drawled. "I'm mad as hell. But I won't interfere tonight."

Lily stared at her untouched drink. "She loves him, Ben."

At his silence she met his eyes. "I know it doesn't make it any easier or right, for that matter, but her motives aren't to hurt him or you."

His thoughts were turned inward. "Kate is young," he said. "She'll recover. We might even be able to palm her off on some threadbare aristocrat."

Lily's temper exploded. "Why you goddamn hypocrite!" she growled. "You haven't heard a thing I've said."

A dangerous light came into his blue eyes turning them icy in their intensity.

Lily ignored the warning signal. "What's so different?" she raged. "Aren't my girls jest as good as Katie? Jest because she's your daughter, you're upset and planning how to cover up this little indiscretion."

He eyed her over his glass. "It isn't quite the same, Lil. Katie has no need to earn her living."

"And she's not. She's with the man she loves. If I miss my guess, Caleb cares a lot about her, too. What's so wrong about that?"

"Not a thing. If he were a younger man . . ."

Lily moved away from the bar to pace the room. She turned on him, her fists set on her hips. "You'd what? Take a shotgun to him? Make him marry her?"

Paradise's eyes blazed now, although his manner was lazy as he stared at her irate form. "Why haven't you said it, Lily? What's the difference between Kate and her mother? I wasn't in any hurry to marry Lacy, was I?"

"Well?" Lily demanded, her eyes flashing with indignation. She was fond of Kate. Damn it, she loved the kid and she wouldn't hear anyone snipe at her. Not even her own father! "Why did ya wait till Lacy was three months pregnant?" she insisted, dredging up the past. "Why didn't ya marry her back in Missouri instead of draggin' her across the country as your own private whore?"

Paradise set his now empty tumbler careful-

71

ly on the bar. "You're on thin ice, Lily. Don't trade on the possibility that your part in this hasn't cancelled out any affection I once felt for you."

"Affection? We shared quite a few nights between the sheets." She leaned closer to him. "Let Katie work out her own life, Ben. The kid knows what she wants. No matter what ya do, Katie will do as she pleases." Lily smiled softly. "She's a lot like you, lover. Let her go."

He sighed, the fury dying just as quickly as it had flared. "I'm getting old, Lily. It's a hard thing to admit or to realize your children don't need you anymore."

Lily slid an arm around him as he slumped wearily against the bar. "She still needs ya. She'll always need ya, just not in the same way."

Paradise stared at the bar, unseeing. "It's going to be one hell of a morning, Lily."

"Yeah, it'll be tough," she agreed. "At least it's peaceful now. Why don't ya catch a few hours sleep?"

He grinned the faint smile she knew so well. "With you, Lily?"

She smoothed his dark brown hair back. "I never did bite, lover."

Ben caught her hand and kissed the back of it gently. "You asked a question a little while ago that I neglected to answer."

Lily smiled quietly. "I didn't mean none of those things I said, Ben. I was mad."

"I want to answer it, Lily."

He was silent, collecting his thoughts. "I loved her, Lily. I think I loved Lacy Phalen the first time I set eyes on her. But she didn't love me.

I had to make her love me, teach her to love me."

Lily thought of the girl Lacy Phalen Paradise had been nearly twenty-five years ago. He was wrong. Lacy had loved him all along. It was her pride that had kept her from admitting it.

"I think that's how Katie feels," she said. "She'll never be happy with anyone but Caleb. Accept it, Ben. She's a good kid. She's just desperate."

He patted her hand absentmindedly, his thoughts on the morning yet to come. "It's not a question of whether I can accept it, Lily," he said at last. "It's whether Caleb can."

Chapter Four

A blanket of fog shielded the city from the first rosy rays of the sun. In the richly appointed room at Madam Lily's Parlor House, Caleb Innes stirred. He lay a moment, staring at the pastel wallpaper and the heavy dark blue drapes. It always took a few minutes when he was ashore to orient himself to the fact that the rocking motion of the sea was absent. Beneath him, this bed was softer and wider than the bunk in his cabin aboard the *Puritan Paramour*. And he wasn't alone.

A lazy smile crinkled the corners of his eyes. He remembered now, not only the joys of last night, but of those yet to come. This morning promised to be very special, for Cathy would no longer be able to hide the lovely body he had enjoyed so intimately in the dark.

She lay on her stomach, the sheet slipping from her shoulders. Her beautiful hair spread over the pillows in a rich fragrant pool, still shielding her face from his gaze. The early-morning sun burnished separate strands so that they glowed deep, earthy red, or glittered like newly minted gold. Her hair was neither red nor gold but a beautifully blended combination of the two.

Now why would she choose to hide such glory? Her wig and mask on the dresser assured him that this was indeed the same woman who had given him such pleasure. Her satin dress was a spill of sunshine against the darkly patterned rug.

Caleb ran his fingers lightly along the curve of her back, barely touching her. His mystery woman, the songbird. She had been a curious and addictive lover, innocent yet knowledgeable when it came to a man's weakness. That alone was mysterious. When added to the fact that he didn't know exactly what she looked liked, it only heightened the excitement he still felt.

She was a woman protected by the shadows. This time they were phantoms he could dispel with a brush of his hand through her hair. It would take only a moment and Cathy would be revealed, her copper-gilt mane would tangle with his fingers as cool and soft as the silks he brought back from China.

Yet he delayed the moment. Once he woke her, the mystery would be gone, Part of her allure would vanish.

He had seen the lovely contours of her face through his touch and taste in the dark. He had sailed them and the lush womanly rises and falls of her body, using his own senses to chart a course toward pleasure. Cathy had responded as his ship did before a strong and steady wind, moving as if she were privy to his thoughts, an extension of him, a part of him.

Why hide her true coloring? Her lovely face? Had it been a ploy to set her apart from the other beautiful women in Lily's employ? To make her companionship more highly prized by the men who frequented the parlor house?

Whatever her reasons, Caleb dismissed them as unimportant at the moment. The sun climbed higher in the heavens with every minute, working to burn the haze from the city. As much as he would have enjoyed spending the day in bed with the songbird, he had a business to run, a ship to ready for its next voyage.

Gently, Caleb drew the sheet away from his sleeping companion. Perhaps he could delay concluding this Iliad just a bit longer.

Her skin was pale, lightly freckled across her shoulders. He traced it from her nape down the curve of her backbone to the delectable swell of her hip. She sighed in her sleep, then rolled over, moving closer to him.

He wanted her again. Again? He was acting like a kid. How long had it been since he found it nearly impossible to leave a woman? Quite a long time. That made this girl extremely special. She had given him back his youth. Or could it be possible he no longer wanted to sample the delights of a thousand ports? Had he grown sated with the women who haunted the wharves, not just the whores but the ladies who spent their afternoon exploring the limits of a man's talents?

The songbird's legs were long and shapely, her stomach almost concave. Slowly, his hands roused her from her slumber, gently stroking her pale flesh, noting every curve and valley with his sight as well as with his touch.

"Caleb?" Her voice was drowsy, breaking on a slightly higher octave than he remembered from the evening before.

"Good morning," he said, and placed a tender kiss on her naked shoulder. "How do you feel?"

Eyes of a luminous lagoon-green blinked from behind her veil of hair. She smiled. "Wonderful," she said, and stretched.

He admired the sensuous arching of her body. It pleased him that she was not embarrassed to be naked before him. Although she had made the decision to sell her body, she still had been an innocent the night before. He was glad she showed no regret for what had passed between them.

"I knew you were beautiful," he whispered, "but I dared not hope for such a garden of delights."

"Was I . . . all right?" she asked, her face still turned slightly away from him.

"More than all right," he said. "Shall I show you?"

He moved to brush the veil of burnished hair from her face, but she forestalled him, leaning forward to pull his head down to her waiting lips. The soft texture of her hair melded with the nectar of her kiss. He savored the taste of her

with his mouth, with his hands, demanding a
rebirth of passion. She moved against him, her
fingers moving with new-found knowledge over
the hard length of his body. She twisted in his
arms, taking the initiative until she straddled
him, her face and shoulders still hidden in a
shroud of red-gold waves.

Caleb caressed her, directing her movements.
They melted together, her body accepting and
molding to his easily now. "Love me, Caleb,"
she insisted, her voice cutting across his memory.

A familiarity that had nothing to do with his
knowledge of her body tugged urgently at a
corner of his mind. Something to do with her
voice? Her accent was tempered, nearly absent.
Her voice wasn't as low-pitched as he remembered. The sensuous pull remained, wrapping
him in an cocoon of passion.

Caleb gripped her shoulders and rolled, pinning her beneath him. Her hair swirled with the
movement, allowing him a brief glimpse of long
dark lashes, of a perfect straight nose. His mouth
found hers and possessed it. She possessed him.
She was a sea siren bewitching him. Her hips
rose to meet his rhythm, matching it with a
frantic need that drove him to new heights of
pleasure.

"Caleb," she whispered again, savoring his
name, the haunting accent forgotten now in
passion. "Caleb."

Her voice cut across his mind like a searing
brand and recognition jolted him from the bed.

The violence of his move frightened her.
"Caleb," Kate cried, and her arms stretched

out to him to reclaim the shattered moment.

He stood unsteadily just beyond her reach, his chest rising and falling quickly as he sought to still his racing pulse. Pictures of her flashed through his mind: Katie at five crawling into his lap; at twelve, scrambling aboard the *Paramour*, laughing as he swung her into his arms; at sixteen, inordinately proud of her long skirts and trying desperately to act grown up.

Knowing the masquerade was at an end, Kate brushed back her hair, and Caleb's stricken brown eyes regarded her with horror.

With a moan of anguish, Caleb turned from her, collapsing to sit at the far side of the bed, his face buried in his hands. "Sweet Lord," he whispered hoarsely. "What have I done!"

Katie, beautiful Katie, her lovely young body sprawled across blood-stained sheets. Her hair a silken mantle that teased, obscuring then flaunting the perfection of high thrusting breasts, the gentle sloping curve of her thigh.

She scrambled to her knees, clutching the sheet to her naked breasts. "Don't hate me, Caleb," she pleaded.

He turned at the breathy touch of her voice. "Hate you, Katie? My God, I've ruined you!"

She flinched at the raw pain in his voice. "Don't say that. You love me. I know you do, Caleb."

Angrily, he gripped her shoulders. "Love you? I was there when you were born. I delivered you! Katie, how could you do this to us?"

His fingers dug into her flesh, and Kate welcomed the sharp pain. "I did it for us," she cried. "I'm a woman now, Caleb. Not a little girl. A woman made to love you. And I do love you, Caleb." Her voice dropped an octave, seducing him. "Let me love you," she purred.

Caleb released her quickly, putting the length of the room between them. "No! I wish to God I could undo, forget what I did." Hurriedly, he gathered his clothing in a bundle. "I'm sorry, Katie. I can't do as you ask."

"Caleb," she wailed in despair. He couldn't leave her. Not now!

Innes resolutely hardened his heart against the shiny wetness of her eyes. "Good-bye, Katie," he said firmly, and closed the door behind him.

Dressed once more, Caleb stumbled to the bar downstairs and poured a double shot of whiskey. He gulped it down, barely tasting the sting, and refilled the glass.

"It won't help," a deep baritone voice said. "I've tried it all night."

Caleb turned to face Kate's father.

"You look like hell," Paradise told him.

Innes grimaced. "So do you. Why didn't you stop me?"

Ben shrugged out of his armchair. His normally immaculate suit was crushed from the erratic sleep he'd caught during his vigil. His tie hung loose, his vest lay open. A light dusting of gray painted the dark stubble along his jaw. "Lily says Kate loves you," he said.

"That doesn't answer my question," the captain insisted. His creased trousers and shirt looked as disreputable as he felt. His hair stood in agitated waves. He ran a weary hand through it. "Hell, I just ruined your daughter, Paradise."

The gambler moved to the back bar, his movements stiff, and filled a fresh tumbler. "I know," he said. "Katherine loves you."

Caleb laughed shortly. "And that's supposed to make me feel better? I'm old enough to be her father."

"It doesn't bother Katie, why should it disturb you, Cal?" Paradise asked.

"Why?" Caleb stared into his glass disconsolately. "Because she's Lacy's daughter. If things had been different, she might have been mine."

Paradise sat the decanter down near Innes's nearly empty glass. "But she's mine," he murmured.

"That doesn't excuse my actions. Why didn't I recognize her earlier?" Caleb finished his whiskey and refilled the glass. He met Paradise's bloodshot eyes. "She deceived you, too, didn't she?"

"Yeah." Paradise sighed and leaned heavily on the polished bar surface. "Why should we have even suspected Katie of such a Machiavellian ploy? We didn't expect to see her performing in a parlor house, so it never crossed our minds that she and the songbird were one. Phael still hasn't realized it."

Ben paused, his face full of pain and weariness. "What are you going to do, Cal?"

Innes stared into his glass. "Are you asking as a father or a friend?" he demanded shortly. He took a deep breath. "Belay that. I'm sorry. I don't know. Right now I'd like to forget."

"And Katie?" Paradise pushed.

Elizabeth Daniels

A vision of Kate surfaced unwanted in Caleb's mind—her eyes clouding with passion, her voice a throaty whisper that caressed his name.

"And Katie." God, would he ever forget Kate Paradise? Caleb wondered. Could he?

Chapter Five

Devin Thaxton pulled nervously at his tie, disturbing the perfection he'd worked an hour to achieve.

She'd kept him cooling his heels in the outer office a full twenty minutes now. The longer he waited, the worse his temper grew. For two weeks he'd sat patiently—no, impotently!—riding the waves waiting for word to sail. The cargo had been loaded long ago as preparations to pull anchor progressed on schedule despite the captain's mysterious disappearance. Captain Innes had rowed into San Francisco the day of their arrival and had not been seen since then. As first mate, Thaxton had kept the swabbies to their tasks and, as the days stretched into a fortnight, he had begun to pray that the captain would not return.

Elizabeth Daniels

His decision to beard the bitch on her own
ground hadn't been easily made. He'd heard a
myriad of conflicting stories about Lacy Paradise, the woman who controlled the western
division of the Puritan Shipping Line. She was
a middle-aged harridan stripped of every feminine virtue by her mannish ambitions. Still, she
was just a woman and he'd never had a woman
refuse him any request. If worded right, he felt
his goal was in sight.

Soon he'd have permission to sail on the tide
and achieve an easy promotion to master of the
Puritan Paramour in the process.

The *Paramour* was an old clipper but still
swift. Given the old routes, Thaxton was sure
he could match or best the speed records from
China to New York. He wouldn't accept progress,
rejecting the suggestion that goods reached their
eastern markets faster via the railroad.

Thaxton paced uneasily.

Lacy's secretary, a small wiry man with thin
graying hair and heavy spectacles, glared at the
arrogant young officer. He hadn't liked the sail-
or's highhanded demand to see Mrs. Paradise.
Now he didn't care for the swaggering way the
man strode about the room, blind to the dark
leather armchairs, the Persian rug, or the litho-
graphs of Puritan clippers that decorated the
room. He had no reason to act superior toward
anyone. The insignia on his dark uniform was
that of a minor officer. The man's broad shoulders and narrow hips probably attracted many
a woman's eye, but the cocky bastard was in for
a surprise if he thought to charm Lacy Paradise,
the secretary thought with satisfaction.

The little man smiled to himself, casting a glance at the mantle clock. Mrs. Paradise had instructed him to keep Mr. Thaxton waiting for half an hour. Perhaps even a moment or two more wouldn't hurt. It certainly wouldn't improve the officer's temper.

Thaxton paused in his pacing to check his reflection in the glass of a lithograph. It depicted the newest ship of the line, its tall masts supporting five tiers of sail, the peacock-blue Puritan banner flying just beneath the Stars and Stripes. He didn't see the ship as he admired his reflection.

The Line uniform with its high cut, wide lapels emphasized his broad chest and trim form. His gleaming blond hair was swept from a side part to disguise a high forehead and grew in thick abundance along his jaw. He was inordinately fond of his bushy sideburns and brushed at them proudly. Yes, the old lady should be rightly impressed, he decided and glanced at the clock.

Twenty-nine minutes. A scowl deepened the tint of his amber eyes and tightened the set of his thin lips. His hands clenched at his side. If he waited much longer, he'd probably strangle the bitch.

Satisfied that the visitor was sufficiently chastised for his impertinence, the secretary got to his feet stiffly. "Mrs. Paradise will see you now," he intoned pompously.

Thaxton turned, irritated at the man's superior manner. It smacked of insubordination. His palm itched to teach the little man a lesson, one he'd be loath to forget.

Thaxton grunted and pushed past the man into the inner room.

Three different sets of eyes looked up at his entrance. A young boy sat at a desk in the corner, a ledger book open before him. He regarded the newcomer with interest, his blue eyes alert. A willowy redheaded woman glanced over her shoulder briefly at him. Her gaze took in his close-fitting uniform and dismissed him, turning to stare out the window at the activity on California Street once more.

The third person caused Thaxton to halt uncertainly on the threshold. She was incredibly lovely. Her pale blond hair was swept back into an elaborate twist on the crown of her head. Wispy curls escaped to cluster around a face that appeared perfect and youthful. At forty-three, Lacy Phalen Paradise showed few signs of aging. The light tracing of lines at the corners of her forest-green eyes only enhanced them.

She smiled in satisfaction at his reaction. Lacy had never actually met Devin Thaxton but Caleb had described him as impatient and ambitious. The captain had also said that Thaxton was very efficient in his duties and would make an excellent ship's master in the future. Without being told, Lacy knew the reason for Thaxton's sudden appearance in her office.

"Good afternoon, Mr. Thaxton. It's a pleasure to make your acquaintance at long last," she said, and stood, her hand stretching across the desk to grip his.

Devin stumbled forward to grasp the slim hand, surprised at the firmness of her grip.

He was unprepared for this vision. Her hair was the palest shade of gold, her skin luminous. Her businesslike dark gray suit hugged an intoxicatingly attractive figure.

His sources had been very misinformed about Lacy Paradise. This woman was no middle-aged hag. "It's a pleasure indeed for me, Mrs. Paradise," Thaxton murmured smoothly. "The captain neglected to tell me you were beautiful as well as intelligent."

Beneath her long dark lashes, he caught a glint of amusement in Lacy's eyes. She drew her hand from his.

"Thank you, but I doubt Captain Innes ever notices my appearance, Mr. Thaxton. We grew up together, as I'm sure you know. Caleb is like a brother," she said. It pleased her to note the slight twitch at the corner of his mouth. He hadn't been prepared for that hit.

She turned toward the young woman perched on the narrow window ledge. "Have you met my daughter Katherine?" she asked smoothly.

The girl turned from the window once more, a look of distaste on her face. The late-afternoon sun set copper lights aflame in her neatly coiled hair. Her emerald silk gown clung to full, high breasts, and an impossibly narrow waist before being caught up in a spray over her bustle. She glared at him angrily before turning back to the view.

Disconcerted by the flash of hatred in her dark eyes, Devin missed his introduction to the boy. The stiffly held back and the insult she had implied by her silence both irritated and intrigued him. What had he done to merit such a cut? He doubted he had met Miss Katherine Paradise previously. Surely, he would not have forgotten such a woman.

Woman? Inwardly, Thaxton grinned. Yes, the girl was certainly no innocent. She exuded a sensuality that drew his gaze back to her repeatedly.

Lacy watched the young man's reaction to Kate with satisfaction. Like her husband, she had always considered Kate's attachment to Caleb to be nothing more than puppy love, which she would outgrow. As a result, she still found it difficult to accept Kate's behavior at Lily Walsh's house.

Kate and Caleb? In a way Lacy felt cheated. The fact that Caleb had never married had seemed a compliment to her, a sign that he languished in part over her.

Despite her insulting lack of manners in slighting Devin Thaxton, Lacy noted that there was a new maturity about Kate. She knew her daughter was eaten with worry over Caleb's disappearance and that the child blamed herself.

"Has Captain Innes sent you, Mr. Thaxton?" Lacy asked, watching for the young man's reaction. She knew as well as he that Caleb appeared to have been swallowed up by the Barbary Coast, so complete had his disappearance been.

The officer started at the husky sound of her voice. Fleetingly, he wondered if her daughter's voice were as titillating.

"Why, no, ma'am. I had hoped you could give me word of him," he replied, hoping he looked sufficiently concerned. "We have been ready to weigh anchor any time this past week."

Lacy seated herself behind the desk and gestured for her guest to take the other chair. "None of the cargo is perishable, I believe," she murmured.

Devin met her eyes with an ingratiating smile. "Nevertheless, I fear we will lose certain markets if we don't sail soon, Mrs. Paradise. In the captain's absence, I had hoped you would give me permission to sail."

She nodded in acknowledgement of his suggestion, raising Devin's expectations. "I believe we will wait for Captain Innes, though, Mr. Thaxton," Lacy said quietly.

A spark of renewed anger lit his eyes. "I fear the captain has met with a misfortune, else we would have heard from him, ma'am," he insisted. "If not, then—"

The boy interrupted, jumping from his chair, heedless of the spray of ink his pen splattered over his papers. "The crimpers," he breathed reverently. "I told ya he'd been shanghaied, Katie!"

The young woman at the window favored the boy with a look of disgust.

Lacy Paradise glared at her boisterous son. "You will return to your assignment, David," she said sternly.

The boy cowed immediately, but threw a rebellious look over his shoulder. "I bet they did get him," he insisted sulking.

The woman ignored his outburst.

"Unlike my son," Lacy said, "I don't believe Captain Innes has met with mischief. Perhaps he has gone into the country or to Sacramento."

Thaxton's temper struggled anew. She didn't believe that any more than he did. Captain

Innes had always been anxious to leave port, to put back to sea, cleansing his lungs of the stench of the city. "It doesn't really matter anymore, does it, Mrs. Paradise? I want your order to sail. Without the captain if necessary." He leaned forward eagerly. "I can handle the *Paramour*, ma'am. I've been first mate aboard her for five years now. Her every creak is like a breath of my own body. She's an extension of it."

Lacy sat back in her chair. Her hands played with a pen on the desk top. It hurt to see such eagerness. It reminded her strongly of a young man her father had once sent to Liverpool and out of her life. Her first love, he'd been. A young man who loved the sea to the exclusion of all else, including her. She doubted Caleb would ever relinquish the sea again.

"I'm afraid I haven't the authority to issue such an order, Mr. Thaxton," she said.

His eyes started, bulging in disbelief. "I don't understand," he insisted. "She's a Puritan ship."

White-gold curls clustered at her brow and twitched from the artful chignon as she shook her head. "Only Captain Innes can make the decision to sail."

"He's missing!" Devin sputtered. "The *Paramour* is your ship!"

He found two pair of glittering green eyes centered on him in anger, one set as dark as the forest, the other as turbulent as the sea. Katherine Paradise had moved quietly away from the window to stand directly behind her mother's chair. They presented a united front determined to protect Caleb Innes's interests.

It was Lacy Paradise who spoke, her voice a low husky threat. "The *Puritan Paramour* was bequeathed to Captain Innes in my father's will, Mr. Thaxton. She holds a contract with the Puritan Line but she most definitely is not mine to command. She belongs to Captain Innes."

He should have been told, Thaxton thought angrily. Now he'd made a fool of himself before these women. Especially the daughter. Unable to stop himself, Devin met the young woman's burning gaze once more. Why did she dislike him? What had he done to merit such hatred?

He stood, his hat clutched in his hand. "I see I've wasted my time and yours, ma'am. Is there anything I can do to assist in the search for Captain Innes?" he asked stiffly at attention.

Lacy relaxed. "Search, Mr. Thaxton? I hardly think that is necessary. The good captain will return when his business is concluded."

Thaxton thought her smile was a little tight. She didn't believe that Innes had gone off to conduct business elsewhere but he'd play the bitch's game. "Yes, ma'am. I'd best be returning to the ship now. Thank you for your time, ma'am."

He snapped a smart salute and left the room. Damn the woman, he thought. He wasn't going to sit idly awaiting Innes's return. A few inquiries wouldn't hurt. If Innes was dead and he could prove it, there might still be a way to gain the *Paramour*.

Kate slumped against the desk as the door closed behind Devin Thaxton. "I'm worried, Mama," she said, her voice tight with pain.

Elizabeth Daniels

"Something must have happened to Caleb."

Lacy stood and gave her daughter's shoulders a reassuring hug. "We'd have heard something," she soothed unconvincingly. "Your father and Phael are both searching for him. They'll find him."

The young woman's eyes were awash with unshed tears. "I didn't mean to hurt him, Mama. I'd never hurt Caleb."

"I know, darling." What comfort could she give Kate when she feared the worst herself? "I know."

Chapter Six

In a dive off Pacific Street, Caleb Innes had come to the same conclusion. He'd stumbled drunkenly from Lily's intent on purging the memory of Kate from his mind. But alcohol had not done the job. He still saw her, her lovely womanly form arching eagerly to accept him, still felt the searing brand of her lips on his. It blotted out other memories, confusing his befuddled mind.

Katie had always been a child who set her goals and pursued them. That he was one of those goals, a long-standing one, he found hard to comprehend. She was a beautiful young woman. Accent on both young and beautiful, he thought. Whereas he was . . . Hell, she couldn't want him.

Yet the thought of Katie, eager, enticing, in the arms of another man, hurt. If Caleb married her, would he be able to watch her fall out of love with him as he grew older and could no longer love her as she needed? Would he be able to watch her go into the arms of a younger, more energetic man?

Katie. The little girl he'd spoiled with special gifts from around the world. Katie. The woman who'd given him back something he hadn't even realized he had lost—the ecstasy of physical love joined to spiritual love.

Had his subconscious known all along that she only could offer him such happiness? Is that why he couldn't forget her? Why he could no longer see Katie as a child in his memories but rather as a vibrant woman?

In desperation, his footsteps turned to China-town. There were no answers, at least not answers he was ready to accept.

Stopping at the place which would offer him a haven, he entered the narrow, smoke-filled, dark, welcoming room. The rows of hard narrow bunks contained both men and women. Orientals and Westerners. Only the dark, slanting eyes of the proprietor gleamed avariciously as they surveyed Caleb's tall form, now clad in casual civilian clothes.

His soul aflame, Caleb took his place on a bunk and accepted a pipe from the proprietor.

The ball of opium gum dropped into the bowl easily, although it was his first experience with the drug. For all his trips to China, the sweet, cloying forgetfulness the drug offered had never lured him. He drew on the pipe tentatively, savoring the strange sensations.

Slowly, the hardness of the unyielding cot

gave way to a pleasing numbness. He no longer hurt, no longer felt. Until she came. Katie. The purity of her features sought him out in the dim cellar, haunted the false contentment of the drug. Lazily, he watched again as she responded to his lovemaking. Her actions were at once wanton and innocent. His name hung on her lips. Her love echoed in his ears and hurt him.

Did she mean to wrench his heart from his body? Lord! Katie! He reached for her to beseech her forgiveness. Not forgiveness for what he'd done, but forgiveness for his love for her. Surely, it was selfish of him not to push her into the arms of a younger man? But that he could not do.

Had he been there days or only hours? Caleb wondered, waking. Time had no boundaries in this poppy-induced paradise—or hell.

What was the lure of opium? It hadn't eased his pain. It had multiplied it with each hallucination. Repetition of each bittersweet moment he'd spent in Katie's arms had somehow made his feelings for her crystal clear. He refused the offer of still another pipe, accepting instead a rude, nearly brutal ejection from the den. His mind still cloudy, Caleb stumbled out into the alleyway, slumped down against a wall, and wept.

How long had he thought of her as a woman? It hadn't been a recent development. He'd been aware of her for a long time. But she was the daughter of his best friend, a girl twenty-three years his junior. She deserved more than he could give her. Yet he loved her. Had always loved her, he realized. From the moment he'd held her tiny squirming form aboard the *Paramour*, she had captured his heart. Now she had enticed his body, his soul.

Caleb gathered the shreds of his self-esteem and pushed to his feet. His stomach growled, reminding him it had been empty for too long.

Teddy Masters considered the lean man as he walked slowly, unsteadily out to the crowded street. The man wore a tan shirt pushed carelessly into denim trousers and a dark leather vest. The scruffy boots, battered hat, and ragged beard made him resemble any miner in from the country. Even the red-rimmed eyes made him look like several hundred of San Francisco's inhabitants. But Teddy recognized the man as a gold mine—a sailor.

Teddy noted the man's rolling gait—the stance of a man accustomed to the tilting deck of a ship. His eyes measured the broad shoulders straining against the fabric, displaying well-developed muscles.

There should be a good bit extra for this swabbie. It wasn't often he delivered an experienced sailor. Few crimps did. They dealt in volume not quality. The skippers, desperate for able-bodied men, paid for whatever they could get.

Teddy watched the man, following him at a safe distance. They crossed the breadth of Chinatown and entered the outreaches of the Barbary Coast. The fact that the man appeared to know his way didn't bother Masters at all. There was no unwritten law in his business that protected local men from a crimper's mallet. Not that that would stop him even if there was, Teddy mused. He wasn't about to let this specimen escape. He'd follow and await his opportunity.

Teddy Masters watched with glee as Innes turned into a dive offering meals as well as a variety of alcoholic beverages. He waited patiently for his prey to order before stumbling in the door.

The place wasn't filled, but a good number of men sat in the semi-darkness, either bent over checker or cribbage boards or morosely studying their glasses of rotgut.

The bartender glanced up from wiping down his counter to acknowledge the new drunken arrival. The flicker of an eyelid identified his readiness to accommodate Masters. Neither was worried about any repercussions or questions about customers suddenly disappearing in this bar. The trap door was kept well oiled for deliveries of shanghaied men.

Teddy signaled back flamboyantly and thanked the bartender profusely for the foaming mug of warm beer.

The sailor, Teddy noted, as he leaned back on the bar, was gazing remorsefully into his own mug. With a wide drunken grin plastered on his thin, flat face, Teddy Masters sidled up to Innes's table.

"Hate drinkin' 'lone," he slurred, and staggered uninvited into a chair. "Bartender,'nother fer ma friend here."

Innes glanced up, his eyes slowly registering the other man's presence. "I'm getting damn tired of my own company at that, mate," he admitted.

Masters registered the nautical term with barely a nod. "Been like that," he agreed foolishly. "What'll we drink ta?"

The bartender, a large man with a blank expression, slid two fresh brews before them. He tested the coin Masters flipped him with his teeth before moving away.

Teddy giggled and waved his mug.

Innes picked up the fresh glass. "Is there any other toast?" he asked with a sad smile. "To all our lovely ladies and their welcoming beds," he said.

Masters's mug sped toward Innes's drink in a show of drunken camaraderie and missed. The dark liquid slopped over onto the table. "To their welcomin' thighs," he amended, and gulped his beer, sending a good portion down his shirt front. Surreptitiously, he watched Innes down a good bit of his drink. The next toast emptied their glasses.

Another round was quickly disposed of, causing Innes to blink to clear his vision. Perhaps it was the combination of alcohol and the dregs of opium clinging to his mind that made the room spin. He grinned at Masters and accepted the offer of another round. The unappetizing stew he'd been served was pushed to the side, forgotten in the easy joviality of this newfound and fleeting friendship. He wasn't in any hurry to confront Paradise, was he? Hell, Ben and Lacy both should know he'd never deflower their daughter and not marry her. He would do so soon. But not just yet.

The foolish grinning face of Teddy Masters came close as Caleb's face hit the table. Innes could see one distorted eye before he passed out.

The suddenly sober crimper lifted the unconscious man's head by the hair, checking his victim's breathing.

"I wish ta hell ya'd not nab the big ones when yer by yerself, Teddy," the bartender growled, returning to the table.

Masters picked up the sailor's hat and dusted it against his leg. "Yer get paid yer share, so quit yer bitchin'," he recommended.

The barkeep dragged Caleb's limp form over his shoulder. None of the other customers paid any attention to his actions. They counted themselves fortunate that it was the stranger who was being sold for duty at sea rather than themselves.

"Ya might help, ya bleedin' bastard," the bartender spat. Masters favored him with a sick grin and stood aside for the big man to proceed him.

The procession moved to a tiny back room where the body of their victim was unceremoniously dumped in a corner. Masters followed the bartender, his step cocky with triumph. "I'll have Mosely get 'im tonight," he declared. "He'll sleep till then, won't he?"

The other man laughed hoarsely. "Damn right he will. A mite longer."

Masters nodded, satisfied as the sailor slid over, dropping heavily to the floor. He tossed the man's hat into the corner and rubbed his hands together in glee. "This one's gonna be lucky fer me, Sam. Yes, siree, I kin feel it in ma bones!"

"Yeah," the bartender grumbled, as Masters and he left the room and he locked the door behind him. "Jes' be damn sure Mosely ain't late."

Lily Walsh jumped from her chair, turning with one hand flat against her breast as the door closed quietly behind her.

"For Christ's sake, ya scared me half out of my wits, kid." She sighed, recognizing her unexpected guest.

It was broad daylight and here was Katie decked out in boy's clothing, her hair tucked up beneath that ridiculous cloth cap. "What 'er ya doin' here? Ya promised the songbird was dead. Remember?" It was exasperating that Katie would risk recognition and exposure by attempting to pull off her boy's disguise during the day.

"Sorry," the young woman mumbled as she ambled into the room. "I had to come, Lil. I had to know."

Lily studied the dark circles beneath Kate's eyes. "I ain't heard from him, Katie. Why should I? He blames me as much as ya."

Kate fidgeted, moving restlessly about the room, examining the clutter of figurines and photographs that filled the tables in Lily's sitting room without really seeing them. "We've got to find Caleb. It's been two weeks," she said quietly.

"It's easy to disappear on the Coast," Lily reminded her harshly. " 'Specially when ya want to. And Caleb wants to, Katie."

"Papa and Phael have been combing every saloon and crib looking for him," Kate continued. "Even Davy put the word out among his friends." She paused, waiting while Lily settled back into her chair and reached for the decanter on the table. "We almost had him, Lily. Quah Cue traced Caleb to an opium den in Chinatown. But he'd already vanished when Papa got there."

Lily added an extra measure of whiskey to her glass. This whole affair was turning her into a lush. She was still amazed that Ben hadn't tossed her out on her rear for her part in the deception. He still might, Lily reminded herself. That thought deserved a healthy gulp of the fiery liquid. Wine had stopped appeasing her conscience two weeks ago. Not that whiskey had helped it, either. But after a few belts, she didn't care anymore.

"No clue to where he'd gone?"

Kate's head shook sadly. "No. That's why I came here. We've got to start looking for him, Lily."

The madam laughed shortly. "How the hell are we gonna find him if your menfolk can't, Katie?"

Kate perched on the arm of the miniature sofa. The upholstery was nearly the same sea-touched color as her eyes. A design of gold threads twisted and curled, entwining in complicated geometric patterns and Kate's fingertips followed the course they took. "We have to. I have to," she amended.

Lily stared gloomily at her glass. "Yeah, I know, kid." She couldn't meet the stricken look in the young woman's eyes. "I guess—"

The click of the latch on her door sent Lily's head snapping about in fear a second time. Katie couldn't be found here. Hell, in broad daylight there was no hiding the fact that she wasn't a boy.

The man entered the room uninvited, as if he had the right to go anywhere he chose in Lily's establishment.

The gun at Kate's side swiveled, its deadly muzzle aimed at the center of his elaborate vest.

The man's brows rose, more in amusement than surprise. "Not a very hospitable greeting, Lily," Bull Run Allen admonished, ignoring the pistol. "Put the toy away, kiddo. I ain't here for anything but business." He strolled easily into the room and poured himself a drink from the sideboard.

Kate's gun remained leveled, her gaze unflinching at his complacent sneer.

"Whatta you want, Allen?" she growled, her voice pitched deeper, as a young man's might be.

A smile creased his face. "Ah, the mysterious songbird," he said. "I wondered how ya came and went without my boys catchin' sight of ya."

The hammer of her gun cocked. "I asked what you want," she repeated dangerously.

Lily's hand tightened on her glass. Katie sounded like her father. Bull Run Allen was the self-proclaimed king of the Barbary Coast. No one was more dangerous than he was, but at the moment, Katie was the more deadly of the two. Lily held her breath.

Unperturbed, Allen turned, holding his glass between two fingers. He opened the lapels of his frock coat, allowing Kate to see he wore no gun belt. "Take it easy, angel," he cautioned. "I'm jest here fer some pleasant conversation."

Kate's eyes never left his face. Beneath his swollen, red nose his smile was calculating. She hesitated, then eased the hammer down, and dropped the gun snugly into its holster. "So talk," she said.

Lily's hand was shaking. She put her glass aside, knocking over a photograph. "I ain't changed my mind, Bull," she warned.

Allen sipped at his drink, studying her faintly flushed face. Lily was worried about something but he was fairly sure that it wasn't him. His eyes slipped to the wary girl. It had something to do with the songbird. He wondered what the connection was between them? Was she Lily's daughter? A relative?

"I've changed my mind, though, Lily," he said. "You don't need my protection."

As the madam gaped at him in astonishment, Allen turned smoothly to Kate. "But you do, angel. I can help you."

Kate stiffened, then before Lily's startled eyes, she removed her cap and shook her head until her coppery hair flared out around her shoulders. "What did you have in mind?" Kate asked.

Allen chuckled. "Red," he mused. "Suits ya better than the black wig."

Kate stood her ground, waiting for his answer.

"Told ya before," Allen continued. "Ya'd be a real money-maker at the Kitchen."

Lily reached for her drink and gulped it. Katie wouldn't do it. She had more sense than that, didn't she?

Kate was considering it, though. Both Lily

and Allen could read it in her face.

"I might be interested," she said slowly, her voice having lost all hint of an accent. But it was still the husky, seductive sound Allen associated with the songbird.

Lily jumped from her chair, and her skirts rustled in agitation. "Katie! You can't! Think what it means."

Kate smiled reassuringly at her friend. "I am thinking, Lily." She turned to Allen, her eyes hard and watchful. "I have a few stipulations you'll have to agree to . . . Ned," she purred.

He grinned. "Katie, is it?" He savored her name. "I'm sure we can come to terms, angel."

He admired her cool, the way she sauntered to a vacant chair and slumped, her legs stretched out, her ankles crossed as if she were still intent on enjoying her role as a boy. Her hand was never far from the handle of her Colt.

"I'm sure we can agree," she said.

Allen was amused at the girl's masculine posturing. He admired the long length of her legs, picturing how she'd look in the short red jacket and black stockings that where the only costume his waiter girls at Hell's Kitchen wore.

Kate's voice cut across his thoughts. "First, I choose my own wardrobe."

The simplicity of the request amused him and he inclined his head slightly in acceptance. He would amend the agreement in the future to his own satisfaction.

"The only entertaining I do is singing," she said.

He frowned. "Now, wait a minute, kiddo. All the drabs in my place can be tossed on their backsides for the right price." His brows drew together in anger. Who was she kidding? He knew she'd taken a man to her bed since he'd last seen her. The kid had lost that look of innocence. There was a certain gleam in her eyes that told him she knew how to please a man. The songbird, with her dark eyes and pale copper-touched hair, would drive a man mad with pleasure.

Kate regarded him steadily. "Then we don't have a deal."

Allen took in her relaxed form once more. The kid definitely hadn't been spawned on the Coast, but she wasn't a new arrival to San Francisco, either. He took in the well-manicured hands, the cut of her boy's suit, even the boots and simply tooled gun belt. All custom-made if he missed his bet. A society brat, that's what she was, bored and spoiling for the wild life. Well, he'd make damn sure she found it and make himself a bundle on her. Once she was installed at the Kitchen, he'd renege on all his promises. What could she say, after all? She was bluffing her way through this game, unaware of the hand he held. Hell, he'd use that beautiful body, then throw her back to her folks for a healthy sum.

His eyes dwelt along every inch of her just as she wanted him to do. He could see the satisfaction in those cool lagoon eyes. As if capitulating, he shrugged. "All right, you got a deal. You can start tonight."

Kate smiled lazily, almost seductively at him. "Not tonight. Perhaps tomorrow. Perhaps not. I'll sing the day you find a certain man for me."

Allen's eyes narrowed. "What kind of a trick is this?" he demanded. "Maybe ya ain't worth this much trouble, angel."

Kate's smile widened knowingly. Her eyes remained hard. "Oh, but I am," she said softly.

Allen finished his drink. She needed to be taught a lesson. She was too cocky. Later would do, though, after she'd started singing at the Kitchen.

"Okay," he growled. "Who's this bucko?"

Chapter Seven

Caleb groaned as consciousness returned slowly. The thin line of light pierced his eyes, causing a renewed explosion of pain. He winced, closing them immediately. His whole body ached. His head felt swollen and beaten like some South Seas native drum and a sharp pain extended across his cramped shoulders. Hell, he hoped the evening had been as enjoyable as the hangover was hellish.

Cautiously, he flexed his sore muscles and the torment spread through his legs and arms. He had escaped the confines of Davy Jones's locker many times, but apparently he had not eluded one particular batch of devils, the crimpers. They held him captive with more physical means than just pain. Ropes held his wrists tightly behind his back and forced his legs into a kneeling position, pulling his ankles up. The position made it impossible to reach the knife he carried in his boot top.

If he still had the weapon, that is. Caleb squinted in an attempt to protect his sensitive eyes. He tried to move. Any shift in position eased his tight muscles. But the foul-smelling gag caused nausea to rise in his throat, threatening to choke him.

As the bout passed, Innes breathed easier. Shanghaied. In a way it was almost amusing. He'd wanted to be punished for what he'd done to Katie, had been trying to punish himself. Now that he'd come to terms with the idea, admitting that he still wanted Katie, hell had caught up with him.

Caleb forced his eyes open. Even the dark hurt. Breathing hurt.

The smell of dust and cheap cigars and whiskey nearly disguised the scent for which he searched. The taste of the sea. It was faintly there.

He strained in the dark, forcing his senses to explore his prison. He was alone, of that he was certain, as if he'd been singled out for some purpose. The room was small and without windows. A closet most likely. The rock and sway of a ship was missing, although he now caught the familiar sounds of lapping water and the creakings of a ship in its moorings.

So he was still ashore somewhere near the wharf. Escape was still possible.

Innes flattened his cheek to the floor. From beneath the narrow door, the sound of men's voices began to penetrate his consciousness. Two, no, three men. He could hear the slap of cards, the jangle of coins being tossed on the table.

"I'll see ya, Teddy, an' call," a gravel-voiced man declared.

Another man laughed. "Read 'em and weep," he advised gleefully.

Caleb heard the disgruntled noises of losers, the rake of coins, as the man named Teddy gathered his pot.

"Hell, the way yer winnin', I'd swear ya was cheatin', Teddy."

Someone else snorted in derision. "He ain't smart 'nuff. How often Teddy ever win, anyway?"

"Hardly ever," the first man said, and spit on the floor. "That's why I'm always ready ta play a hand with the cuss."

Teddy chuckled with them. "Knew it was ma lucky day when I spotted that swabbie, lads," he declared. "We'll get a right proper copper fer that one."

Caleb frowned. The man's voice sounded familiar.

"That why ya got 'im tussled up like a plucked chicken, Teddy?"

"I ain't takin' no chances on losin' him," Teddy declared, his voice taking on a wheedling tone. "Let's have another hand."

A chair scratched back across the wooden flooring. The noise jarred Innes's nerves, sending a fresh stab of pain through his drug-swollen head.

"Not fer me," the gravel-voiced man said. "What makes ya think that fella's worth any more than t'others?"

Teddy chuckled. Caleb heard the ruffling sound of cards being shuffled. The effort was broken, uncoordinated, far different than the smooth flow of cards through the hands of a professional gambler. " 'Cause Bull Run Allen's a lookin' fer him," Teddy announced.

Caleb's eyes narrowed in suspicion as he strained to catch every movement, every word from the outer room. A chair tilted back, creaking with a man's weight. "How'd ya know that?"

"Word's out on the street. Allen's lookin' fer a tall, black-haired sailor boy with a scar jagged close ta his eye. Jest like our man in there," Teddy answered cockily.

Caleb let his eyes close a moment while he puzzled over this new and confusing knowledge. What could Ned Allen want with him? Bull Run had his finger in every form of vice the city offered, but Caleb had never even seen the man until the night at Lily's. What was the connection? Was there a connection?

"Got the scar all right, but are ya sure he's a swabbie?" the third man demanded. "Ain't dressed like one."

Teddy snorted. "I been crimpin' long 'nuff ta know a sailor when I sees one," he declared. "The way he walks, things he says. Hell, even the way he swills his licker and eyes the whores. I kin spot 'em. Trust me, Charlie boy."

One of the men spat again, giving the rough flooring a new coating of tobacco juice. "How much ya figure we'll get fer him?"

"Two, three, maybe even four times the usual. Ol' Bull Run must want 'im pretty bad," Teddy said. "Come on. Another hand, lads."

In his narrow prison, Caleb rolled painfully away from the door. There had to be something he could use to cut or fray the ropes. Something the three crimpers had overlooked.

He wasn't proud of the fact, but he'd bought shanghaied men often enough in the past to know the system. The lack of able-bodied men willing to endure the hard life at sea fed the pockets of unscrupulous men along the Barbary Coast. There were many hidden trap doors where a drugged man could be dropped into a waiting skiff to be rowed out into the harbor and to a new home aboard a China-bound clipper. Desperate shipmasters took hearty men any way they could get them. A shanghaied man awoke at sea already subject to a captain's will, forced to learn the sailing trade or suffer the stinging rebuke of a cat-o'-nine-tails. Wages were paid, but they rarely amounted to more than a short drunk the first time the ship put into port.

The fact that he was still ashore meant that Allen had something else in mind for him, Caleb decided. But what?

His bonds and the narrow width of the cell limited his movement. Still, escape was not impossible. First he'd need to dispose of the ropes then find a weapon. He was sure now that he'd been relieved of his knife. Surprise would be the only equalizer. If he missed his guess, at least two were large men and all three were dangerous.

Caleb inched back, his fingers, limited by the

ropes, stretched, combing the thick coating of dust on the floor. Any sharp-edged object would do. A broken piece of glass, a forgotten tool. Agonizingly slow, he searched every inch of space, each of his movements controlled and silent.

The rope stretched taut between his ankles and wrists, cutting into his flesh. His hands were almost numb as they fumbled along, scrapping the rough boards. Pain clouded his mind, beat at his straining senses.

At first, the cool touch of metal didn't fully register. Then his fingertips explored the length, the breadth, identifying the object.

The building was a rough shack thrown together with used materials. In daylight, Caleb guessed it would be possible to see through the wide-spaced seams of the building. The cool snap of sea-scented air crept through the cracks as if bent on clearing his head. His fingertips gathered splinters from the weathered boards, yet now they tested the ragged edge of a rusted, bent nail protruding from the lower back wall.

Cautiously, he edged against the wall. His wrists strained, sawing the stretched bonds against the dull-edged bit of steel.

The work was slow, tedious, and all of his concentration was trained on the rope. He could barely hear the gnawing whisper of fiber against metal. Ignoring the scream of cramped muscles and cut flesh, Caleb worked steadily.

In the alleyway, a man peered through a crack in the ill-fitting shade. The three men seated around the rough table were passing a near empty bottle. One chewed monotonously on a chaw of tobacco, his expression bucolic, contended. Another frowned, his voice a low growl as he disputed with the slight, nervous Teddy Masters. Their stupid expressions assured the silent watcher of their inability to react quickly.

At a signal, his men merged with the shadows. Their dark clothing blended into the concealing night, cloaking the glints of steel slung low on their lean hips.

Ned Allen moved from the window, adjusting the line of his pale frock coat. The head of his cane came up smartly, rapping sharply on the weathered door of the shack. The startled oaths and bumbling crash of a chair within brought a sinister smirk to his lips.

"Yeah?" The voice that growled from behind the heavy panels of the door sounded disoriented. Perhaps even a bit frightened, as any sensible man would be of a late-night caller in this section of the city, Allen thought. His grin widened in pleasure.

"Masters?" he shouted. "I've come fer my package."

The sharp intake of breath was audible even through the door. "Get the hell outta the way," Masters hissed. The sharp order was nearly drowned by the rasping scrape of a rusted bolt being drawn.

Teddy threw open the door, unmindful of the easy target he presented in the lighted entryway. His pinched face was flushed and jovial. "I got 'im, Bull. He's tied up pretty as a package fer ya."

The two other men retreated, leaving Masters alone to parlay over the merits of their merchandise.

Allen pushed past the small man. "Where is he? I ain't 'bout ta buy a pig in a poke."

Teddy grinned widely, feeling the twin intoxicants of good fortune and cheap whiskey. "Show 'im the swabbie," he urged his cohorts.

Caleb blinked owlishly as the door to his cell was ripped open. The ruckus had warned him, giving him time to move away from the wall. He lay back, attempting to hide the frayed ropes from his captors.

A big man dragged him from the compartment, tossing Innes's hobbled form on the floor at Allen's feet.

Teddy pulled Caleb's head back, his hand clenching a handful of dark hair. "Your man, ain't he, Bull?" He grinned, sure of himself and of the identity of his prisoner. "Can't be more 'n one black-haired man with a scar like that in the whole state!"

Allen barely recognized the bruised and filthy man. Masters's hold forced his captive to kneel submissively, his head pulled back at an awkward angle. Only the cool steady gaze of the captain's dark eyes reminded Allen of the proud man he'd encountered a fortnight before at Lily Walsh's house.

A long smear of dust coated the captain's cheek, clinging like gray mold to a dark, ragged growth of beard. A pair of snug-fitting denim trousers, a cotton shirt, and a loose dark leather vest had replaced the custom-tailored uniform of the Puritan Line giving the captive a rakish, lean look. Like a timber wolf, Innes's eyes burned with a fearless, feral intensity as they met Allen's.

"Cut him loose," Allen ordered sharply.

Teddy chuckled with glee. He pulled a knife from his boot top and slashed at the ropes. "Sure, Bull. Your man, ain't he?"

Caleb flinched as blood rushed back into his numbed limbs and the pain cleared the last of the drug clouding his mind. Remaining seated on the floor, he tugged the gag loose and rubbed his wrists cautiously.

Teddy slipped the knife back into his boot, his movements careless and unconcerned that his victim was now free and within easy reach of the weapon. The crimper waved his arm in the direction of the table and the lone bottle in its center. "Have a drink," he urged Allen. "Ta celebrate our bit o' business." Again he chuckled.

Allen took the whiskey, tossed off a mouthful and instead of returning it to Teddy, passed it on to Innes, still seated on the floor, the gag hanging loosely around his neck.

Without a word, Caleb accepted the bottle and tilted it, quickly downing the fiery liquid.

"Hey," Teddy protested, making a grab for his property.

Allen stopped him, his cane raised to form a barrier between the crimper and the sea captain. "How long you had him, Teddy?" Allen demanded.

The wiry little man looked puzzled, then belatedly frightened. His accomplices moved back, hoping to blend with the rough-hewn walls and escape Bull Run Allen's notice. Teddy swallowed loudly, his eyes starting anxiously from his head. He'd made a mistake. He'd nabbed a friend of Allen's! The hard glint in Ned's eyes sent Masters's heart beating faster, louder, until it almost drowned out the questions the king of the Barbary Coast spit at him.

Nervous, Teddy pulled a kerchief from his pocket and mopped at his damp brow. "Not long, Bull. Few hours. I was real careful with him, Bull." Wildly, he turned to Innes, his expression terrified and pleading. "Tell him. I didn't lay a finger on ya!"

Caleb got slowly to his feet, stretched his stiff shoulders in a rolling motion. He towered over Masters by a full head. Quietly, he considered the now trembling crimper.

Teddy retreated from the glint in the seaman's eyes. He swallowed loudly. This weren't no regular swabbie! Death was in those dark eyes, and it was measurin' him fer a coffin.

Innes tilted the bottle once more, savoring the sting of whiskey against his cracked lips.

"I treated ya good!" Masters's voice rose in terror.

Allen's narrowed eyes drilled the cringing man. "That the way ya see it, Captain?" he snapped.

Teddy's eyes widened. Sweet Mother of Jesus! He hadn't shanghaied a swabbie but a ship's master!

Caleb lowered the bottle and shrugged. "Yeah," he drawled slowly. "For a crimper, he treated me like family." Caleb didn't understand Allen's role in this farce. He had convinced the little weasel that he'd shanghaied a friend, an equal, a partner. Whatever Allen's reason, Caleb welcomed release from his prison. But he'd be damned if he dropped his guard and allowed himself to be lulled by Allen's actions.

Teddy relaxed visibly at the captain's words. "If I'd known yer were a friend o' Bull's, I'd never a tied ya up, Cap'n," he babbled.

Allen's lips stretched in a mirthless grin. "Sure, Teddy. I believe ya," he said, reaching into the inner pocket of his coat. "Promised a reward, didn't I?"

Masters glanced triumphantly at his silent compatriots as they stood dumbly to the side, out of harm's way. He grinned happily.

The grimace froze on his face as the bullet thudded into his chest, knocking him back against the wall. As Teddy Masters's body slid to the floor, Allen turned to face the two silent henchmen, his gun trained on them.

"Get out," he spat.

They wasted no time but hurried toward the door with crablike movements, afraid to take their eyes from the still-smoking metal threat in Allen's fist.

"I wouldn't follow 'em too closely, Captain," Allen recommended, perching on the edge of the table. "Any of that rotgut left?"

Innes passed the bottle to him. He was unmoved when gunshots erupted in the alley. Allen intended to leave no witnesses. "Nice of you to spare me," Caleb murmured. "Why did you?"

Allen laughed and laid his gun on the table within easy reach. In the dim light, his nose appeared to glow. "Cautious bastard, ain't ya, Innes?"

"I survive."

"Yeah, I guess ya do," Allen mused. "Don't thank me, though. You're a wanted man and the price was . . . ah, temptin'."

Caleb's brows drew together. Wanted? What was Allen getting at? Had Paradise reconsidered and put a warrant out for his arrest? "Dead or alive?" he asked.

Allen decided he liked Innes. The man had a cool head, and that casual tone implied the answer didn't really matter. Dead or alive. It was all the same to the captain.

"Alive," Allen said. "That little redhead wants ya that way. 'Healthy' is the way she put it." He took a pull on the bottle. "The kid's got grit."

The kid? Redhead? Caleb pondered the sly smirk on Allen's face. Katie! The stubborn set of her jaw, the snapping lagoon-green of her eyes flashed in his mind. Again he saw her at Lily's, her lovely hair hidden beneath the black wig, her yellow gown clinging to her ripe womanly form. The thin set of her lips as she faced down Bull Run Allen.

Why hadn't he connected Allen and Katie?

He couldn't let Allen guess his true feelings, though. Ned wasn't a man to turn your back on under any circumstances.

Caleb shrugged as if uninterested. Better to give Allen the impression he considered Kate just another woman he'd sampled and forgotten.

Apparently at his ease, Caleb ambled over to Teddy Masters's body. Hunkering down, he stripped his knife from the man's boot, balancing its familiar weight lightly in his hand before tucking it away. He continued searching, emptying Masters's pockets, systematically reclaiming his possessions.

"God, this stuff is bad," Allen declared, tossing the empty whiskey bottle in a corner. It shattered, spewing tiny shards at Innes's feet.

Caleb stood, hefting a chamois bag. The clatter of coins had improved since Masters had taken it from him. He tucked it away in the inner pocket of his vest. "What's on the roster now. Allen? Am I a prisoner or a free man?"

Allen's smirk was crafty. "Up to you, Captain," he insisted. "I'd appreciate it if ya stopped by Hell's Kitchen. There's a new act ya might be interested in seein'."

Feeling his safety depended on a close proximity to Allen, Caleb agreed. "Sure," he drawled amiably, his New England accent flattening the word. "My plans are flexible."

Allen hefted his gun, testing the metal. Satisfied that the barrel had cooled, he replaced it in an inner pocket. "Hope ya can ride then. Captain," he said, and left the shack.

Devin Thaxton swept the cap from his head in order to get a clearer view of the sedate brick-fronted building. It bore no sign to broadcast the nature of the business conducted behind the dainty lace-edged curtains. To all appearances, it was merely a private residence.

Thaxton set his cap back at a jaunty angle, and glanced once more at the piece of foolscap in his hand, comparing the address written there with the numbers on the door.

The fact that the house sat squarely between a gambling den and a bordello belied any possibility that this home survived as a private, domestic oasis on the edge of an area of rampant vice such as the Barbary Coast. Still, Thaxton was hesitant to approach the door.

Could his informants have gotten the wrong address? They weren't men to frequent a first-class parlor house. From all reports, the prices at Madam Lily's were exorbitant, far beyond the pockets of a Puritan Line sailor. Beyond his own resources for that matter.

He'd been careful in sounding out the *Paramour's* crew. He'd singled out loyal Puritan men, men who had sailed thousands of leagues with Captain Innes. A shared bottle and a few ribald jokes had loosened their tongues.

Thaxton had learned more than he bargained for in regards to Innes's relationship with the Paradise family. It would take a miracle to wheedle control of the *Paramour* from under Captain Innes. Even if Lacy Paradise had lied about Innes's ownership of the vessel, Devin doubted she would ever relinquish the command to him. As the captain's former sweetheart, she guarded Innes's claim jealously.

Their past relationship certainly explained the Paradise woman's defensive attitude. But what of the daughter? Unadulterated hatred had spit at him from her lovely green eyes. For what reason? He was a stranger. A man who was used to reading interest in a woman's look, not distrust or disgust.

Disheartened by the numerous mouthings of the Paradise name. Thaxton had watched the rum bottle make another circuit among the tars.

Lily Walsh's name came up in the early morning hours. He heard her name, saw the admiration on the men's faces, long before he recognized that she was the straw for which he grasped. The more he heard, the better she sounded. He was sure Innes had not overlooked the lovely madam this trip. It had been over three months since any of the crew had seen a woman from their own world. The tiny almond-eyed creatures of the Orient had never satisfied Thaxton. He found them spiritless, pathetic in their docile attempts to please him. He preferred the robust, buxom women of the Western culture. It was a preference he shared with Innes, Devin knew. The captain would have made Madam Lily's establishment one of his first ports of call in the city.

Once the idling ship had settled into the rhythm of the day the next morning, Thaxton had left the bosun in charge and rowed himself into town, dropping anchor, so to speak, not far from Lily Walsh's front door.

Behind the scant cover of lace curtain, Dora Acton peered down at the watching man. He stood in the center of the street, his legs braced apart, oblivious to the traffic or the raucous calls of drivers as they passed. He was a handsome fellow. She could tell his features were comely even from her second-story perch. She admired the deep golden color of his bushy sideburns, the way they reached nearly to his chin. They were slightly darker in color than the sun-touched waves that peered from beneath his hat. She liked the way he wore the cap, cocked casually on the back of his head. The blue-black uniform fit him snugly, allowing her a glimpse of broad shoulders, a nipped-in waist, and long muscular legs.

As she watched, the man glanced away, a wide rakish grin on his sun-bronzed features. He called an answer that she couldn't hear over the rumble of wagons in the street below. She could hear the squeals of the whores in the next house, however.

Dora turned to check her reflection quickly. The lavender peignoir was attractive, allowing ample view of her gently rounded charms. Yet it wasn't tawdry or cheap, not like the bawds' gowns next door. Dora patted her gleaming brown curls and licked her lips. Nightly, she thanked the Lord that she had found a place at Madam Lily's. The threat of the common bordello, the houses familiarly known as the cowyards, still hung over her. When her looks deteriorated or she failed to please the customers, where would she go? Too many of her profession had descended into the varied levels of hell that the Coast offered—from the parlor houses to the cowyards to the dance halls to the streets. It wasn't the path Dora chose to follow. Somehow, she'd leave Lily's for a better life.

Dora turned back for a last glance from her window. She was sure the man saw her this time. She fluttered the drape in a coy gesture, then swiftly left the room to intercept him.

Most of the girls would still be asleep at this hour of day. Dora had found mid-morning her best hunting time. It was when she was assured of being the only woman at Lily's available to entertain visitors who presented the proper golden enticement.

There were only two ways to escape the life of a whore. One was to become a madam with a house of girls. The other was to become a wife. To accomplish either one in some style required a man with money and only men with money frequented Madam Lily's.

Thaxton grinned once more at the scantily clad women hanging from the windows of the adjacent building. One had managed to display her large breasts as she leaned over the windowsill calling lewd suggestions to him. They were the type of women he normally sought to ease his needs. They knew how to cater to a man, to judge his desires and fulfill the fantasies of a long voyage. And yet, he suddenly desired another kind of woman, one who gave herself without the benefit of his open wallet. A woman who comported herself well, coolly as a lady would. A lovely woman who combined a quiet smile with a spark of spirit, of animation. A woman like . . . aye, like he surmised Miss Katherine Paradise to be. He'd been unable to get her off his mind since that ill-fated meeting at the Puritan Line office. There was a haunting quality about her that held him in thrall.

Devin pushed thoughts of her aside as the house before him beckoned, recalling Thaxton to his purpose. He caught an enticing, brief glimpse of a young woman at the upstairs window. She wore something pale and flowing and the curtain fluttered as she smiled at him knowingly.

Thaxton grinned and shoved the scrap of paper back in his pocket. There was no longer any doubt that he had found the correct address.

Whistling, he ran lightly up the porch steps.

Zack opened to the rapid tattoo on the door. He didn't know the man in the entranceway but he did recognize the dark wool uniform the officer wore.

Devin's whistle stopped abruptly when confronted with the giant. "Do I have the pleasure of being at Madam Lily's?" he asked with a quirky half-smile. What if he had gotten the wrong address and the temptress in the upper window had been nothing more than a wanton wife?

Zack nodded shortly, still holding the door against intrusion. "Who sent ya?" he growled.

Nonplused by the big man's unfriendly attitude. Thaxton's smile widened. "My skipper, in a way. Heard he appreciates the quality of the young ladies who board with Madam Lily. You might know him. Captain Innes of the *Puritan Paramour*?"

The huge guard stiffened. Could this popinjay really be from the *Paramour*? Could he have a message from the ship's missing master?

Seeing Zack barring the handsome young man from entrance to the house, Dora stopped posing on the staircase and swept gracefully down, her lavender gown trailing from step to step. She couldn't remember Zack ever taking Lily's orders so literally before. The members, as the madam called them, were few and very select but new prospects had never been turned away as abruptly as Zack was doing to the very personable man on the doorstep. She swept into the hall with the light of battle in her eyes.

The bodyguard's first inkling that he was no longer alone in the entranceway came when the stranger whipped his cap from his head and peered appreciatively past the giant.

Dora smiled, and her lashes fluttered coyly as she surveyed the visitor at closer range. Beneath classically arched brows, his amber eyes burned as they traveled familiarly over her. "I'm so glad you could come this morning," she cooed softly. "Do let him in, Zack. I was expecting him."

Zack glanced down at the petite woman, noting the steel in her gaze. In a pig's eye, he thought. Dora was an adventuress always on the lookout for an easy bankroll. If she thought this sailor boy was a greenhorn to pluck, she was on the wrong track. The man was determined to gain entry to the house. Zack read it in the stern set of the fella's jaw. He eyed the young officer once more. Could be she was taken with the man's features. Even Dora had a soft spot for a handsome face and there weren't many of those among Lily's clientele. Members were chosen by their financial assets rather than their physical ones.

Recognizing a flicker of indecision in the guard's broad face. Devin beamed and offered his hand to Zack. "First officer Devin Thaxton of the *Puritan Paramour*," he declared brightly.

Dora's lashes swept down to hide the glint of avarice that flickered in her eyes at the mention of the man's ship. The Puritan Line was an extremely prosperous shipping concern. The cut of the man's uniform was clearly that of a custom tailor. It was molded to his shoulders.

Thaxton's smile widened as the giant ignored his hand and he noted the fury gathering in the little brunette's face.

Dora glared at Zack's large back. Exasperated, she stamped one foot. "Really, Zack! Mr. Thaxton doesn't have all day. Let him in!"

Devin admired the gentle jiggling movements her termagant action caused within the deep-cut neckline of her gown. "I promise to behave," he said. Not that it was expected, he thought. The little spitfire would be all over him in a minute.

Zack scrutinized Dora's pouting pink face, recognizing the storm brewing behind her sulking features. What harm could there be in letting the man keep the little bitch entertained for a few hours? The sailor was nearly slathering he was so intent on her. Innes, when he returned, was sure to vouch for his man. With a shrug, Zack opened the door wider. "Come on in then," he growled. "Jest hope ya can ante up fer the service, slick."

Dora ran a practiced hand over the hard breadth of muscle, following it across Thaxton's naked back. "Must you leave?" She pouted prettily.

Devin drew on his second boot and stood up, reaching for his shirt. "You were saying something about Captain Innes," he said, one brow arched questioningly at her.

"Come back to bed and I might tell you, lover." Dora smiled and let the sheet slip across her breasts, nearly exposing them anew. His money rested on her dresser and it was hours until

Lily's regular clientele arrived. Why was he so eager to leave?

Devin continued dressing.

"Oh, all right," she declared, capitulating. Her voice was sulky, irritated that she couldn't lure him back beneath the sheet. "The last I saw your precious captain, he was going into the songbird's room." She flounced back against the pillows, her dark curls wiggling with the movement. "No one's seen him since that I know of. The songbird hasn't sung since then, either. But no one knows where to find her or what her name is."

Thaxton shoved his shirttail inside his trousers. "The songbird?"

Dora glared at him. "Don't tell me you don't know about her," she insisted. "That hussy didn't have anything to do with anyone till your captain came in."

"Where can I find her?"

Dora laughed shortly. "I don't know. Nor do I care. She's not one of the seamstresses, just a bitch from outside."

Devin smiled crookedly at his reflection in the mirror and adjusted his collar. Whoever she was, the songbird had not made friends among the inmates at Madam Lily's. She seemed the only key to Innes's disappearance, though. He hoped the information was worth the week's salary he'd just paid.

"Have you seen this songbird lately?" he asked.

Dora wished he'd drop his braces, climb back out of his trousers, and into bed. It wasn't often that she actually enjoyed earning her living but the young officer had been absolutely glorious in bed. Dora sighed. "Once or twice."

Devin waited patiently.

Dora could feel his eyes on her, could sense that he no longer saw her as a desirable woman. If he did, he wouldn't be standing there demanding information about the damned mysterious songbird. She wished she knew where to find the woman. She hadn't taken any business away from the girls at Lily's but she had certainly made them all feel like pale substitutes in the men's eyes. Depression was easily come by in their profession and they hadn't needed the songbird to throw it in their faces.

"She's been visiting Madam Lily in the afternoon lately. They talk about your captain. I overheard the songbird say his name," she allowed.

Thaxton shrugged into his jacket. "At what time does she usually arrive for these visits?"

Dora's shoulders heaved. "I don't keep a timetable on the bitch," she snapped. "She dresses in boy's clothes when she's here." Her voice implied a slur that any woman would demean herself so.

Pleased at last with a constructive answer, Devin bent over and kissed her pretty pouting lips. His hand slid to caress her breast.

Dora's hands clutched at his lapels. "You will come back, won't you, lover? I'd like it. A lot," she purred.

He disentangled her grasp. "Aye, I'll be back," he lied. "After I locate my skipper."

She licked her lips and parted them invitingly. But he was already at the door.

"This songbird," Thaxton said, one hand on the door knob, "does she come in past the gorilla in the hall?"

Dora bounded from the bed, the sheet draped loosely around her, molding to her body seductively. In one movement, she grabbed a figurine from the dresser and hurled it at him. "The damn songbird again!" she screeched. "Go to her, damn you! You'll find the bitch sneaking in the back door!" Hell! If she ever found the songbird alone, she'd tear the woman's hair out. She'd scratch her eyes out. She'd mark her face so that the songbird would be forced to hide behind that damn mask with good reason!

Thaxton didn't hear the abuse she hurled in his wake. He was already halfway down the stairs.

Chapter Eight

Caleb sat in the saddle uneasily, his awkwardness a source of amusement to the stony-faced men who accompanied him. The short ride to Pacific Street was accomplished in silence with the riders surrounding him like an honor guard, insuring his continued cooperation.

Until he discovered what Katie's connection with Ned Allen was, Caleb knew he had few options. He had to remain adaptable to Allen's whims.

The alleyways along this particular section of the Coast were narrow and deadly. They carried names with unsavory reputations as well, such as Pike Street, Murderers' Corner, and Deadman's Alley.

Allen's group kept to the center of the street, well away from unseen danger, their eyes alert, their pistols ready. Ned Allen might term himself a monarch of the Barbary Coast, Caleb thought, but even kings took no chances in this domain.

Allen reined in at the front entrance to his main establishment and dismounted in a single, fluid movement. Caleb climbed stiffly from his saddle, uncomfortable from the short time he'd endured the unfamiliar gait of a horse. Allen strode toward the doorway quickly but Caleb lingered a moment, surreptitiously studying the layout. He wondered whether, once he passed the screen that separated the street-level saloon from the curious stares of passersby, he'd ever come out alive.

Hell's Kitchen and Dance Hall was loud and garish and the sounds of music and boisterous drunken voices poured from the open doors to lure men in.

The night itself was cool, touched by the winds that raced in to shore. And as Caleb entered Allen's gin mill, he found the air stifling. Smoke hung heavy in the air, a man-made fog that never rolled out to sea. The aroma of whiskey, beer, gin, and rum mixed with the sweat of bleary-eyed men and the cheap perfume of faded women. The noise was deafening, the sound compacted by the narrow room and the closely packed crowd.

On the stage at the far end of the room, four gaudily dressed women were dancing. Their steps were far from synchronized but the audience didn't seem to mind. Men shouted for higher kicks, for faster movements. The women were perspiring with their efforts, the brightness of their smiles dimming as they gasped for breath.

Allen ignored the entertainers. He stood on the threshold, obviously enjoying the sights, the sounds, the smells of his establishment.

Still encircled by the three gunmen, Innes stepped into the saloon. A voluptuous brunette, wearing a short red jacket, black stockings, and high-heeled red slippers sidled up to Innes, pressing her lush body against his suggestively. "Oooh, Mistah Allen, ya brought me a present," she cooed, eyeing the captain.

Allen laughed shortly. "Etta's mighty taken with you, Innes."

As they expected him to do, Caleb ran an appreciative eye over the straining buttons of Etta's jacket and the stocky legs displayed beneath the short hemline. A plump white section of flesh rose above her bright garters. He smiled down into her painted, upturned face. "This the entertainment you promised, Allen?" he drawled lazily.

Etta wiggled closer, her hands boldly exploring the breadth of Caleb's chest.

Allen slapped her sharply on the backside and Etta jumped with an indignant squeal. "Later." He smirked. "Thought ya might want ta see yer little songbird first."

Etta sniffed and moved off to solicit another newcomer.

Innes stared after her disconsolately. "Songbird?" he echoed, hoping he sounded convincingly curious rather than worried. "Lily's girl? Is she the one I should thank for your . . . er, timely intervention?"

Allen frowned. The kid had given him the impression Innes meant something to her. She'd been cool but a bawd didn't bargain for a man unless she fancied herself in love. Yet here was Innes appraising every tart the Kitchen offered, as if no one woman meant any more to him than the next.

"Yeah. The redhead," Allen said casually, watching Innes from the corner of his eye.

The captain continued to look over the room, his gaze lingering on various women almost longingly.

"Redhead?" Innes echoed. "Thought Lily's girl had black hair. Like some fandango dancer."

"And I thought ya knew her better than that," Allen said, his voice a little harder. He signaled for the group to follow him across the room to a newly cleared table before the stage. He directed Innes to sit near center stage and took the chair opposite, a position that would enable him to keep both the sea captain and the songbird, when she came on stage, under observation. The three thugs grouped themselves around the outer edge of the table, an impenetrable wall between Caleb and freedom.

The captain appeared unconcerned. He lolled back in his seat, his eyes on the short, chubby legs of the dancers. Up close, it was possible to see that their gowns were frayed and stained, their black stockings much mended.

Innes's smile was as bemused as the drunken men around him. When one of the waiter girls brought over a bottle of whiskey and glasses, he lifted his drink toward the ponderous women on the stage, in a toast to their performance. His mind tacked in a different direction, though.

If Katie was behind the curtain, set to perform as the songbird in Allen's saloon, events beyond his wildest imaginings had taken place during the two weeks he'd absented himself. But was it all tied to Bull Run's visit to Lily's? To Kate's mysterious performances as the songbird? Or was it something else? Allen said that the songbird had arranged for his rescue from the crimpers.

Just the fact that Allen knew her true hair color was enough to frighten Innes. Caleb swore silently. Sweet Lord! What rig was Katie running now?

In the small room behind the stage, Kate listened to the raucous hoots and howls of the audience. Her pale face stared blankly back at her in the mirror. She'd already received word of Allen's arrival and Lily had gone to verify Caleb's presence. Soon, Kate knew, she would have to fulfill her side of the bargain.

The door scraped open to admit the madam's neat form. "Bull's got him, Katie." Lily sighed, both relieved and nervous of the consequences of the young woman's deal with this particular devil. "They're sitting out there just in front of the stage."

Kate's eyes questioned anxiously. "Is he all right? How did he look?"

Surrounded by Allen's men? Caleb was a damned prisoner, Lily thought. Would he forgive Katie this latest start? "Sure, he's fine," she soothed brightly. The kid was as pale as a ghost, jumping at the least noise. She was right to be nervous. The Kitchen was the worst den of vice on the Barbary Coast and Katie had walked into it with a damn chip on her shoulder. "Got himself a beard, too. Looks good in it," she continued.

Kate fidgeted with the cosmetic containers that littered the rough surface of the dressing table. She had always become the songbird behind a convenient disguise. Tonight the wig and mask were gone. She would be exposed, open to harassment from any man who recognized her. Judging from her brother Phael's activities and those of his cronies, there was a very good chance that some of her audience would be familiar men of the social elite.

"Ya gonna be all right, kid?" Lily asked quietly. "Ya don't look too good."

Kate smiled weakly. "I'll be fine now that Caleb has been found," she answered. "Did you notice if Papa . . ."

" . . . got the message?" Lily met Kate's worried eyes. "Ain't seen a sign of him yet."

Kate took a deep, determined breath, then let it out slowly. "I'll have to go through with it then."

She stood and ran her hands down over the tightly clinging white satin dress. The neckline was lower than she was accustomed to wearing. It left the upper curves of her breasts exposed. The hemline was short, displaying her softly rounded calves and slim ankles. Allen had insisted she leave her own hair uncovered. It was piled in a mass of curls and topped by a white ostrich plume that bobbed and swayed when she moved.

White. It had been Allen's idea as well to dress her in the virginal color. She wondered why he'd been so insistent. Bright, fiery red would have suited his tastes far better.

Lily glanced over her shoulder as a fresh burst of laughter exploded in the main room. Just overhead, she could hear the rhythmic squeak of a mattress as one of the waiter girls plied her trade. Bull had been against Lily accompanying Katie to the Kitchen but the madam had no intention of letting the young woman out of her sight. It was one thing for the kid to brazen things out at Lily's parlor house, but Hell's Kitchen wasn't a place for Ben Paradise's daughter. Lily fervently hoped the message she'd sent to the Paradise Palace saloon reached Ben.

The plump, far from talented dancers had left the stage amid a chorus of whistles, yells, and stomping feet. While waiting for the next act, Caleb leaned back in his chair, appreciatively ogling the procession of waiter girls who trooped by. The glimpses of full breasts and tender thighs would have cheered him in other circumstances but Katie's safety was his only concern now and it depended on his performance in convincing Allen that his interest was easily diverted. Caleb gulped down a shot of fiery rotgut whiskey, savoring the burn, gaining resolve from the warmth it spread through his veins.

Allen watched the captain avail himself of the bottle and the sloppy smile on his face. The sailor had tossed off his drinks quickly and now radiated inebriated contentment. He seemed perfectly happy to enjoy the particularly rowdy brand of hospitality offered at the Kitchen. The women, the booze. But Allen was skeptical. Despite Innes's behavior, Ned doubted that the captain was as unaffected by the girl who had bargained herself for his deliverance.

As if conscious of his host's suspicions, Innes added his voice to the catcalls when the curtains parted on stage to reveal the angelically pure form of a young woman.

She stepped forward to center stage, her head held high, ignoring the shouts of the audience. The bell-shaped skirt of her white gown swayed with each step she took. The ridiculous plume in her reddish-gold hair bobbed. The whistles and shouts nearly drowned out the piano player's heavy-handed playing of the opening bars of her first song.

Allen glanced at Innes, hoping to catch a change of expression at the songbird's entrance. Caleb's face maintained its pleased, slightly lecherous grin.

The songbird's reaction was much more satisfactory, Allen felt. Her eyes sought the captain, her gaze caressing his features. She flushed slightly at the fixed grin he wore. Yet when he winked outlandishly, she brightened immediately.

"Sing us a song, darlin'," Innes called out as loudly as the men around him.

She appeared to gain courage from his presence. Her dark eyes swept the audience contemptuously, her smile knowingly superior as she faced them. Her very movements changed, dazzling and damning the ogling men.

"Any request, handsome?" she purred. Her voice had the sultry pitch Allen associated with the mysterious songbird but the accent was missing now. Her hands went to her hips as she struck a saucy pose.

Devin Thaxton slumped further in his seat, his eyes trained on the stage as the songstress's voice washed over him. It was as insistently luring as the song of a sea siren. Her appearance was more intoxicating than any of the rotgut he'd drunk while waiting for her to come on stage.

The girl on his lap wiggled enticingly. "Want me ta sing fer ya, sweety?" She giggled. "Privately, o' course. Only cost ya a couple dollars."

He had recognized the singer immediately, had known her identity when he'd seen her in the boy's clothing earlier that day. Hell's Kitchen was the last place Thaxton would have thought to find Miss Katherine Paradise. He still struggled with the shock he'd received when she arrived at Madam Lily's that afternoon and was quickly admitted through the alley door.

After leaving Dora, Thaxton had quickly purchased a civilian suit. The plaid was a little loud for his taste but it blended well with the down-at-the-heels crowds of the Coast. His uniform had stood out, made him easy to notice, had branded him as a stray in their midst. It was not a thing he wished when his intent had been to follow the songbird to the love nest she apparently shared with his missing superior.

At first the tall, slim boy with the cocky stride hadn't impressed him. It was only when the youth had headed for the alley and the parlor house's rear entrance that Devin's interest had been piqued. Edging closer, he caught a glimpse of red-gold hair and a delicate profile before she had disappeared from sight. Although he'd never seen the songbird before, something told Thaxton that he had found the quarry for whom he searched. Not a quarter of an hour later, she had emerged once more, this time with another woman who wore a blue dress. Katherine Paradise had carried a dress box and been impatient with her companion's short stride.

"Damn it, Katie," the older woman had sworn. "You know these narrow skirts won't let me keep up with you. Slow down. Caleb will still be waiting when we get there. Allen's not about to louse up this deal."

The young woman had shortened her stride but continued to display nervous energy for the short walk to Hell's Kitchen. Thaxton had followed at a distance until they disappeared within the notorious saloon.

Now Devin's eyes covered the white-gowned vision on stage, feasting on the full rise of her nearly naked breasts and the bit of shapely leg that her shortened skirt allowed. Could this be the same haughty Miss Paradise from the Puritan Line office? She strutted across the stage, her hips swaying provocatively, her voice seducing her audience.

"Hey," the woman on his lap demanded irritably. "Ya hear what I said, Mister?"

Thaxton turned back to her with a smile. He kissed her, his tongue plunging within her parted lips, luring her back to complacency. "I'm

139

gonna need strength to enjoy you, Dulcie," he said, and coaxingly indicated his empty beer mug.

Pleased by the renewal of attention, she kissed him back, her arms around his neck, gratified at the way his hand strayed up her thigh. "Sure, sweety," Dulcie purred, and hurried away with a flirtatious look.

Temporarily rid of the waiter girl, Thaxton turned his attention back to the stage.

Katherine Paradise appeared to be enjoying herself. The white gown emphasized her features, and highlighted the blush of innocence that still clung to her. Her actions were not those of a maiden, however. Her accentuated walk, her body movements, were calculated to arouse her audience. Laughing, she bent toward a tall, bearded man at a front table, then blushed as her gown gaped away from her breast. The crowd went wild, their calls causing her color to darken.

Thaxton settled back in his chair. Tonight he would enjoy Dulcie but she was merely a substitute. One day he would take his pleasure with Katherine Paradise. He could almost feel her squirming beneath him, see her lagoon eyes cloud with passion at his touch.

"Miss me?" Dulcie demanded, sliding onto his lap once more. She was pleased at the bulge of his trousers against her buttocks. She put his fresh glass of beer on the table and snuggled closer. "Wouldn't ya like ta go upstairs, sweetie? We could have a good time," she purred.

On stage, the songbird finished her final selection and departed, peeping coquettishly over her shoulder before disappearing.

"Dulcie." Thaxton murmured, "why don't we go somewhere a bit quieter?"

Kate rushed through the dressing-room door, slamming it thankfully behind her. She felt as if she'd been holding her breath, running for her life. Leaning back, she gulped the cool, relatively smokeless air of the tiny back room in relief.

Lily hurried toward her, her blue skirts swishing in agitation. "You were wonderful, Katie."

It hurt to see the way Lily's lips were thinned with worry. Dear cheerful, easily duped Lily. Kate felt a prick of conscience. She had dragged Lily into one scrape after another and the woman hadn't uttered one word of rebuke. She'd warned but never scolded.

"Allen won't be satisfied with just one show," Lily said.

"He's entitled." Katie sighed. "He kept his side of the bargain. I'll have to keep mine." She plucked the plume from her hair. If Caleb hadn't been there encouraging her, lending her moral support, she could never have gotten through the performance. Yet, when he sailed, she would still be bound by her promise to Ned Allen.

Kate shivered at the thought and made an immediate change in plan.

"Unhook me, Lily," she urged. "I'm not out of the fire yet, but I'll be damned if I'm going back out there again tonight."

Lily hesitated. "Is that smart, kid? You don't know Bull Run Allen like I do."

Kate moved away from the door, pulling pins

from her hair. It fell in luxurious waves around her shoulders. "And he doesn't know me," she said, her voice hard.

Unaware that his prize was preparing to leave, Allen got to his feet and pulled an unprotesting, bleary-eyed Caleb Innes with him. "Stay here," Allen ordered his henchmen. "The captain and me is jest gonna congratulate our little songbird personally, ain't we, Captain?" he murmured, his voice dangerously low.

Caleb grinned happily and lurched unsteadily to his feet. "Damn good idear," he agreed, his New England accent heavier as he slurred the words.

Allen led the way to an alcove near the stage and held the curtain aside for the captain to proceed him.

Near the bar, two men finished their drinks and staggered into the crowd, slowly working their way toward the stage door.

The lewd calls of the audience still rang in Kate's ears. Even the thickness of the door didn't soften the sound. Hurriedly, she slid out of the white dress and pulled her trousers on, not bothering to remove her frilly drawers or silk stockings. She wouldn't stay a minute longer. Now that she knew Caleb was safe, and where he was, she was sure her father could provide the means to extricate the captain from Allen.

Ned Allen didn't bother to knock. Privacy wasn't a commodity he dealt in at Hell's Kitchen. The women who worked for him were owned by him.

As the door opened, Kate caught a glimpse of Allen's pale frock coat and turned away. Her back to him, she shrugged into her shirt. The lace frills of her corset reshaped the contours, curving the fabric so that she no longer could pass for a boy. But Kate didn't care, as she fumbled with the shirt studs, quickly fastening the closings.

"Funny," she said. "I don't remember leaving the door open, Lily. A big wind just blew in."

Caleb hung back in the shadows of the doorway. She hadn't seen him follow Allen, but at the moment that suited him very well. He was still confused about Katie's involvement with Allen. Her nettling tone of voice baited the man. If she had indeed opened negotiations with Allen to locate him, why was she so hostile to the man? Her actions were sure to irritate Allen, to increase the danger to them all. Didn't she realize Allen was not only ruthless, he was deadly?

"Whadda ya think yer doin'?" Allen demanded sharply.

Kate kept her back to him. "Dressing. If you were the least bit thoughtful, you'd have provided a dressing screen. Or were you planning to sell tickets for private performances?"

Lily hadn't dared to glance up, but busied herself in repacking the white dress away. She was in awe of Katie. Imagine ripping up at Bull Run Allen and getting away with it. The man seemed to enjoy the battles. But how long would it be before the novelty of the kid's attitude wore off and it began to irritate Allen? What would happen then?

Elizabeth Daniels

Lily straightened, prepared to divert Allen's attention to herself if need be. Then she noticed the bearded man standing silently in the background. "Caleb," she whispered.

Kate spun at the sound of his name.

Innes grinned loosely, intent upon preserving his drunken shield. Kate looked even more desirable in male clothing. The straight line of her trousers showed the long length of her legs to perfection. The open collar of her shirt displayed the soft curve where her neck met her shoulder and dipped toward the high thrust of her breasts. Her red-gold hair fell in lush waves to her waist, begging a man to bury his face in its fragrant length.

He seemed different, Kate thought. Almost a stranger. She had been too tense, too preoccupied while on stage to take in the changes to his person. Not just the clothes, although the denim trousers, rough shirt, and dark vest made him seem harder. No, Caleb looked older, almost haggard. His eyes were hollow, the usually warm brown color now flat and lifeless. His full black beard was shaggy, unshaped. It made him appear harsh, disreputable, dangerous. What had she done to him?

"Nice show," Caleb said, as if unsure what was expected of him.

"Caleb." Kate breathed his name. She longed to run to him but Ned Allen's presence prevented her. "Are you all right?"

"Fine, fine." Caleb slurred the words and grinned drunkenly, continuing his own charade with Allen.

Allen was immune to the unease in Kate's

144

eyes. He strode toward her and caught her wrist. "You've got another show to do! If need be, I'll be glad ta rip those damn trousers from ya and personally squeeze ya back inta that costume."

His threat jolted Kate back to the danger of the situation. This was no time to sort out her relationship with Caleb. First Allen had to be appeased. But in her own way.

She pulled away from the dandy's grasp and brushed an errant lock of hair back from her brow. Her chin rose challengingly. "Another time, Bull. I never said I'd do more than one show a night. Or that I'd even sing more than once, if you recall."

Allen's face was nearly as red as his bulbous nose. "You'll do as many shows as I tell ya to!" he thundered.

Kate stood her ground, her eyes narrowed. "The debt's paid. End of the game."

Allen stood over her, his stance threatening. "It ain't a game, angel."

"Oh, but it was." As if totally at ease, Kate sat down before the dressing table and leaned back, her elbows brushing against the jars of face paint, lip rouge, and cheap perfume. The pose pulled the fabric of her shirt tight across her breasts. "It was a bet."

Allen glared at Lily. "Is that right?"

Lily was speechless. She stared at him, her mouth suddenly dry, her breathing shallow.

"Lily wouldn't know," Kate said. "I wagered that you could succeed where the authorities failed when it came to finding a missing man," she lied. "Becoming the songbird was all part of the plan."

Bull Run turned to Innes but the captain's drunken grin and slumped body against the door molding convinced him the man knew nothing of the songbird's plots. Allen ignored him and swung back to tower over the relaxed girl. He moved quickly and grabbed a handful of her hair.

"No games, kid." His voice was vicious, tight, and deadly as he bent toward her. "We had a deal. I find Innes for you. You belong to me."

The cool touch of honed steel against his throat took Allen by surprise. "Let her go," Innes ordered, his voice dangerously calm. The drunken slur had disappeared. Only the faint scent of whiskey hung in the air between them. Where the captain had looked incapable of action moments before, the knife that now rested intimately along Allen's jugular was steady and sure.

"I said, let her go," Innes repeated. The blade pricked Allen's skin.

Kate's eyes were large and luminescent as they met Ned Allen's furious gaze. Slowly, he relaxed his grip on her hair. Once free, she moved quickly away from the men.

"See if there's something to tie him up with!" Innes snapped the command without glancing at the women. He hauled Allen around to face him, the knife now pressing against the man's ribs.

Lily stared at the suddenly reversed diorama, her limbs partially frozen in shock. One moment Caleb had lounged in the doorway, looking as if he'd put away the best part of a jug of bad whiskey, and the next he was a dark angel visiting death on the damned.

Kate was shaking. Whether with fear or fury, Lily couldn't tell. The kid's face was white, drained of color and life, and Lily couldn't move. It was all just a dream. A bad one. But Kate had no problem following Caleb's order. She ripped open the dress box and began shredding her petticoat. When she had a number of lengths, Kate returned to Caleb's side.

Allen was complacent. He sat quietly in the chair, biding his time. But even when the girl reappeared at the captain's side, Innes's attention didn't waver.

"He's got a gun in his inside pocket," Caleb said.

Gingerly, Kate removed it, checked the cylinder, then cocked the hammer. She aimed it at the center of Allen's chest.

Innes watched the way Allen's eyes followed Kate's actions. "She knows how to use it, you know," he said, and dropped the knife back into his boot. He yanked Allen's hands back and tied them fast together.

"Don't worry," Allen growled as the captain bent to bind his ankles. "I ain't stupid enough to let some bawd shoot me."

"She wouldn't have to," a deep voice said from the doorway. A tall man in ill-fitting clothing stood there, a Colt in his hand. "I'd do it for her."

"Papa." Kate didn't look away but kept her gun trained on Allen. "You did get the message."

Allen's head twisted in quick succession from the armed young woman to the deadly man in the doorway. "She's your kid?" His tone was almost conversational.

147

Ben Paradise nodded. "One of them," he conceded. "Put the gun down, princess. I think we should leave now."

Although securely bound in the chair, Allen wasn't prepared to let things lie. "The kid and me's got a deal, Paradise," he growled. "I mean ta see it paid in full."

Ben's eyes hardened to cakes of blue ice. "You were paid in full, Allen. She's not performing anymore. The songbird's career is over."

"It ain't no game," Allen persisted.

Kate put the gun aside, far away from Allen. If he managed to get loose, she had no intention of making things easy for him. From the thoroughness of Caleb's work in binding him, she doubted Allen's escape would be achieved very soon. "It was a bet," she insisted once more.

Innes's hand came down heavily on Allen's shoulder. "You understand about bets, Bull," he said. "Any more of that cloth, Lil?"

Still slightly paralyzed with fear and shock, Lily stared down at the remains of the petticoat, surprised to find she held it in her hands. Slowly, as if she moved in a dream. Lily handed it to him.

Innes wadded the fabric up and shoved it in Allen's mouth, silencing the king of the Barbary Coast. "Time we left."

Kate quickly shrugged into her short sack coat and wound a muffler around her throat as a further disguise. She swept her hair up and tucked it beneath the cloth cap. "Thanks again," she told Allen.

Paradise's gun dropped back in his holster, but his hand stayed near it, ready for further

148

trouble. He motioned for the others to precede him. The women hurried out of the room and back toward the stage, Lily with the dress box clasped to her as if it were a life line, Kate cocky once more now that she was free of Allen's control. Innes delayed a moment, his eyes watchful. They weren't out of it yet.

"Phael's watching at the stage entrance," Paradise said, closing the dressing-room door quietly behind him.

The captain retrieved his knife from the sheath in his boot and held it close to his body to disguise the gleaming blade. His eyes scanned the dark hallway. "This is too easy."

"Damn right it is," Paradise agreed. "Allen's not one to forgive and forget. He misjudged this time. He won't the next."

With barely a sound, the two men moved through the shadows to join the women and Phael. Behind them, there was a thump, as if something heavy had fallen. The sound of shattering glass was muffled by the closed door. Innes and Paradise exchanged a solemn glance. Allen wouldn't be a prisoner in his own saloon for long.

Paradise held Innes back a moment before they joined the others. "I'm putting Lily out of business," he said. "Lawson and Sparks will get her out of town. It would be best if you left, too."

"That doesn't protect Katie," Innes pointed out.

Even in the shadows, it was possible to see Paradise's face was stiffly set. "Just get the hell out of here, Cal," he said. "Let me worry about my daughter."

Chapter Nine

The couple stood on the dock, staring out at the harbor. They had done it often in the past, stood together in companionable silence with the salty tang of the sea surrounding them, the gentle lap of waves against the wharf the only sound to disturb them.

Those other times were a very long time ago, Caleb thought. It had been a different harbor then, a different ocean. He had been a different man, a young man. A man unwilling to commit himself to a girl with dark gypsy eyes.

Lacy. His childhood companion. His first love. She had haunted him over the years, just as her daughter did now.

Her daughter. His hands trembled at the thought. He kept them in his trouser pockets, afraid that they would reveal his emotions, would show that he'd never been so terrified in his life.

The sea could throw its worse at him, hurricane winds, torrential rains, Atlantean swells. He stood close-hauled, reveling in the challenge, determined to best Davy Jones yet again.

But a slip of a girl had accomplished what all of Neptune's minions had failed to do. She had bested him, had scuttled the serenity of his bachelor existence. There was something horrifying about the ease with which Kate had reduced him to this state of fear.

How had it happened? Had he been subconsciously sailing this course for years? And if he had, why wasn't he more prepared? Why didn't he have the answers that he so desperately needed?

When he looked at Lacy Phalen Paradise, Caleb didn't see the successful woman behind the western branch of the Puritan Shipping Line, didn't see the mother of seven children. He still saw the girl she had been. The girl he had left behind him twenty-five years ago.

Time had barely touched Lacy. Her hair was still the same white-blond he'd once loved to touch. Her lips still asked to be kissed. Many men had lost themselves in her dark, gypsy eyes, had dreamed of her slim, womanly form. She had been the belle of Boston, an heiress. Her fortune, her beauty, the Puritan Line had all been his for the asking once. And he had thrown everything away rather than commit himself to one woman, rather than commit himself to love.

He had always been able to conjure up Lacy's

form, her smile. Her image had always been a comfort to him, her happiness a talisman, a balm to his soul. Long ago he'd condemned himself to nearly three years in a warehouse in Liverpool, had temporarily given up the sea rather than offer her his heart and hand. He'd thought he was being noble, a martyr, when all he'd actually been was afraid.

Now the decision must be made once more. This time was no easier than the last. Perhaps worse.

The breeze whipped at their clothing, tore long pale blond strands of hair from Lacy's neat chignon. She brushed them aside, as unconcerned about the dishevelment as she had been as a girl. Her eyes appeared fixed on the distant masts of the *Puritan Paramour* as the ship rocked gently at its mooring, rising and falling with the choppy waters of the bay. Her adventures had begun with the clipper's first sailing. She had been married aboard the ship, had given birth to Kate in the captain's cabin.

"Have you talked to her?" Lacy asked softly, her eyes still on the harbor.

Caleb didn't look at her. "No."

"You should."

"Aye."

Lacy turned, her eyes solemn. "Caleb, if your heart—"

"Damn how I feel," he growled. "I'm doing the right thing."

She was silent a moment, then placed her gloved hand on his arm. "Let's walk," she suggested.

Walking was better than talking, but Caleb

knew she had both in mind.

But when Lacy didn't say anything more, it was Caleb who felt the need to speak.

"It's just a short voyage," he explained.

"I know."

He didn't want understanding. Caleb wanted her to rage at him, to force him to defend himself, to force him to battle the indecision that plagued him. "Ben told me it was wise to get away just now," he said, his voice churlish.

It had been two days since Ned Allen had kept him from being shanghaied, two days since Kate had sung at Hell's Kitchen. Two quiet days in which they had heard nothing of Allen or his henchmen. No one thought Bull Run had forgotten them. They knew he was merely biding his time, waiting for them to relax their vigilance.

And, somehow, through it all, Lacy had maintained a composure that Caleb found maddening. She was still calm, strolling along the waterfront, her touch light on his arm, her cloak whipping in the wind, her tread soft and measured.

"It is very wise for you to pull anchor now," she said.

Wise or not. Caleb felt the need to explain himself, to make this voyage sound necessary and quick rather than an escape, even a temporary one. "I'll be back in a few weeks."

Lacy nodded, accepting his nebulous statement. Caleb wondered why she didn't ask for a more specific time frame, why she wasn't pinning him down to a schedule.

"It's perfect," she said. "That's why I want to ask you a favor."

A favor? Caleb didn't like the way Lacy had led up to it. He felt guilty enough to be running away again, but he needed time to think.

They all expected him to marry Kate. No one had said so. It was their silence that pushed him toward making a commitment. It wasn't enough that he loved Kate. He had to correct a wrong, one that Kate herself had committed. He had just been the innocent but very willing accomplice.

He knew marrying Kate was the right thing to do. But he'd been shying away from pledging himself to one woman for so long, it wasn't something he could agree to easily.

It wasn't just the idea of promising he would love only Kate. Caleb was convinced that he would never love or even want another woman the rest of his days. It was the accoutrements of the married state that unnerved him. A home. Children. Those things were part of a landlubber's life, not his.

"You want me to talk to Kate before I go, is that it?" Caleb demanded shortly.

Lacy laughed at his irritability. "No, it isn't. I want you to take David with you as a cabin boy."

Innes stopped walking abruptly. "Is this his penance for being involved in Kate's little adventure?"

Lacy urged him on further down the quay. *Kate's little adventure. What a telling phrase,* she thought. Her daughter had plunged him into a situation not of his choosing and now it was all a "little adventure." Lacy wondered if Caleb even realized he no longer used the childhood epithet,

Katie. Her daughter had become a woman to him. She was Kate, his Kate.

"I thought the trip would keep David out of further trouble," Lacy explained as they continued strolling along the wharf. "Even if I thought it was a punishment for his recent activities, I doubt my precocious son would think so."

Caleb watched a gull come in for a graceful landing atop a pier piling, still reluctant to meet her eyes, still afraid he'd see other requests for favors lurking beneath her long dark lashes. Ones he wouldn't be as willing to grant quite yet. "All right, I don't mind having Davy aboard. But what about his schooling?"

"He's bright. He can catch up. For now, learning about the shipping business from another perspective will keep him happy." She turned her head to watch the sea bird as they moved past it. Their presence didn't disturb the gull. It was used to the activity of the docks.

"As you know, Phael is hopeless," Lacy said sadly. "He has no interest in the Line. He'll never go back and take over management of the Boston office as the captain and I had expected him to do." To Lacy, "the captain" always referred to her father. Sean Phalen had died in his sleep a few years earlier while sailing to New York on business. Now the main office of the Line was run by Lacy's staid cousin, Harry Phalen, and his son, Harold.

"Phael is perfectly happy being . . . well, feckless," Lacy said with a disappointed sigh. "But David is different. He's interested in the business."

155

Elizabeth Daniels

"In the Puritan Line? Or in sailing?" For him, Caleb thought, it had always been the sea, the feel of the wind in his hair, the feel of a deck beneath his feet. It wasn't something he could easily give up.

"At the moment, I don't think even David knows," Lacy admitted. "So we'll send him off to the Sandwich Islands with you to find out. You'll both be back for the holidays and hopefully this business with Ned Allen will have been forgotten by then."

Their steps had lead them back to the tip of California Street. Caleb turned up the roadway, his steps automatically heading toward the Puritan Line office. "Do you really believe Allen ever forgets anything?" he asked.

"No," Lacy admitted. "But the man has numerous enemies. I was hoping that he would become involved in another contretemps, one that would overshadow Katie's escapade."

It took only a few strides to reach the brick building that had served as headquarters for Lacy's shipping business since before Phael's birth. Caleb paused outside and glanced up at her office windows. They looked out on the bustle of activity below, on the comings and goings of sailors, freighters, and merchants. How often had he come along this very street and glanced up to see a little girl's nose pressed against the glass as she waited for him? The sight had always made him feel lucky, special.

She wasn't there now. She had grown up but she still waited for him in the mansion on Nob Hill.

Lacy watched him, the eagerness in his eyes,

156

the disappointment that replaced it when the window remained empty. Katie had always known when the *Puritan Paramour* was due into port, had always kept a vigil for him. Her perch in the window had allowed the little girl the first glance of Caleb when he docked. Katie never squealed or shouted when she spied him coming up the street. She had merely taken off, her red-gold pigtails flying in her hurry to meet her favorite captain. They had returned together back then with Katie's face alight, her skinny arms around his neck, her cheek cuddled close to Caleb's as he carried her. Lacy had thought it was a game with them. A game similar to the one she had once played with him, welcoming him back to Boston with loving caresses and tender kisses. Lacy had planned to marry Caleb Innes when she played those games. She just hadn't realized that Kate had had the same goal.

Lacy's hand on his arm tightened. She stood on tiptoe and pressed an impulsive kiss to his freshly shaven cheek.

Caleb looked startled and pleased. "What was that for?"

"Old times." Lacy took two steps toward the door before pausing and turning back. "You really should talk to Katie."

It was a different window Kate Paradise stood before, one which gave her a spectacular view of the harbor. Over the years, the roofs of other buildings had obscured the panorama but it was still magnificent.

The Paradise home had been one of the earliest houses on Nob Hill, predating the mansions of the railroad barons. Rising three stories, it had long ago sacrificed a moderate ballroom for additional bedrooms. It sat astride two long narrow lots, allowing for well-tended gardens on either side, and a small carriage house to the back.

The upstairs parlor had always been Kate's favorite room. The wide bow-shaped windows not only framed the view of the growing city and the bay, they allowed light to flood into the room even on cloudy days.

The sun spilled in this particular afternoon but its cheerful appearance did little to lighten Kate's mood.

Behind her the sound of cards continued. Cards being shuffled, dealt, turned over. Her sister, Winona, never tired of playing, whether it was repeated games of patience by herself, afternoons of whist with her friends, or poker with Phael and his cronies.

"Damn."

Kate turned at Wyn's muttered exclamation. "The cards winning this round?"

Wyn glared at one particular card. She held it up to the light. "You know I never lose at patience," she said. "I cheat. I did a lousy job marking this card. Even Phael could spot it."

As far as the two sisters were concerned, their older brother lived in a fog, unaware of what went on around him. They had both been surprised at the part he had played in Kate's rescue from Hell's Kitchen, but seriously doubted he would be able to repeat the performance. His siblings felt he exaggerated in retelling the tale. They were sure that it was their silent, but

amused, father who had played a more perti-
nent part in the rescue.

Wyn laid the marked card on the table and
ran a well-manicured finger along the edge,
smoothing the nick she'd put in it. "Come play
a game with me. I don't care what. Fan-tan,
casino, two-handed euchre. Anything."

Kate turned back to stare out the window.
"Ask Lisa."

Wyn wrinkled her nose. "No thank you. The
only game she wants to play is snakes and lad-
ders."

"Well, you liked playing that when you were
nine, too."

"Never," Wyn insisted. "When I was that age,
I could already clean Uncle Caleb out at poker."
She paused, stared at her cards, then stacked
them all back together in a neat pile.

"Uncle Caleb," Wyn mused. "I suppose I'd better drop the uncle now."

Kate continued her vigil, watching down the
street for a familiar figure to come in sight.

"I don't think he's coming," Wyn said. "After
all, the *Paramour* is setting sail tomorrow."

That got Kate's attention. She spun from the
window, took two agitated steps into the room,
and halted. Her hands were pressed together,
her cheeks suddenly pale. "Sailing?"

Wyn was stunned at her sister's reaction. Kate
had always known the *Paramour*'s schedule. "Oh,
Katie, I thought you knew!" she murmured sadly.
"He'll be back. We all know that. Then you'll get
married and . . ." Her voice trailed off, unsure of
what the future would be.

Kate took a deep breath. "Yes, of course. The

ship has been ready to leave for weeks. It has already been delayed long enough."

Wyn looked a bit relieved when Kate sat down across from her. "Unc . . . I mean, Caleb probably would prefer to be right here with you," she soothed, shuffling the cards, and dealing a hand before Kate could refuse to play a quick game. "But you know how business is. How often has Mama been unable to attend some function because of a late docking or a scrambled manifest?"

Kate nodded. She even picked up the cards that Wyn flicked across the table, little aware that she held them, or what game her sister had decided they were playing.

Caleb was sailing and he hadn't told her. No one had told her. Had they all assumed, like Wyn, that she knew the *Paramour* would be pulling anchor?

It was more than just that. Caleb was avoiding her. They hadn't been alone together since he'd left her that morning at Lily's. She had no idea of how he felt about her. Did he love her as she had long believed, or was he repulsed by her scheme to be with him that one wonderful night?

Wyn took it for granted that Caleb intended to marry her, but Kate wasn't nearly as sure or if he would for the right reasons. She had given herself to him, relinquished her virtue to him. She had not done it to gain his name. Nor did she want Caleb to feel he had to marry her because she had spent a night in his arms. Kate wanted him only to love her, to want her by his side.

Instead, he was sailing away from her and she couldn't let that happen.

Kate stared at her cards.

"Coon-can," Wyn said. "We're playing coon-can. Match your ranks or suits. Your turn to draw."

Kate picked a card from the deck and absent-mindedly slid it into her hand and discarded an unknown card. It didn't matter how she played. Wyn would cheat if she really wanted to emerge the victor. What was more important was the need to come up with a new plan.

There was really only one avenue for her to pursue. If Caleb were sailing, that meant she had to be on board the clipper the next morning when it left the harbor. How to accomplish that feat was the problem.

Wyn formed her first melded set—three jacks—drew a new card, and tossed her discard seemingly all in one flowing movement.

Kate lagged behind, her mind churning with possible ploys to get on board the *Puritan Paramour*. Each had a major flaw. Caleb would see her, would recognize her.

She took another card, stared at it. The fourth jack. A club. She slid it between others of the same suit.

What she needed was a fellow conspirator, someone like Lily had been, setting up the framework within which she had moved as the songbird. Finding someone aboard the *Paramour* who was willing to go against the captain's will was more difficult, though. Lily had been a romantic, lost in her own dreams, and eager to help Kate pursue the man of her choice.

Strangely enough, it had been Lily who emerged the victor from Kate's plot. The parlor house had been shut down, but in losing her business Lily had found two very eager suitors ready to take her away from danger. Both Zack Lawson and Luther Sparks were vying for the honor of offering the former madam their heart and hand in marriage. Overcome with surprise and emotion but unable to choose between them. Lily had left with them for the ranch the big men had bought out near the former gold-rush town of Sonora.

Lily was far out of Ned Allen's reach now. Soon Caleb would be, too. But what about herself? Kate wondered. It hadn't been Lily Walsh or the captain who had made a deal with Bull Run. It had been the songbird. She was the one from whom he would plan to exact further payment.

Kate had heard her parents tell Lily that leaving town was the safest measure. Were they planning to remove her as well? If so, where? To Sonora with Lily? Or. . . .

Boston.

Dear Lord, it would be Boston! Allen's grip on the underworld probably spread out from the Barbary Coast, from San Francisco itself into the countryside. But it would not reach across the continent, could not touch her in New England.

It was just the sort of plan her mother would hatch. It didn't matter that long ago Lacy Phalen had run away from Boston, away from the influence of her cousin's wife, Abigail, and the woman's brother, William Quire. Kate knew her mother had found true happiness with Ben Paradise. Since both William and Abigail were dead, even her father would see no danger to Kate in Boston. Quire had died in the fire that had destroyed the original Paradise Palace saloon months before Phael had been born. Abigail had succumbed to pneumonia during a particularly wet winter and died only a few years later. There had never been anything to fear from Harry Phalen, who now ran the Puritan Line office.

They would send her to Boston. Kate was sure of it now. Far away from Ned Allen but also far away from Caleb Innes. Although his family was from Massachusetts, Caleb's sisters had married and moved away years ago. When the youngest had followed her husband to Indiana. Caleb had made the Pacific his new home and the Paradises his family.

"Your draw," Wyn said.

Kate stared at her sister. Wyn looked confident. She held only three cards in her hand now, the others laid on the table in neatly ordered fans displaying sequenced suits or like numbers. Kate still held all ten of her cards.

Did Wyn know what was being planned? Kate frowned slightly, considering whether she should demand to know everything Winona knew.

Wyn misunderstood Kate's look. "I'm not cheating," she insisted. "It wouldn't be fair to you. You're just not concentrating."

Kate took another card, slid it into her hand, and contemplated the pasteboards. She wouldn't go to Boston. Too much time, too many miles,

Elizabeth Daniels

would lay between Caleb and herself. No, there was only one acceptable plan. That was to be aboard the *Puritan Paramour* when it pulled anchor. If only she could think of someone. . . .

There was a light knock on the door before the motherly face of Edith Turney, the housekeeper, peered inside. "Excuse me, ladies. There's a Mr. Thaxton asking after Captain Innes. You wouldn't happen to know where—"

Kate's triumphant exclamation cut off the rest of the woman's question. "Ha!" She tossed a card toward the discard pile. It skidded across the table, face up. Kate was already slapping down her hand. The ten cards created a neat, single fan shape. "Ace, king, queen, jack, ten, nine, eight, seven, six, and five," she announced. "All clubs. I win."

Mrs. Turney smiled softly, amused at the expression on Winona's face. It wasn't often that the girl lost at cards. "About Mr. Thaxton . . ." Edith said.

Kate was already on her feet. "Oh, I'll see him," she offered. "It will take a few minutes for Wyn to recover from her loss anyway." Before her sister could stop her, Kate swept from the room.

Devin Thaxton stood within the curve of the bay window that graced the front parlor of the Paradise mansion. From this height, he had a panoramic view of the bay. It was a clear afternoon, the sky a paler shade of blue than the harbor waters. Thaxton could see the small island of Alcatraz and beyond it to the shores of Angel Island. But it was the

164

beauty of the San Francisco bay that drew him, its surface glittering like the facets of a diamond under a warm sun. The tall masts of docked ships rose like a defoliated forest and danced among the whitecaps. Here and there, the sky was tainted by the smoke that streamed from the stacks of steamships as they maneuvered to a mooring or chugged out to sea. But Thaxton preferred the beautiful grace of the sailing ships, their sheets unfurled to catch the wind, moving with the even measured tread of a lady across the choppy waters.

He had fallen in love with the clippers when he was only a boy back in Baltimore. Since then he had wanted nothing more than a permanent berth at sea. It had taken long years of pleading before his parents agreed to let him ship out. He'd been eighteen and ignorant of the caprices of a ship. But learning his new trade was so much more exciting than studying for the law as his father had wanted, that Devin absorbed each lesson with an unquenchable thirst. Within five years, he had achieved the status of first mate aboard the *Puritan Paramour* and settled into his real love affair with the sea. The power of command, even the limited sort that a first mate held, was a drug as addictive as opium, as thrilling as he found each breath of salt-tinged air.

During those years he had served under Captain Caleb Innes who had praised his work and had depended upon him to oversee the daily business aboard the clipper. The fact that Innes had absented himself from the ship without a word to the crew for a number of weeks proved that the captain felt his first officer was competent.

But Thaxton didn't want to be just another competent mate. He wanted to be master of his own vessel. He had expected to be promoted to captain status for the last year. The Puritan Shipping Line had commissioned the construction of a number of new vessels and as each neared completion, other mates, men with far less experience than Thaxton, had gained the higher rank and a command of their own. Thaxton had been patient, certain that opportunity would come his way. It wasn't just any ship he wanted. He wasn't interested in the newly christened clippers. It was command of the older, more gracefully designed ships that he craved.

In his wildest dreams, it was the *Puritan Vista*. But there was little chance of that fantasy ever coming true. Gernsheim, her first mate, would take over when Captain Marshall retired. Devin had thought his chances of gaining the *Puritan Paramour* much better.

In the last few years, Innes had become more involved with the merchants and sugar planters in the Sandwich Islands. He had purchased land on both Oahu and Kauai. Each move his captain made led Devin to believe he was preparing to resign from the sea. While it was true that Innes had often expressed relief at leaving the crowded ports of both San Francisco and Canton, settling in the islands would be far removed from city life. The tropical weather, combined with endless beaches and the constant sound of the surf, was a sailor's dream.

But not his. His dream went no further than command of the *Paramour* and Devin was willing to do anything to get her.

The dream had nearly vanished the day he'd gone to the Puritan office and heard Lacy Paradise calmly announce that the *Paramour* was no longer hers to command, that the clipper belonged to Captain Innes. Another man would have crumbled, would have gotten stinking drunk, cursed Innes and the whole Paradise clan. Another man would have ruined all his chances of future success. Thaxton had been desolate, but only for a short while. Anger had burned brightly within his soul. It had remolded his being, reshaped his thinking. Patience was no longer the route to his desires. Cunning had taken its place.

Thaxton turned away from the view to survey the room to which the housekeeper had guided him. It was richly furnished with ornately patterned upholstery and Oriental carpets. The distinctive tooling of the dark wood furniture was a repeated smooth curve that reminded Thaxton of curled waves. The same design had been carved into the upper molding of the walls. It was a room that shouted of wealth, yet it wasn't sterile. There was visible evidence that this room was the favorite meeting place of a robust family. Twin settees were arranged to enjoy the warmth of the wide fireplace. A pair of comfortable wing-back chairs were tucked into the embrasure of the wide bay window, a table perched between them with a temporarily discarded needlework frame tossed on its highly polished surface. Other hard-backed chairs were placed against the walls. A wooden boat lay beneath one, evidence that this was a household where young children played.

Not all the Paradise children were interested in toys, though.

Thaxton's attention went to the portrait that hung over the mantle. He had been drawn to it almost immediately and had reserved the pleasure of studying the painting for now, knowing that standing before it would give the impression that he was fascinated with the subject matter.

In a way, he was.

His feet planted as if he still stood on the deck of a ship, his hands clasped behind his back, Thaxton let his eyes move over the picture. The portrait was of three young women all dressed in gowns of green velvet. The styling of their dresses and coiffures denoted the differences in their ages. The youngest's hair was drawn back to fall in pale yellow ringlets down her back. Her dress was demure, cut high to her throat, and decorated with a trim of lace. The broad sash at her waist turned into a childish bow in the back. The middle girl was already a beauty, a vibrant mirror image of Lacy Paradise from her white-gold hair to her exotic eyes. Her gown conformed to her blossoming figure and had a swath of fabric draped modestly across her breast. A simple ribbon encircled her slim throat.

But it was the portrait of the third young woman that drew Thaxton's eye. He knew her immediately. Not just from the red glow in her soft-hued hair but from the thrill of excitement that ran up his spine just looking at her painted image. Unlike the gowns her sisters wore. Katherine's made no effort to hide the fact that she was no longer a girl. The neckline dipped toward an enticing display of flesh, skimming across the gentle fullness of her breasts and hanging just off her shoulders. The cut drew attention to the slimness of her waist and the curve of her hips. Her red-tinged hair was swept up in a simple arrangement, softened by wayward curls spilling loose at her brow and near her ear lobes. Her only adornment was a pair of diamond earrings that hung like glistening tear drops just above her collarbone. While the other girls looked at some distant spot, Katherine's lovely eyes seemed to gaze directly at him.

"The portrait was done four years ago," a soft voice said behind him. "My sisters, Winona and Amelia, are very like my mother, don't you think?"

Thaxton turned to face her, pleasantly surprised that this time Katherine Paradise was not displaying hostility at his presence. Her approach had been silent. Now she drew the sliding doors of the parlor closed and paused with curiously bright light in her eyes. A beam of sunlight from the bay window haloed her, turning the loosely flowing hair into a veil with copper threads entwined with gold. It was held back with a simple black ribbon but the girlish styling didn't lessen the allure of her woman's body. The severe cut of her ivory waist and dove-gray walking skirt played up the innate sensuality rather than disguised it. Yet it was difficult to believe this young woman was the daring songbird, until he looked into her deep green eyes and saw that other woman watching him.

"Your sisters are very like Mrs. Paradise," he agreed. "But I prefer your style, Miss Paradise."

Kate took a seat, her back to the light, and motioned for Thaxton to be seated on the settee opposite her. "Compliments, sir? You surprise me."

She was cool, so in control. He wanted to disturb that complacency, wanted to see the fire she had displayed at their first meeting, even if, like then, it denoted hatred. But first he wanted something from her.

"Surprise you, ma'am?" Thaxton said, his voice pitched to show amazement at her statement. "Not nearly as much as you surprised me the other evening."

Her eyes narrowed slightly. It was the only sign that he had disturbed her calm pose. "I'm afraid I don't understand," Kate said as if she were truly sad to be so obtuse. "But then, you told Mrs. Turney you were looking for Captain Innes, I believe."

She couldn't turn the subject that easily, though. Thaxton leaned forward, his forearms resting on his knees, determined to keep her off balance. "I lied. I was hoping to see you again, Miss Paradise."

Kate looked down at her hands, which were soft and graceful in her lap, enticingly pale against her dark skirts. He wondered what it would feel like to have them skimming over him in a gentle caress.

"More compliments, Mr. Thaxton?" Her voice alone was thrilling. "I don't think you really know me."

"I'd like to get to know you, Miss Paradise," Thaxton said. "Know you very well. I haven't been able to get you off my mind, not since I recognized you the other night at Hell's Kitchen."

He waited, wondering if she would tell him he had been mistaken.

"The Kitchen?" Her lips curved in amusement. It didn't lighten the suspicion in her eyes. They stayed as dark and unreadable as any sheltered lagoon. "Such a low gin mill, Mr. Thaxton. I'm surprised you patronized it," Kate said smoothly, her voice dropping to a more intimate level. Devin felt the tingle of anticipation ripple along his spine once more. "There are other more elite saloons where I'm sure you would be welcomed. My father's, for instance," she suggested.

Devin allowed himself a gentle smile to lure her into his trap. She hadn't denied being at Hell's Kitchen but she hadn't admitted it, either. He took the next move, letting his gaze drop to admire the thrust of her breast, the curve of her waist. "I enjoyed your singing. You have an unusually lovely voice."

His perusal didn't disturb her. She seemed to expect it. "Is that all you enjoyed, Mr. Thaxton?" Kate asked quietly. She sounded amused but he had seen the slight flare of anger in her eyes.

Devin leaned back against the cushions of the settee and crossed his legs like a man completely at ease. "The dress, Miss Paradise. You are quite . . . lovely, shall we say, in white."

171

"Lovely wouldn't be your first choice of words, though." It was a statement rather than a question.

"No." He watched her silently a moment, wondering if she fought to keep such tight control of her emotions. "No, lovely is merely a polite word," he said.

Kate got to her feet, moved over to a side table, and picked up a bibelot. Her head was bent, studying the trinket. "And what word would not be polite but much more apt?"

"Intoxicating. Or perhaps, erotic."

She laughed, the sound spilling like a cascade, bright and sparkling. "Erotic, Mr. Thaxton? How very amusing." Kate replaced the bibelot on the table and turned to face him. "Have you come to blackmail me then?"

Thaxton got to his feet and took two paces to her side. He loomed over her but there was no hint of fear or distrust in her dark eyes. "I have come, Miss Paradise, to ask you to drive out with me."

Chapter Ten

It felt good to be at sea once more. Caleb took a deep satisfied breath of the salty air as he stood on the quarterdeck, his feet braced, his body swaying naturally to the rise and fall of the ship. The day was clear, the winds favorable, and more important, the city was behind him.

The *Paramour*'s sails had filled quickly, taking the ship in a southwesterly direction, as if eager to reach the island of Oahu and the harbor at Honolulu. Due to the delay in their original sailing, there were only a few passengers—a married couple, a middle-aged spinster, her brother, and a shoe drummer. The cargo had undergone a slight alteration. Instead of goods for China, the hold had been pared down to domestic goods— cloth, tools, books—items that the Americans living in the Sandwich Islands craved. Little bits of home. Civilized items to diminish the beauty of the natural paradise they'd found.

Caleb cared little what his actual cargo was. Thaxton had taken care of it in his absence, seeing that it was stowed away properly, fretting over the manifest. Innes wouldn't have been surprised if the man had memorized every item down to the exact number of nails in a keg.

He was lucky to have such an efficient second-in-command. Thaxton had kept the men busy during the captain's absence, his only loss the cook's helper, a boy who had run off the day they had dropped anchor in San Francisco Bay. The first mate hadn't been able to find a replacement until just before they had sailed. Innes was surprised Thaxton had found the time even to ask around for a new cook's boy. He had probably had his hands full keeping the crew together and out of jail in the city.

But everything was fine now. They were underway, the sheets were full, the day was bright, and he had gained another month or more in which to come to terms with the future.

There was only the nagging knowledge of his cowardice in combat. The sea would work its magic, though, and diminish even that. It had been cowardly to send Kate a brief note rather than visit her as Lacy had urged. But despite the fact that he hadn't committed himself in words, Caleb felt he had a lifetime yet in which to converse with Kate. When he returned would be soon enough. For now, he had returned once more to his first mistress, the sea.

At his side, young David Paradise stood a bit unsteadily, his dark knee britches and sack coat a sized-down version of a Puritan officer's uniform. The lad hadn't shown the least sign of being stricken with seasickness. However, the same could not be said of the new cook's boy. Innes had only caught a glimpse of the newcomer, but he hadn't been reassured that the kitchen recruit would adapt to life at sea. He was tall and looked rather gangly, but that could be the result of his oversized clothing, Caleb thought. Perhaps being in the cook's hands would fatten him up, help him grow into the shapeless shirt, baggy trousers, and worn jacket. Other than the boy's clothing, though, Innes had no idea what his newest crew member looked like. The lad's face was nearly hidden behind thick wire-rimmed glasses and the knitted cap he wore low on his brow.

At the moment, the cook's helper was hanging over the side of the ship, the visible part of his complexion a distinct green.

By comparison, David's face was glowing with excitement. The wind had whipped his cheeks to a rosy red and tangled his mop of straw-blond hair. His blue eyes sparkled as if, like the sea, they harbored constantly moving swells that glinted where the sun touched each crest.

"This is better than I thought it would be," David confessed, his gaze moving quickly from the men checking the rigging to those busy at various chores on deck. He avoided looking at the gagging cook's boy, though, either from embarrassment or disgust. Innes wasn't sure which. When the boy had seen the new arrival, his face had been wiped clear of any emotion, his expression as stoic and watchful as a Chinaman—or a poker player.

Innes dropped a hand on David's shoulder. "I'm glad you feel that way, Davy. Let's hope you don't change your mind the first time we hit a storm or when we reach the doldrums and are becalmed."

"I'll still like it," the eleven-year-old assured him. "Grandpa Phalen said he thought I had sea water in my veins. He used to take me out to the ships when he visited." The boy's eyes saddened. "I was still pretty little the last time he was in Frisco, but I remember everything we did. I miss him."

Caleb knew exactly how David felt. Sean Phalen had been a substitute father to him, had guided his steps from the time Caleb had begged to be a cabin boy, until he'd been given his master's papers and the *Paramour*. He could still hear the old captain's voice, the chuckle that seemed to underlie every serious inflection. There had only been one time when Captain Phalen had not seemed amused during one of their interviews. That had been the day he had suggested Innes marry his daughter, Lacy, or remove himself from Boston to quiet the gossip that linked their names.

Innes turned his thoughts away from that particular memory. There tended to be a natural progression from the decision he'd made that day, to the one he had yet to make. But the future wasn't something he cared to dwell on now.

"Your grandfather was a wonderful man," Caleb said. "Quite a sailor, too. If he was right about your aptitude, it will still take one hell of a lot of work to make you a ship's captain."

"I'd like to be one, sir." David's attention moved from the ship to the miserable soul at the rail. "Where will Tom Caitlin, the cook's boy, be sleeping, Uncle Cal . . . I mean, Captain Innes?"

David's concern amused Caleb. But it was a good sign. A ship's officer had to care for his men. Since the cook's helper and David had both come aboard recently, it was only natural that some bond would form.

"The cook has his own quarters near the galley," Caleb explained. "But his scullion bunks in the fo'c'sle with the crew."

David continued to stare at the sick boy. "Could he stay with me?" he asked. "I mean, I know cabin boys don't usually have a cabin all to themselves. And won't the crew think it's a little strange that I do? It would look like I wasn't really one of them. Like . . . like . . ." He searched for the right word.

"As if you were being favored?" Innes suggested.

David brightened immediately. "Yeah! 'Cause I'm both a Phalen and a Paradise. 'Cause my mother runs the Puritan office."

Caleb appeared to give the idea serious thought. Usually the clipper carried two cabin boys. One of them, young Jason Quinn, had been left on the island of Kauai with a missionary couple on the *Paramour*'s last voyage. He had broken his ankle during shore leave and was under their care while he mended. Quinn had been more upset about losing his position aboard the *Paramour* than he had been about his injury, so to soothe the lad Innes had promised not to replace him. The other cabin boy had outgrown his duties and when the opportunity to be a third mate appeared, had moved aboard another Puritan ship.

It wasn't usual for a cabin boy, especially one like David who would most likely become the major stockholder of the Puritan Line, to share quarters with a lowly cook's boy. But since David was aboard only for this short cruise, Innes decided to make an exception. The two boys would have very little interaction, the duties of each taking them in different directions.

"All right," Caleb said. "But don't feel that you need to play nursemaid until he gets his sea legs."

David's head was full of new words, new visions. The phrases had dripped from Captain Innes's tongue, as sweet sounding to David as if they had been honey. Clew lines, hunt lines, reef tackles, leech lines, clew garnets, downhauls. It was a musical language. Like a litany he repeated the names of the sails, from the top of the mast nearly to the deck. The royal, upper topgallant, lower topgallant, upper top'sl, top'sl, lower top'sl, lower sheet.

As he opened the cabin door, he'd almost forgotten his request to share his bunk with the cook's boy and the huddled bundle of shapeless clothing laying in the tiny lower berth startled him at first. The pile groaned as the ship plowed into a particularly stiff swell.

"You're not going to be sick again, are you?" David demanded, far from considerate of the sufferer's feelings.

"No," the shapeless bundle said, its voice gruff.

"At least, I don't think so."

David closed the cabin door. The room was extremely small. The bunks were built fore and aft into the side of the starboard bulkhead, one upper, one lower. Neither appeared long enough to accommodate a man. Opposite the bunks was David's trunk and a worn carpetbag that belonged to the cook's boy.

David climbed into the upper bunk and sat with his feet dangling over the side. "Serves ya right," he said.

"A little compassion . . ."

"Ha!" David swung his feet back and forth. The miserable cook's boy caught at his ankles, stilling the movement.

David peered down into his roommate's pale, haggard face. "You're gonna get caught, Katie," he announced smugly.

"Caitlin," she growled. "I'm Tom Caitlin. The cook's helper." She gagged a bit on the word "cook," though.

"Cap'n's bound to notice ya if ya use big words. *Kate*–lin," David pointed out. "How'd ya manage ta get on board anyway?"

Kate curled her knees up and crossed her arms over her still-rolling stomach. "Thaxton," she murmured, her eyes closed. "He recognized me at Hell's Kitchen."

David whistled low. "Blackmail, huh?"

"Do we have to talk?" she moaned. "I feel . . . sick."

David swung off the bunk and moved to his trunk. He threw back the lid and rummaged in it a moment. Kate heard the distinct sound of something being broken, cracked in half. "Here.

179

Maybe this will help," he said, handing her his treasure.

Kate opened her eyes and struggled up on one elbow. "What is it?"

"Peppermint. Edith sent it along in case I felt seasick." He sounded very superior and cocky not to be struck down with the malaise.

"It won't help," Kate said, but took the piece of candy and sucked on it anyway.

David grinned. "I'll bet the cook's got a cure ya could try. Somethin' nasty tastin' made with sea weed and raw eggs and . . ."

Kate groaned again. "Please, Davy. I'm sick enough without your help."

He surveyed her silently, taking in the darned stocking cap that covered her hair and was pulled down to disguise half of her face. The wire-rimmed glasses slid down her nose, the ear pieces bent a bit out of alignment. Her pants and shirt looked like she'd raided Phael's closet, except their brother would never have worn such tatty articles. Her jacket was yet another size bigger, ensuring that there was no hint of a softer, womanly form beneath the rough clothing. The suit she'd had made for her excursions to Madam Lily's had been natty, a bit dandified. David had longed to have one just like it. But there was nothing about Kate's latest disguise that he cared to imitate. For once, he was quite happy with his knee-length trousers and fitted sack coat.

David sat on the floor and leaned back against his trunk. "If Mr. Thaxton is blackmailin' ya, how come you're playactin' again?" he asked.

Kate sucked on her piece of candy. The fresh

taste of the peppermint did make her feel a little better. A very little bit better.

"Well, he isn't blackmailing me really. I made a deal with him . . ."

David's expression showed just how disgusted he was with that news.

"I asked him to get me on board," Kate said.

"Why?"

"To be near Caleb."

"Why?"

"You wouldn't understand, Davy."

He chuckled. "That never stopped ya from tellin' me before, *Kate*–lin."

She relented. "I'm afraid he'll decide not to come back for me."

"Why won't he? Isn't he gonna marry ya?"

"That's just it, Davy. *I don't know*."

"So ya stowed away."

"I did not. I'm working my way . . ."

David cocked his head to one side, watching her. "I bet ya let Mr. Thaxton think that ya'd sleep with him if—"

"*David*," she hissed. "I did no such . . ."

But her brother obviously thought differently, and the idea disgusted him even more. "I ain't helpin' no more, Katie," he said.

"Just don't tell Caleb that . . ."

"You gotta tell him you're aboard." David was adamant.

Kate took a deep breath. "Okay. I will. But not yet. We've got to be farther away from San Francisco."

"Why?"

"So he won't turn the ship around and take me back, of course." She struggled to get out

181

of the bunk. "Just don't give me away, Davy."

When he didn't answer right away, Kate joined him on the floor. "Please, Davy."

He stared at her a moment before shrugging. "Okay. But only if ya promise you'll tell the cap'n soon."

"Soon enough," Kate temporized. At his intent look, she gripped his hand. "I promise."

"And tell him I didn't have nothin' ta do with gettin' ya aboard." David looked quite ferocious now. "I been in 'nuff trouble 'cause of you."

Kate nodded. When David scrambled to his feet, she held on to his hand a moment longer. The peppermint he'd given her had eased the misery in her stomach. It allowed her to think a bit more clearly and that only brought new problems to the surface. "Davy. How did you recognize me?"

He pulled his hand away and puffed out his chest proudly. "I'm not as dumb as Phael," he said. "I know my own sister."

"But if you knew me, then . . ."

"Naw. Grownups are stupid, *Kate*–lin. I'll bet ya could walk right by Uncle Caleb and he wouldn't see you." David grinned. "He'd only see Caitlin, and wonder if it was safe ta eat his stew, seein' as such a grubby galley boy had a hand in it."

Kate wasn't as sure. Now that her mind was functioning again, she had one last question before her younger brother left the cabin. "Davy." Still seated on the floor, she stared up at him. "What are you doing aboard the *Paramour*?" Her voice was suspicious of this latest surprising development.

David laughed. "Me? What else? I'm being punished!"

Dora Acton sat forward in the closed carriage and checked her appearance once more in the tiny hand mirror. It wouldn't do to have even one curl out of place during this interview, one which she had requested. She had chosen her gown carefully, intent on finding the exact color to play up her eyes yet not look indiscreet. She had checked every fold of the silk dress, making sure it enhanced her figure. The flounced hemline, draped apron and bustle were of a fashionable dark blue-and-green tartan. The same fabric was repeated in a ruff that framed her face. The tight-fitting jacket and straight-fronted skirt were a deeper shade of blue. She had worn no jewelry, feeling it would detract from the impression she wished to make. The only accent to her attire was the smart tilt to the *lamballe plateau chapeau* perched forward on her brow. Dora had been sparing with cosmetics as well, playing up her best features as she supposed the wealthy women who lived on Nob Hill did. She wanted to give the impression that she was a lady, not just an expensive whore.

There had been a number of options available when Lily Walsh's parlor house had closed so suddenly. The girls had each been paid off with a generous bonus to tide them over while they looked for employment elsewhere. With a nest egg to support her, Dora was in no hurry to settle beneath another madam's thumb, though. She wanted a protector, someone who would support her in style, either as a mistress or as a wife.

Dora's friend, Zoe, the pretty ash-blonde, had immediately purchased widow's weeds and a train ticket to Denver where she planned to look helpless whenever she was around single, wealthy men. With her life as a prostitute behind her, Zoe had every confidence that her period of fictitious mourning would be short. She had asked Dora to accompany her, but had looked relieved when the brunette had declined. Dora understood her friend's thinking. One widow had a much better chance of success; two widows would have been glaringly suspicious.

Dora had been tempted, though. The plan met her own ambitions very well, but it left out one very important element—spite.

Very little had been said when Lily's house had been closed, but Dora had kept her ear to the wall and discovered the circumstances behind Lily's sudden retirement. She had been surprised to find that Ben Paradise was the actual owner of the establishment. He had never been involved with the day-to-day business, and he certainly hadn't played the part of Lily's flash man. His visits had been short and always very public. Dora had never caught him sneaking back into the house for a midnight session with Lily. No, clandestine visits had been his daughter's prerogative.

Dora still found it hard to believe that Katherine Paradise had been the mysterious songbird. Why would a wealthy woman want to steal away to the Barbary Coast? Katherine Paradise had everything that Dora wanted—a beautiful home, a rich wardrobe, and no need to let grossly fat old men paw her just to keep her stomach filled.

Not that Dora had ever been very hungry. Her father ran a modest hostelry in Pittsburgh. Her mother cooked meals to be served in the attached dining room, and Dora and her sisters had been expected to keep the rooms spotless, the water basins filled, and the mattresses turned.

But Dora had found another use for the mattresses by the time she was sixteen, and had managed to keep her activities from her family for nearly a year before being discovered in bed with a ribbon drummer. Her mother had cried, and her father had lectured and taken a hickory stick to her backside. Her mousey sisters had smirked superiorly, as if they considered their lack of looks a blessing rather than a curse. Dora had stolen away, boarded the first train out of town, and worked her way toward the fortune she was sure awaited her in the West.

The money she had accumulated in her account at the bank was far from a true fortune, but it proved to Dora that she had taken the right step in leaving Pittsburgh and her family far behind.

The step she was about to take was a departure from her original dreams for the future, though. Zoe would have seen it as a step down if she had known about Dora's plan, but Dora saw this meeting as the first move toward her ultimate goal. Katherine Paradise's lark had cost Dora dearly. Lily's house with its wealthy and lonely patrons had been the perfect setting for an ambitious woman. It would have only been a matter of time, Dora was sure, before she would have lured one of the men into a marriage proposal.

But the songbird had ruined all that. Not only had she distracted the men Dora had stalked, but her escapade had resulted in Lily Walsh's house being closed. The monetary going-away present had been generous, but it didn't make up for all the lost time or for the opportunities that were now gone.

Dora thought briefly of the younger men as well. Particularly Phael Paradise. He hadn't even been clever enough to recognize his own sister but had casually shrugged Dora aside in favor of the mysterious songstress. Then Devin Thaxton had spent a pleasant afternoon with Dora but had shown more animation over information about the songbird.

The songbird. Dora was sick of hearing that name. It seemed to ring in her ears even now that Lily's was closed and Katherine Paradise had returned to her comfortable home among the wealthy families of Nob Hill.

She should leave San Francisco, Dora knew, but before she did there was a bit of business to be transacted. And the man she was about to meet was the key to gaining satisfaction for her injured ego. Once she had managed to slap Katherine Paradise's smug face, Dora could shake the dust of San Francisco from her skirts with pleasure.

Assured that her appearance reflected just the right balance between decorum and sensuality, Dora tucked her mirror back into her purse and stepped down from the hired carriage.

*   *   *

Ned Allen stood back from the hazard table, two paces behind Demas, the dark-featured sharp who ran the game. He watched the croupier's moves, but he also watched Barnabas Freel, a Barbary Coast ranger who continued to win steadily.

Bets had been placed on the stenciled layout and coins had been piled on particular numbers or on combinations. The three dice rattled as they tumbled inside the cage. The clatter was sweet music to Allen's ears. The thing that jarred him was the reduced take from this particular table.

The cage came to a rest, and the dice settled, showing a triple—three identical faces, each of four dots.

Allen's gaze swept the table, noting that only one man had wagered a good bit on the chance that the dice would hang together. It was a long chance, one that paid thirty to one, and had been paid too frequently at this table.

"Dang blast it!" another player grumbled. "If ya ain't the luckiest cuss!" The modest bet he'd placed on the pips showing an even total was lost. Although twelve dots peered through the bars of the dice cage, the fact that it was a triple, a raffle, wiped out what would have been his good fortune.

Freel, who had won with his outside bet, grinned widely and offered to stand the table a round of drinks. Two men, who were preparing to leave, changed their minds and stayed, pushing a coin or two back on the table.

The cage rolled again, the rattle sounding

loud despite the noise of the saloon. The men held their breaths, wondering if this time luck would smile on them. The dice settled. One, four . . . four.

The player who favored evens, slapped his hand down against the rim of the table in disgust. "Lordy! I cain't win fer losin'!"

Freel chuckled and scooped up his winnings. This time, instead of staking his coins on a triple, he'd moved to the next best paying bet, a single number—four. With twin fours showing in the cage, his bet had paid double. "All comes from livin' with the gypsies," he claimed. "Old woman tol' me ma lucky number was four, and danged if she warn't right!"

"Wal, them damned pips have been showin' four all night," the other player said. "Ya'd think they was a gettin' tired by now."

The men laughed but the players opposite the winner sobered first and eased away to other games.

"Damn curious bit o' luck, ain't it?" Ned Allen commented, coming up to the table. His hands on the cage, he rocked it back and forth, allowing the dice to slide. "In fact, I'm willin' ta bet I can spin 'em three separate times and a four will show on one or more die each time."

Freel bristled. "Listen, I ain't cheat'n, Bull," he growled. "Hell, how could I? It's yer spread, yer bird cage, yer bones."

"Sure," Allen said. "The gypsy told ya to plunge on four. I heard ya."

"Yeah. So ya can't expect me ta bet against a four showin' up, can ya?"

Two of Allen's henchmen moved up behind Freel. One Year Tim, an Irishman and combination master of ceremonies and head bouncer at Hell's Kitchen, stood behind the silent, sweating croupier, Demas.

Bull Run spun the cage. The three die tossed, then settled, and showed a five, a one, and a four. Allen barely waited for the display to be noted before he turned the cage again. This time two fours appeared.

Freel swallowed loudly.

Allen tossed the cage a final time. Before the dice settled, Demas tried to make a run for it. One of Allen's gunmen shot him down before the croupier had taken two steps.

Sweat was pouring from Freel. He stared at his former partner lying still on the saloon floor. The gunshot silenced the crowd for the space of two heartbeats. In that time, the cage had stopped turning for its third time to display three identical faces—fours.

Freel sank weakly against the table. "It warn't ma idea, Bull. Swear!" he whimpered. "Was Demas. All his . . ."

Allen jerked his head at the men behind Freel. "Get rid of him."

Freel wailed and tried to dodge free. The thugs just grinned and beat his flailing arms down. As they dragged him out of the saloon, Allen calmly opened the hazard cage and spilled the dice onto the table. At a word, the Irishman turned over his pistol to Ned, who brought the handle down sharply on each of the die, smashing them one by one. Among the splinters of ivory were tiny lumps of metal.

One Year Tim whistled softly. "They was loaded."

Allen brushed off the table and motioned to a man who waited apprehensively near the bar. "Take over, Hutton." He passed the empty cage to the new croupier and dipped a hand in his pocket for new die. "Don't try to run the same rig Demas did."

Hutton nodded, keeping his eyes from the body on the floor. At a signal from Tim, Demas's body was dragged out of the saloon. As if drawn, players returned to the table.

"How'd ya know Demas had monkeyed the bones?" the Irishman asked, following Allen from the room.

Bull Run laughed shortly. " 'Cause ma gypsy ain't partial to four as ma lucky number," he said. "And a little help from the blacksmith makes damn sure the house wins on my numbers."

The noise of the saloon was muffled in the upstairs room of Allen's office. A narrow window faced the alley in back so that noise from the street was reduced as well. As she sat in the uncomfortable chair, Dora Acton tried waiting patiently, her face and skirt both arranged to please the eye and give the impression that she was a woman who could not be manipulated. She'd been sitting there, her backbone straight and as stiff as the preacher's wife back home. But over an hour had gone by and Bull Run Allen hadn't come to see her yet.

Dora's nerves prickled. She got to her feet and moved to the window to look down on the alley. She saw two rough-looking men drag a third man out and proceed to beat him. Dora turned away quickly and took her seat again. It wasn't healthy to witness some events at Hell's Kitchen and Dance Hall.

There were other things she couldn't ignore. The walls were thin. She could hear the waiter girls come and go, could count their practiced moans, groans, and screams. Dora wondered just how much each sound was worth in gold, and how much the drabs she'd seen were able to keep for their performances. She doubted they made as much in a month as she had in a single night at Lily's.

But those days were gone, behind her. She was playing for higher stakes now. Not just for money, but for the satisfaction of getting revenge. Once exacted, she would be on her way out of San Francisco, following Zoe's example. Which city would she choose? Should she try New Orleans? New York? Or stay in the West? There were the more recent mineral strikes in Colorado to consider, and the newly rich, lonely men of Leadville made excellent prospects as spouses.

Down the hall, a woman was screaming. Dora tried to ignore the sound. It was cut off quickly. In the silence that followed, Dora was back on her feet, this time pacing the room.

Ned Allen heard the rustle of silk skirts when he paused outside the door. The woman's tread was soft, unlike the awkward stomping steps of his waiter girls. He rather liked the gentle sound. But he knew it was an act. The woman who waited for him had been one of Lily Walsh's girls. She had cultivated a bit more class than was necessary at Hell's Kitchen. But it wouldn't take much time to bring her down to the same level as the other women. Booze and a never-ending line of men waiting to toss her on her back would take care of Dora Acton's illusions of grandeur.

He remembered her from his visit to Lily's. A well-rounded brunette with big blue eyes and a dimpled chin. She was the kind of woman he usually sought out but this time it had been Dora who had requested the meeting.

Allen smiled to himself and opened the door.

Dora spun, startled by his sudden appearance, and one plump gloved hand flew to her breast. "Oh, Mr. Allen," she breathed, relaxing as he closed the door behind him. She gave him a simpering pout. "You were so long, I feared you had forgotten me."

"What man could forget ya, angel?" he said smoothly, and picked up a whiskey bottle from the sideboard. Without asking, he poured a shot in a glass and handed it to her. He tossed his own drink off quickly and refilled the tumbler, watching her from the corner of his eye. "Whadda ya want?"

Dora tasted her drink, wrinkled her nose at the sharp biting taste, and set it aside on the desk. "You go right to the point, don't you?"

"I'm a busy man." He crossed the room, and leaned back against the desk just in front of her. They were so close now, her skirts spilled over the toes of his boots.

Her head cocked to the side as if she considered the statement worthy of dispute. "I thought we could join forces," she murmured at last. "Now I'm not so sure."

Allen allowed a smile to curve his lips. "So ya wanna join my girls, do ya?"

Dora's form stiffened at the mere idea. "Absolutely not. I believed we had a common goal. But . . ."

"But what?" Allen set his glass aside and leaned forward. He cupped her face between his hands and slid his fingers along the ribbons that bound her hat in place. Slowly, he drew the bow loose and removed her hat.

Dora took a deep breath. Allen's gaze dropped to the way the tight-fitting bodice strained across her breast. She felt more at ease now, more in her element. She had been using her charms to get her way with men for four years. She'd been very successful in convincing them to give her everything she wanted. Allen would be no different.

"What do ya think we have in common, angel? You're a high-class whore."

"And you are a powerful man," Dora said. Her hand stole to the collar of her dress. She played with the top button, teasing him.

"So?"

One by one, the buttons of her bodice were loosened. "And I know we both want the same thing," Dora purred.

Allen's smile widened. He picked up his whiskey and took another sip. "And what might that be, angel?"

Dora plucked the pins from her hair, letting it tumble in rich dark waves around her shoulders. "The songbird," she said as her lashes dipped coyly. "I want to see her ruined."

Chapter Eleven

"Oh, bloody hell," the cook muttered, looking at his helper's soft, torn hands. "What did ya do 'fore the first mate took yer on, Caitlin? Pick pockets?"

Kate flinched as the plump, pasty-faced man poked at the freshly broken blisters in her palms. "No, sir. Ma uncle was trainin' me ta work in his bank."

The cook snorted. "Ya got too shifty a look fer a countin' house."

The spectacles slid down the bridge of her nose and Kate tried to pull her hands away so that she could push them back in place. But the cook's grip was inflexible.

She had been repulsed by Bledsoe when Thaxton had introduced her to him as Tom Caitlin, the new cook's boy, the day before. At the time she'd thought it had a lot to do with her queasy stomach and the greasy sheen of the cook's face. Now that she'd overcome the worst symptoms of seasickness, the man had put her to scrubbing every surface in sight and she had other reasons for disliking Bledsoe.

"I ain't a damn fingersmith," she snarled, struggling to free her wrist from his grip.

"Quit actin' like a ruddy fish and stand still." Bledsoe leaned forward, sneering into her face. "Ya ain't what ya say ya are."

Kate turned away from the blast of garlic on his breath but Bledsoe jerked on her arm, insisting that she face him.

"I seen ya watchin' what goes on, Caitlin," he sneered. "I seen the way ya been watchin' the captain in pertic'lar. Like ya was lyin' in wait fer yer chance to pick his pocket."

"I ain't," she said. "Let me go so's I kin ready them vegetables fer yer pot."

Bledsoe's bushy eyebrows drew together over his nose. "Even with them lilylike hands ya ain't no bleedin' clerk."

"Yer dreamin'," Kate insisted.

"Yer been warned. Don't know what ya did 'fore, but I ain't standin' fer trouble from no guttersnipe."

"I ain't . . ."

He dropped her wrist, flinging it away in distaste. "Hell, yer as soft as some woman."

Afraid Bledsoe would guess her secret, Kate shoved the spectacles back in place, blurring her sight of the cook's face. "Ya callin' me a damn catamite?" she bristled.

Bledsoe laughed nastily.

"I ain't one," Kate growled. " 'Fore comin' aboard I visited Hell's Kitchen itself."

Bledsoe only looked more amused. "An' got yerself a case o' the clap, huh? Calm down ya randy little bantam."

Kate continued to glare belligerently. "I won't have ya, 'er anybody else, thinkin' I—"

"Stow it, Caitlin. We got work ta do. Ya see that bucket o'er there? Shove yer hands in it."

Feeling she had defended her charade sufficiently, Kate pushed up her sleeves and bravely plunged her hands into the obnoxious-looking mixture. Almost immediately, she pulled them out, her eyes tearing with pain.

"Stick 'em back in!" Bledsoe bellowed. "An' keep 'em in there as long as I tell ya to."

Kate gritted her teeth and did as she was told. The torn flesh on her hands burned as if it were being licked by flames. It took all her will power to keep her hands submerged in the liquid. She wondered if this was the cook's way of punishing her for standing up to him. "What is this stuff?" Pain made her voice little better than a tight whisper.

"Salt brine." Bledsoe chuckled. "Best thing in the world fer tore-up hands. Dipped fresh off the pork, jest fer yer pleasure, ma fine young bandy rooster."

When she started to pull her burning hands free, Bledsoe shoved them back in the bucket. "Don't take on so. The saltpeter in there won't ruin ya fer the ladies. Jest souse fer a bit. Ya'll heal fast 'nuff ta be a help ta me then."

It felt as if the brine was eating her flesh away. Kate was convinced her hands would resemble raw meat. They had already been red and chapped from the strong lye soap Bledsoe had given her. The soapy water had stung but that pain was minimal compared to the touch of the salty preservative that oozed into the abrasions now.

Bledsoe was watching, waiting for her to cry out or pull back. Kate wouldn't give him the satisfaction. Stoic, she kept her hands submerged, her teeth clenched, her feet balanced against the sway of the deck.

"That's 'nuff," the cook announced at last. "Bind yer hands up with them rags over there and get started choppin' turnips."

Dinner was long past and Kate had come on deck to toss a bucket of scraps off the stern. She dawdled in returning to the hot galley, enjoying the sea air and rosy red colors of the sunset off the starboard bow.

David joined her at the rail. "Not pukey anymore, are ya?" he asked, a bit leery of her answer.

"Fine now," Kate mumbled. She still had twinges but the thought of Bledsoe's gloating face was enough to toughen her will and ignore the sensation.

David glanced up at the billowing sails and, as if two days at sea had given him the expertise to forecast the weather, nodded sagely. "It'll be a good day tomorrow," he said. "We should make excellent headway."

Kate set the empty bucket between her ankles and leaned on the rail. She stared out at the horizon. "Thought ya was still tryin' ta learn different kinds o' knots," she said gruffly. In the event that a crew member or one of the passengers overheard them, Kate was careful to keep her voice disguised whenever she met her brother outside of their cabin. Within it, she rarely spoke above a whisper, fearing the sound would carry beyond the bulkheads.

"I am studyin' knots," David announced. "Cap'n says my half hitch is almost perfect. Soon as I can get the sheet bend and a midshipman's hitch, I think he'll let me into the rigging." His eyes were still on the creaking yards above them. The *Paramour* sported three masts and was running with every sail unfurled, taking advantage of the favorable wind. The clipper plowed into the crest of each swell eagerly with an enthusiasm that belied her age.

Their grandfather had enjoyed bragging about how he'd had the ship built to his specifications in 1847. He never tied of retelling David how she'd put to sea in the summer of '48 and rounded the Horn en route to harbors in both Canton and Hong Kong. Since then the *Paramour* had sailed around the world in search of new markets, new trade products. She'd withstood both rough seas and time. David knew that the steamers could do the run to China in less time but they were dependent on bases for re-coaling. While the Puritan Line had ordered a number of the steamships, it was the reliable clippers of earlier years rather than the new steamers that remained the mainstay of the fleet.

Kate also thought about the *Puritan Paramour* and, despite the ship's age, she was still a spritely lady. Kate closed her eyes and listened to the now familiar creak of the ship. When it was docked, she had been aboard the *Paramour* frequently, scrambling up the rope ladder nearly from the time she could walk. The vessel was nearly as familiar as home, and she wanted it to be *her* home.

Did Caleb realize that? she wondered. Did he know she had no intention of staying behind whenever he sailed? That she wanted to be at his side at all times?

The *Paramour* had been under his command for over twenty years now. He had walked these decks, watched these sails. He knew the clipper's every sound from the soft sighs of the sails to the groans of the masts and the creaks of the deck.

The sounds had become music to Kate's ears already. Every night she lay in her bunk and listened to the ship. It whispered, telling her secrets she needed to know to win Caleb's heart. But Kate didn't know the language, didn't understand what the *Paramour* murmured. At times she wondered if the vessel was laughing at her. It had been Caleb's mistress for so long, that surely even the thought of his now preferring a flesh-and-blood woman was ridiculous. The *Paramour* already knew how to play the coquette, already knew how to manipulate the captain to get her way.

The prow dipped into a particularly stiff swell and spit back a playful spray of sea water. Kate jerked back involuntarily, feeling as if the clipper had doused her on purpose in an effort to dampen her dreams.

The movement brought Kate's hands up to ward off the mist. The rags that bound her palms looked like fingerless gloves in the dim light.

"Geez," David said, his eyes wide. "What did ya do to yer hands?"

Kate pulled away, trying to hide the makeshift bandages. "Nothin'," she growled. "I been doin' work I ain't used ta, that's all."

"Let me see 'em." David insisted.

Kate turned from him, retrieved the bucket at her feet, and moved back toward the galley. "Leave me be. I ain't gotta listen ta ya, too. Jes' that Bledsoe."

But David had no intention of letting his sister shrug him off that easily. He dogged her steps until Kate reluctantly returned to their tiny cabin and unwrapped the bandages. He took one look at the inflamed blisters and reddened skin and left the cabin.

Kate didn't blame David for running. The destruction of her once lovely hands brought tears to her eyes that had nothing to do with pain.

Devin Thaxton lay on his bunk, his eyes closed. He hadn't slept for two days now and he was dead tired. His body cried out for rest, but his mind wouldn't cooperate. It raced with thoughts of the future, with dreams that, for once, had a chance of being realized.

He'd volunteered for the late-night watch, manning the wheel during the blackest hours. The distractions of daily chores were missing then and a man's mind could drift at his leisure. There was just the feel of the wheel beneath his hands, the sound of the wind in the rigging, the scent of the sea surrounding him. During those hours, the *Paramour* was his. Not a Puritan ship, not Innes's ship. His. She responded differently, quivering beneath his touch like the woman she was. Like a lover. Thaxton felt those hours flew by all too fast, disappearing as he reluctantly faced the dawn. The night held the best hours of the day, the dark hours for his darkest thoughts.

It wasn't just the *Paramour* that filled his mind now. It was the way fate had supplied him with the means to win all that he craved. Thaxton was still amazed at how easily it had all been.

He had planned to woo Katherine Paradise, to make her fall in love with him and thus secure him a captain's post. Ordinary methods would not suffice, though. She would have laughed if he had quoted poetry, had brought her flowers. No, he had been sure that intrigue was what would win her. A woman who masqueraded as a songstress on the Barbary Coast obviously had found her daily round tedious, her other suitors boring. So Thaxton had teased her with his knowledge of her secret life. If it had come to blackmail to get his way, so be it. But he had doubted it would be needed.

She had surprised him with her eagerness to join him for a ride the afternoon before the *Paramour* had sailed. But subsequent events had blurred that early amazement.

Kate. He thought of her by her nickname now. It fit her far better than the more formal Katherine. A woman called Katherine would lack the fire that burned in Kate. She would never have consented to a drive, would never have sung at a parlor house or at Hell's Kitchen.

But Kate . . . ah, Kate.

In his mind's eye, Devin could picture her as she had looked that day in the buggy. The breeze had tossed her glorious red-gold hair letting long strands of it curl against his arm as they sat side by side. She had donned a form-fitting, gored paletot that matched her gray skirt. A simple boater had tipped forward at a jaunty angle over her brow. He had enjoyed another view of her delicate ankles and shapely calves while helping her into the buggy and had felt the slimness of her waist upon assisting her down when they reached Point Lobos.

It had been at Kate's direction that they had driven to the cliffs that faced the Pacific Ocean. The winds were brisker on that side of the city but the view was unhampered by the sight of land in the distance. After so many weeks in the harbor, Thaxton had felt like a man newly released from bondage.

Kate had breathed in the ocean's scent, her eyes closed. "It's beautiful here," she had said, huskily. "Thank you for acceding to my wishes and driving the distance."

He would have gone wherever she wished. Not just because she was the key to his future, but because she was a beautiful and vibrant woman.

"My pleasure," Thaxton said.

She turned from the view, placing her graceful hand on his arm as they strolled along the cliff. "You love the sea, don't you."

It hadn't been a question. Thaxton let his own fingers cover hers, felt the faint flutter of indecision before she relaxed. "I am enamored of the sea," he said. "Each ocean is as lovely and unpredictable as a woman. What man wouldn't be enchanted?"

Kate looked ahead rather than at him. "And you find me unpredictable, Mr. Thaxton?"

He laughed. "Very. But that intrigues me, ma'am."

"Because I was the songbird?"

"Perhaps."

A particularly strong gust tore at her hat, whipping her hair in a tangle across her pert nose and kissable lips. Kate made a grab at her boater before it blew off. She brushed locks of hair from her face. "Oh, but, Mr. Thaxton," she insisted with an alluring grin, "I'm nothing like the songbird. Believe me, she no longer exists."

He wasn't listening to her any longer. His gaze was on her lips, on the pesky strand of hair that clung determinedly to the corner of her smiling mouth. Gently, he brushed it away, then cupped her face between his hands in an intimate caress.

Kate pulled away, took two skipping, flirtatious steps away from him, swinging her hat in her hand. "Have you seen the seals?" she asked brightly. "Or Cliff House?"

Thaxton followed, content to wait patiently. "That Gothic monstrosity?" he asked of the popular resort.

"You prefer a different style of architecture?"

"I prefer ships to houses."

She had moved to the edge of the cliff once more, standing close to the sheer drop. "So do I," Kate said, her voice a sigh that barely carried over the sound of the wind. "Amazing, isn't it? The only time I've ever been aboard a ship has been while it was anchored in the shelter of the harbor. Yet I love them. Especially the *Paramour*."

Devin stood close to her, his arm nearly brushing hers. Below them, rocks jutted from the shallows. There were no seals in evidence today. Only the constant roar of the surf and the cry of gulls as they soared on the wind currents. The roof of Cliff House was a blemish on the scene as far as Thaxton was concerned. The building jutted out over the shoreline, braced on the side of the slope. There were few visitors at the moment to enjoy its luxurious furnishings and elegant meals. No ladies in swirling ball gowns to bound to the exuberant sound of a polka or sway to a languid waltz in the ballroom.

He preferred the music of a hornpipe, the graceful flap of the sails, the rhythm of the sea.

The young woman at his side wasn't looking at the impressive construction of Cliff House, either. Her gaze was turned west to the distant horizon. "I was born aboard the *Paramour*," she said. "One day I'd like to sail away on her."

"You have but to book passage to accomplish that," he said.

"To where? China?" She smiled gently. "What reason could I give for going there? No, my family would never countenance such a voyage. They would prefer to send me East, to Boston perhaps."

She sighed and held out her hand to him. "We should be getting back."

Thaxton clasped her fingers in his. She hadn't worn gloves and he reveled in the soft touch of her skin in his hardened hand.

"If I commanded a ship, I'd take you to Boston. To Canton. To the gates of Siam if that is where you wished to go."

Kate grinned at him. "How very gallant, Mr. Thaxton. But you won't be surprised, I'm sure, if I tell you I don't believe a word you say. It sounds far too romantic."

"You make me feel both gallant and romantic, Miss Paradise."

A gust of wind caught at her skirts and tossed her already tangled hair once more. The black ribbon came undone and sailed off, cavorting on a particularly strong updraft. Kate made a grab for it. She was an enchanting, disheveled sea witch. She was the songbird. She was the brass ring for which he had waited.

Thaxton swept her close and stared down into her mysterious lagoon eyes. She didn't struggle within his arms but stood quietly, her hair swirling around them. "Mr. Thaxton," Kate murmured, her voice pitched to an intimate almost husky level, "would you help me get on board the *Paramour* tonight?"

That had been two days ago and Thaxton hadn't been able to sleep remembering how she had felt in his arms.

With his hands behind his head, he stared at the ceiling. She was only two cabins away but he barely recognized the enchanting minx who had evaded his attempts to kiss her when they'd stood on the cliffs at Point Lobos. He still was unsure of how she had maneuvered him into agreeing to smuggle her aboard as the cook's boy.

Kate had arranged to meet him at the wharf late that night. Fool that he was, he'd been too bewitched to refuse her anything. He had returned with her to the mansion and spent a few moments conversing with Lacy Paradise before taking his leave. Kate's mother had looked puzzled when she had seen him. Her expression had deepened when Kate had blithely announced she looked forward to renewing her new friendship with him when the *Paramour* returned. Perhaps Mrs. Paradise was merely trying to anticipate her daughter's next flirtation with scandal. Thaxton was sure that the songbird's sudden retirement from the stage was due to the discovery of her adventure by her parents.

He had left the mansion and headed for a dark corner in The Albatross, a dim bar on Columbus Avenue, and a bottle of rum.

She wouldn't appear, he'd told himself. It was too outrageous a stunt even for the woman who had saucily tread the stage at Hell's Kitchen.

But Kate had been at the wharf that night, her lovely womanly curves lost in baggy secondhand clothing, her beautiful eyes hidden behind the bottle-thick lenses of a pair of spectacles.

She had actually swaggered up to him, given a sloppy salute, and introduced herself as Tom Caitlin. *Kate*–lin, for God's sake! There was no end to the woman's daring, which, of course, made it impossible for him to stop thinking of her or to sleep.

The rapid pounding on his door jarred Thaxton from his mental stupor. Before he could call out an answer, young David Paradise burst into the cabin.

"Pardon, sir," the boy mumbled, conscious of his hasty action before a ship's officer. There was no apology in his blue eyes, though, which were as cold as ice. "Would you have some salve for sore hands, Mr. Thaxton?"

Thaxton swung out of his berth. "Rope burns?" he asked. "You have to be more careful while practicing knots."

David stood just inside the door, his fists clenched, his jaw set in stern lines. "It's not for me, sir."

Thaxton turned from the medical chest, holding a jar of cream. "Then . . ."

The boy's brows were knit in a distinct scowl. "It's for *Kate*–lin, sir. The cook's *boy*. Bledsoe used brine on them."

Thaxton slowly straightened. He had wondered if the new cabin boy would recognize his roommate. The lad's emphasis on his sister's name was proof that her charade had been penetrated. "It is the usual procedure," he said carefully. "A seaman's hands have to be hard."

"But these aren't a seaman's hands, sir," David hissed, his voice as dangerous as it was possible for an eleven-year-old's to sound. "You know that. They are my sister's."

Thaxton was quiet a moment, his mind still lingering on the way Kate's touch had affected him such a short time ago. Her hands had been so graceful, so soft, and that bastard Bledsoe had plunged them into salt brine. Good Lord!

Thaxton had just disappeared through the door of the boys' cabin when Caleb Innes left his own quarters. David froze in the companionway, looking uncomfortable and suspiciously guilty, the captain thought.

"Is there a problem, Davy?" Innes asked.

The boy looked down at his shoes, then abruptly stood straighter, and stared up at the captain. "Yes and no, sir. It's just the cook's boy. He's never done work like this and his hands got torn up."

"It happens," Innes pointed out. "You've been working on your own set of blisters."

David's shoulders squared even more. "This is different, sir. You see, *Tom's* hands got really tore up bad and the cook made him hold 'em in brine and . . . well, sir, I don't think he can work tomorrow."

Caleb frowned. Bledsoe was a sadistic devil. The cook hadn't been a member of the crew for long but they'd already lost three cook's boys because of the man's abuse.

Innes looked thoughtfully at the furious child who blocked his way. David would hate to be compared to his mother, but Caleb recalled a very young Lacy Phalen standing in much the same stance, her dark green eyes blazing. David's look had a touch of reckless danger in it, his anger reflected in a controlled icy glare reminiscent of his father. The arctic blue of his eyes gave the boy's look a sharp edge.

"You're fond of Tom, aren't you, Davy?" Innes said.

The boy's chin raised a fraction. Lord, so like Lacy. So like his sister, Kate.

"Yes, sir. I don't think the cook is treating *Tom* right."

The slight emphasis David put on the other boy's name was puzzling.

Innes nodded and clapped a hand on the bristling child's shoulder. David was tall for his age and sturdy. His personality was quite different from that of his older brother, Phael. As Lacy had said, Phael was feckless and lacked ambition. But David would be a very different type of man, one of whom Caleb knew he'd be proud.

"Would you like me to talk to Bledsoe?" Innes asked.

David's face lit with hope. "Would you, Uncle Cal?"

It was the first time since they'd pulled anchor that the boy hadn't caught the slip and corrected his form of address.

"Certainly. Should I view the damage to Tom's hands first?"

Beneath his palm, Innes felt the boy stiffen again. "No, sir. Mr. Thaxton had some salve. I'm sure *Tom* will be fine now, Cap'n."

"Good. Now you get some sleep. I'll be checking your progress on those knots in the morning." Innes patted David's shoulder, urging him back toward the cabin he shared with the injured Tom Caitlin.

Caleb climbed to the quarterdeck and took the wheel from Raush, the man on watch. "Tell Bledsoe I want to see him," he ordered, his voice deceptively calm.

Raush grunted. "Thought cook only served the crew them nasty-tasting meals," he said. " 'Spect the passengers 'er used ta better, Cap'n."

All the better, Innes thought, as the seaman

moved off toward the cook's quarters. Bledsoe would think it was merely a complaint about the food that was the reason for this interview.

The cook took his time answering the summons. When he appeared, his step was uneven. He heaved himself up the ladder and staggered to a halt before the wheel.

Innes looked past him at the way the sails responded to the slight adjustment he'd made to the course. He was tacking, taking advantage of the change in winds and the current. There was no such thing as sailing directly to any port anymore than it was possible to travel as the crow flew on land. Rather than mountains, rivers, and other natural obstructions, at sea it was the ever-changing winds, the suddenness of storms, or the lack of a breeze, as much as the currents, that dictated a ship's route.

"I see you've been drinking again, Bledsoe," Innes said.

"Just a taste, sir, to wash away the dryness in me throat. Cookin's a thirsty business, Cap'n."

"Is that what you do aboard my ship, Bledsoe? You cook?"

The man blinked. " 'Course I do."

Innes turned the wheel slightly. "There are others who would argue with you on that head."

"Don't like ma cookin', do they?"

"No one likes your efforts, Bledsoe. But it isn't just your cooking I find offensive."

The cook's face twisted in an unpleasant grimace. Innes recognized it as the man's innocuous smile. "I don't un'erstand. I stay in ma galley and don't have no truck with the others, Cap'n."

"Except for your helper," Innes said, his voice still deceptively soft.

Bledsoe's smile turned into a scowl. "He been whinin' ta ya 'bout his work?"

Innes signaled to Raush to take the wheel again. "Keep her on this course awhile longer," he instructed before turning back to the cook.

"How many helpers have you had aboard the *Paramour,* Bledsoe?"

The question appeared to take the man by surprise. "Couple."

"This is the fourth boy you've abused, Bledsoe. Four different lads have done your bidding and three of them have jumped ship the first chance they got. Why do you suppose they left?"

Innes's tone carried more steel in it now. He towered over the pasty-faced cook but Bledsoe stood his ground. "Ungrateful, that's what I'd call 'em," he said of his former helpers.

"Ungrateful? Try scared stiff, Bledsoe!" Innes thundered as he grabbed the cook by the front of his shirt and hauled him close. "I'm warning you. One more of your sadistic little games and I'll make an example of you to the crew."

When the captain released him, Bledsoe's rum-soaked breath came out in a whoosh. "The cat?" His voice quavered.

"Familiar with its lash, Bledsoe?" Innes purred, his voice dangerously soft again. The cat-o-nine-tails wasn't used often aboard the *Puritan Paramour.* It had proven to be an effective means of punishment, though. Perhaps because it was used so frequently on other ships, it was a familiar and accepted penalty for disobedience at sea.

"At the moment, a whipping seems tame, Bledsoe. Keel hauling has a damn better ring," Caleb said. "This is the only warning you'll get. Sober up. You'll have no help tomorrow. I'm told that Caitlin's hands are quite useless to any of us right now."

As the cook ambled away, his step listing worse than the deck, Innes caught the tail end of a muttered curse. Caleb leaned on the rail, looking out at the peaceful sea. The moon was just rising, spreading a milky sheen over the surface. Damn it all! As shorthanded as they were already, when the ship dropped anchor in Honolulu, Bledsoe was out of a job. And if Innes had his way, the cook would be blackballed from gaining a berth with any other ship. Enough cook's boys had suffered already.

Chapter Twelve

Unknown to Captain Innes, the cook's boy insisted on resuming his post in the galley the next day. Bledsoe was careful to give Tom Caitlin a wide berth and the simplest of tasks. It was well he did so since the first mate stopped by the galley often throughout the day, twice to examine Caitlin's hands and smear cream over them before rewrapping the bandages.

Bledsoe was disgusted at the tender care Caitlin received. He had been aboard many ships and had administered the same treatment to green boys and shanghaied men alike who had ripped their uncalloused hands on the ropes. He'd seen far worse cases than Caitlin's broken blisters and chapped fingers. The rigging could strip layers of skin away. A bit of brine-soaking had made real men of swabbies.

The cook watched Caitlin with disgust. The boy hadn't complained to him, but he sure had whined to someone. For a scruffy water rat who couldn't see beyond his nose without those damn spectacles, who was still so soft he couldn't stomach a bit of pain, Caitlin was being treated like a bloody rajah. But the captain had threatened Bledsoe with the cat. Him! A man who'd shipped with the *Paramour* for near half a year now. There was something strange about Tom Caitlin, the cook decided. Thaxton was putting in as many appearances in the galley as a smitten swain and the new cabin boy fluttered around like a damn gull.

Bledsoe left his helper weeping over a bowl of onions. As he looked at the boy, he saw there wasn't a hint of fuzz on Caitlin's face, no meat on his bones. With tears running from his eyes, dampening down those damn long lashes, the boy was as pretty as a simpering miss.

Bledsoe stomped from the galley into his narrow quarters and fished out the bottle of rum, his private stock. He'd smuggled numerous bottles aboard during the long weeks the clipper had sat in the harbor. A quick snort or two and he didn't mind the sickening attention Tom Caitlin was getting.

Hell, despite the boy's mealymouthed boasts of his visits to the whores, he was probably as eager to perform for a randy sea ranger with a gold coin as was any dockside doxie.

The squall appeared out of nowhere when they'd been at sea a week. The mid-morning watch had just sounded three bells when the call came.

Kate had been in the galley long before dawn, up with the men on the early dogwatch. Bledsoe wanted the coffee going by four-thirty in the morning and rather than bestir himself, had turned over betimes duties to his helper. Kate had come to savor the time alone in the galley. It wasn't stifling yet from the heat of the cook stove, and without Bledsoe glaring at her, the chores were finished quickly. She had the stove fired, the coffee done, and breakfast started before the cook ever made an appearance, breathing rum fumes as he roared at her.

Considering she'd never spent much time in the kitchen at home, Kate felt she'd made excellent progress in her abilities to cook a meal. While he supplied simple, but elegant, meals for the captain and passengers, Bledsoe kept the crew's fare to watery stews and hard biscuits, neither of which had much flavor. Whenever the men complained, Kate kept a weather eye out for signs of a storm in Bledsoe's face. She had learned to dodge blows rather well in the last week.

Her hands had healed but they were far from the graceful hands of a lady. She had cut her nails to short stubby lengths for her masquerade as Tom Caitlin but now they were broken and jagged. Her fingers were rough to the touch and on occasion still hurt but pride kept Kate working without complaint.

By mid-morning Bledsoe had retired to his quarters to cradle his rum bottle, which gave Kate a break. All too soon the cook would return to preside over the preparations for the next meal. When the call rang out for all hands, she was surprised to see Bledsoe stumble out on deck. Without a word to anyone, he went to the lines and waited for the order to drag on them.

Kate stood in the galley hatchway torn with indecision. Was the cook's boy expected to be on deck or in the sheets? And for what precise duty? Off the port side, dark clouds were rolling toward them. The seas were building, rocking the *Paramour* so that the deck tilted to an alarming degree.

The passengers had retired to their cabins at the first sign of rough weather. David had described them briefly to her—the plump middle-aged Orloffs, the thin-faced Erbes, who were brother and sister, and the sanguine Mr. Yarbrough. The only one David liked was Yarbrough, the shoe drummer who made snide comments when Miss Erbe tried to flirt. Not that Mr. Yarbrough received the sly glances. The spinster was interested in Captain Innes.

What woman wouldn't find Caleb attractive? He was a paragon, his black hair alive with blue lights, his soft brown eyes warm with laughter. He was straight and slim as a mast and, when he smiled, the intriguing scar at the corner of his eye gave him a rakish appearance no woman could resist.

All the same, Kate had taken a dislike to Miss Erbe. Her first glimpse of the older woman should have squelched her jealousy. But since the woman had been clinging to Caleb's arm

and batting her meager lashes, Kate's hatred
only burned brighter.

She rarely saw the captain, so Kate took advantage of every chance she had to be on deck when
he held the watch.

Now, up on the quarterdeck, Caleb stood at
the wheel, his stance seemingly immovable, his
hands steady. His eyes were on the sky, on
the sails as they snapped and shook. David
stood poised near the captain, his whole being
radiating an eagerness to follow the men aloft.
Thaxton was stationed on the main deck, strad-
dling the open-weave design of the main cargo
hatch cover. As Innes shouted an order, Thaxton
relayed it to the men, his voice carrying over the
rising shrill of the wind.

Ponderously, the ship turned, putting her
stern to the storm. On all three masts, the
sails blossomed out again, filling with the wind.
The *Paramour* plunged ahead, plowing her nose
into the rising swells. A moment later the sheets
slackened again and the ship bucked as a wave
struck broadside.

Kate lurched against the galley hatchway,
bruising her shoulder. Out on deck, Thaxton
staggered and swore. The wind tore the sound
of his voice away, pushing it into the storm.

Thaxton glanced back toward the wheel, then
shouted another order to the men above him.
They scrambled out along the yards. Lines were
drawn up quickly, pulling the sails one by one
into neatly reefed bundles.

While the men worked, the seas climbed higher, the winds became sharper. The clouds rolled
ever closer, grew denser, and emptied, lashing

the *Paramour* with a biting, cold rain.

"Caitlin!" Thaxton's voice was as loud as a crack of thunder.

Kate jerked her attention away from the swaying masts, from the agile men who inched out to the far end of the rain-slicked yards to fight the wind for control of a sail.

"Sir!" she answered, looking to where Thaxton stood. Despite his rain slicker, within moments Devin was dripping wet, his cap gone in the wind, his blond hair plastered to his skull.

"Bank the stove. Every coal drenched, mind you. We don't want to chance a fire."

She had turned to do his bidding when the next wave struck. The force threw Kate off her feet and she slid across the narrow room, striking sharply against the bulkhead. The fall knocked the wind from her temporarily, and her glasses had fallen off. As the deck tilted in a new direction, they slid along the bulkhead just out of reach. Kate scrambled after them and scooped them up before they smashed into the sturdy cabinet where the crockery was stored. Without the spectacles obscuring a good part of her face, Kate was sure her masquerade would be uncovered. With her latest mask in place once more, she hurried to bank the coals that still glowed in the iron stove.

David arrived just as she finished. Water streamed from his clothing. He smiled at her in an attempt to appear excited but his eyes reflected fear. He jumped as a bolt of lightning split the sky to be followed by a deep roll of thunder.

"Cap'n sent me. Said since neither of us is an experienced sailor, we were to stay here," David announced.

It was the best news Kate had heard in a long time. Since Caleb had no idea that the cook's boy was a female in disguise, she'd feared hearing an order to join the men out in the storm. Thaxton, of course, knew her real identity, but she doubted that he could make an exception to an order if the captain insisted.

Kate motioned for David to join her on the floor. They sat wedged into a corner, their feet braced against the tipping deck, their shoulders pressed close together.

"What's happening out there?" she demanded. "Are we riding the storm out?"

David shivered in his wet clothes. "Tried to outrun it but the winds kept changing." His teeth chattered.

Kate longed to put her arms around him, to comfort her little brother. He was only eleven years old. She didn't blame him for being scared. She was afraid of the storm herself.

But the cook's boy couldn't offer solace to a son of the Puritan Line so she gave him a bracing smile instead.

"We'll be okay. You think the captain, Mr. Thaxton, and the crew are as green as we are?" she asked.

"No," he murmured. "But I don't feel so good, Katie." David shook with cold and his lips looked a bit blue.

"You need some dry clothes. That's all," she said bracingly.

He nodded miserably. "And a blanket."

219

The deck tipped sharply again. Outside, the curses of the men rose over the scream of the wind. It would be quite awhile until it was safe to fire the stove once more and warm the galley. There was no telling how long the storm would rage. If David wasn't warm soon, Kate feared he'd become very ill. She stared into his face, then brushed back the damp locks of his hair.

"Stay here," she ordered, and crawled across the galley to the cabinet where she knew Bledsoe had stowed one of his rum bottles. With it and a tin cup in her hand, Kate scuttled back to David's side. Moving now with the tilt of the ship, Kate poured a small portion of rum into the cup and pushed it into her brother's hands. "Sip this."

David blinked at her. "It's rum," he said. "You know Mama won't . . ."

Kate brushed the objection aside. "You're a sailor now, Davy. Drinking rum is part of the job."

When he hesitated, Kate pushed the cup to his lips. "It'll warm you up, brat."

David sputtered as the first tentative sip burned his throat but Kate was adamant that he finish it. With her finger at the bottom of the cup, she tilted the rest down his throat. She hadn't poured much more than a couple tablespoons of rum out for him. Not only had she worried about how David's system would take to the alcohol, she was also afraid Bledsoe would notice if a full shot was missing.

"I do feel a bit warmer," David said, gasping a bit for breath.

"Good. You stay here," Kate instructed, sticking the rum bottle back into hiding.

"Where ya goin'? Uncle Caleb said to stay here." Still shivering, David wrapped his arms tight across his chest.

"I'll be right back," Kate promised, and got to her feet. The deck tipped drastically again, but she was ready for the lurch this time as she braced her shoulder against the molding around the hatchway.

"Katie!" David's voice was no longer brave as it rose in terror.

She peered at him over the top of her glasses and winked at him. "Relax, Davy. I'm just going to get you that blanket. I'll be right back."

Kate left before he could argue.

It was a devil's storm. Neptune was throwing the full fury of his forces at them once more.

Caleb stood at the wheel, fighting to keep the *Paramour* afloat. In spite of the rain slicker he wore, Innes was drenched but he barely noticed the discomfort. His whole attention was on the battle he fought with the sea, one he'd fought numerous times and had always won. He would this time as well. He knew the clipper, every inch of her, knew what she could handle, knew how to handle her.

It was a personal battle now between him and Neptune. The sea king wanted the *Paramour* for his collection of dead ships, wanted to show his power in besting the puny beings who sailed his domain.

The ship bucked, the wheel jerked, as yet another wave crashed over the rail, swamping the deck. The last of the sails was being furled and most of the men were out of the rigging and below deck, no longer swaying out over the boiling ocean. Storms had a way of making the masts look like poles and the men nothing more than fish bait. Only two men remained topside, still struggling against the wind in the shrouds.

Thaxton stood on the quarterdeck as well, his face turned up as he watched the men in the rigging. Rain rolled off his oilskin poncho and dripped off the end of his nose.

"Where in hell did this storm blow from?" Thaxton shouted. "An hour ago there wasn't a sign of it."

"Look on the bright side," Innes thundered back, trying to be heard over the storm and grinning widely. There was something in the savage weather that brought forth an answering wildness in his soul. "If we're lucky, it'll push us clear through the doldrums."

The storm stirred something within Thaxton as well. He felt the excitement, the challenge in this continuing war they waged with Neptune. His face cracked in a smile and he laughed. "Never! We'll still be manning the pumps a month from now if this keeps up!"

As if the mate's comment had summoned a fresh deluge, a new mass of water rushed at them from starboard and crashed down on the deck. The *Paramour* staggered and wallowed in the trough between the swells, then bobbed back up. High on the mast, the nearly reefed remaining sail tore from the men's hands. It flapped out in the wind, pulled at the ship, and ripped loose to disappear among the rising waves. One man was flung wide, caught by a hungry sea, and disappeared from sight. The other made a frantic grab for the lines, slipped and fell, one leg and one arm entangled in a web of ropes.

Thaxton bolted forward a step, slipped on the running deck, and fell heavily. The ship lurched and swung the sailor in the rigging so that he smashed against the mast.

"Take the wheel," Innes roared as Thaxton pulled himself up. The first mate had barely grasped the wheel before Caleb was off the quarterdeck and climbing through the lines.

Kate paused in the companionway outside the cabin she and David shared. She had bundled dry clothing for her brother inside the blankets she carried. Although she'd donned a rain poncho and shapeless oilskin hat, Kate's own things were damn but only her feet were soaked. Her clothing felt clammy but she could stand the slight discomfort. Once the storm began to die down, her duties would center on refiring the stove and brewing coffee to warm the crew. Staying in the comparative warmth of the galley was better than a closed cabin.

The wind buffeted her when Kate stepped from cover and the rain was sharp and stinging. She kept close to the shelter of the outer bulkhead and worked back toward the galley, her feet sliding along the slick deck. A fresh wave crashed over the rail, drenching her trousers to the knees. An abandoned oilskin jacket washed along the deck to lay at her feet.

She recognized the slicker immediately. She'd seen Caleb wear it numerous times over the years, turning up in it at the mansion or the Puritan office on dismal San Francisco days.

Surely, in this storm he would have it on. Unless something had happened to him.

Kate's head snapped up. Caleb! Her eyes swept the deck as thoroughly as one of the storm-driven waves. Thaxton was at the wheel, his eyes fastened to the swaying masts.

Kate turned her face into the storm, squinting against the beating rain. The masts stretched tall and straight, combing the sky. The yards shook, flexing as the storm shook the ship yet again. As the *Paramour* dropped down between swells, the man dangling above jerked like a marionette.

He wasn't alone. Stripped of his confining rain slicker and uniform jacket, Caleb worked his way up the mast. Each movement was methodical, yet he covered the distance quickly.

"Kate—!"

The wind tore the sound of David's voice away so that it was impossible to tell if he'd called for Caitlin or used her own name. He was leaning out the opposite companionway, his young face dripping with rain, his expression tight with fear.

Kate scooped up the captain's oil coat and hurried to her little brother's side within the sheltered archway. The outer blanket was soaked, but within its folds David's clothing was still dry. She thrust the bundle at him but David didn't move. He too concentrated all his attention on the drama above them in the rigging.

Caleb reached the lower topgallant yard and inched his way out along it. Kate held her breath. Unlike the other cross beams of the mast, the three topgallant yards were separate entities, spanning only half the width of the ship. They stuck out at right angles from the mast, the arrangement splitting the sail on one side into two adjustable sections. There was no corresponding length of timber to balance the yard of the lower topgallant. One end was lashed to the mast while the other stretched to the tip of the reefed sail. The yard bent, curving downward slightly as Caleb worked his way out to the man entangled in the ropes. Innes stretched out an arm, caught the dangling man, and drew him to safety. Within moments, the captain had cut the ropes that bound the sailor, and was helping the injured man back toward the mast. Together, step by cautious step, Caleb guided the seaman's descent. With David pressed close to her side, Kate held her breath as she watched the two men slither back down to the deck. She turned away only when Caleb disappeared from sight toward the forecastle with the crew member draped over his shoulder.

The storm continued for the rest of the day, but the worst was behind them. In the galley the stove was refired and coffee brewed. Kate was busy keeping up with the demand for it, and with dispensing the rations of rum that accompanied each cup.

The passengers sent a representative, like Noah's dove, to ascertain if there was food available, then kept within their dry cabins.

Caleb and Thaxton spelled each other at the wheel. The crew manned the pumps, working through the night to rid the *Paramour* of sea water. The men were soaked through and chilled but the combination of rum-flavored coffee and the cadence of the sea chanties they sang kept the rhythm of the pumps smooth.

Bledsoe lent his strength at the pumps, leaving the simple galley chores to his helper, which suited Kate. The less she saw of the cook, the better.

When the clipper sailed free of the storm and below decks the water level had fallen, Bledsoe stumbled to his quarters with only a token cuff at her, which Kate managed to dodge easily.

The next morning the sun returned. Kate was up with the dogwatch again, had completed her chores, and was leaning against the bulkhead, her spectacles pushed down to the end of her nose so that she could admire the sunrise. The galley porthole framed the first rays as they spread pale fingers into the sky, pushing away the night. The same warm glow was reflected in the glint of the softly dancing sea swells.

The sight was soothing, not only because of the beauty of the rising sun, but because it meant she was one day further away from San Francisco. In another day or so she would feel safe enough to accede to David's wishes, and confess her true identity to the captain.

What would Caleb do? she wondered. Would he be pleased to find she was aboard? Would he be angry?

Kate sighed softly. She really hadn't thought about what would happen when Caleb discovered her latest escapade. She hoped he would be touched that she was so determined to be with him. But he was a different person aboard the clipper, a distant personality, the captain. His orders were relayed through Devin Thaxton. His time was spent on the quarterdeck at the wheel or in his cabin going over charts. Since it was David who served the passengers and officers dinner in the captain's day room, she hadn't even been able to catch a glimpse of him at meals.

It was time to decide what she would say to him, how she could convince Caleb that nothing mattered to her but being at his side. Other sea captains' wives traveled with them, setting up housekeeping in the two narrow cabins that comprised the captain's quarters. That was the future Kate wanted. To be his partner in everything, not just a pair of welcoming arms that waited patiently in his home port.

She knew enough of Puritan contracts and manifests to be a working helpmeet. She had been training herself for a life as Caleb's mate all her life. Now if only the captain could be convinced to see things her way.

Bledsoe's step was uneven but light. He'd learned long ago to move about a ship as silent as a cat, even when he'd spent the night with a bottle of rum.

He stood in the doorway, blinking blearily at his young helper. Caitlin was bad luck. The cook had had a comfortable berth aboard the *Paramour* until Thaxton had stuck him with the scurvy little rat.

Bledsoe had his suspicions as to why Thaxton had chosen Caitlin for the position. The first mate had always acted too damn prissy when they were in port, and wasn't happy with the dockside whores. Caitlin's appearance aboard proved why Thaxton sneered at the little slant-eyed doxies in Canton and ignored the brassy sluts in San Francisco. Bledsoe had gotten a good look at Caitlin's pretty little face. If Thaxton didn't like women, the cook's boy was sure the next best thing.

If Thaxton came to the galley just now, Bledsoe thought, he'd find his little laddie love a damn fetchin' sight. The sunlight spilled in the open porthole giving Caitlin's face a warm glow. With the boy's spectacles riding low on his nose, it was easy to see his thick, long lashes. Pretty as a bleedin' girl.

Bledsoe heaved himself into the galley. "Quit lollygaggin', ye damn laggard," he roared at Caitlin, swinging a knotted fist at the boy.

The cook's helper dodged the cuff easily, stepping just to the side. It was a move he'd made frequently, getting just out of Bledsoe's way a moment before the blow struck, and Bledsoe had come to expect Caitlin to dodge him. But now the fact that his helper avoided the punch enraged the cook and like a bull, he lowered his head and charged the boy.

Kate sucked in her breath and ducked under Bledsoe's arm. She danced just out of the range of his fists as the man turned. There was scant room to maneuver in the narrow galley and the air was tainted with the scent of rum on the cook's breath. He turned, huffing in fury.

"I ain't lollygaggin'," she insisted. "Was jest waitin' fer ya ta tell me what yer wanted done."

"Friggin' little bastard," Bledsoe growled, and made another grab.

Kate evaded him once more, and this time picked up a skillet to defend herself. Bledsoe's attacks were often half-hearted but the cook was drunker than usual. And the hatred in his eyes burned as hotly as the coals in the galley stove.

"Hell, Bledsoe," she said sharply. "I ain't done nothin' wrong. What's the matter with ya?"

The cook wasn't listening. He closed in, his fists clenched and burning for action.

Kate dodged to the side and swung her makeshift weapon at the same time. It connected with Bledsoe's shoulder and glanced off. He bellowed with rage and took another grab at her. The blow swiped alongside Kate's head, dislodging the set of her cap, knocking her wire-framed glasses to the floor. She made a grab for them, but Bledsoe swooped down, catching the back of her jacket. Kate tore loose for only a moment. Bledsoe had her cornered. She swung the skillet in a swipe that kept him temporarily at bay. The cook grabbed the front of her shirt with one hand and drew back his fist.

Kate kicked out. Her foot made contact with his shin and Bledsoe laughed. She kicked again, smashed at him with the skillet. His grip dragged her up off her feet so that she dangled an inch off the deck. She squirmed, twisting in an effort to avoid the blow. Bledsoe delayed delivering it, savoring the moment a bit longer.

Kate's foot struck out once more and made contact with the cook's groin. Bledsoe swore and his grip loosened. But there hadn't been enough force to the blow to fell him. Kate squirmed away, making a dash for the hatchway and the relative safety of the open deck. Bledsoe lurched after her, made a grab, and stumbled against Kate. His fingers caught the knit cap and pulled it off. Kate tumbled toward the companionway, knocked off balance by Bledsoe. Her hair spilled down, straggling around her shoulders.

Bledsoe's roar was deafening. "A woman!"

Kate scrambled to her feet and flew toward the doorway—and ran smack into the broad, unyielding chest of Captain Caleb Innes.

Chapter Thirteen

A subdued and nervous group sat around the table in the captain's day room. Bledsoe had been taken below in chains to await punishment for attacking another member of the crew. The news that the cook's boy was really a woman had spread quickly so that when Kate was escorted from the galley, all eyes had stared at her.

Now the cabin door was shut on their curiosity and what amounted to a trial was about to begin.

Kate sat upright in her chair, her backbone stiff, her chin set at a stubborn angle. Her hair was matted and straggly after being confined beneath the knit cap for a week. But for the sake of neatness, she had plaited it in a single braid. She had straightened her jacket but there was little she could do about the rest of her appearance. It was impossible to look her best in her disguise, but she wanted to look as presentable as possible if for no other reason than that it boosted her flagging spirits.

David was hunched in his chair, his expression a slight bit rebellious. He had caught a chill during the storm and was forced to swipe at his nose often with a bunched up handkerchief. Thaxton lounged in his seat, endeavoring to look the complete innocent. Before he had smuggled her aboard, Kate had promised to absolve him of all responsibility in the matter. If she were caught, Thaxton was to swear he had no idea that Tom Caitlin was not what he professed to be.

Now that the time had come, Kate wondered if the captain would accept her explanations. Caleb's expression was closed and hard and contained anger was evident in each of his movements. After an intent, but brief, scowl in her direction, he had ignored Kate's presence in the cabin.

Caleb stood at the head of the table, his hands braced along the back of a chair. He looked straight at Thaxton. "Explain," he ordered sharply.

Before the first mate could answer, Kate jumped in. "Mr. Thaxton is innocent," she insisted. "He didn't know I was anything other than a boy inquiring for a position aboard the *Paramour*."

Caleb glanced at her and his eyes glittered with tightly controlled fury. "I wasn't addressing you, *Kate*-lin," he snapped, and turned back to his first officer. "I'm interested in learning how Mr. Thaxton plans to explain his actions."

On the top of the table, Thaxton's hand clamped tightly into a fist. He made an effort to spread his fingers, stretching them to ease the tension. "What reason had I to doubt an urchin?" he asked, his voice calm. "We needed a cook's boy. It was the night before we sailed and I was desperate to fill the position. Perhaps I didn't look as closely as I should have at this particular recruit. If you consider that a dereliction of my duty, Captain, I apologize."

"I'm not speaking of then," Innes said. "A harried man can make a mistake on a dark night, especially when confronted with such an unconscionable adventuress."

Kate shifted in her chair nervously.

"No, I'm speaking of your blindness during the voyage thus far," the captain said.

Thaxton kept his eyes directed on his superior's face. "I don't understand, sir. To what are you referring?"

Caleb stared the man down. "Correct me if I'm mistaken, Mr. Thaxton. Did you not administer to Caitlin's hands our second night at sea? Did it not occur to you, upon close inspection, that the cook's boy was no boy at all?"

Thaxton remained silent.

"And you," the captain continued, turning that hard glittering gaze on David. "Don't tell me you didn't recognize your new cabin mate as your sister."

Out of the corner of his eye, Caleb noticed that Thaxton didn't display surprise over Kate's identity, which confirmed his impression that the man had known who she was all along.

David stared down at his lap, his face tight as he fought the tears that surfaced in his eyes.

Kate hurt just looking at her miserable little brother. He'd been so thrilled to be a part of the crew, so insistent that she confess her charade that first day. Kate rallied to his defense. "Davy didn't—"

"Quiet!" Innes thundered.

Both David and Kate jumped in their chairs. They'd known the captain all their lives, but had never heard that note of wrath in his voice before. David cringed in his chair.

"I'm waiting for an answer, David." There was no softening in Innes's voice. No compassion for the boy. On his ship, his word was law. If David was serious about a career at sea, the boy had to learn that his family name counted for little aboard ship. It would be his knowledge and expertise with a ship that made him a respected member of the crew.

Not only Kate and David had undermined his authority, but Thaxton, his first mate, had crossed the line. It was time to reestablish order. In spades!

David kept his head bent. "I knew her right off," he admitted. "That's why I asked if we could . . ." His voice got fainter and fainter until it finally trailed off.

"But you didn't report her presence to me," Innes said.

Kate started to open her mouth, then snapped it shut as the captain threw a warning glance at her.

"I told her to tell you," David murmured. "And

Katie promised to, only after we were farther away from Frisco."

"And what reasoning did she use to convince you that continuing this masquerade was wise?"

"She said that you'd turn around and take her back," David said miserably as the tears spilled onto his cheeks. Surreptitiously, the youngster brushed them away with the back of his hand.

Innes waited a moment more, his unflinching gaze moving from David's bowed head to Thaxton's sternly set face. He turned his back on them, moved to the porthole, and stared out at the distant horizon. "We have a number of cabins vacant. Caitlin will be be confined in one until we dock in Honolulu. She will have no contact with either the passengers or the crew. That includes you, David. If anyone asks about her, you are both to answer that we have no idea of Caitlin's true identity, but that she will be put ashore on the island of Oahu. After a wardrobe change, Miss Paradise will join us there as a passenger to return to San Francisco. Is that understood?"

Caleb turned slightly to glare back over his shoulder. David nodded in acceptance, and Thaxton inclined his chin in a terse movement. Only Kate refused to answer him. She stared at the table top, one finger tracing the grain of the wood. Damn! The woman was incredibly stubborn!

Innes hunched his shoulders and returned to a contemplation of the view. "I'm glad you agree," he murmured sarcastically. "Dismissed."

The three conspirators avoided looking at

each other, and pushed their chairs back, the legs scraping over the hardwood floor. Thaxton strode stiffly, his shoulders and the set of his jaw reflecting his smarting ego. David hung his head, his sniffles a combination of his cold and the tears that were awash in his eyes. Kate's steps lagged.

Innes let them get nearly to the door before he snapped one last order. "Stay where you are, Caitlin. I'm not finished with you yet."

David looked frightened and grasped Kate's hand. She squeezed it and gave him a quick, cocky smile. She kissed his forehead and pushed him on his way.

When the cabin door closed, Kate sank back down in her seat and waited.

Caleb's shoulders hunched forward, straining the fabric of his uniform jacket. His arm was braced against the bulkhead as he continued to stare out the porthole. "Good Lord, Kate," he murmured after a few moments, his voice no longer sharp with anger. It was weary and full of hurt. "What the hell do you think you're doing?"

She longed to go to him, to comfort him. Instead, she stayed in her chair, her hands twisted together in her lap. "I wanted to be with you," she murmured.

Innes sighed but kept his back to her.

"I love you, Caleb," Kate said. "When you didn't come for me, I was afraid."

He laughed, the sound dry and hollow. "You afraid? The woman who thinks nothing of manipulating a man like Ned Allen? Pardon me if I doubt you, madam."

Kate got slowly to her feet and moved toward
him. She reached out to touch the inflexible
breadth of his shoulders, then pulled her hand
back, unsure of herself. "I was afraid you
wouldn't come back for me."

"So you disrupt my crew."

"I only . . ."

He turned suddenly and seized her arms. His
fingers bit into her skin. "We sailors are a super-
stitious lot," Caleb snarled, a wild glitter in his
eyes. "The shape of a cloud, the sight of a bird,
anything can set the crew off. But do you know
what the worst omen is, my dear? A damn woman on board."

Kate shrugged him off. "That's ridiculous.
There are other women aboard as passengers."

"They keep to themselves. They don't infiltrate the crew."

"Many captains have their families aboard,"
she insisted. "Not only wives but young children."

"Damn fools they are, too," Caleb snapped.
"The sea isn't a gentle giant. Hell, the storm we
just endured was tame compared to Neptune's
real rages. We lost a man to that little blow,
Kate. There's another man lying in the fo'c'sle
with cracked ribs and a broken arm."

Kate turned her back to him. This was not the
Caleb she knew. Her love would understand her
reasoning, would want her by his side. "It's not
the same," she said. "There was no danger to
me. I wasn't in the sheets or even on deck for
very long."

"How the hell long do you think it takes to
be swept overboard?" he thundered. "Do you

237

think Triton's spear isn't as eager to pluck you as a man? Lord above, woman, if the ship goes down, you'd be just as damned as anyone else aboard."

There was a satiric bite to each of his words, as if he were ridiculing her, belittling her intelligence. Kate swung angrily to face Caleb, her eyes narrowed and glowing dangerously. At her sides, her fists were clenched tightly.

"What else is there, Captain? A damned mythical sea serpent looking for a tasty lunch?" she spat. "Do you honestly think that if Neptune or Triton or Davy Jones or fate claimed the *Paramour*, that I'd want to go on living?"

He snorted in derision. "You're being ridiculous."

"Captains go down with their ships, don't they?"

Caleb's smile was sardonic. His voice was much quieter when he answered. "Not unless they are incredibly cursed by ill fortune."

"And you aren't, Caleb. Which means there is no reason why I can't be aboard with you."

He turned away from the softened look in her eyes. The endless view of the sea was much easier on his nerves right now. He needed to disassociate his feelings, needed to convince Kate that this latest lark of hers was not forgiven. But gazing down into her lovely upturned face, seeing the warmth and passion in her eyes, undermined his intentions. He hadn't been able to stop thinking about Kate since the night she'd given herself to him. The promised forgetfulness of opium hadn't materialized. Even his addiction to the sea hadn't cured him. Had he been aware of her presence on board all along? Had he really been so blind as to not recognize her as the scruffy cook's boy?

"There is an unwritten commandment of the sea, Kate," he said. "No woman can ever be part of a crew. You broke that law. Therefore, this cruise is cursed. You may have fooled us for a while, but Neptune knew your identity. In retaliation he has claimed one member of the crew, possibly maimed another, and sentenced Bledsoe to be flogged."

She touched his arm. His muscles were tense beneath her fingers. "You don't believe in curses."

"Don't I?" Caleb continued to gaze at the wide expanse of ocean and sky. "The crew does."

"But you're the captain."

"Not an enviable position if it comes to mutiny, my dear."

They were both silent, he watching the sea, she watching him.

"Ah, Kate, what am I going to do with you?" Caleb murmured at last.

She took a deep breath, summoned a bright smile. "Marry me?"

The passengers' conversation around the captain's table that evening was animated. As if they had merely been waiting for a familiar theme to surface, the passengers had locked on the scandalous behavior of the nameless young woman who had disguised herself as a boy to join the crew.

"One hardly dares to guess at what this young person's intentions were," the plump Mrs. Orloff declared in ringing tones. Her dark eyes gleamed with barely suppressed excitement.

Mr. Yarbrough, the tall, thin drummer, absently played with his dinner fork, readjusting its angle near his plate. "The mind boggles, indeed," he murmured. "Had I only dreamed that entertainment was available so close at hand, I could have whiled away the better part of this dreary voyage."

"Really, Yarbrough," snapped Mrs. Orloff's husband, a rotund man with a florid complexion. "Ladies present, you know. Can't sully their delicate ears with that kind of talk."

"Oh, I don't mind," Miss Erbe insisted. The bloom of youth was gone from her hollow cheeks and her backbone was as straight and stiff as her corset stays. Her eyes glittered with the fervor of a crusader. "I am quite used to the cruder side of life. You see, my brother, Horace, and I have been working with the more unfortunate members of society," she announced proudly.

"The dregs," Horace Erbe murmured. His build was slight, but his manner was far from a replica of his sister's. The set of his mouth was a bit rebellious, like that of a petulant child.

Miss Erbe cast him a disapproving look and turned her attention back to the Orloffs. "We are touring the island missions, you see, so that we can make a report to the devoted back home who support our brethren in the field with contributions of both money and prayer. There is never too much that we can do toward the salvation of the savages."

"Very noble," Mrs. Orloff agreed. "But I doubt if anything can be done for this . . . this . . ."

"Soiled dove?" Yarbrough suggested.

Mrs. Orloff frowned. "You men tend to surround these unfortunate women with an aura of romance."

"They are poetry to my soul," the drummer murmured dreamily. "In fact, I feel an ode coming on. Perhaps the good captain will lift the quarantine on the young lady so that I can get her opinion on my stanzas."

"You are disgusting," Miss Erbe said. "It's men like you who fuel the system, who allow young women like this poor unfortunate no chance to escape a life of degradation."

Yarbrough smiled faintly. "But it is little adventuresses like this one who enliven the tedium of my life, dear lady. Surely, you would not deprive me of such a lifting of my spirits?"

"I would prefer that your spirits were dampened, sir," Mrs. Orloff declared.

Yarbrough's lips stretched in a leer more than a smile. "Speaking of which," he said, "I wonder if the good captain has another bottle of that excellent brandy to offer this evening."

The door opened partway through the drummer's comment to admit Captain Innes, Devin Thaxton, and David, the cabin boy. The youngster carried a tureen of soup and the appetizing smell of beef broth filled the cabin.

The captain removed his cap and bowed his head briefly in the direction of his guests. "I hope you will forgive our late arrival, ladies and gentlemen," Innes murmured as he closed the hatch behind him. "We have had a slight change in personnel in the galley this afternoon. Judging from the aroma coming from that bowl though, the alteration has turned out well."

Raush, the seaman who had complained about Bledsoe's meals, had been very eager to replace the cook. Based on the crew's reaction to their own dinner, Raush was proving to be a deft hand with a ladle.

Thaxton took his seat at the foot of the table with barely a nodded greeting to the passengers. At Miss Erbe's query on his health, the first mate admitted to a slight headache. She offered to supply him with headache powders from her own supply. Thaxton gave her a wan smile but declined the honor.

"How very kind of you, ma'am," Caleb said as he settled in his chair at the head of the table. Before Miss Erbe could launch into further cures that she recommended for the sufferer, the captain directed his attention down the table to where the shoe salesman lounged back in his seat. "I hope I can interest you in a fine claret this evening, Mr. Yarbrough?"

Yarbrough looked quite eager at the suggestion. Mr. Orloff's interest was piqued as well but after a careful sidelong glance at his spouse, he subsided into a quiet contemplation of his empty dinner plate.

David served the soup with stiff-lipped dignity, barely looking at the guests or the officers. When the boy left the cabin to return to the galley, Mrs. Orloff leaned over her plate and pinned the captain with an intent expression.

"Do tell us, sir, how is the poor prisoner?" she demanded.

Caleb spooned a bit of soup, savoring the aroma. Raush had a light touch with spices but the end result was far more pleasant to the taste than Bledsoe's cooking had been. "Are you speaking of the former cook, ma'am?" he asked. "It is kind of you to inquire, but the man attacked a member of the crew. I would advise that you and Miss Erbe keep to your cabins in the morning."

"Whatever for?" Horace Erbe demanded.

"To avoid witnessing the man's punishment I should think," Yarbrough said. He helped himself to a piece of bread, tearing off a chunk from the hard crust loaf. "Flogging, is it?"

Mrs. Orloff gasped. "And what of the young person? The female?" Her tone was a blend of repugnance and fascination. "Surely, you would not whip a woman!"

"Of course he wouldn't," Miss Erbe declared, her complexion flushed with fervor. She gave Caleb a simpering smile. "Captain Innes is a true gentleman."

Caleb finished his soup. "I was sorely tempted to administer a touch of the cat to this particular lady," he murmured.

"But in the spirit of Christian charity, you are restraining the impulse, dear sir," Miss Erbe declared.

"On the contrary," Caleb said with a slight smile. "It is because I fear the wrath of my fiancée should I even attempt such a punishment."

Miss Erbe stared blankly at him a moment. "Your fiancée?" she repeated in failing tones.

Mrs. Orloff rushed to her rescue. "My dear sir! We had no idea that we should be offering you congratulations! Did we, Almira?" Her tiny dark eyes darted to Miss Erbe.

"You never said a word." The spinster mumbled her words.

Horace Erbe barked a short laugh. "Why should he, Mira? It's not like we was bosom buddies!" He wasn't immune to curiosity, though. "Who is the lucky gal?"

Caleb finished his soup. "I'm not sure any of you would know Miss Paradise," he said.

"Hmm," Mrs. Orloff pondered. "Paradise?" She jogged her husband's elbow. "Wasn't that the name of the man who—"

"Miss Paradise?" Thaxton echoed faintly. "Miss *Katherine Paradise*?"

Puzzled by the inflexion of disbelief in his first officer's voice, Innes inclined his head briefly.

Thaxton's face was pallid. "You never mentioned . . ."

"The arrangement is not of long standing," Caleb said, turning to Mrs. Orloff, a smile curving his lips. "Miss Paradise is one of the heirs to the Puritan Shipping Line, ma'am. Perhaps it is through that connection that you are familiar with the name."

Horace Erbe chuckled. "Smart move aligning yourself with a thriving business."

Innes looked down the table at Thaxton. "A very necessary one," he said. "But my wife-to-be is a spirited young woman. Wouldn't you agree, Mr. Thaxton?"

The first mate's complexion was nearly white. He stumbled to his feet. "If you will excuse me, sir? Ladies, gentlemen. I fear I am not up to enjoying supper with you," he mumbled, and quickly left the cabin.

*   *   *

Thaxton leaned heavily on the rail, his arms supporting his weight, his knuckles pressed painfully into the wood. His eyes were turned away from the beauty of the setting sun. If another ship had sailed into sight or land had crested on the horizon, he would not have seen it for his vision was turned inward.

Damn them both, Devin raged silently. Damn Innes for always getting there before him, first in commanding the *Paramour*, and now in whisking Kate Paradise from his grasp as well. Damn Kate herself for luring him into believing fate could be altered.

Oh, he could see it all now. Her flirtatious smiles, her coy retreats. She had so beguiled him that day on the cliffs that he hadn't questioned the smooth reasons she spouted for wanting to sail clandestinely aboard the *Paramour*.

He knew better now. Devin had stumbled from the captain's cabin still in a fog of disbelief. Young David Paradise had just entered the companionway, bringing the next course of the evening meal to the captain's cabin. Thaxton waited patiently for him to return, dragging the boy within his own quarters for privacy.

"Did you know your sister is going to marry Innes?" Thaxton growled as soon as the hatchway was closed behind them.

"Sure," the boy said, displaying a total lack of interest. "Have to, my sister, Amy, says, to protect Katie's reputation."

Thaxton frowned. "Because she was smuggled aboard the *Paramour*?"

Elizabeth Daniels

"Naw. 'Cause Katie tricked him when she was the songbird and they . . . er. . . ." David ground to a halt and blushed bright red.

Thaxton's eyes narrowed. "He bedded her?"

David swallowed loudly and looked away.

"When?"

David tried edging toward the door. "I got chores ta do, Mr. Thaxton," he said.

Damn the bitch! Devin fought down the rage that threatened to engulf his mind. "What reason did she give you for her presence on board?" he snapped.

The boy's hand was on the hatch bolt. "Ta be with the captain." He drew the door open. "Katie's a bit impatient," David said, and left quickly.

Now again at the rail with the sting of the spray on his face, Devin closed his eyes and pictured the vixen who had coerced him into helping her.

The wind at Point Lobos had whipped her red-gold locks into an abandoned tangle. Her lagoon-green eyes had shimmered with unspoken promises. She had felt so right in his arms.

But it hadn't been just Kate herself that had tempted him that day. It had been the opportunity she had unconsciously dangled before him, a chance to woo his way to the only thing Devin wanted, a command of his own.

He had heard the legends of the sea sirens, the beautiful women with the alluring voices who lured sailors to their death. Had it been Odysseus who bested them? He couldn't remember. The classical education he'd had was as much to blame as his weakness for attractive women.

The dangers encountered by an ancient Greek hero would not threaten him. It was just a story passed down through the ages.

Unlike a Homeric hero, he could not stop his ears with beeswax or have himself lashed to the mast to save himself. This siren had been on land and she had played the lady in distress like a veteran of the boards.

"I need your help, Mr. Thaxton," Kate had said that fateful day.

Her scent had filled his head. The feel of her even temporarily in his arms had intoxicated him. "Devin," he murmured. "My name is Devin, Kate."

"Devin," she repeated.

Chills had raced along his spine. His embrace had tightened, drawing her closer.

Kate had played with a button on his uniform jacket briefly, then spun away from him. "I need to leave San Francisco." She had stared out to sea. "You see, I made a mistake in singing at Hell's Kitchen," she confessed. "Now Bull Run Allen is adamant that I return."

She kept her back to him, twisted her hands nervously. "It was a lark. I thought I could perform that one night and disappear. He didn't know who I was. Just that I was the songbird. But I was recognized."

Such a sad tone of voice, such an affecting posture. How could he resist the tremor of fear? The desperation in her eyes?

Fool. What a damn fool he'd been! She hadn't wanted to elude the gossip of San Francisco society or even the determined owner of Hell's Kitchen. All Kate had wanted was to get on board the *Puritan Paramour* so that she could continue her affair with Innes.

Blind, that's what he'd been. The good captain had put as much effort into his own performance, acting not only surprised but angry when she'd been discovered. Perhaps Innes's anger was real. She'd probably been sneaking off to the captain's cabin each night. But now that the crew and passengers were aware of her presence, Kate and Innes would no longer be able to indulge in midnight trysts.

They had both deceived him, both led him on, Thaxton decided. Innes in keeping him from gaining command of the *Paramour*; Kate in luring him on with dreams she had no intention of fulfilling.

He had been gullible once but no more. He would watch his chance and when the time was right, Devin Thaxton would have his revenge.

Chapter Fourteen

When the *Puritan Paramour* sailed into Honolulu harbor, Caleb Innes realized that, once
again, he had been fairly successful at avoiding the future. There had only been one
concession, his offhand announcement of his
engagement to Kate. It had surprised him
as much as it had Devin Thaxton. Not even
Kate's blatant suggestion that she marry her
had managed to push him to the point of
agreeing. It had been the simpering of Almira
Erbe that had brought him to the sticking
point.

Had it been just a defense against the unwel-
come attention that Miss Erbe was determined
to shower on him? Or had he wanted to warn
Thaxton off? His first mate had shown a distinct
preference for Kate during her week aboard as

Caitlin. The fact that he had taken Caleb's announcement rather hard showed that the man had been attracted to her.

What man wouldn't be? She was lovely to behold. She was an heiress, but more important, Kate had spirit.

Actually, it was extremely complimentary to have so much energy expended on attracting his attention, Caleb admitted. She could have her pick of young men the world over and she wanted him.

But there was much to be desired in Kate's courtship ritual. Disguises, clandestine meetings, and unwitting accomplices littered her schemes, making Caleb feel like he was center stage in some melodramatic play, or caught in the pages of a dime novel penned by Ned Buntline.

The problem was, he was never sure how the story ended. He knew how Kate wanted it to end, but since her plots tended to draw dangerous characters like Ned Allen along her course, the finish could not be as simple as a walk down the aisle.

He hoped that being locked in her cabin had given Kate time to think through all the ramifications of her acts. Yet, somehow, he doubted she had used the time in self-evaluation. She had probably plotted some new scheme and would drag him along in her wake as if he were nothing more than a skiff.

Of course, he'd known all along that in the end he would marry Kate. It was the only honorable thing to do after the night he'd spent with her at Lily's parlor house.

Fortunately, Thaxton was the only member of the crew who had heard his announcement. When they had changed places at the wheel later that night, Caleb had asked Thaxton to keep the news to himself. A public announcement would come later. Much later.

Since Kate was under a social quarantine in her cabin, she was still unaware of her new status. David had not been told, either. It was far easier to announce his intentions to strangers than to those closely involved.

He wasn't avoiding a confrontation with Kate, Caleb told himself. He was just working up to it slowly.

The first step had been admitting to himself that he loved Kate. The second was announcing to the world, at least the small part of it that had sat around the table in the day room, that she would be his one day. Now it was just a case of pushing himself to name that day. The day his life would change. The day he would relinquish his freedom for the shackles of matrimony. The idea alone was enough to make Caleb break out in a cold sweat.

When Oahu was sighted, the knot in his stomach should have eased, not tightened. The tension of keeping the well-meaning Miss Erbe and the lecherous Mr. Yarbrough from Kate's cabin would be gone once they dropped anchor at Honolulu. Ridding himself of his passengers was first on Caleb's list. Gathering additional crew members came second. Raush was in his element in the galley but a cook's boy was needed. Perhaps Jason Quinn's ankle had recovered sufficiently for him to rejoin the ship as cabin boy. A trip to Kauai would be a break in the schedule, but it had to be a brief one. Counting the man lost at sea and Bledsoe, two additional seamen were needed before they had a sufficient crew for the return voyage to San Francisco.

Kauai. It was another hundred sea miles from Honolulu to the westernmost isle, which was the site of numerous sugar plantations as well as missionary settlements. But, more important, the spectacular beauty of the beaches and the jungle waterfalls made Kauai Caleb's favorite of the eight islands.

He had left the injured Jason with the Reverend Ephraim Needham and his wife, Miriam, a mission couple stationed in the town of Lihue. The Needhams were fixtures in the settlement, knew everyone, and more important for a man in the merchant marine, they were a link to what items the owners of the profitable sugar plantations desired. His own property backed up to theirs, and Ephraim acted as overseer for the minimal cultivation done by the natives.

The more he thought about it, the more convinced Caleb became that a visit to Kauai was necessary. He would take David and Kate with him. Thaxton could see to the distribution of the cargo in Honolulu.

Perhaps on Kauai he could come to terms with the future, could find peace of mind, could get to know the young woman who was so determined to be a part of his life.

Kate whirled in a circle, holding a polonaise dress of buttercup silk before her. It seemed a lifetime since she'd felt pampered and extravagant. Her disguise as Tom Caitlin had gotten her in trouble once more, but it had also gotten Kate just what she wanted. She had managed to get aboard the *Paramour* and to stay near Caleb.

She had seen little of him, it was true. Either she had been too busy slaving in the galley with Bledsoe or she'd been locked in the narrow cabin. Caleb had accompanied David when he brought her meals or replenished the basin of water. Few words had been exchanged.

It had been impossible to tell the captain of her love for him with her little brother in the room. And it had been equally impossible to talk to David with Caleb waiting impatiently in the companionway.

There had been two breaks in the daily routine. The first had been when one of the woman passengers had tried to visit Kate. Miss Erbe's insistence that she would wean the misguided Caitlin from Satan's path had amused Kate. She had only heard the rather one-sided argument the fervent missionary had conducted with the captain outside the locked cabin door. The end result had been the book of sermons that arrived with dinner that night. To ease the boredom of her days, Kate had actually read them. Rather than feel an urge to reform her ways, after finishing the overly pious sermons, Kate felt more inclined to shock Miss Erbe with a further display of spirit than to thank the woman for lending her the book.

The second event had been a far more interesting contretemps with Mr. Yarbrough. That enterprising man had managed to pick the lock of her cabin late one night. His timing had been poor, though. The watch was changing, and Caleb had caught the drummer just as Kate's door swung open.

But now all that was behind her. She was aboard a smaller ship with Caleb and David, bound for another of the islands. The *Paramour* still rode peacefully in the Honolulu harbor as her crew busily unloaded cargo.

And Tom Caitlin was officially dead, quietly disposed of along with the ragged, oversized clothing Kate had worn.

After dropping anchor, Caleb had gone into town with the passengers and had returned with what Kate was sure had been the least attractive gown he could find. Attired once more in feminine apparel, Kate had been allowed to join Caleb, Thaxton, and her brother for meals in the captain's quarters. She had soaked the last grubby remnants of Tom Caitlin away with a luxurious bath the one night they had spent ashore at a hotel. Her wardrobe had been built with substantial purchases at the shops in Honolulu but there had been no time to enjoy the sights of the city. At dawn, Caleb had hustled her aboard a small sailing ship for the journey to Kauai.

The light-weight buttercup gown settled over her petticoat with a slight rustle. Kate smoothed the skirt into place and allowed the tiny Kanaka woman Caleb had hired as her maid to fasten the many tiny, covered buttons down her back. The overskirt of the dress was attached to the bodice and hung straight down in front before being looped up at the sides and draped at the back. Although the bodice had a modestly scooped neckline as befitted a day dress, the styling accentuated the narrowness of her waist and the gentle curve of her breast. With the help of her new attendant, Kate's hair was swept back from her face and allowed to cascade in loose curls down her back. Wispy little curls clustered at her temple and at her ear lobes.

The apparition in the mirror pleased Kate. Fleetingly, she wished she had earrings or a locket to wear, but she was content with her wardrobe. And more than ready to show how grateful she was for the openness of Caleb's pocket in paying for her new clothing.

When Kate went up on deck to join David and Caleb, she once more looked like a lady, complete with a frilled parasol to protect her complexion. The rough, work-worn texture of her hands was hidden by short, lace gloves. A fringed shawl of delicate hand-painted Chinese silk protected her against the bite of the sea air.

Unfortunately, she found Caleb was not topside to enjoy her entrance.

David was not impressed. He barely looked around before yelling for her to join him at the rail.

Oahu had fallen far behind them, and Kauai was still only a haze on the horizon. But David's enthusiasm wasn't for the beauty of the islands. His gaze was on the depths of the sea.

"Look! More dolphins, Katie!" he cried, leaning over the ship rail, his feet off the deck.

Kate yanked at the back of his shirt to pull him to safety. "Don't go swimming with them yet," she recommended.

"Oh, I won't." David promised off-handedly. "Cap'n says I can go diving along the reefs. Look! A school of something!"

"Tuna," Caleb identified, coming up to them. Since all three were traveling as passengers on the small interisland craft, he hadn't worn his Puritan uniform. But there was little difference in the styling of his conservative suit and the military cut of his uniform. Even the color was dark. Instead of the blue-black of the Puritan Line, it was tailored in a rich, deep, warm brown. The same color as his eyes.

David was still entranced by the sea, his eager gaze following the school of tuna, then flashing to the shadows of other large fish. They had identified dolphin, marlin, and sailfish on the short journey already.

Had she ever been that enthusiastic about things at his age? Kate wondered. Then she looked at Caleb, at the way his eyes squinted against the glint of the sun on the white caps, at the affection he showed her little brother. Yes, she had been blindly enthusiastic when she was eleven. She still was. Over Caleb Innes.

David's fascination was far reaching. Everything he saw, everything connected with sailing or ships had taken on a new aura for him. His first sight of one of the flimsy-looking outrigger canoes had left David nearly breathless with excitement. The daring Polynesian men skimmed along the swells in the fragile-looking craft hunting the larger species of fish. The interisland ship had already passed one such group of fishermen earlier. Kate had seen them from the porthole of her small cabin, and heard

David's shrill shouts of excitement.

While David was preoccupied with the sea, Kate turned to Caleb, hoping to see an encouraging light in his eyes. She had chosen her gown carefully, knowing that the buttercup coloring was complimentary to both her dark eyes and red-gold hair.

His face was shadowed by the angle of her parasol. The clean, masculine angles of his face were softened by a faint smile. His brows arched as if in faint surprise. His black hair, usually brushed back in a casual manner, had been tossed by the sea breeze into a boyish tangle.

He seemed a completely different man from the stern captain of the *Puritan Paramour*. He was once again the Caleb she knew.

In turn, Kate thought Innes appeared to be studying her. His eyes covered her slowly from the tips of the white shoes peaking beneath the hem of her skirt to the arrangement of her hair. The sun had brought out freckles on the bridge of her nose and tanned her cheeks during the week she had played cook's boy. Though the coloring was just begining to fade, Kate hoped Caleb didn't find it offensive.

His eyes lingered at her lips until Kate felt breathless. But he didn't compliment her in words. "How are your hands doing?" he asked.

"Fine."

"It was a damn fool thing to do, Kate," Caleb said.

David turned from the rail. "Yeah, it was," he agreed. "When will we reach Kauai, sir?"

Caleb continued to watch Kate. "In a few hours."

"Can I go diving then, Cap'n?"

Innes chuckled, tucked Kate's hand on his arm, and turned to join David at the rail. "Not today. First we visit the Needhams and see how young Quinn is doing."

The feel of Caleb's sleeve beneath her fingers was comforting and Kate felt as if he'd finally forgiven her. Surely, on Kauai she would have a chance to spend time with him, to talk to him, to convince him that he needed her by his side. Without the responsibilities of his own ship riding on Caleb's shoulders, he seemed younger, more carefree.

Perhaps she had been reckless and thoughtless in sneaking aboard the *Paramour*. Yet Kate was glad that she had done so. She had seen Caleb Innes in another light, had seen him in the guise of commander, a king aboard his vessel. As a member of the crew, she had been privileged to hear the men's opinion of Caleb, of his abilities, of his fairness. It was a fine line that he trod as master of the clipper. He couldn't be too inflexible or hard; he couldn't be too soft or easy. During the storm, Kate had seen Caleb climb a slippery mast to rescue one of his men. He hadn't asked others to free the tangled seaman, he had done the dangerous job himself, had risked his own life to save one of them. He had then shrugged off the man's thanks with a hearty laugh and bound up the swabbie's injuries himself. No, she would never regret her adventure as Tom Caitlin.

But he had been so many different men lately. Not just a ship's captain with the courage to rescue his men but a man with the daring to hold a knife to Ned Allen's throat. A familiar family visitor who brought presents to her younger brothers and sisters and a bearded ruffian who yelled encouragement to entertainers at Hell's Kitchen. Her passionate, eager lover and the distraught man who had run from her bed the next morning.

She loved each of the men he was and found that her new knowledge made him more attractive, more fascinating. Made her feelings deeper and his continued distance all the more painful. If only Caleb would find her just as intriguing.

He wasn't looking at her. His gaze was on the sea. The ever-moving sea. He had placed her hand on his arm, but Caleb wasn't touching her. The action had been more polite than possessive.

At the captain's side, David had squirmed his way up on the rail again. "Then I can go to the reefs tomorrow?" the boy asked eagerly.

Caleb laughed and ruffled the youngster's straw-colored hair. "No promises. I've got a spyglass in my cabin. Why don't you go get it?"

David was off at a run.

The breeze fluttered the ruffles of Kate's parasol, tossed the fringe of her shawl, let her skirt whisper secrets. Caleb kept his attention on the ocean, leaning both forearms on the rail. Kauai was closer now but still little more than a growing haze in the distance.

Unable to stand the quiet between them, Kate drew her hand reluctantly from his arm and closed the parasol. "What does happen when we reach the island?" she murmured. "Are you going to follow Miss Erbe's suggestions and place me at a mission until I reform my ways?"

Caleb straightened slowly. He waited a moment, his eyes still on the horizon, as if he pondered her question. Then he turned. His eyes were dancing with laughter, his mouth was curved in a crooked grin. "No, minx," he said softly, his deep voice vibrant and tender. "I don't think you can mend your ways."

"I could try if you wish," Kate offered.

"That would never be my wish." Caleb caressed the delicate curve of her jaw with the back of his fingers. His gaze dropped briefly to her lips once more.

Kate stared into his eyes, her own sparkling with hope and love.

"Don't ever change," he said.

She leaned toward him, her lips parted.

Caleb put an admonishing finger against them. His eyes were still twinkling with amusement. "But let's not rush this particular fence quite so fast, my love. On Kauai life begins anew for us. Why don't we become acquainted first?"

Kate stared at him a moment. "Acquainted? As if we were strangers?"

"Ah, but you see, my darling Kate," he said, and raised her hand to his lips, "from this instant on, that's exactly what we are."

Strangers. Perhaps they were that in truth, Caleb thought. He had known her all her life, but he knew nothing about her.

As a child, Kate had been partial to cherry pie, Caleb recalled. She would steal into the kitchen and eat the cherry filling, leaving the crust barely touched. Did she still do that? What was her favorite song? Did she like to dance?

And why did she love him? And he knew she did love him. Blindly. She thought he could do no wrong. How wrong she was. How beautiful.

Caleb watched Kate from across the width of the Needhams' parlor. She sat quietly, as if in repose, her lips gently curving as she listened to her hostess describe life in Lihue. There was no sign of the harridan who staked her reputation, her safety, her life, to be near him. Kate was the polite society butterfly now, seemingly spiritless and obedient.

He wanted to kiss the facade away, to turn her back into the wildly dangerous woman who had enchanted him. But now was not the time. Miriam was talking quickly, her hands flying to illustrate her speech as elegantly as if she were painting pictures with them as the *hula* dancers did. Caleb knew Miriam would be shocked at such a comparison, of course. She only approved of very young girls performing the native dance, and then only in the evening. The sensuous, swaying movements were too licentious in the eyes of most missionaries, especially the women.

But they wouldn't be to his Kate, Caleb thought. She'd probably insist on learning the *hula* and would shock society by performing it upon her return to San Francisco and end up in yet another scrape.

Caleb smiled widely at the thought, his expression at odds with Miriam's description of a recent bereavement in the colony.

Miriam was too caught up in her story to notice Caleb's bemusement but Ephraim was more alert. He began telling an amusing anecdote about Jason Quinn's recovery. At the conclusion, he invited Caleb to escape the closeness of the house with him, and enjoy a pipe on the *lanai*.

"Not often that I indulge in a smoke," Ephraim confessed, stretching out his legs and tilting his chair back against the house. He filled the bowl of his pipe lovingly, struck a match, and drew a few times on the stem. Ephraim sighed in contentment. "Miriam says I'm a bad example to the natives."

"You are," Caleb agreed, peeling his suit jacket off and draping it around the back of a chair. Rather than sit, Caleb leaned casually against one of the porch supports. "Sounds like young Quinn is ready to report back to duty," he said.

The reverend nodded. "Wasn't a bad break," he said of the cabin boy's injury. "The young heal quickly."

Caleb grunted. He looked off down the dirt road to where the jungle gave way to the neat fields of his own small sugar plantation.

"Pretty girl, your Miss Paradise," Ephraim mused. "Polite. Well behaved."

"At the moment," Innes agreed.

"Spirited?"

"A vixen."

Needham chuckled. "What's she doing here?"

Caleb sighed deeply and pulled a chair next to his old friend. "Smuggled herself aboard my ship," he said. "I couldn't leave her in Honolulu.

Besides, her brother is along to lend countenance to our traveling together."

"Young David's not much of a chaperon," Needham pointed out. "What are you going to do with her, Cal?"

Innes leaned forward, his elbows on his knees. He avoided meeting Needham's eyes. "Marry her. I think."

Caught inhaling, Ephraim choked on pipe smoke. Once he had recovered, the reverend nodded sagely. "Have to," he agreed.

Caleb smiled wryly at his friend. "That's what everyone seems to tell me. As an old friend, you could at least try to talk me out of it."

Needham studied his pipe. "How?"

"With horror stories of married life?" Innes suggested.

"Dear Lord!" the reverend breathed in horror. "Miriam would burn my ears for months on end if I dared."

Caleb laughed.

"Miss Paradise is a lovely young woman," Needham said.

"Aye." Caleb stared back at the scenery again. "That's the trouble. She's so young."

"There's nothing wrong with that. Many men take wives who are years younger . . ."

"I've known Kate all her life."

Needham didn't appear to see a difficulty in that.

"She's an heiress."

The reverend fingered the bowl of his pipe. "Very fortunate for you, Cal. Weren't you talking about expanding your own interests the last time you were here? The American population on all the islands has grown in the last few years. At this rate, some counter-hopping Yankees will take it into their heads to overthrow the *iolani* and request territorial status for the whole chain. Did it in Texas, didn't they? Tried it again in California with the Bear Flag Rebellion."

"That doesn't mean anyone will think the islands are worth the trouble," Innes said.

Needham frowned. "Things have changed a lot since Captain Cook sailed into Waimea Bay nearly a hundred years ago, Cal. The *ali'i* don't have the power or control they did back in Kamahameha's time. Whale oil brought foreign nations in, but now sugar is the real king. And it's Americans who own the plantations."

"So you think I should marry my heiress to ensure that I get my share of island wealth?" Caleb asked.

Needham chuckled. "You want a small fleet of interisland commerce ships, don't you? What better reason could there be for marrying Miss Paradise than financing that venture?"

Caleb's eyes were on the distance rather than his friend. "Maybe that I love her?"

Ephraim drew deeply on his pipe and blew smoke rings into the evening light. "Ah, my friend," he murmured softly, "you are indeed hooked and netted."

Chapter Fifteen

Kate enjoyed the warm hospitality of Miriam Needham's home, and the slow, lazy pace of each day on Kauai.

From the time of their arrival, David asked endless questions about his promised diving adventure along the coral reefs. His new friend, Jason Quinn, had told him stories of strange, multicolored fish that lived along the reef and David was anxious to see them for himself. With a crafty glance at Miriam, he even claimed that the experience would undoubtedly be educational. Kate had nearly choked on her tea.

David developed a fast friendship with young Quinn and was full of the tales the older cabin boy told. He was even inclined to see Jason's broken ankle as a manifestation of his new friend's intrepid nature. Kate was quite tired of hearing Jason's praises sung.

It was quiet, and relaxing to be with the mission couple. The Needhams were good people but not as overtly sanctimonious as Miss Erbe had been. Good works were merely a matter of course for the Needhams. They treated the Kanakas warmly, as friends, neighbors, and family.

The domestic setting affected her little brother as well, Kate found. Without being told, David remembered to wash before meals and displayed his best manners. The rest of their siblings wouldn't have recognized the young gentleman he had become. In spite of his boyish enthusiasm for the strange new sights he encountered, David appeared to be growing up before her eyes.

Or perhaps she was just more aware of the things around her. The sun seemed warmer, brighter, the earth more lush and fruitful, the people gentle and loving. The very air she breathed was enhanced, sweeter, more vibrant. And with every hour, she fell further in love with Caleb Innes.

How could that be possible? Kate wondered. Hadn't she loved him before? Was it because she was growing to know his many sides? He was no longer just the idol of her childhood. Now he was a very mortal man with flaws. A man who could hurt, who could rage. Who could love her.

They took frequent walks together, accompanied by a tireless David. Caleb didn't touch her but when he looked at her, Kate felt as if she'd been caressed.

He was the Caleb she knew and yet he wasn't. He was less than he'd been, and more than she could ever dream of wanting.

She was no longer afraid that he would leave her. When he spoke now, Caleb's speech was sprinkled with endearments. They weren't the tender love words her father often used. To Ben Paradise, his wife was his "dearest heart," and he had never used that particular phrase for any of his daughters. It was Lacy's alone. But Caleb had never been that way. Kate had always known the captain loved her mother. She had often heard Innes fondly call Lacy "little puritan," a tribute to her fanaticism with personally running the Puritan Shipping Line. Caleb had extended the affectionate term to Kate long ago. Unlike her mother, though, Kate had always rated a more possessive phrase. "My little puritan," he'd called her.

The words weren't as poetic as those she'd heard from countless young men on starry nights. They were better. When Caleb spoke, he labeled her as his. "*My* dear, *my* darling girl. *My* love."

Kate's heart filled each time she heard his voice. Even when he was answering one of David's endless questions or talking local politics with Reverend Needham.

She walked in a happy haze, content for once to leave the timing of their courtship to Caleb. They took excursions, occasionally heading north or driving around the southern curve of the island. David marveled at the moaning cry of the lava rocks each time the sea pushed up in a geyser-like plume of water at the Sprouting Horn. Kate watched her younger brother enjoy his fill of scouting along the reefs of Poipu Beach and again around Anahola Bay. While David babbled about fish in shades from deep red to orange, yellow, blue, green, white, and black, Kate collected shells in as many varied shapes, colors, and sizes. At her side, Caleb strolled along the sand, apparently happy to either talk or share the intimacy of silence with her. He identified oyster, cockle, cowry, horn, and moon shells. He pointed out flocks of sooty terns, feeding albatross, petrels, masked boobies, various noddies, and red-tailed tropic birds.

It was all familiar music to Kate—the sound of the surf, the cries of the birds, and Caleb's quiet voice. She had heard them before on the beach below Cliff House when he had joined the Paradise children for picnics over the years. But this time she shared him only with David and even her brother's enthusiastic babbling could do nothing to ruin these precious hours.

When the trips turned inland, a truly exotic world opened before Kate. Sandy beaches gave way to tropical jungles, to massive lava cliffs, rushing streams, and majestic waterfalls. She saw fields of sugar cane, of taro, sweet potatoes, and rice. She tasted *hala kahiki*, the pineapple, and the once-*kapu*, forbidden to women, flavor of the banana.

The scent and beauty of flowers was yet another marvel. Nowhere else could the fragrances be as intoxicating, the colors more vibrant. In a land of frequent rain showers, even the often-seen spectrum of a rainbow paled next to the flowers.

Caleb delighted in purchasing necklaces of the blossoms, the *leis* woven by the natives. Bedecked with sweet-smelling pedal crowns of deep purple, scarlet, gold, yellow, or bright orange, Kate felt like a queen, his queen. But, while Miriam Needham's home became festooned with wild ginger, orchids, and bright *halapepe* blossoms, Caleb kept his distance.

They had been on Kauai for ten days when Kate's patience ended. It happened suddenly, erupting with as much destructive force as Waialeale, the volcano that had built Kauai.

The day had been damp, the rain falling steadily all morning and casting a pall over the group gathered under the Reverend Needham's roof. Miriam had tried to entertain David by teaching him various Kanaka words. But once he knew he was a *haole*, a foreigner, and had mastered a rather tongue-twisted version of *Mele kalikimaka*, Merry Christmas, David lost interest. When Jason Quinn proposed a game of *konane*, a native game similar to checkers, David was quick to agree. His head was bent over the pebble game pieces the rest of the morning.

Kate sat at a window and watched for Caleb's return. He had gone out with Ephraim just after dawn.

She had spent her life waiting for his return. She had endured it with whispered promises to herself. One day, Kate had vowed to herself all those years, one day she would grow up, would grow into his world, would become part of his life, and the waiting would end.

That "one day" was so close yet so far.

Did Caleb lay sleepless each night as she did? Did he dream of her as she did of him? Did he long to have her in his arms once more? In his bed?

It had been nearly two months since she had tricked him into making love to her at Lily Walsh's parlor house. Two long months with only memories to hold close. Since then, there had been no tender kisses, no loving embraces. Yet there was no doubt in anyone's mind that Caleb was courting her. Kate had often noticed Ephraim's gaze linger on her, then turn to Caleb with an obvious nod of approval. Miriam had mentioned the captain's attentions, commenting that few younger men were as gallant when they sought a wife.

Well, she didn't want Caleb to be gallant, Kate stormed silently. She wanted him to be passionate. She wanted to be in his arms, to be his lover. It didn't matter if she was his wife. It had never mattered to her what status society gave her as long as Caleb wanted her at his side. He had never married. Perhaps he had made some wild vow when another woman had broken his heart. Not all men wanted a wife. Some preferred a mistress and if that was all she could ever be to Caleb, then so be it. Kate was willing to be shunned by polite society as long as she was with Caleb.

But while they stayed with the Needhams, Caleb was never more than just politely attentive. For the sake of propriety, he wasn't even staying in the main house with Kate and David. He slept in a separate building further back on the property. Once they returned to Honolulu and the *Paramour*, he would be the aloof captain of his ship once more. She would be shut out of his cabin, out of his life.

Kate stared unseeing at the windbreak of golden-stemmed bamboo and the dripping leaves of the banana trees. Once, Miriam had told her, banana trees had been planted near the temples. The natives had believed that the constantly fluttering leaves would speed their prayers to the gods. Pele, the volcano goddess, Ku, the war god, and Lono, the fertility deity, had long ago been replaced by the Christian God. Kate hoped the banana leaves would wave her own prayers closer to being answered. It didn't matter which deity answered, she decided, as long as one of them did so soon.

Patience, Miriam Needham would undoubtedly counsel her, was a virtue to be pursued by any woman who loved a man of the sea. But patience had never been one of Kate's qualities. She had been lulled into temporary contentment in the aftermath of her adventures on the Barbary Coast and aboard the *Paramour*. The quiet, lush beauty of the island and Caleb's nearly constant attendance were intoxicating. Time seemed to stand still but all too soon they would be returning to Oahu, to San Francisco. What lay ahead in the future? Happiness or heartache?

Kate watched the rain, and waited for Caleb. Patience be damned, she thought.

*   *   *

Caleb sat on the floor of his *lanai* late that night, his only companion a bottle of rum. One leg drawn up, his arm resting negligently on his knee, he contemplated the moon.

He never tired of island life. It had a pace so different from the frantic gait of a city or the measured tread of life aboard a ship. The days he spent on Kauai were always peaceful, quiet, lazy. Some called it Eden. When combined with the thrill of sailing the high seas, perhaps it was. He could give up neither. But his idea of a true paradise was tied to a woman. One particular woman. Kate Paradise.

Caleb studied the moon without really seeing it. Soon it would be time to return to the *Paramour*, to return to the responsibilities of running his business. He had let it slide these last weeks, allowing Devin Thaxton to handle the business in his absence. He had not settled things with Kate, either. It was so much easier not to. Just thinking about actually proposing, of actually vowing to love her, still terrified him. So he spoke of it to friends, to strangers, in an effort to gain courage. But he never mentioned it to Kate.

Kate.

Caleb took another pull on his rum bottle, savoring the bite and burn of the alcohol, waiting for the numbing sensation that made sleep possible.

The clouds had lifted in the afternoon, leaving the day muggy, the air clinging. But the night was beautiful. It let his mind wander to the past, to other such nights. Anything to keep him from thinking about the future.

He'd been enchanted with the islands during his first visit, over twenty years ago. It had been his maiden voyage as master of the *Puritan Paramour* and his first crossing of the mighty Pacific.

His first mate that voyage had been Giles Vinton, a man who served as advisor as much as officer, guiding Innes through the unfamiliar waters. Vinton had moved on the next year to a command of his own. But before assuming the mantle of captain himself, Giles had provided Caleb with a voluptuary's knowledge of the islands. It was at Giles's side that Innes had sampled the delights of a *luau*, tasting *imu*-baked pork, *opihi* shell fish, seaweed, sweet potatoes, *poi*, breadfruit, coconuts, bananas, and guavas. Vinton hadn't stopped at food but had taken him to a house where the *lomilomi*, a massage, eased tense muscles, before the sight of beautiful *wahines* in native dress made a man tense for different reasons.

Caleb tipped the rum bottle to his lips. How long ago those days seemed. How perfect the women were in his memory. How sensuous their motions as they performed the swaying movements of the *hula*. They had worn the *pau*, a long length of cloth wrapped around their figures from hips to knee, and the *kihei*, a mantle that was draped under one arm and tied on the opposite shoulder. As the drums increased their tempo, the dancers had discarded their *kiheis* and swayed just in low-slung *pau* and flower blossoms, their long inky-black hair hanging straight to brush their gyrating hips.

Elizabeth Daniels

Golden days they had been with golden-skinned, dark-eyed women. But those days were gone. Civilization had surged over the Kanakas, clothing them as completely as any New England churchgoer. The beauty was still there, just disguised and tamed. Vinton had mourned its passing, found himself a wife, and was now the proud father of four children. But Caleb had tried to hold on to the primitive beauty of those days.

The pleasant scent of *iliahi*, the sandalwood tree, surrounded Caleb. The Needhams had bowed to his wishes in constructing the hut like the thatch-sided building of the natives. It was his alone, his retreat. The inside was decorated simply with furniture of *koa* wood and samples of feather work, in particular a flowing cloak of red-and-yellow *o'o*, *iiwi*, *mamo*, and *apapane* feathers. The servants who cared for the hut told him he possessed the same wealth as the *ali'i*, the Kanaka nobility.

Mats of palm leaves covered the floor. Sheets of tapa cloth were used on his bed. The steady rain earlier in the day had soaked the tightly bound thatch of the roof and walls. A leak had developed near the doorway, but Caleb ignored it. This small hut was all the home he had ever needed. It and his cabin aboard the *Paramour*. But it was no longer enough. He wanted more. Earlier he had known exactly what but the rum had blurred the image in his mind now, making those desires nebulous. All but one.

She was a wraith that came to him each night in his fantasies. A joke played on him by the *Mu*,

274

the pixy creatures who had inhabited Kauai long before the Kanaka. But when he reached for her, he clutched at nothingness.

So he knew the pale figure moving toward him was nothing but a spirit. Perhaps a water sprite come to fill his befuddled head with *hoomalimali*, sweet flattery.

She stood hesitantly before him, her long hair turned silver by the moonlight, her dark eyes mysteriously shadowed, her thin gown and robe fluttering softly in the breeze. A bowl of fruit rested in her hands.

"You're late," Caleb said.

"I am?" the vision murmured, her voice soft, low, sensuous.

"Some would say about ten to fifteen years too late," he mused.

The moon gave her skin the sheen of a pearl and made her lips as lush as the pedals of a camellia. She floated toward him, moving onto the *lanai*. In a graceful flow of draperies, Kate sank to her knees at his feet. "And would *you* say that I'm too late, Caleb?" she whispered.

He felt her touch on his soul, on that part of him that had stayed free for so long.

"No." Caleb put a hand to her hair. It was like silk, cool, soft, exotic. He took a long breath and let it out slowly. This was no dream. She was here, her lovely face glowing with love. "I thought you would come to me two days ago," he said.

Kate grinned and held up the bowl of small yellow fruit. "I brought you a gift."

"In appeasement?"

Her smile was impish now. "In hunger."

"So you brought *lilikoi*." At her puzzled expression, he translated. "Passion fruit."

"Is that what it is called? Shall I peel one for you?"

"That's not the best way to eat passion fruit, my love." Caleb slid his knife from its sheath, chose a ripe piece, and sliced off the stem end. "You scoop out the seeds with your tongue," he said, and, watching her face, demonstrated the process.

Kate accepted the fruit from him. "Like this?" she asked, her eyes on his. The pink tip of her tongue slid into the heart of the fruit, collected seeds, and retreated. The sweet, exotic flavor filled her mouth, surprising Kate. Her eyes widened with pleasure. "It's delic—"

The word was lost as Caleb's lips brushed hers gently. "I'm glad you like *lilikoi*," he murmured huskily, and kissed her again, his lips as light against hers as the evening breeze.

Kate slid her arms around his neck. "Does passion fruit always affect you this way?"

"You affect me this way," Caleb said, and gathered her close.

He tasted of passion fruit and rum as Kate's lips brushed against Caleb's briefly, teasing and tempting him. She sampled the fruit again, then shared the cloying flavor of the seeds with him in another kiss.

"Have you really waited two days for me to come to you?" Kate purred. Her head tipped back in enjoyment as his mouth moved along her throat.

"Longer," Caleb said against her skin. "I've waited all my life."

Kate arched under his touch. As his mouth moved lower, she slid out of her robe. It shimmered as it fell back to display the transparent nightgown beneath.

She was moon-drenched silk, creamy, white, and irresistible. The light highlighted her body through the fabric, displaying each delightful curve. It was impossible not to touch her, not to enjoy the fullness of her breast in his hand, or the heat of her lightly covered flesh against his.

The neckline of her gown dipped low and he pushed it from her shoulders. He sampled the taste of her skin, slid his tongue along her collarbone, and placed a lingering kiss in the hollow of her throat.

Kate shivered with pleasure and leaned closer to him, relearning the beloved feel of his body against hers. She had longed to experience these delicious sensations again, had tried to relive them in her memory. But it had been impossible.

"You're cold," he said as she quivered against him.

Kate trailed fleeting kisses along the rough line of his jaw. "I didn't dress for warmth," she murmured. "I thought perhaps you'd be kind enough to supply that."

"I might." His mouth claimed hers hungrily. She felt so right in his arms, tasted so right. There had never been another woman who filled him with such longing, such tenderness. Such love.

She was breathless when he released her. Her eyes were as bright and dark as the sea at night.

Elizabeth Daniels

Caleb stared down into them, amazed at the depth of his emotions for this slip of a girl.

"God, but I love you, Kate Paradise," he murmured in awe. "Will you marry me?"

Chapter Sixteen

Dora Acton stood just within the portico of St. Mary's Cathedral, looking out at the rain. A modest veil draped forward over her face, its slight covering neither diminishing the style of her hat nor disguising the loveliness of her features. It allowed the man who had just left the church an ample view of her dismayed face.

Dora waited until he was closer before beginning her performance. Her timing had been off the first few times she had tried to lure a victim. After weeks of practice, however, the game had become second nature to her.

He was nearly abreast of her now, looking at the leaden sky, shaking out his umbrella. He was portly. His suit was dark and, although obviously tailor-made, stretched a bit over his expanding paunch. A watch chain was draped across the wide expanse of his richly figured waistcoat. Dora knew she had him hooked when he placed his bowler hat at a rakish angle and gave her a sidelong, appraising glance.

"Oh, dear," she said in a plaintive tone and cast a worried look at the steadily falling rain.

The man paused on the church steps. "Problem, ma'am?"

Dora smiled as if embarrassed. "The rain," she said. "I was running late for Mass this morning and came away without my umbrella." She glanced to the slick street, then back at him helplessly. "Do you think this shower will last long?"

"Hard to tell," he answered.

From the corner of her eye, Dora saw that he was taking in the way her dove-gray redingote clung at her narrow waist before flaring out over her hips. It was double-breasted with a rich black velveteen collar that drew attention to her generous breasts. She moved as if to descend the steps and brave the shower, carefully lifting her skirts just high enough for him to catch a glimpse of her slim ankles.

"I suppose I shall just have to risk a drenching," Dora said with a light, half-frightened little laugh. She raised her skirt a bit higher and stepped out into the rain.

The man sprang forward, his umbrella held over her tiny form. "Nonsense, ma'am. Can't have a pious woman like yourself getting wet."

Dora looked up at him, her blue eyes wide and innocent. "That is so kind of you, sir. But really, I cannot impose. I live just a short distance away and it is God's rain, after all."

"Wouldn't think of letting you get wet, ma'am. My pleasure to help. Play the Good Samaritan, you see?" He laughed a bit nervously. His complexion reddened. "I'll see you safely, and . . . heh heh . . . dryly to your door."

Dora's lashes fluttered. "If it would not take you away from your business, then I would appreciate your escort, sir."

"Absolutely. Strangers well met on the church steps, that's what we are," he said.

He chattered nervously as they went down the hill, crossing the few blocks to the neat little house that Dora indicated was hers. Dora maintained a well-bred demeanor and, upon reaching the door, invited her gallant escort in to warm himself with a cup of tea before continuing his journey. Lured by the soft expression on her face, the man closed his umbrella and followed her inside.

Dora unpinned her hat and allowed him to help her off with her coat. "I'll just put the kettle on," she said. "Do make yourself comfortable in the parlor. I'll be back directly."

Her skirts whispered over the floor, swaying subtly with each natural twitch of her hips. She knew he watched her every movement.

In the kitchen Tom Heath, her partner, was waiting. Heath was a tall, handsome fellow who posed as a mild-mannered schoolteacher. In fact, he was a very talented actor and confidence man. Without a word, Heath got to his feet, straightened his suit coat, and brushed back an unruly lock of his light brown hair. He consulted his pocket watch and held up five fingers to indicate how long she had before his entrance. Then, turning up the collar of his jacket against the rain, Heath gave her a cheeky grin and eased out the back door. Dora returned to the front room.

The waiting man turned at her entrance, the photograph of a stiffly posed couple in wedding finery in his hand. "I think I know this fellow," he said.

Having absolutely no idea who the people in the picture were, Dora gave him a warm smile and replaced the frame on a side table. "My cousin and her husband," she said. "It will be just a moment or so until the tea is ready." She cast a surreptitious glance over the room and noted tiny details. It was very rare for Heath to find such a nice setup for them, especially on a damp day. It had taken him only moments to pick the lock and to settle in earlier. Using a home in the owner's absence meant that if a disgruntled victim complained to the police, there was no way for Dora or Heath to be traced. It also saved the expenses of hiring a lodging for their confidence game.

This particular house appealed to Dora. She wasted little time admiring the pattern of the rug or the delicate carving that decorated the mantle. She looked for usable props or the lack of them. A sewing basket sat near her own side chair. Unfortunately, there were no decanters of spirits to offer her guest.

"I'm sure you would probably prefer brandy or some other type of liquor," Dora murmured, her eyes downcast in humility. She glanced aside at the clock. She needed to speed things up or she would not be able to compromise the portly man.

"My husband doesn't tolerate spirits of any kind in the house."

"Tea's fine," the man said, and looked uncomfortable. He too glanced at the clock. It was just going on nine, barely mid-morning.

If the rain and her luck held, there would be time to relieve a few more businessmen of their wealth before evening. It was time to dispatch her current gallant.

Dora bent and took an embroidery frame from the sewing box. She smoothed the neat stitches done by another woman, plucked the needle from the cloth, and pushed it down as if resuming her own work. As planned, the point stuck the tip of her finger. Dora jerked back in exaggerated surprise, dropping the needlework to the floor.

"You've hurt yourself," her visitor said, bounding forward. He was nearly on his knees before her, his head bent solicitously over her hand.

Dora looked down at the tiny drop of blood that welled from the miniscule puncture. "It's nothing," she murmured, and gave a little laugh. "I suppose you'll think me foolish . . ."

His expression said he found her lovely.

"But I'm a bit nervous. I mean, we are strangers, and . . ."

"Perfectly understandable," he said, still hovering close to her side.

"I wouldn't wish for you to think I'm ungrateful for your assistance," she continued.

"There's no need to explain," he insisted, her hand still clasped in his.

Dora's hand fluttered free and landed in uncertain confusion against the front of his waistcoat. "It's just that—"

Footsteps dashed up the front steps, and keys jangled at the door.

Dora's mouth formed a perfect little *O* as she threw herself into the kneeling stranger's arms as if frightened. "My God," she breathed. "My husband!"

Heath burst into the room, then stood poised in the doorway. His hair was wet and plastered to his head. Droplets glistened on the shoulders of his jacket. His eyes narrowed in fury when they fell on the stranger. With a theatrical roar, Heath launched himself at Dora's guest.

The man got to his feet in a hurry and stumbled back. He pushed Dora's clinging form between him and her supposedly enraged spouse.

"Philanderer!" Heath stormed, his hands reaching for the other man's thick neck.

Dora threw herself at her partner, her supplicating pose the equal of many she'd seen performed on the stage. "No, dearest!" she cried. "You mistake the matter!"

Heath's features were contorted in exaggerated rage. "You were in his arms!"

"I was not!" she declared stoutly, and cast an apologetic look at their victim.

"I don't believe you!"

The frightened man tried to ease his way toward the door but Dora cut him off, clinging to his arm. "Tell him," she urged tearfully. "He is such a jealous man. He believes all men find me . . . attractive."

Heath was breathing quickly, his fists clenched at his side. "I know you," he stormed at the trapped man. "Not just your kind and the

284

ways in which you trick gentle, defenseless women. I know your name, where you do business."

Heath paused a moment as if considering his new position. "I can ruin you for your evil work this morning."

The portly man tried to brush Dora off but she continued to cling to him, preventing his escape. "I did nothing but help this lady home in the rain," he insisted.

"I don't believe that," Heath snarled. "And neither will the men with whom you deal."

The stranger paled at the implication that Heath would be so ungentlemanly as to start rumors about him. He had done nothing wrong but he had enemies who would be glad to besmirch his name with a tale whether it was true or not.

"I'll do anything you wish," the man babbled, and wiped nervously at his perspiring upper lip. "I was not here today. I have never seen your wife."

"Ha!" Heath cried. "You've sullied her fair name and I intend to do the same to yours."

"But I'm innocent!" the man insisted. He glanced down into Dora's tragic face, noting the tears that sparkled on the tips of her long dark lashes. "I'll pay you to say nothing of what occurred here today," he offered rashly.

Heath looked thunderstruck. "You think you can buy my silence?" he demanded.

"Please," the stranger pleaded. "For the sake of my own wife's happiness, if not for yours." He fumbled in his inner pocket for his wallet and thrust a handful of greenbacks at Heath.

"You can't buy something as sacred as a woman's honor," Heath said, his arms folded across his chest in refusal, his voice hard.

The hapless victim was shaking now. He pried Dora's fingers from his arm and folded the notes into her hand. He added his pocket watch to the cache. "Tell him," the man pleaded.

Dora blinked, allowing a single tear to course down her cheek. "I'll try," she promised tragically. "Perhaps I can convince him. Go now, before he becomes violent."

Their victim needed no second chance. He grabbed his bowler and dashed out into the rain, leaving his umbrella behind.

Heath moved quickly to the window, twitched a corner of the curtain aside, and watched the man hurry down the street.

"Right, my sweet," he said. "Let's get out of here before the real owners return."

Dora was already buttoning her redingote. She glanced in the hall mirror and jammed a long pin through her hat to hold it in place.

"You were superb, Tom," she said.

"As usual," he agreed, and dropped a quick kiss on her upturned mouth. "No time to count up our profit now. Allen wants us to meet him."

Dora let him pull her quickly through the house and out the back door. Heath snapped open their victim's umbrella and drew her close against him beneath it.

"What's Allen want?" she demanded crossly. "I want to get warm and dry. We've got two days until we're to see him. Don't tell me you've been holding out on his share!"

Heath clucked his tongue. "Course not, sugar. Hell, Allen's the one who made us a team, isn't he? I owe him something for that."

She cuddled closer to him beneath the umbrella. Her heels on the pavement clicked quickly as his long strides forced her nearly to run to keep up. "We're a wonderful team," she agreed. "Both in bed and out."

Heath laughed. "Then lets get this meeting over with and back to that cozy, dry bed."

Ned Allen was waiting in the sample room at the rear of the corner grocery at Grant and Sutter streets. If local customers were in search of liquor that day, they did their shopping on the opposite side of the board partition without tasting the merchandise, or they patronized another corner shop.

The surroundings were grim. A rough table and a couple of chairs sat in the center of the room. A small, rain-streaked window let in very little light, but Allen hadn't lit the oil lamp on the table. He preferred to keep to the shadows, to watch the expressions on the faces of his employees.

When Dora and Heath entered the room, they had no choice but to take the seats facing the window, their backs turned toward the door. Allen kept his own back safely against the wall. He was amused that the couple moved their chairs close together. A month ago they had both been strangers, Dora an unemployed whore, Heath a down-on-his-luck hustler dodging the police. Together they were a successful confidence team, milking susceptible men with Dora's guileless blue eyes and Heath's realistic rages.

"How's business so far?" Ned asked softly.

"Better this week," Heath answered, glancing aside at his lovely partner.

"The rain helps," Dora added.

"That and the churches. Dory's attended a lot of services lately," Heath said.

"And passed our own brand of collection plate," she said.

Ned Allen nodded. "Good. I have another job for you both. Something different."

Heath's jaw tightened. "How different?"

Allen smiled grimly. "A little sleight of hand for you, a few languishing looks from Miss Acton."

"You have someone in particular in mind?" Heath asked carefully.

Allen wasn't looking at Tom, though. His gaze was centered on Dora. "Yes. Someone Miss Acton knows very well."

Phael Paradise crossed Portsmouth Square at a jaunty pace. He'd spent the morning at the Paradise Palace, his father's first-class saloon, had stayed on to lunch there with a few of his cronies and planned his evening's entertainment.

There were many long hours before dark, though, and Phael was undecided on how to fill them. He could stop in the Puritan Line offices and play at being interested in the business or he could find another bored soul and while the time away with a hand or two of cards. Neither prospect pleased him.

The earlier rain had left a pleasing bite in the air. The dust in the streets had settled and each breath he took was fresh and clean, almost like being in the countryside. Almost, but, thank God, not much! Phael could think of nothing more stupefying than being forced to live outside the city. What did a man do with only fields and trees to look at? He needed the saloons, the illegal gaming houses, the beautiful, agreeable women of the city.

He was almost to the corner of Clay and Kearny when he heard a sweet voice call his name.

"Phael!" the woman cried again, waving one slender gloved hand to get his attention.

A wide grin spread over his handsome face. "Dora! I haven't seen you in weeks. Thought you'd left town," he said, strolling to where she stood waiting for the Clay Street Hill horse-car.

She was as neat and petite as he remembered—and just as shapely. The cinched waist of her dark redingote showed her womanly figure to advantage. A ridiculously tiny hat was perched forward over her brow, barely anchored in her rich, dark brown hair. A flirtatious smile dimpled her cheek, and her big blue eyes gleamed with excitement.

"I'm taking a bit of a holiday before deciding what next to do," she said. "How have you been?"

"Lonely." Phael took her hand in his.

"Poor darling," she cooed. "If only I'd known."

Phael's smile widened. "Well, you know now," he said.

Dora cocked her head to the side and stared up at him. Her dimple deepened. "Would you like me to do something about it?"

"If you're not busy."

Dora slid her hand along his arm. "Why don't I show you where I live?" she suggested. "So you can visit me when your spirits are low."

Phael dropped his hand over hers. "I was hoping you'd suggest that," he murmured, and drew her away just as the horsecar arrived.

There was an air of good breeding in the room, and it was not reflected just in the quiet manner of the men who sat at the tables, or in the rich furnishings of the house. Only men of wealth could afford to patronize this particular gambling hall. Illegal though it was, the clientele was very select, and strict rules of behavior as well as income were adhered to. No loud laughter was heard inside these doors, no uproarious hilarity. The players at each table were dressed with taste and simplicity. Only their demeanor and acceptance at the club shouted of wealth. During daylight hours these same men gambled in mining stocks, railway stocks. Now that the sun had set, it was the turn of a card that their money rested upon.

When Phael entered, he paused to scan the room. He had already put in an appearance at a ball, acting as a temporary escort to Wyn and Amy. He had danced with the daughters of his mother's business acquaintances and with his sisters' friends. He had even enjoyed a brief, but encouraging, flirtation with a bored young matron. But it was only at the tables that he was truly comfortable each evening.

Across the room, a man was signaling to him, a broad smile on his florid face. Phael had to think a moment before he came up with a name to match the face. Birk. He only knew the fellow slightly, but there were other faces he did recognize at the table. Petrie and Ansel, two of his father's friends.

"Looking for a game?" Birk asked as Phael joined them.

Ansel glanced up. Unlike Petrie's tall, bulky form, Ansel was a thin man with a balding pate and pale blue eyes. The cards ran through his fingers like water flowing in a brook, smooth and barely riffled. "We're looking for a new lamb to fleece," he said with a grin. "Birk here claims we've sheared him good, but you've always got a nice piece of wool to hand over, Phael. Care to join us?"

Phael laughed and accepted Birk's vacant chair.

"Good luck," Birk said with a thin smile and moved off to watch the play at another table.

The fourth man at the table was a stranger, a young man with soft brown hair and a studious demeanor. He wore a pair of gold-rimmed spectacles and sat a bit hunched as if he spent his days bent over ancient tomes in a dusty library. He was introduced as Thomas Carleton Heatherwood, a visitor in town from Vermont, sent West by his doctor in the hopes that a change of air would cure his breathing condition. Heatherwood claimed the trip had done wonders. It had enabled him to enjoy smoking once more.

Seeing that as a cue, Petrie signaled for a box of cigars. Ansel dealt out the next hand of cards. Phael helped himself to a cigar when the box was presented, as did Mr. Heatherwood. Both men shared a light and inhaled the rich flavor with pleasure before picking up their cards.

Heatherwood stared closely at his poker hand, adjusted his glasses, and drew thoughtfully on his cigar.

Phael lounged back in his chair, barely glanced at his hand, but raised the bet on the table when his turn came.

"Even though you always lose, I'll be damned if I care to play with you often, Paradise," the man directly across the table growled, matching the bet. "Looking at you unnerves me."

Phael smiled slowly. "Why's that, Petrie?"

"You make me feel time's peeled back and it's '51 again. That's when I lost a very nice little piece of property to your father," Petrie explained. "You've got his manner."

Ansel chuckled. "Fortunately, you haven't got Ben's cussed luck," he said. "How many cards you need, Heatherwood?"

The Easterner peered at his poker hand again before requesting three new cards.

Phael took two, Petrie four. Ansel hesitated, grumbled softly, then took four cards as well. From the disgusted snort he gave, his hand hadn't improved.

Heatherwood emerged the winner. His brows rose in delighted surprise as the pot was pushed toward him. "Did you come to California for the gold then, Mr. Petrie?" he asked. "I've read extensively about the early years. Fremont, of course, and various travel guides. But actually meeting someone who was part of the excitement is . . . Well, it leaves me nearly breathless."

"Well," Petrie drawled slowly, chewing on the end of his cigar a bit. He accepted the deck of cards from Ansel and shuffled deftly. "Things weren't as nice as they are now. Things were rough," he said, tossing cards onto the table before each man. "Young Paradise there was born above his father's saloon. Wasn't much law then, either."

Ansel swept up his cards, arranged them to his satisfaction, and nodded sagely. "Damn right there wasn't. Had to be the law ourselves. Was it '51 when the Committee of Vigilance had to put down riots near the docks?"

Petrie moved his cigar to the other side of his mouth and decided not to push his luck that hand. He tossed his cards down on the table and leaned back. "Griswold's office, wasn't it? Bunch of sailors upset about some captain's treatment of his men."

"Yeah. What was his name now?"

Phael raised the bet when his turn came. "Waterman," he said. "Captain Robert Waterman."

"Yeah," Ansel murmured again in agreement. "Damn, how the hell do you know, Paradise? You were just a baby then. I remember you. Slobbery little bastard, always drooling over the ladies."

Petrie laughed. "Haven't changed much, Phael, have you?"

Heatherwood contemplated his cards, then folded. "Waterman. I've heard that name."

"Captain of the *Sea Witch*," Phael said. "He holds the fastest record for a clipper from China to New York."

293

"Damn! And you know about it?" Petrie demanded. "Don't know what the world's coming to."

Phael grimaced. It was no secret that he had as little to do with his mother's business as possible. He turned to the puzzled Heatherwood to explain. "My family owns the Puritan Shipping Line. Waterman worked for N. I. & G., the competition."

Petrie's cigar had gone out. Rather than relight it, he signaled for a waiter to bring drinks. Heatherwood requested a mixed cocktail with an exotic-sounding name. The other men asked for whiskey.

"Bet your mother would have killed to have Waterman on a Puritan ship before that incident," Petrie commented.

Heatherwood's eyes moved from one man to the other. "What exactly did Captain Waterman do to rile a mob?"

Petrie shrugged. "Killed one of his men, if I remember it right."

"Not the kind of master we want aboard a Puritan," Phael said.

Petrie shook his head in wonder. "Damned if I don't think you're an imposter tonight, Paradise. Never thought I'd see the day when you'd spout information about the Line."

Phael let the comment slide and drew deeply on his cigar. He helped himself to another shot of whiskey from the bottle that had been left on the table.

He was feeling very pleased with himself. Perhaps that was the result of the afternoon in bed with Dora. He had been very fortunate to run into her earlier. Dora had never told him what she'd been doing at Portsmouth Square. But then, he hadn't asked, either. He preferred to think of their meeting as pure luck.

The cards were falling his way that night as well. Heatherwood won a number of hands, but the majority of games were his. It was a pleasant change. Usually, he left the table with empty pockets and a desire to appease the loss with an hour or so in some lovely cyprian's arms.

He wondered if Dora would mind a late-night visit. She'd always been very soothing over his losses. It would be a nice change to have her help celebrate his wins.

The players at the table changed as the older men left, seeking other games. Phael's luck held, though. Between Heatherwood and himself, they collected a small fortune. He was thinking more and more about showering Dora with currency and making love among the greenbacks. One last hand, then he'd go, Phael decided.

Playing the role of Thomas Heatherwood, Tom Heath settled the gold-rimmed eyeglasses more firmly against the bridge of his nose. It was the signal for which Kappa had been watching since replacing another player in the game an hour before.

Heath hadn't been pleased at the turn of events. All morning he'd been thinking about spending the remainder of the day between the sheets with Dora. The fantasies had been a pleasant way to while away the time at the house they'd borrowed as he waited for Dora to reel in her latest dupe. Theirs was a very profitable team. It chafed him that Ned Allen took half of everything they earned—if "earned" was the right word for what he and Dora did in milking stupid men. He'd considered suggesting to Dora that they take the game elsewhere. New Orleans, maybe. Allen only saw them once a week to take his share. He was a dangerous man to cross, but they could be aboard a train and headed east before Bull Run knew they'd skipped out on him.

But Allen had other plans. Not only for Heath but for Dora. She'd spent the afternoon in bed with another man. Phael Paradise.

He hadn't known Paradise and Allen had given no reasons why he wanted the man brought low. But after a day of stewing alone while Dora entertained Paradise, Heath had his own reasons for seeing that the man came out a big loser at the tables tonight.

It hadn't been easy keeping his mind off what Dora was doing with the mark. Heath had pictured Paradise as an older man, portly and easily led, just as their other victims had been. Discovering that Paradise was none of those things had been a bit of a shock and the fact had grated on his nerves all evening.

So when he recognized the signs of a winner preparing to leave the table. Heath was quite ready to play his part in the charade that would ruin Phael Paradise.

The poker hand was dealt and play proceeded quickly with Paradise once again raking in the pot. As he collected his winnings, Kappa quietly drew a derringer from his inner pocket and accused the table at large of cheating.

Phael paused and then leaned back in his

chair. "Who exactly do you feel cheated you?" he asked, his voice dangerously quiet. "Me, perhaps?"

Kappa, another confidence man in Allen's employ, pointed to the pile of greenbacks. "Looks rather obvious to me," he snarled. "How'd you do it? We all had a hand at dealing and you won hands you didn't deal."

"My lucky night," Phael said.

"You damn well made it your lucky night." Kappa looked closely at each player in turn. A good-sized crowd had gathered as play was always quiet at the club and arguments were few and settled away from the premises. "Who the hell was working with you?" Kappa demanded.

Heath waited until the tension had built sufficiently. He liked timing his entrances. It was a carry-over from his days with the theatrical company.

Kappa leaned threateningly over the table. "Which one of you is in on it with him?"

Heath fidgeted with his spectacles and looked from face to face with just the right amount of fear building in his expression. Everyone but Paradise was looking at him.

Heath pushed back his chair. It fell over. A nice touch, he thought. "I couldn't help it!" he said, his voice pitched to a desperate, frightened croak. "I couldn't refuse to help him!"

Phael barely moved. Only his brows rose in a brief flicker of surprise. A rising murmur of disgust rose from the men now crowded around the table. Some stared in disbelief at Phael while others shook their heads sadly as they contemplated the shambles of the man they knew only as T. C. Heatherwood, late of Vermont.

Heath broke into a babble that sounded close to tears. "You see, I owe Paradise a lot of money. He said, if I helped him win tonight, that he would discharge the debt."

Petrie pushed through the crowd until he towered over the still form of the accused. "What have you got to say, Paradise?" he asked sternly.

Although apparently still relaxed, Phael's eyes had narrowed. It was impossible to figure out what game Heatherwood was playing or how he had become the victim. Phael watched Heatherwood's performance a moment longer before replying. "He's lying."

"Oh, my dear lord," Heath moaned, apparently trying to pull himself together. He straightened his spectacles more firmly on his nose and squared his shoulders as if going into battle. "Do not damn me so, sir! You may have forced me to help you cheat these men, but I draw the line, I tell you, at lying to them as well."

Phael leaned forward in his chair, his teeth bared in a snarl. "Heatherwood is lying."

Heath stood silent, sure that his performance had been successful.

Kappa picked up his cue. He grabbed the deck of cards and splayed them in a fan across the table. "There's got to be some marking on them," he insisted, sorting through the cards while the other men leaned forward curiously. It took Kappa only a moment to find what he wanted. "Damn," he breathed. "Will you look at that!"

Petrie whipped the card from his hand. "At what, man?"

"The markings on the back," Kappa said, pulling yet another card from the pack. "Here in the corner. They're slightly different, aren't they?"

Petrie peered closely. "Hell, I don't see any difference."

But other men claimed the markings were distinctive, not enough to cause comment, but enough for a professional to know exactly what hand another player held.

Petrie glared down at Phael. "What do you have to say for yourself, boy?" he demanded.

The condescending form of address tipped the scales. Phael came to his feet in a rush, pushing over the table, and the crowd fell back. "I was not cheating," Paradise growled as his gaze lit on one face after another. "You all know I couldn't read the markings even if the deck were fixed. If I could, do you think I would have been losing to all of you all these years?"

A few men chuckled in agreement, yet no one suggested that any of the other players was at fault.

Kappa's jaw was thrust forward stubbornly. "But you were winning tonight," he pointed out.

Phael faced his accuser. His fists were clenched but he didn't move. Kappa wasn't taking chances, though. He eased back into the crowd.

"I think you'd better leave, Phael," Petrie said quietly. "Perhaps it would be best if you didn't come here to play again."

Phael glared at the older man a moment longer before pushing his way out of the room.

Tom Heath had already melted from the scene.

Chapter Seventeen

Stunned by his ostracism from the club, Phael stood on the street, unaware that a slight drizzle had begun to fall. It wouldn't be only this particular gaming house that closed its doors to him, he realized. Once the story circulated around town, there wouldn't be a single game open to him. No man would trust him, either for a friendly hand of cards or in a legitimate business deal. In just a few moments, his reputation had been blackened, destroyed.

And the devil of it all was that he was innocent. Not only innocent, but incapable of pulling off the very thing of which he was accused.

If he had been born with Winona's talent with the cards, at least he would have been able to recognize the fact that the game was rigged. By Heatherwood, obviously. The man had won nearly as many hands as Phael had. But he hadn't seen the danger, hadn't known there was a trap waiting to be sprung.

If he hadn't been so ready to accept a providence that dealt him nearly perfect hands that night, he would never have even stayed at the same table for so long. In the past Phael had roamed from game to game, never playing more than an hour before straying toward what he hoped would be a more profitable venture at a different table.

Why had it happened? Why hadn't he left the game earlier? Why had Heatherwood chosen him as the dupe? Had he been just waiting for a suitably blind player?

Phael turned the collar up on his coat and set his hat low over his eyes. Moisture dripped from the brim but he barely noticed it. A cab drew up alongside him, but Phael didn't hear the driver call down to him. His mind was busy sorting through the events of the evening. The vehicle kept pace with him for nearly a city block before turning off in search of a more eager fare.

Would Heatherwood have been content with any wealthy young man or had he been looking for someone with the Paradise name? It seemed impossible. Heatherwood had been at the table before Phael had even arrived at the club. It had been ill fortune that led him to that particular game. It had been . . .

Birk. Damn it all! Birk had called him over, offered him a chair at the table, had lead him to Heatherwood's game!

Phael hunched his shoulders against the damp night and continued walking. There were few others out on the street. Those men and women who were scurried quickly from their carriages to the warmth of a well-lighted building. Phael's long strides took him past them, through the damp, ill-lit streets.

What did he know of Birk? Where had he met the fellow? What had the circumstances been? Had it been over a convivial bottle of whiskey? At a card table? At one of the society parties to which his sisters insisted upon dragging him?

Hell, there had to be a link somewhere. Something that would explain who hated him enough to plot such a thorough ruin.

Other men could count their enemies, knew who they were and how to placate them. Enemies were made over played-out mining stocks, over misinformation concerning the route of a proposed railroad, over women. But Phael had never cared enough about anything but a good time to hurt anyone. He couldn't think of a single enemy he had ever made. His father had a few, but they wouldn't have waited years to strike back at him. They wouldn't have done so through his son. The enemies Ben Paradise collected preferred one-to-one showdowns.

Where had he met Birk? Under what conditions had he seen the man recently, other than that evening? Phael frowned, his mind on the questions that filled his mind rather than the path he tread.

His footsteps had followed the trail of his earlier thoughts, bringing him to the boarding house where Dora Acton lived. Phael glanced up at her window. A soft warm glow showed against the drape. Was she entertaining another man? Or was she trapped inside by the weather, longing for some company?

Phael's hand froze on the latch. Birk's face flashed before Phael's mind with striking clarity. He had the answer! He knew where he'd seen Birk now. It had been at Hell's Kitchen. Birk had been at one of the tables in Ned Allen's gin mill the day Katie had made her last appearance as the songbird.

The main door to Dora's boarding house swung open, beckoning Phael into the welcome warmth. He moved inside automatically, his steps leading him up the staircase toward the room where he'd spent the afternoon enjoying Dora's freely offered charms.

Birk, he thought. Birk! What had he ever done to the man? Hell, if he remembered correctly, the only time they'd ever played a hand together, Birk had neatly cleaned out Phael's pockets. A man didn't plot your ruin when he could just as easily take your money.

But it wasn't Birk who had a grudge. It was Ned Allen. The memory of Birk playing roulette in Allen's establishment was enough to convince Phael that he'd found the enemy at last. Birk had the social pull to get in the door of the elite gambling halls but he wasn't particular who financed him as long as the money kept coming. Allen had the resources to keep Birk happy.

Why had Allen come after him, though? Phael wondered. Did Bull Run know he'd had a hand in Katie's escape? Or was he merely using the most convenient member of the Paradise family to exact his revenge?

Lily Walsh was far from Allen's grasp. Innes had sailed, and, if the note Kate had left was to be believed, she had been aboard the *Paramour* as well. Guards had been posted at the Puritan Line warehouse and the employees at the Paradise Palace Saloon had been alerted and armed. The younger Paradise children were kept under close surveillance and when the older girls attended a party, Phael had been asked to stay with them until his father arrived.

Precautions had been taken everywhere except with him. They had thought he would be careful, would be able to handle an attacker if Allen made a move. He'd been avoiding his usual haunts in the Barbary Coast and had watched the alleyways. But he hadn't thought to be on his guard in the elite gambling club.

Phael paused on the landing before Dora's door. He checked his pocket watch, wondering if his parents had returned yet from the ball. Knowing Amy's determination to marry into one of the old, moneyed families, he doubted anyone would be able to pry her from the party until the last moment. It would be another hour or so before he could confess his stupidity. Time in which he could use Dora's sympathetic, softly rounded form to bolster his own flagging spirits.

Phael rapped lightly on the door to her room.

At the tentative knock, Dora felt her throat go dry. She glanced to the door, then back to the man who waited in the shadows, his legs crossed negligently as he lounged in the only comfortable chair. He had arrived barely half an hour earlier and made himself at home. To pass the time, he had asked her to disrobe, slowly dropping each item of apparel to the floor as she removed it. She had been posing for him on the bed since then, moving as he requested, her naked flesh touched by nothing more than Ned Allen's eyes.

He looked toward the door, a slight smile of satisfaction on his face. "Answer it," Allen said quietly.

Dora moved slowly, unsure of what the evening held for her. She picked up a silk robe, shrugging into it, shivering a bit as the cool touch of the cloth caressed her skin. She tightened the sash, pulling the fabric close over her breast. Her bare feet were silent as she crossed the room.

"Yes?" she called, and found the sound loud. She glanced aside at Allen. A small movement of his fingers urged her to say more. Dora cleared her throat. "Who is it?"

"It's me," a man's voice whispered. "Let me in, will you, Dory?"

Swallowing was very difficult now. Something seemed to be contracting her throat. "Phael?" she croaked.

"Open it," Allen murmured. He was on his feet, easing back behind the dressing screen in the corner.

She had gone to him, Dora reminded herself. She had performed, enduring the touch of his cool, cruel hands, all because she wanted petty revenge on a woman known as the songbird. She hadn't known that Allen had bigger plans, that his net was spread to catch more than just one young woman in his trap.

Now he had used her to lure Phael into danger, had used her to ensure that Heath would do as he was told as well. She had been wrong to think Ned Allen was just another man to do her bidding. She was being forced to do his.

Dora eased the door open. "What are you doing here?" she whispered hoarsely at Phael. "I didn't expect to see you until tomorrow, as we planned."

Phael pushed past her, turned, and shut the door to ensure their privacy. "I had to come, Dory. I needed you tonight."

Dora stared at him. She hadn't moved from the door. She was afraid to glance at the corner where Allen was hidden from view.

Misunderstanding her silence, Phael gave her a weak smile. "You don't mind, do you, Dory?" He put his arms around her, holding her close. His chin rested lightly against her dark, flowing hair. The feel of her curvaceous body next to his allayed the terrors of the future he had yet to face.

Her hands fluttered, not quite embracing him, not quite repulsing his advance. "Phael . . ."

"Just let me hold you," he said.

He tugged gently at the sash of her robe. When it gaped open, Phael slid his hands inside the loosened folds, caressing her waist, her ribs, moving up to cup her full breasts.

Dora pulled away from him. "Don't," she said, and pulled the garment closed. She grabbed at the door, wrenched it open. "Get out!" Her voice dropped to the merest whisper. "Please, Phael," she pleaded. "It isn't safe for you here."

Phael didn't move and Dora wondered if he'd heard her, if he understood he was in the danger. Phael Paradise had treated her cavalierly in the past, alternately ignoring her and enjoying her, so she had no reason to try to protect him. But she was trying to and Ned Allen wouldn't like that.

"Heatherwood," Phael growled, staring at the man who stood in the hall, his hand reaching for the doorknob. "Is he the reason you want me to leave, Dora?"

"Tom!" she squealed.

Before Heath could react, Phael had launched himself forward. Heath took the blow on his chin, and staggered back in surprise against the doorjamb. When Dora moved toward him, Heath waved her back. He rubbed his jaw, eyeing Phael. "I suppose you think I deserved that," he said. "I don't. I was just following orders."

"Whose orders?" Phael demanded, still bristling. His fists were raised, prepared to deliver another blow or to defend himself. "Ned Allen's?"

Heath came into the room and shut the door quietly behind him. "Yeah, Allen."

"You destroyed me," Phael said. "My past, my family, they all count for nothing. It only takes one blemish to damn a man. And you made damn sure it was a dandy." He was breathing fast, trying to regain control of his temper, and wondering why he even bothered. "I should kill you for what you did."

"I think not," Ned Allen commented quietly as he stepped from behind the screen, a long-barreled pistol in his hand. Rather than train it on either of the men, Allen aimed the deadly muzzle directly at Dora. "I have a different ending in mind for this little story," he said.

Dora backed up against the side of the bed, one hand pressed to her mouth to keep from screaming. Her eyes were wide with terror.

The threat to Dora kept both Phael and Heath still.

"Let her alone," Phael said. "You've had your revenge, Allen."

Bull Run chuckled softly. "Because yer reputation is in question, Paradise? That's just the beginning. Get undressed, Miss Acton," he said. Without taking his eyes off the two men, Allen hedged toward the window. He moved the curtain, signaling his men below. "Ya see, angel, Paradise came here tonight to forget his troubles fer a while. I knew he would. It's a pattern. A bad night at the tables, and he heads for the nearest welcoming bed." The gun moved infinitesimally. "Come on, angel, I said drop the robe."

Barely daring to move, Dora let her robe slide to the floor. She looked to where Heath stood frozen near the door. *Help me*, she pleaded silently.

Heath didn't read the message in her eyes. His own had closed. His face was pallid, nearly as white as the fresh sheets on her bed, and he swallowed loudly.

Phael's glance flickered over Dora and returned to Allen, his look dark and glittering with restrained malice. "Let her go," he said, his voice pitched low in a savage growl.

Allen ignored him. "Get in bed, Miss Acton," he instructed. "Paradise came here tonight because the luck ran against him at the tables tonight."

"Thanks to you," Phael said.

Allen declined the honor. "Not me. It was Heath here who juggled the hands. As you know, the doors ta that particular gambling den are closed ta me. I wish I could have been there. I understand it was one of Heath's better performances. His best is yet ta come."

Dora held the sheets clutched to her breast. Her breathing was shallow. "What do you mean?"

The door opened and two gunmen eased into the room. At Allen's signal, one gave Heath a rough push toward the bed. He stumbled forward, catching at the footrail to keep his balance.

"It's a very simple story we intend ta show the police," Allen said. His gun trained on Dora's cringing form. "Paradise arrives ta find the man who fingered him as a card sharp in bed with his favorite tart."

Heath's complexion grew even paler.

"He jumps ta the obvious conclusion that they planned his ruin together," Allen continued in a conversational tone.

Heath looked up, his eyes red-rimmed. "Why would I—" he stammered in a croaking voice.

"Not you," Allen sneered. "Your talent is in duping marks. It was the lovely Miss Acton who planned it." He mused a moment, studying the participants in his little drama. Only one displayed courage—Phael Paradise—which surprised Allen.

"Ya see, Paradise had thrown her over fer another bawd and she wanted revenge," Allen said.

Dora's eyes were wide with fear. "But I didn't . . ."

"The waiter girl who showed you ta my office knows you came ta me, angel," Allen reminded.

"But that was over the songbird . . ."

At his sides, Phael's fists opened and closed in frustration at the mention of his sister.

Allen smiled thinly, pleased with the reactions of his players. He lowered his gun and dropped it out of sight in the pocket of his frock coat. As if there had been no interruption, Allen continued to outline his plan. "Ya find the guilty lovers together. There is a struggle."

Phael's jaw was stiff, his face expressionless as an expert poker player.

Which Phael Paradise was not, Allen thought. Curious that the young man chose this time to develop a backbone. But fortunate for him that young Paradise's timing was so bad.

"What do you suppose happens?" Allen asked.

Paradise leaned casually against the polished top rung of the footboard. He folded his arms across his chest and essayed a faint smile. Allen had never seen him look more like his father or as dangerous.

"I would guess," Phael said, "that during this fictional struggle someone dies."

Dora gasped and reached for Heath. The con man slumped at the foot of the bed, unaware of her, his shoulders shuddering as he wept in fear.

Phael looked at Heath in disgust. "Which one of us?" he asked, his voice hard.

Allen's teeth showed in a feral grin. His eyes moved from Heath to Dora, lingered a moment, then returned to meet Phael's unflinching gaze.

Chapter Eighteen

Kate leaned on the railing of the *Puritan Paramour*, enjoying the cool touch of sea spray on her face. The coast of California was in sight and Caleb was at the wheel, tacking the vessel toward the harbor entrance.

Jason Quinn rushed up to her side, a cocky grin on his face. "Cook wants to know if you'd like a cup of coffee, Mrs. Innes. Made fresh, he says."

Kate smiled. She loved the sound of her new name. Mrs. Innes. Mrs. Caleb Innes. "I'd love some," she said. "Thank Mr. Raush for his thoughtfulness, Jason."

He gave her a sloppy salute, a trick he'd picked up from David. She might be the captain's wife, but having Davy take her august position seriously was fairly impossible.

With the hot mug of coffee warming her cupped hands moments later, Kate continued to watch the shoreline.

She and Caleb had been married by moonlight, joined both by God and by passion. No ceremony could have been more beautiful or more quickly dispensed with.

Although Reverend Ephraim Needham had been privy to Caleb's intentions and feelings about her, he was still rather startled to be awakened in the middle of the night.

"Married? Now?" He had yawned and stretched his back. His eyes were puffy with sleep, as he donned his robe, leaving it half open over a night shirt that ended just above his ankles. Scuffed slippers had covered his feet. "Can't you wait until morning?"

Caleb's grip on Kate's hand had tightened. "No," he had said simply. "It can't wait."

Miriam materialized at her husband's side, her dark hair with its light sprinkling of gray woven in a thick braid, her nightgown hidden in the voluminous folds of her robe. "But there have been no banns published," she insisted. "No arrangements made."

The pressure of Caleb's hand increased. He looked down into Kate's upturned face, his eyes shadowed, his jaw clenched with tension. Kate's throat tightened with a surge of love.

"Please, Ephraim," Caleb requested, his voice hoarse, nearly strangled.

The Needhams exchanged a long glance, silently communicating.

"All right," the reverend said.

"But not in night clothes," Miriam added. She stared hard at the Kate. "Especially not the bride."

So she had been married in the buttercup gown, a wilting *lei* of white blossoms draped around her neck, a hastily woven crown of flowers taking the place of a veil. A sleepy David had given her away, a stunned Jason Quinn had become his captain's best man, and Miriam Needham had stood in as a combination proxy mother-of-the-bride and witness. After the brief ceremony, Caleb had carried his new wife back to the thatched hut, the strain in his face wiped clear now that the momentous step had been taken.

The crew of the *Paramour* had welcomed the bridal pair aboard a few days later. Raush had prepared a veritable feast, and Caleb had issued extra rations of rum for each toast to their future, of which there had been many.

The cabins were full on the return trip to the mainland, and David had given up the luxury of his own quarters to move into the forecastle with the other men. He had developed a new swagger to his step, Kate noticed, and was inclined to thrust his chest out in a boastful manner. Being the captain's brother-in-law apparently had given him an elevated status, one not usually achieved by a lowly cabin boy.

Only Devin Thaxton remained withdrawn, polite but distant, and Kate didn't blame him. She had tried to apologize for the way she had used him in getting aboard the ship as Tom Caitlin, but Thaxton excused himself, pleading duties.

He had never accepted her apology, and had continued to maintain a cool distance from Caleb as well.

His first mate's attitude bothered Caleb. He had discussed it with Kate late at night in their cabin and had asked her advice on the availability of Puritan ships. When they docked, he said, he was going to request that Thaxton be given his master's papers and a ship of his own.

Kate had snuggled in her husband's arms and mentioned that the captain of the *Puritan Vista* wished to retire. The *Vista* had been built along the same lines as the *Paramour* but she was a much younger clipper. Like the *Paramour*, she had followed the currents to China on a regular schedule, a route of both familiar ports and familiar waters to Thaxton. The opportunity seemed nearly custom-made for the first mate. His mind relieved concerning the future of his first officer, Caleb had settled down to the more pleasant prospect of pleasing his lovely wife.

It wasn't Devin Thaxton's future that preyed on Kate's mind as the *Paramour* eased into San Francisco harbor, though. She had been gone for nearly six weeks, but she doubted if Bull Run Allen's thoughts had been far from the songbird in that time. Had he been searching for her? Or would he realize that she had sailed with the *Paramour*?

With Allen's wide-flung underworld interests, word of the clipper's return would reach him quickly. She and Caleb would have to be on their guard the moment they set foot on the wharf.

Kate turned her attention to the crew, who were busy securing the ship, their activities overseen by both Caleb and Thaxton. As the departing cabin boy, David had already completed his chores and stood on the quarterdeck, a spyglass trained on the docks looking for familiar landmarks. At the rail Kate was content to admire the city from afar. If she had her way, it would no longer be her home. She had questioned Miriam Needham extensively about life in the Sandwich Islands and the growing opportunities but she had not broached her idea to Caleb yet. There were a few records at the Puritan office that she wanted to check to verify her facts, but she was sure that her husband would see the same profit margin in her figures. Caleb had owned a share of the *Paramour*'s cargoes for a number of years and knew how to improve them. Kate was sure he would agree to her proposal, especially if she made it at an opportune time.

It was David's salty and rather obscene exclamation that drew Kate's mind from the pleasant contemplation of the future. He had obviously picked up a few bad habits during his weeks with the crew.

"I beg your pardon," Kate said in frosty tones. "You know what will happen if you say a thing like that around Mama or Papa, Davy. You won't be able to sit for at least a week."

He wasn't listening, though. He strained forward, as if moving the telescope closer would change the scene he was watching. "The Puritan office," David whispered, his voice shaky with fear. "It's gone."

Kate was at his side immediately. "What do you mean it's gone? You're just looking in the wrong direction." She took the glass from him and adjusted it to her eye.

But David had been correct. The brick building on California Street was no longer there, just the shell of it remained, the burned-out interior exposed to the elements.

"Dear God!" Kate breathed. "Get Caleb, Davy. Hurry. But don't let the crew or passengers know about this."

The boy was off quickly. Despite the cool breeze that whipped at the whitecaps in the bay, perspiration had broken out on Kate's brow. She lifted the spyglass again, studying the ruins.

It had been more than just the Line office. It had been the warehouse where goods were stored as well. For over twenty years, Lacy Phalen Paradise had conducted business from the structure. It had survived earthquakes, fires, and mob scenes, but it had not obviously survived Ned Allen's fury.

Kate brought the scene into better focus. Her view was obstructed by the ships moored at the docks for unloading. Their bulk did not minimize the extent of the destruction. The whole second story of the building was gone. Charred fingers stretched skyward from the ground level. Boards had been nailed over the gaping, open windows that faced the street to discourage looters. Kate doubted many of the goods stored there had escaped destruction. The building looked as if it had been dynamited, either by the arsonist or by the fire fighters.

When Caleb joined her at the rail, Kate handed the glass to him. "The Puritan office," she whispered, still in shock. "I killed it."

The passengers and their baggage were rowed into the city, but there was no shore leave for the crew of the *Paramour*.

Caleb assembled them all on deck and described what he had seen. Guards were posted and watches reinstated. The bosun and Thaxton would share command, alternating shifts, while Innes went ashore to ascertain the safety of the Paradise family. Although he ordered both his wife and David to stay on board, neither paid him any heed. While Caleb returned to his cabin for the gun he rarely carried, Kate and her brother quietly climbed down the rope ladder and into the waiting skiff. Innes looked at their pale, determined faces a moment, then, without argument, signaled his men to cast off.

They avoided the ruins of the Puritan office and hurried quickly through the streets. On Portsmouth Square, the Paradise Palace Saloon still stood, but its sturdy doors were barred and bolted, the windows tightly shuttered. Even destruction by fire over twenty years earlier had not caused the Paradise to close to business. The tightness in Kate's throat increased. What would they find when they reached the Paradise home further up the hill? Would it be boarded up as well? Burned out?

Her hand clasped tightly in Caleb's, Kate followed as David led the way through Chinatown and up Washington Street toward the mansion. She didn't breath easily until the house was in sight, not only whole but bustling with activity.

Lacy herself greeted them at the door and David threw himself into his mother's arms and squeezed her hard. One arm around his shoulders, Lacy hugged her tearful, contrite daughter. "We're all right." With her arms around her children, Lacy smiled softly at Caleb, including him in the welcome. "All of us are fine," she said.

"But, Mama, the office . . ." Kate began.

Lacy kissed her daughter's cheek briefly, and dropped another kiss on David's straw-blond hair. Then she released them and moved over to hug Caleb. "It can be rebuilt. We've done it with the saloon, why not the warehouse?" she asked brightly.

Caleb wasn't deceived by her cheerful facade. He read the strain in her eyes, felt the tension in Lacy's shoulders as he returned her embrace.

She clasped his hands tightly, trying to assure him without words that, despite the recent problems, she was fine. It was then that she noticed the ring on his left hand.

"It's done then?" she asked.

Caleb nodded. "A quiet but legal ceremony."

Lacy sighed, closing her eyes briefly. "Then something has gone right," she said, and turned back to her children. "Your father's upstairs. We both want to hear all your news."

But when they were all gathered in the upstairs parlor, the recent events in San Francisco were the main subject of conversation.

Ben Paradise pushed back the ledger over which he'd been poring when they arrived. He kissed the bride, shook the groom's hand, even thanked his son for filling in for him at the wedding. A toast to the newlyweds' happiness was delayed until dinner, though.

"The fire was two days ago. Very little was rescued. We've been trying to rebuild the accounts, satisfying merchants' demands through other sources. The Line will pull through with its reputation intact," Paradise explained.

Kate sat down at the makeshift desk and sorted through some of the papers. It was a bit surprising to find her father involved with the shipping line. His interests had always been in an entirely different direction. Precise business hours and paperwork had never appealed to him. He preferred the relaxed, social atmosphere of his saloon. Most of his successful stock transactions had taken place during a congenial game of poker.

"We had a bit of luck," Lacy explained. "Two of the ships were delayed by a storm, so we didn't lose those cargoes. With the *Paramour*, that makes three holds ready for distribution. We should have a new building to store things in by next week sometime."

"And new reinforcements to guard it," Paradise added.

Caleb leaned forward in his chair. "You're moving fast then."

"Not fast enough," Ben said.

David had gone off in search of a snack. Now he returned with an apple and a glass of milk. He perched on the arm of his father's chair. "Where's Edith?" he asked. "There was nobody in the kitchen."

"Edith is with your sisters and the baby in Sonora. Which is where you will be tomorrow as well, Davy," Lacy said, and picked David's dripping milk glass off the ledger. "With Zack and Luther to watch over them, we felt Lily's new home was a much safer location for the children."

Kate had been going through a stack of orders. "Phael shouldn't be in Sonora," she said. "I know he isn't fond of business, but he should be here helping you."

Ben and Lacy exchanged a worried glance. Lacy's hands twisted together, the first very visible sign that she was extremely worried. Ben's fingers covered hers, squeezing them gently. The lines around his mouth were strained when he answered, his voice low.

"Phael is in jail. For murder."

Bartlett Freel stared into the speckled mirror, studying the bruises on his face. The color had faded to a sickly yellow-green. But his body still felt the affects of the kicks and blows he'd received after being dragged into the alley behind Hell's Kitchen. No one had come to his rescue. He wouldn't have been stupid enough to help another man, either, Freel admitted. He'd already been incredibly stupid in believing Demas when the man had said milking Allen would be easier than thieving from a Chinaman.

It had been until Bull Run had gotten suspicious.

Freel was luckier than Demas had been, though. He was still alive and he doubted

Allen knew that. His henchmen had left Freel for dead.

That had been their mistake. He intended to make sure Allen knew they'd failed, meant to make him realize it big.

Chapter Nineteen

Phael sat on the narrow bed in his cell, staring blankly at the opposite wall. He was unshaven, his once immaculate clothing now muddied and torn.

Caleb had to clear his throat before the young man noticed he had visitors.

David fretted at the captain's side, quiet now that they were actually inside the jail. In the coach on their way to see Phael, the boy had railed at fate and had declared his older brother incredibly stupid.

If getting arrested for murder was stupid, then Caleb was in complete agreement with his cabin boy. But Phael wasn't mean. No one who knew him well believed he had killed Dora Acton. The police had found him in the room with a citizen who claimed to have heard a shot and rushed into the room. But Phael didn't know if he had shot the woman. He couldn't remember.

At the slight pressure of Caleb's hand on his shoulder, David shot forward to grip the cell bars. Caleb stayed back in the shadows to allow the brothers time together.

"Phael?"

The prisoner looked up, stared unseeing at the two figures outside his cell, then ran a hand along the back of his neck.

"Back from the islands already?" he asked with a weak smile. "How was the trip?"

"All right," David answered. "Mama and Pop are sending me to Sonora today. But I had ta see you first."

Phael's eyes glistened with emotion. "Thanks, squirt. Who's your jailer on the trip?"

David wrinkled his nose in distaste. "Wyn's friend, Leigh Underwood."

"Lord! I wouldn't inflict that harridan on anyone. Sounds worse than this." Phael waved one hand in an elegant gesture that encompassed more than just his narrow cell.

"We'll get you out, Phael," David promised rashly.

Caleb moved closer to the cell. "I know you've been over this before, but could you tell us what happened?"

Phael closed his eyes a moment and took a steadying breath. His voice was low and nearly devoid of emotion as he recounted the scene in Dora Acton's room.

He moved quickly through the earlier events— being accused of cheating; of going to Dora's; of finding not only the man who had accused him of cheating there but Ned Allen as well.

"We were all just staring at each other," Phael said. "Dory, Heatherwood, and me. Each of us wondering which one Allen was going to kill or if each of us was about to die." He ran a shaking hand through his dark hair. "Then everything went black. I've got a lump on the back of my head, so I suppose Allen had me knocked out. When I came to, Kappa was standing over me with a gun pointed at my chest swearing he'd heard a shot and found me standing there with a gun in my hand."

Bent forward, cradling his head between his hands, Phael paused in his tale. "Allen wasn't there and neither was Heatherwood. Just Kappa. And Dory's body."

David leaned on the bars of the cell. "I know you didn't do it, Phael," he said. "You couldn't."

"Damn right I couldn't," Phael murmured, and threw his little brother a wan smile. "It was all I could do to keep from shaking, I was so damn scared. I couldn't have hit the side of a barn much less kil . . ." His voice trailed off and Phael swallowed loudly.

"You'll get off," David said. "Everyone knows you're a rotten shot."

Phael chuckled hollowly. "Thanks, Davy. Thanks a lot."

Caleb turned the tale over in his mind. He had known Allen was a vicious enemy, but hadn't conceived of the scope the man would go to with his revenge. "No, you didn't kill Dora, Phael," he said. "Most likely Allen or one of his men did."

Phael nodded slowly. "Could be Kappa for all I know. He and Heatherwood had set me up at

the gaming club earlier. They made it look like
I was an unscrupulous card sharp."

David snorted. "That's Wyn, not you."

Caleb saw the lopsided smile Phael gave Davy.
"Could this Heatherwood have killed Dora?"
Caleb asked.

Phael surprised his visitors with a bark of
laughter. "The frigging bastard was worse than
I was," he said. "He just cringed at the foot of
the bed and cried. He wouldn't even look at
Dory. In any case, they tell me no one has seen
him since that night."

And no one would, Caleb thought, unless
Heatherwood, or what was left of him, washed
ashore.

"Allen claims he was nowhere near Dora's
boarding house. And he's got witnesses swearing on stacks of Bibles that he was in his saloon,
in clear sight of the whole room, all night,"
Phael continued. He studied the floor of his cell
a moment, then looked up. "I hear you married
Katie, Cal," he said. "Congratulations."

Caleb's mind was far from his bride at the
moment. "This Kappa," he demanded. "What
do you know of him?"

"One of Allen's men, I guess," Phael said.

Caleb stretched one hand up to grip the bars
and leaned closer. "Obviously," he drawled.
"What the hell else?"

But Phael was no help. When the jailer came
and told the captain it was time to leave, Caleb
passed Phael a flask of brandy and ordered him
to pull himself together, to think for a change.

Thinking was not Phael's strong suit, Caleb
mused later that night. If Phael was going to

327

escape the hangman, it was going to take more than just thinking anyway.

With the Puritan office in ruins and the Paradises trying to salvage the business, the job of clearing Phael's name had been handed to a Pinkerton detective. Caleb hadn't seen the man. He'd only heard Ben and Lacy arguing about calling in a stranger.

Caleb's mind was in complete agreement with Ben. Paradise wanted to ferret out Allen himself, to beat a confession out of him if necessary.

"You think I can't clear my own son's name?" Ben had stormed.

But Lacy had always been equal to any battle. "Allen's a killer," she shouted back. "Do you think I want to lose you, too? Dear God!" Her voice had quavered and Caleb knew she was fighting tears. "Where will it all end, Ben?" she whispered.

So the Pinkerton man had been hired.

Unlike Paradise, Caleb kept his plans to investigate to himself. What was needed was evidence that linked Kappa with Ned Allen. Evidence that, if it existed, was hidden at Hell's Kitchen and Dance Hall.

The night was balmy, nearly starless, but a breeze wound its way through the city streets.

The Kitchen was little changed in atmosphere and clientele from the last time Caleb had been there. He'd borrowed a shapeless jacket and cap from Raush aboard the *Paramour*. A further disguise of a patch over his left eye hid the identifying scar. Caleb stuck the stubby remains of a cheap cigar between his teeth, then sauntered through the door and past the screen into the smokey confines of Hell.

The sound of drunken revelry was nearly deafening. On stage, one of the tawdry performers was trying to make headway despite the noise of the crowd. The tables were full of intense men watching the outcome of a roll of the dice, the spin of a wheel, or the turn of a card. Their smiles a bit forced and faded, the waiter girls in their short revealing costumes paraded between tables, delivering rotgut whiskey or beer to leering customers.

Caleb made his way to the bar and ordered rum, then took his glass and roamed from game to game, as if undecided about which to join. His eyes watched for familiar faces.

He took a seat at a monte table where he could watch the hallway that led to the back of the building. After half an hour he was sure it also led to Allen's office.

The last card was turned over, making the house the winner once more. Caleb downed the last of his rum and pushed to his feet. Another man took his place immediately, his eyes nearly feverish as he watched the new layout of cards.

Caleb was a few feet from the archway when Ned Allen came through the main door. He barely glanced at the crowd but made his way across the room with a burly man tagging along at his heels, talking urgently.

Caleb melted back into the crowd quickly. He knew that voice, knew the man. He'd last seen him leaving the *Paramour* in Honolulu Harbor. Bledsoe.

Chapter Twenty

The creaks and groans of the *Paramour* had become as soothing as a lullaby to Kate. Although her parents had urged Caleb and her to stay with them at the mansion, protected from Ned Allen's rage by armed guards, they both had declined. Caleb wouldn't leave his crew and vessel to weather this particular storm alone. If Allen went against his ship, Caleb intended to repel any boarders personally. He had urged Kate, however, to accept her parents' hospitality but she had no intention of being parted from him during the long hours of the night and Caleb hadn't argued.

They had spent many hours in San Francisco either at the mansion or at the hastily cleared Paradise Palace. While Kate worked with her mother attempting to reconstruct the Puritan

Line files, Caleb and Ben had supervised the storage of recently arrived cargoes. The saloon had closed its doors to one type of clientele, and opened to another. Tables and chairs had been replaced by crates and barrels of goods. The long, highly polished bar had disappeared beneath a flurry of manifests and orders from local merchants. The arrangement was crowded, and fortunately of a temporary nature. Her father already had workmen clearing the lot on California Street and carting away the charred remains of the Puritan Line office. An architect had been hired to design a larger building to replace it. The warehouse manager had been given the job of locating and leasing more suitable premises near the docks while construction progressed on the new building.

Although she had rarely set foot inside the saloon before, when Kate visited the Paradise Palace she had felt a sense of bereavement. The gleaming wooden floors were scuffed and marred by the packing crates. The glitter of crystal chandeliers was dulled. Cargoes, rising to the ceiling, demanded every inch of space. The mirror behind the bar had already met with an accident. An edge of a carelessly handled box had smacked it with just enough force to send a jagged crack racing across the surface. Where once the Paradise Palace had been spacious and grand, an elite gathering place for wealthy men, it had shrunk to the status of a paltry storeroom under the avalanche of Puritan cargoes.

If the defilement of his own business by the needs of his wife's shipping line hurt Ben Paradise, his daughter had seen no sign of it in his demeanor. From the moment he arrived, his black suit coat was abandoned and his shirt sleeves rolled up as he had assisted in the placement of cargo. He had a ready smile for the workers, his own high spirits lifting the morale of any Puritan man haunted by the specter of the recent fire. Only survivors made it in San Francisco, Ben had told them, and you just had to know when to dodge the punches fate delivered.

The Paradise Palace itself had burnt to the ground during one of the many fires the city had endured in 1850. But Ben had been back in business as soon as the ashes cooled. Kate knew he would be once again, after the Puritan Line office was reestablished in quarters near the docks. It had been his decision to close the saloon, to use his own three-story building to store merchandise. If he regretted that choice, Kate doubted that her father would ever let anyone know, not even her mother.

Paradise had turned command over once a day to Caleb while he visited Phael in the city jail, and Kate had noticed that it was after those brief visits that Ben's facade cracked a bit. He looked tired and haggard when he returned, his jaw tight, his eyes haunted. But he had said nothing, and merely returned to work.

Kate wondered if her parents managed to find any ease to their tension. Her mother worked tirelessly on the Puritan accounts and only once had Kate found Lacy quiet. She had been sitting in the embrasure of the bay window, staring listlessly out at the bay.

"Mama?" Kate had dropped to her knees, taking her mother's hands in hers.

Lacy squeezed Kate's fingers as a faint smile graced her face. "It's nothing, darling. I just miss my babies," Lacy had said quietly, then abruptly changed the subject. "Did you find the tea sets at the Paradise? There should be five available yet to fill the new order."

Business was her mother's answer to everything, Kate thought. But it wasn't hers. She found it impossible to relax when ashore. It was only when she had returned to the *Paramour* in the evening that the tension eased. The presence of armed men at the house on Nob Hill and at the Paradise Palace didn't make her feel safe. If anything, she was far more tense, waiting for Allen's henchmen to attack the mansion in force. Aboard the *Paramour*, surrounded by familiar crew members and open water, she had a sense of security that was lacking in the city.

Even Devin Thaxton's frequent consulting of his pocket watch that evening at supper did not disturb the contentment Kate felt aboard the clipper. But it bothered Caleb. He barely finished Raush's delightfully prepared meal before returning to the deck. Left alone in the day room with Thaxton, Kate sought a safe avenue of conversation. Polite words about the weather would be ridiculous, yet more personal topics were equally taboo. She had used Thaxton to get what she wanted and it had been despicable of her, but necessary at the time to get aboard the *Paramour*. In his place, Kate knew she would feel resentment at such cavalier treatment.

Thaxton had never said a word to her, though.

He had avoided contact with her as often as possible and Kate was a little surprised when he lingered at the table after Caleb left the cabin.

"Would you care for more brandy, Mr. Thaxton?" she asked, determined to put the past behind them. Caleb had already requested that Thaxton be given command of the *Vista* when she returned to port. In all the excitement, Kate wondered if Caleb had remembered to relay the news to his first mate.

Devin checked the time once more. "Perhaps a little more, Mrs. Innes," he agreed, tucking the watch back into his vest pocket. "But only if you join me. Although we've been on the same ship for weeks now, I don't believe that I've taken the time to congratulate you on your marriage." He paused, his hand suspended over the decanters on the table. "You were drinking the chablis, weren't you?"

Surprised at his mention of her wedding, Kate nodded and allowed him to refill her goblet. "Thank you. I didn't really expect you to be so gracious."

"I'm sure I wasn't the only man whose dreams were dashed," Devin said, stretching to replace the decanter on the tray. His arm brushed against Kate's glass causing the delicate crystal to wobble. Thaxton steadied it, his hand spanning the rim a moment before he handed it to her. "Your marriage was sudden," he continued. "Perhaps it caught me off guard. Otherwise, I assure you, Mrs. Innes, I would never have been ungracious to you. I hope you will allow me to make amends."

Kate smiled and sipped at her wine. The taste

was sharp, even a bit bitter. She had barely sampled it during the meal. "That's hardly necessary, Mr. Thaxton."

"Please," he said, his lips curving in a smile. His eyes watched her. "At least join me in a toast to your future."

Their goblets clinked companionably. "May it be everything you so richly deserve," he said.

Kate swallowed and restrained an impulse to wrinkle her nose at the pungent taste of the chablis. She must make a mental note not to purchase any more of that particular vintage, Kate thought. Something a bit sweeter was more to her liking.

"Speaking of things to celebrate," she said. "Has the captain told you about the *Vista* yet?"

Thaxton finished his brandy. "The *Puritan Vista*?"

"Yes, that's right. Captain Marshall has indicated that he would like to retire from the sea, and Mr. Gernsheim, his first mate, is more interested in gaining a berth aboard one of the steamships. I may be ruining my husband's surprise in telling you this, but Caleb has asked that you be given command of the *Vista*. She returns from China at the new year. Mother is seeing that your master's papers are ready by the time the *Vista* pulls anchor again."

He stared at her, the smile wiped from his face. "My own ship?"

Kate nodded. The movement started a slight ache at her temple and she rubbed at the spot absentmindedly. "Are you familiar with the *Vista*? She's very like the *Paramour*. The same design was used. She carries a little more

335

tonnage and because she was launched perhaps five or six years ago, the *Vista* has every modern convenience."

Thaxton sat up straighter in his chair and consulted his pocket watch once more. "Hell," he muttered under his breath.

The pain was spreading out from her temple quickly and Kate frowned. "You don't seem very happy, Mr. Thaxton. I thought you'd be pleased with the promotion."

"When did Innes arrange this?" he demanded.

The headache made her sight a bit blurry, like the outermost edges of a studio photograph. "The evening we returned to San Francisco," Kate said. "Why?"

Thaxton scowled and pushed back his chair. "Why wasn't I told?"

Her head was swimming now and the soft glow of the oil lamps was too bright. It hurt Kate's eyes. "I suppose it slipped Caleb's mind. With the Puritan office sabotaged, and my older brother accused of murder, we've both been rather preoccupied." Kate leaned forward, resting her brow on her hand. "I'm sorry, Mr. Thaxton. Would you mind getting me a glass of water? For some reason, I suddenly feel dreadfully ill."

"Damn." Thaxton's voice was tortured. "The *Vista*." Again he pulled out his pocket watch and barely glanced at it. "Lord, Kate," he groaned. "I wish someone had told me."

She didn't hear him. *I'm seasick again*, Kate thought. How ridiculous. Yet she recalled the misery of her first day at sea only too well. The slight fever that dampened her brow, the nagging headache, the nausea. How could she be seasick? She'd gained her sea legs weeks ago. The gentle rise and fall of the ship as it rode at anchor in the bay was minimal. The rocking of a cradle was more abrupt.

Thaxton didn't bring the water she requested. He lifted her to her feet and half-carried her into the adjoining cabin. He placed Kate on the bunk and turned to search the drawers of Caleb's desk.

Kate was barely conscious of his movements. She lay quietly, her eyes closed, one hand pressed to her throbbing brow, the other to her heaving stomach.

The first mate grabbed her shoulders, forcing Kate to sit up. She winched with the movement.

"Listen," Thaxton said. His eyes were no longer cold and watchful but burned with fear. He pressed something into her hand, forcefully closing her fingers around it. "Do you know how to use this?"

Kate looked down at the long-barreled pistol. It was heavier than her own gun. "Yes," she murmured, confused at the unflinching edge of command in Thaxton's voice.

"Good." He glanced quickly around the room, took a ladderback chair, and wedged it against the door to the day room. He pocketed the key to the door that lead to the narrow companionway. "Allen's men will be here any minute."

Kate jerked upright. "Allen!" The motion sent her head spinning with pain.

"There's no time to explain," Thaxton said quickly. "I slipped a drug into your wine. Fight it. And shoot any bastard that comes through the door."

He'd drugged her? At Bull Run Allen's order?

Kate leveled the gun at him and cocked the hammer back. "Does that included you?" she asked, her voice low and dangerously quiet.

Thaxton took a deep breath and looked down at the weapon. The barrel was steady and very close to his abdomen. "Yes, it includes me," he said. "Just let me warn the captain first."

She stared into his eyes a heartbeat more, then eased the hammer back into place. "Go," Kate ordered.

Devin took the stairs to the quarterdeck at a run. If only Innes had told him about the *Vista*, the only ship he'd place above the *Paramour*. And she was to be his. Or would have been.

"The captain," he gasped at the bosun. The man leaned back against the rail, enjoying the night, a pipe held between his teeth. Smoke reeled in lazy swirls in the air. "Have you seen the captain?"

Unaware that there was an urgent need for speed, the bosun cupped the bowl of his pipe and clenched his teeth on the stem to hold it steady. "Headed ta the galley last I seen," he said from the side of his mouth.

"Alert the crew," Thaxton snapped. "We've crimpers headed this way."

The bosun's expression didn't change. "Crimpers, huh," he mused.

"I said now, Mister!" Thaxton thundered. He was off the quarterdeck and headed for the galley before the bosun moved.

He could see the shadow of Innes's form in the doorway, half-turned to make some comment to Raush, the new cook. Thaxton was only a few feet away when the first dark-clothed men came over the side.

"Crimpers!" Devin shouted. "Arm yourselves!"

The boarders were everywhere, swarming up the lines from skiffs at the waterline. The light went out in the galley a moment before Raush and the captain entered the fray. Knives and belaying pins flashed as the *Paramour*'s men defended themselves.

Thaxton grappled with a faceless man, struggling to avoid a blow from a heaver. He drove his fist into the fellow's face, staggering forward a bit when the man went down. A hand gripped his arm and jerked him back on his feet.

"Well met, mate," a familiar voice said just before a fist hammered into Thaxton's midriff.

Caleb stood out from the crew, his tall form highlighted against the night. A knife flashed in his hand, keeping Allen's crimpers at bay. His teeth were bared in a grimace of near pleasure.

Ever since he'd seen Bledsoe at Hell's Kitchen, Caleb had been uneasy, unable to relax. He'd spent a good part of that night waiting for a chance to search Allen's office but the hallway had been as busy as the wharves when a ship docked. There had been a parade of men and women staggering through the archway to and from the beds on the upper floors. At last Caleb had given up and returned to the *Paramour* and Kate.

Tonight there had been something in the air, though. Something almost tangible. The night had been incredibly dark, lit only by a sliver of moon that hung low in the sky. The air was balmy with scarely a breeze to curry the swells.

It had been quiet. Too quiet.

When Thaxton's voice had rung out the warning, Caleb had been almost glad that the waiting was over.

At his back, Raush was braced in the galley hatchway, a cleaver in one hand, a mallet in the other. "Go on, Cap'n!" the cook yelled. The mallet connected nicely with a crimper's skull, felling the man at Innes's feet. "We've got 'em. Save yer lady."

Caleb sidestepped as another man came at him. "Want all the fun yourself, do you, Raush?" he shouted.

The cook chuckled and the cleaver swung out causing the boarder to jerk back, his stomach muscles sucked in, his head forward, a target for Raush's mallet. He crumpled to the deck.

Two men rushed at Caleb. His knife flashed, connected with one crimper's shoulder, and pulled free. He twirled, dodging the second man, kicking out sideways at the attacker. The man tumbled back, leaving a space around Innes.

"Leave 'im," a harsh voice snarled as more men came over the rail and lunged toward Innes. "He's mine."

Caleb dropped into a crouch, his knife held at the ready. "That you, Bledsoe?" He peered into the dark, trying to distinguish the former cook from the other crimpers. Having seen the man with Ned Allen, he wasn't surprised that Bledsoe had led the boarding party.

"Yeah. Come as a special favor ta Davy Jones ta fetch ya, Cap'n." Bledsoe pushed slightly ahead of the other men, brash and disdainful of their aid. "Ol' Neptune's been waitin' fer yer bones a long time."

"He'll have to wait a bit longer," Caleb said as around them the sounds of battle continued. It was impossible to tell if the crew was holding their own. New waves of boarders seemed to spill over the rail as their fellows fell back. Allen was taking no changes, and Caleb thought fleetingly of Kate, then pushed her image to the back of his mind. At the moment, she was probably holding her own as well as any of the crew.

The crimpers behind Bledsoe had Thaxton in their grip. He hung between them, his head bowed, his feet dragging, like a puppet they'd forgotten they held. As Innes's gaze flickered over him, Thaxton's head raised an inch.

His decision was made in a split second to get past Bledsoe to Thaxton and back to the cabin where Kate was.

Caleb's savage grin widened with anticipation. "What do you say, Bledsoe? Care to take my regrets to King Neptune personally?"

The former cook fumbled at his belt. "Ya can take mine," he snarled, and leveled a revolver.

Kate managed to douse the lights when she heard Thaxton's warning yell to the crew. He'd locked the door, but that was no guarantee of safety.

Her mind was growing duller every moment.

She splashed her face with water to fight the lassitude, and pinched herself. She tried to concentrate on the sound of fighting outside the cabin, on the scuffle of boots on the quarterdeck above her.

Still the languor increased and the weight of the pistol in her hand grew heavier. She forced herself to keep it trained on the door.

They had come for her. Allen had sent them for her. Perhaps if she went with his men, the crew and Caleb would be safe.

Foolish thought. Allen meant to destroy everything and everyone she cared about before he got to her. Her brother, Phael, had been the first on the list, then the Puritan office and now it was the *Paramour*'s turn.

One by one, Bull Run struck at those she held dear. He would save the songbird until last.

The gun wavered, dipping toward the floor, and Kate forced it up again. She put two hands around the handle to support it but the muzzle tipped down again and her eyelids flickered closed.

The shot on deck jerked Kate temporarily from her stupor. She slid off the bunk, stood weaving, staring at the dim outline of the door. Footsteps and yells sounded in the companionway and moved closer to her cabin. The sound of splintering wood came from the day room.

It took all her dwindling strength to lift the revolver, to hold its deadly barrel steady.

The voices were outside her door now. Something crashed against the wood, splintering it.

Kate gritted her teeth with the effort to remain conscious and took careful aim.

The panel collapsed with a loud groan, and without waiting to see the faces of the men who tumbled into the room, Kate pulled the trigger.

Chapter Twenty-One

Bledsoe stood with his feet wide apart, his hands on his hips as he bent toward his captive. "We'll, if it ain't Tom Caitlin," he snarled.

Kate glared up at him through a tangle of hair. "I beg your pardon?" she said in a freezing tone, clipping her words as precisely as a society matron.

His hand swung, striking her sharply on the cheek.

Her reactions slowed by the dregs of the drug in her system, Kate didn't dodge quickly enough and the force of the blow knocked her off her feet.

"Leave 'er alone, ya damn fool," the other man in the room said. "Allen don't want her looks ruined. He's got plans, ya know."

Bledsoe's stance didn't change. He rolled his

shoulders, reliving the pain of the lash. "An' I got ma own reasons ta teach the bitch some manners," he insisted.

"Ya damage the songbird and Allen'll make sure ya ain't around ta worry 'bout nobody's manners," the other man said.

Bledsoe snarled but backed off, turning to stomp from the room, leaving the other man to guard Kate.

She lay quietly a moment, catching her breath. There was still a haze in her mind. She had no idea how she'd gotten ashore much less back to Hell's Kitchen. There was no doubt in her mind that she was in Ned Allen's saloon once more. Not only did she recognize the room, the tiny backstage dressing area she'd used before her last performance as the songbird, but she knew the man who leaned back against the closed door watching her. One of Allen's henchmen.

She struggled up on her elbow and wiped at the trickle of blood from her broken lip with the back of her hand.

Dawn was in its early stages. Outside the narrow window to the east, rays of light stretched upward into the night sky and probed into the fog that blanketed the city.

Things were quiet at the Kitchen this early in the day. There was the occasional sound of a wheel spinning in the saloon as a weary dealer accommodated an early customer. But the stage out front was silent. Even the sound of squeaky mattress springs from the crib-like rooms above was missing.

Kate slowly got to her feet and sat down before the dressing-table mirror. She tried to straighten her tumbled hair, using her fingers to comb the tangles free.

"What happens now?" she asked the man at the door.

"Beats me, sugar," he said. "Guess we both wait ta find out."

Kate studied his reflection in the mirror a moment. "Thank you for interfering a moment ago."

He chuckled, his voice low and harsh. "Honey, it was ta save my own damn hide, not yers."

"All the same, I appreciate it."

"Maybe ya oughta wait till ya find out what Bull Run's got planned fer ya, 'fore ya thank me," he suggested.

Kate fought down the rush of fear. What would Allen do with her? What had he done to Caleb and the crew of the *Puritan Paramour*? Was Caleb even alive?

She closed her eyes, gathering her courage. She tried to remember what had happened before she had lost consciousness.

Three men had tumbled through the broken door of the cabin. They had been dressed in dark clothing and their faces smeared with dirt to cloak their midnight raid. The first one through the door had held an ax in his hand. He'd swung it in a frightening arc before two shots from her revolver downed him. The next two went down before the volley as well. The three lay in a pile, like discarded dolls, blocking the cabin's entrance. No one followed them. But someone would soon, she'd known.

The gun was empty and she had no idea where Caleb kept the ammunition. The unfamiliar weapon was so heavy and she was so tired that Kate let the pistol drop from her hand.

It took all her strength to knock free the chair Thaxton had wedged against the day room door. Once through the arch, she kept her balance by leaning heavily against the long table in the center of the room, working her way to the splintered and gaping doorway.

The sounds of battle were waning. Other than those she had fired, she had heard just one shot. If it had indeed been an army of crimpers Allen had sent after the *Paramour*, silent weapons would have been their choice. Gunfire would attract the crews of neighboring vessels and bring reinforcements to the *Paramour*'s rescue.

The reports of her pistol had been muffled by the bulkheads. The single shot topside probably hadn't disturbed the men on watch aboard the other anchored vessels.

Kate stumbled down the companionway, and stood in the hatchway. Her eyes sought and found Caleb. He had stripped off his jacket, and had bundled it beneath the head of the man who lay on the deck before him. A man who wore the uniform of a Puritan officer.

Caleb ignored the crimpers who surrounded him. He snapped an order, demanding aid for Thaxton. Raush hesitated a moment, his cleaver raised in a threatening motion. The crimpers moved nearer, their very stances threatening. Caleb's voice thundered, causing all but one of the boarders to halt his movement. Raush disappeared back into the galley and emerged a moment later with water and bandages.

The man who led the crimpers had his own orders, though. He signaled his men to close in. Raush was allowed to administer to the wounded man, but Caleb was dragged from the scene and forced over the rail to the skiff waiting below.

Kate sagged against the molding of the companionway. The brisk touch of a light sea breeze against her face had revived her briefly but it was losing the battle as well. Kate took a step forward as Caleb disappeared over the side.

A hefty arm snaked around her waist and lifted her off her feet, swinging her in a swift circle. "Gotcha, girly," a gruff voice said near her ear. "Lookee what I got me!" he caroled to his companions in glee.

Kate didn't remember any more as at that moment she'd been more than ready to let the drowsiness claim her. Sleep was all she could think about. Even the sight of Caleb in the crimpers' hands had failed to penetrate the vacuum in which the drug held her. So she had let go of reality, knowing it would return later with a harshness she would be unable to avoid.

Now, as she sat once more at the dressing table behind the stage at Hell's Kitchen, time was catching up with her.

A sharp rap on the door signaled the beginning of the gauntlet. The henchman stepped to the side, allowing two other men to enter the room. They dragged a familiar, beloved form with them and dumped him in the middle of the floor.

Kate was on her knees beside Caleb immediately. His face was bruised and battered. His lips were cracked, his eyes dulled with pain. He gasped and grabbed her arms in an agonizing grip when Kate helped him sit up.

Her eyes flew to the men who stood over them. "What have you done to my husband?" she demanded.

"Husband, huh?" Ned Allen mused, strolling into the room. His frock coat was immaculate, his boots highly polished. His linen was a blinding white that rivaled his diamond shirt studs. In his hand he carried a cane, whirling it nonchalantly. "Thank you, Katie. The good captain was bein' foolishly gallant in keepin' that bit of news ta himself."

Kate touched Caleb's damaged face tenderly. "Are you all right?"

He tried to grin but grimaced in pain instead. "Depends on what you have in mind," Caleb mumbled. "I'm still alive, at any rate. Thaxton may not be."

Allen set the tip of his cane on the floor and leaned forward on it with the air of a gentleman of leisure. "Thaxton," he mused. "Stupid act fer a Judas. Bledsoe is determined to kill you, Captain. I thought that was what Thaxton had in mind as well. It surprises me ta find he had changed his mind. I wonder why he did?"

"Thaxton acted as any officer would," Caleb said.

Allen looked amused. "In jumpin' between you and Bledsoe? In takin' a bullet meant fer you?"

"In warning the crew."

Ned's smile grew more pronounced. "He knew the crimpers were comin'. Helped plan it. We had a deal. I remove you so he could take over the ship. And he'd deliver a real prize." His gaze lingered on Kate.

Caleb leaned heavily on her shoulder and forced himself to his feet.

What had they done to him? Kate wondered as she saw Caleb grit his teeth and one arm press tightly across his midriff, his hand cupped around his ribs.

He made an effort to stand upright and just watching him hurt her.

Her arm firmly around her husband's waist, Kate looked up into Caleb's injured face. He was in no shape to best Allen's men. If they were going to escape with their lives, it was up to her to accomplish the feat.

Kate squeezed Caleb's arm, hoping he would understand it was a message of love. Then she faced Allen.

Her chin rose, set in a challenge. Her shoulders were squared, ready for battle. She stepped away from Caleb and gave Ned Allen a slow smile.

"Now you've got me," she said. "Was the chase exciting enough? Was it thrilling?"

Allen chuckled. "If yer plannin' on strikin' a bargain, angel, let me point out yer not in a spot ta do so."

Kate took two steps closer to him, her hips swaying seductively. "I think differently . . . Ned," she purred.

Caleb lurched forward. "Kate—"

Allen's cane snapped up, a barricade between the couple. "Let the lady have her say, Innes," he said. "Whatcha have in mind, kiddo?"

"Well," Kate drawled, her voice at a new husky level, "I've been thinking . . ."

Bartlett Freel paused in the alley, his body pressed flat against the wall. The sound of Bull Run Allen's voice startled him at this time of day. He had expected the proprietor of Hell's Kitchen to be in bed, to be drowsily unaware that his fate was about to change.

But Allen wasn't asleep. He was just beyond the window to Freel's left, chatting with some tart who thought her charms more appealing than those of any other whore. Allen was playing with her, leading her on. In the end, he'd toss her to the crowd. It wouldn't be the first time Allen had gotten one of the women so drunk that she passed out, then charged one man after another for the pleasure of using her any way he liked. Allen even charged those who wanted to just watch the fun.

Freel waited for the minutes to tick by, for his heart to slow its rapid beating. He listened to the conversation and wondered if it was possible to exact his revenge as planned. Then he moved silently toward the rear door.

Kate moved closer to Ned Allen, laid her hand on his chest, and ran her fingers along the lapel of his coat. "We'd make a wonderful team," she cooed. "I like excitement, and I know you can deliver it."

Allen's men exchanged glances and smirked. Even in her soiled dress with her hair tumbling about her shoulders, the songbird had all the airs of a first-class bawd. She was beautiful,

351

but there was something else about her that just might make her Allen's equal. She was ruthless in going after what she wanted and she'd managed to snub Bull Run in the past, a feat in itself.

Ignoring her husband's battered form, standing unsteadily just a few feet away, the songbird was attempting to seduce the man behind her abduction.

Allen hadn't forgotten him, though, or the stoic way the captain had endured each blow his men delivered. "What about Innes?" Ned asked, his voice amused but far from bemused by her actions. "You were awful hot fer him once."

"It's over," Kate said, her voice a throaty purr. "I liked him better before I met you."

Allen studied Caleb a moment, taking in the increased waver in the captain's stance. In another moment the man would topple over. Innes was certainly no threat. Not with three of his own armed henchmen a pace away to take care of any foolish attempt the captain might try to make to reclaim his wife—or to leave her.

The songbird was another case. Allen made it a rule never to trust a woman who wanted her own way. This one was too damn cocky and sure of her charms. She needed to be taught a lesson. It was something he'd looked forward to doing since the night he'd heard her sing at Lily Walsh's house.

"You forgettin' ya married yer fine captain?" Allen asked, moving the cane so that the heavy knob stroked her back.

Kate smiled and parted her lips suggestively before answering him. "It was his idea to be wed," she said. "I was bored that day, so I agreed."

Allen glanced back at Caleb. The captain's hands had clenched into fists, his eyes burned with hatred, but he made no move. Allen doubted he could.

Kate's hands were flat against Ned's chest, moving down over the ornate fabric of his vest. She looked at her own fingers as if admiring the breadth of his chest, then raised her head to meet the look in his eyes. "I hate to be bored, Ned," she murmured huskily. "Why don't you let Captain Innes go? Send your men away. Then we could have a more private talk."

"Jest let yer husband walk out of here? Think again, angel." The head of the cane moved back down her spine, over the flowing drape of her skirt to rest against the back of Kate's thighs. Allen applied a bit of pressure, forcing her closer.

Kate moved nearer readily. Her hands slid intimately across Allen's chest, just as Lily had taught her so very long ago. "The captain was shanghaied once," she said. "Make it so again."

"You want him ta live, that it?"

"He wasn't a bad lover," Kate answered silkily. "In fact, he taught me things you are going to love."

Allen wasn't finished toying with her. "What about yer brother?"

"Phael?"

"Don't you want him outta jail?"

"Why? There was never any love lost between us," she declared pettishly. "If you want to tell me later how you managed to frame him, I'm sure the story will amuse me for a short while."

Allen looked down into Kate's upturned face. His lips stretched in a sneer a moment before he caught her questing hand. "Nice try, angel," he said. "But I know when a bawd is tryin' ta pick my pocket. You can't get my gun that easy." He gave her arm a vicious twist.

Kate dropped to her knees and cried out as something cracked in her wrist.

Caleb sprang forward. His fingers closed around Allen's throat before the watching gunmen could react. They dragged Innes off, pulling at his arms, delivering blows to his already injured ribs.

The scene amused Ned Allen as he stepped out of his men's way, his back to the open door.

It was the moment Bartlett Freel had been waiting for and he stepped quickly inside.

Kate looked up as the flash of the knife blade descended with a force that drove it deeply into Bull Run Allen's back.

Surprise registered in his eyes a moment, then the king of the Barbary Coast sank to his knees and tumbled forward onto the floor.

"Hold it!"

Freel spun, still in a crouch. A uniformed man grabbed him and smashed him forcefully against the wall. He sank down near Ned Allen's lifeless body.

The men grappling with Caleb froze, staring in disbelief as the police spilled into the room.

A roughly dressed man entered in their wake. "Mrs. Innes? Captain?" he asked politely. "I'm Marcus Kantor of Pinkerton's. Ben Paradise sent me."

Epilogue

They didn't look much like the victors.

Harsh new lines were etched on Ben Paradise's face. His arm was stretched across the back of the couch behind his wife, and Lacy held her husband's other hand in a tight grip.

On the opposite sofa, Caleb looked the worst of the adventurers. His face was various shades of black, blue, and yellowish-green. He moved stiffly, his cracked ribs bound tightly in place. Kate snuggled next to him. She had sustained the fewest injuries. Only her broken wrist was bandaged and supported by a sling.

Phael had pulled up a chair between the two sofas. He was drawn and pale from his sojourn in jail. If his family noticed the sadness that haunted his expression, no one mentioned it. Only time would tell if Dora's death and his arrest would change Phael.

Marcus Kantor, the Pinkerton man, stood facing his audience. Kate had barely recognized the quiet-looking man when she'd answered the door earlier. Although he'd retained his long bushy sideburns, the bearded, scruffy man who had led the police to Hell's Kitchen had disappeared. Kantor wore a dark suit and a pale gray silk vest. His indistinct brown hair was slicked into place. "It really wasn't difficult," he said, as he related his tale. "All I had to do was infiltrate Hell's Kitchen.

"Allen was so sure of himself, so sure of the control he held over the participants, he never looked for their weaknesses. Like Etta, the waiter girl who kept my interest in his business secret. Her room was next to Allen's office. While I kept my ear to the wall, she was obliging enough to bounce the bedsprings to give my frequent visits a"—Kantor smiled wryly—"shall we say bit of color.

"Then there is Thaxton, who made his deal with the devil during a weak moment."

Kantor glanced at Caleb. "I understand Mr. Thaxton is recovering from his own wound."

Innes nodded. "If he hadn't jumped in front of me when Bledsoe fired that shot, I doubt very much that I'd be here today."

Kate entwined her fingers with Caleb's and squeezed them tightly. "Devin has atoned for his mistake as far as I'm concerned," she said. "Are you going to let him have the *Vista*, Mama?"

Ben chuckled. "You know your mother better than that, princess. Thaxton will have to grovel a bit, but in the end he'll have his master's papers and his ship."

"Bledsoe, as you know," Kantor continued, "was rounded up with the rest of Allen's men. Your testimony that he led the men who over-ran your ship will keep him from the sea for quite a while. Fortunately, none of your men had been delivered to other ships yet. We found them all together, although perhaps a bit battle-worn."

Caleb smiled faintly. "They'll have plenty of time to recover. The *Paramour* won't be putting to sea very soon," he said. "Not only am I in no shape, but the Puritan office could use an extra hand yet."

Phael moved uneasily in his chair. "Perhaps I could help," he suggested, uneasy about the reception his offer would receive.

Lacy's eyes filled with tears of pride for her oldest son. "We'd be glad to have you there, darling," she said quietly.

"How did you get Kappa to confess, Mr. Kantor?" Kate asked.

The Pinkerton man chuckled. "I didn't, Mrs. Innes. When I arrived at his lodgings to brow-beat him into going to the police, his landlady informed me that he was at the police station. When he heard Allen was dead, apparently he panicked. Fortunately for you, Mr. Paradise, he witnessed Dora Acton's death. Allen him-self pulled the trigger, muffling the shot with a pillow. You were already unconscious, compli-ments of a blow to the back of your head. Kappa himself discharged the revolver a second time to attract the attention of the other boarders in the house before 'discovering' you in her room. He also confessed to being involved in the card swindle as well."

"Petrie says you're welcome back at his table anytime, Phael," Ben added.

Phael looked down at his hands. His lips were tightly pressed together. "And Heatherwood?" he asked.

Kantor spread his hands in a helpless gesture. "We will probably never know what became of him."

Phael took a deep breath and let it out slowly. "Poor Dora," he said. "Why did she have to die?"

"Apparently Allen felt she was expendable," the Pinkerton man answered. "He arranged things so that she reentered your life the same day your reputation was blackened at the gambling club. Ruining you wasn't enough. There was always the chance that your family name would be enough to overcome any disgrace. From what I've been able to discover, Allen wanted to ensure the complete devastation of Mrs. Innes's family. Even if you weren't hanged for Miss Acton's murder, it was fairly safe to guess that the evidence he had concocted would be sufficient to send you to the penitentiary. Thus your freedom would be forfeited.

"Fortunately, the only man who will be charged now is Freel for Ned Allen's murder," Kantor continued. "If Bull Run hadn't been preoccupied with your performance, Mrs. Innes, Freel may never have gotten close to Allen."

Kate looked uncomfortable. "I was just trying to get out of there with my life," she murmured.

Caleb snorted. "Like hell. She was selling me onto a damn whaler."

"I was not!" Kate insisted indignantly.

"Feathering your nest at my expense," Caleb added.

Ben and Lacy exchanged an amused glance. "Speaking of nests," Ben said. "We've been wondering what domestic arrangements you two are planning to make. Will Kate be living aboard the *Paramour*?"

"Yes," Kate said.

"No," Caleb countered. "You know what I think about that, my dear. I'm not a damn fool. I'll not expose you to the dangers of the sea."

Her shoulders squared. "Don't make my decisions for me, Captain Innes," she snarled. "I am not one of your crew members. You can't just snap orders at me."

Lacy and Ben got to their feet. "Let me stand you a drink, Kantor," Ben suggested. "Phael, why don't you come along?"

"Why don't you return for dinner, Mr. Kantor?" Lacy invited, leading the way out of the room. "We would be very pleased if you'd join us."

Left alone, Kate and Caleb stared at each other a long moment.

"I love you," she said. "Even though you're pigheaded."

"Termagant," he murmured fondly. "Come here."

She snuggled back against him, careful not to disturb his bandaged ribs. Caleb's arms gathered her closer. "Perhaps we can compromise," he suggested. "I could take fewer voyages and you could swear off smuggling yourself aboard."

"I couldn't do it," Kate said as she placed her hand against his chest. Her fingers smoothed upward in a coquettish movement. "Caleb," she purred, "what do you think about starting an interisland shipping service? Miriam Needham says that—"

Caleb kissed her quickly, thoroughly. "Lord! Are you ever your mother's daughter." He stared down into her eyes. They were so unlike those of his first love, Lacy. So very right for his last love. "But, God, do I love you, Katie," he murmured huskily.

Author's Note

Although 99.8% of *Paradise In His Arms* is pure
fantasy, my imagination failed when it came to
creating a few things. Caleb Innes, Kate Paradise, and her family are indeed fictional. I can't
say the same about Ned Allen, One Year Tim,
Bartlett Freel, and the infamous Hell's Kitchen
and Dance Hall.

During my research of the Barbary Coast, I
discovered these three men and the Kitchen, and
they fit the elements of the story so well. But they
were only names. Given their place in history, I
plucked them free, manipulated them, and gave
them personae.

Ned "Bull Run" Allen's appearance, nickname,
and his flashy way of dressing are matters of
historical fact. He did indeed own Hell's Kitch-
en. It was located on the corner of Pacific and

Elizabeth Daniels

Sullivan's Alley in the Barbary Coast area of San Francisco. He owned other gin mills as well and styled himself the "King of the Barbary Coast."

One Year Tim ran things at Hell's Kitchen for Allen, but very little else about him was discovered through research.

The same can be said of Bartlett Freel. He was in fact a Barbary Coast ranger, one of Allen's competitors. He is credited with being the man who stabbed and killed Ned Allen, although it was in his own place of business rather than at Hell's Kitchen as I have portrayed. And it was not in November 1873.

Whenever possible, for the sake of authenticity, I have used descriptions contemporary with the time period. Primary sources have included photographs of San Francisco in 1873 and accounts published in 1876 concerning the physical appearance and the numerous confidence games and vices rampant in the Barbary Coast area. Diaries and journals of seamen stationed aboard clippers in the nineteenth century, and in the 1870s in particular, were consulted and supplied wonderful tidbits such as the brine episode.

Caleb Innes, Lacy Phalen, Ben Paradise, and Lily Walsh first appeared in my earlier novel, *Bird of Paradise*. Originally, there was no plan to continue their story. Caleb had other ideas, though, and *Paradise In His Arms* is the result. Wyn and David Paradise are already clambering for attention and will return with further adventures.

One last note to my readers. Authors are always curious about how their "children" strike you. There are no report cards issued, but we have the same anxieties for the characters in our books as we do when our offspring go off to kindergarten. I would like to issue an invitation to my readers to tell me how my fictional children have behaved. Positive or negative comments will be welcomed by:

Elizabeth Daniels
1953 N. Decatur Boulevard
Maildrop #330
Las Vegas, Nevada 89108